W9-CNC-210

SMALL TOWN GIRL

Also by LaVyrle Spencer

LaVyrle Spencer

SMALL TOWN GIRL

DOUBLEDAY DIRECT
LARGE PRINT EDITION

G. P. Putnam's Sons
NEW YORK

G. P. Putnam's Sons
Publishers Since 1838
200 Madison Avenue
New York, NY 10016

ISBN 1-56865-320-4

Printed in the United States of America

**This Large Print Book carries the
Seal of Approval of N.A.V.H.**

Many thanks to the people who helped me
during the research and writing of this book:

Ruth Reed, friend
Dr. David Palmer, consultant
Connie Bennett, fellow writer
Reba McEntire, inspiration and consultant

This book is dedicated to all the editors I've worked with through the twenty years of my writing career. Each has brought me knowledge and friendship. Each has been wise and supportive. Each has made me a better writer. I've loved and enjoyed you all.

Star Helmer
Damaris Rowland
Leslie Gelbman
Lisa Wager
Chris Pepe

And to one more person whose unwavering support has been behind me through all my years with
Putnam Berkley:

David Shanks

Wow, David,
you're absolutely the greatest!

SMALL TOWN GIRL

Words and music by LaVyrle Spencer

May 27, 1996

One-way traffic crawlin' round a small town square Eighteen years've passed since she's been there Been around the world, now she's com-ing back Wider-eyed and noting what this small town lacks Can't re- turn

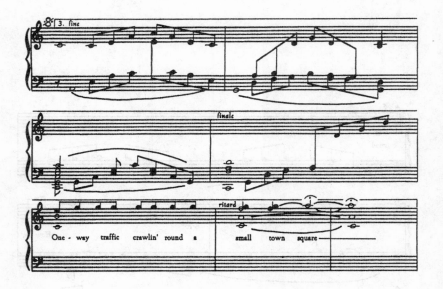

One - way traffic crawlin' round a small town square ——

Verse 3

Heard a lot of talk about the boy next door
He's a part of yesteryear I see no more
Circumstance took us eighteen years apart
Took him just one night to soften up my heart
Say good-bye
Mustn't cry.

Verse 4

Hometown girl departing on a one-way flight
Something deep inside her somehow set a-right
Runs her tearful eyes across the faded kitchen wall
Whispers, Mama, please don't change at all
Must return
There's more to learn.

One-way traffic crawlin' round a small town
square...

ONE

THE BLACK 300 ZX with the smoked windows looked completely out of place in Wintergreen, Missouri, population 1,713. Heads turned as it downshifted and growled its way around the town square behind Conn Hendrickson's lumbering Sinclair fuel oil truck and Miss Elsie Bullard's 1978 Buick sedan, whose speedometer hadn't seen fifty since she drove it off the showroom floor. On the open road, Miss Elsie cruised at forty-five. In town, she preferred a genteel fifteen.

The Z came up short behind her, its stereo booming through the closed windows. The brakes shrieked and its rear end vaulted, drawing attention to the Tennessee vanity plates.

MAC, it said.

And MAC said it all.

Four old men stood out in front of Wiley's Bakery with coffee on their breath, sucking toothpicks, following the car with their eyes.

"There she is."

"She's back."

"Showin' off some, too."

"Shoo-ey. 'At's some car she's herdin'."

"What's she doin' here anyways? She don't come back too often."

"Her momma's havin' her other hip surgeried. Come back to help her out awhile's what I heard."

"How can she see out them there windows?"

"Always figgered people who needed windows that black got somethin' to hide, ain't that right, Delbert?"

They watched the sleek machine follow right on Miss Elsie's tail. The traffic around the town square moved one-way, counterclockwise, and on this lazy Tuesday in April, Miss Elsie, just off her volunteer stint at the Three Rivers Nursing Home, was hankering for a strawberry ice-cream cone from Milton's Drugstore. She putt-putted around four sides of the square at the speed of a candle melting, searching for just the right place to park; the Z followed her around three, a scant yard off her heavy chrome bumper.

Inside the sports car Tess McPhail interrupted her singing and said aloud, "Move your ass, Miss Elsie!"

For the last five hours she'd been listening to her own voice on a rough cut off the upcoming album she'd been recording in Nashville for the past several weeks. Her producer, Jack Greaves, had handed the tape to her on her way out of the studio yesterday, and said, "Give it a listen on your way up to Missouri, then call me when you get there and let me know what you think."

The tape continued playing as Tess impatiently tapped the leather steering wheel with a long persimmon fingernail.

"Elsie, would you *move* it!"

Miss Elsie, her sprouty white hair creating a fuzzball silhouette, retained a two-handed death grip on the wheel and continued around the square at the same snail's pace. She finally reached the corner, turned left and got out of Tess's way while Tess squealed around a right, speedshifted, laid on the gas, and burned her way up Sycamore, muttering, "Lord o' mercy, *small towns.*"

This one hadn't changed since she'd left it eighteen years ago. Same red-brick courthouse in the town square, same tired storefronts around it, same old World War II veterans watching the traffic and waiting for the next parade to give them something to do. Same aging houses along Sycamore. Though the hickories and elms were bigger, most places looked just like when Tess had graduated from high school. There was Mindy Alverson's house: did her parents still live there? And what had happened to Mindy, Tess's best friend back then? That was where Mrs. Mabry used to live. She had taught geometry and could never instill the tiniest flicker of interest in Tess, a girl who had drifted her way through any class that wasn't related to music or creative arts, insisting she wouldn't need it, not when she was going to be a big country western singer after she graduated. And there was the house where that snotty Gallamore girl used to live, the one who landed the lead role in the class play the year they did *Oklahoma!* Tess had wanted to play the part of Laurie so badly she'd cried when the cast had been announced. Everybody said she should have gotten it; it was only because Cindy Gallamore's father was on the school board that she got picked instead.

Well, she'd shown Cindy Gallamore, hadn't she? She wondered what old Cindy was doing now. Probably giving herself home perms and changing diapers in one of these dismal little cracker boxes while Tess McPhail's latest number-one country hit wafted from the radio behind the piles of dirty dishes on Cindy's kitchen cupboard.

Tess reran the tape of "Tarnished Gold" one last time, listening with a critical ear. Overall, she liked it. Liked it a lot, with the exception of one single harmony note that continued to bother her after listening to the cut perhaps fifty or sixty times during her drive up.

She passed Judy and Ed's house on Thirteenth Street. The garage door was up and a car was visible inside, but Tess went on singing harmony with herself and gave the place little more than a hard-edged glance. Judy and her damned peremptory summons.

"Momma's got to have surgery on her

other hip and this time you're taking care of her," Judy had said.

What would Judy know about the demands of a major career? All she'd ever done was run a beauty shop. Why, she hadn't a glimmer of what it meant to be pulled away from your work midway through recording an album that a whole record label was planning to release on a date that had been set more than a year ago.

But Judy was jealous, always had been, and throwing her weight around was how she got even.

The last thing Judy had said on the phone was, "You're going to be here, Tess, and don't try to get out of it!"

Then there was Tess's middle sister, Renee, on the other side of town, whose daughter, Rachel, was getting married in four weeks. It was understandable that Renee had plenty to do during these last few weeks before the wedding, but couldn't they have scheduled it and the surgery a little further apart? After all, Mom had known she needed this second hip replacement ever since she'd had the first one two years ago.

Tess turned onto Monroe Street and memories rolled back while she traveled the six-block stretch she had walked to elementary school every day for seven years. She pulled up at the curb in front of her mother's house, killed the engine and stared at the place. Lord, how it had deteriorated. She unplugged her cellular phone, got out of the car and stood beside it, pushing her narrow-legged jeans down off her calves, a size-seven woman in oversized sunglasses, cowboy boots and dangly Indian earrings made of silver and turquoise, with hair the color of an Irish setter and fair, freckly skin.

Her heart sank as she studied the house. How could her mother have let it get so shabby? The post–World War II bungalow was made of red brick, but the white wood trim was peeling and the front steps were listing badly. The yard looked just plain pitiful. The sidewalk was pitted, and the arbor vitae had grown taller than the living room window. Dandelions spangled the yard.

What does Mom do with all the money I send her?

Years past, Mary McPhail wouldn't have stood for any kind of weed disgracing her lawn. But that was when her hips were healthy. Tess reached into the car, shouldered an enormous gray bag of bread-soft leather, slammed the door, then headed for the house. Walking up the cracked sidewalk she was reminded of how her little girlfriends used to push their doll buggies along it while she took Melody, her singing doll, and put on performances on the front steps.

As she approached those steps now, her mother appeared in the door above them, beaming. "I *thought* I heard a car door!" Mary McPhail's joy was unmistakable as she flung open the screen door and both of her arms. "Tess, honey, you're here!"

"Hey, Momma." Tess vaulted up the three steps and scooped her mother up hard. They rocked together while the door sprang shut and nudged them inside a tiny vestibule. Mary was half a head shorter and forty-five pounds heavier than her daughter, with a round face and metal-rimmed glasses. When Tess pulled back to see her, there were tears in Mary's eyes.

"You sure you should be up walkin' around, Momma?" You could still hear southwest Missouri in Tess's voice.

" 'Course I should. Just got back from a tour of the operating room and they drawed some blood and made me blow into some little plastic tube to see if I got 'nuff air in my lungs to withstand the operation, and I do, and if I can manage all that, I can hug my daughter hello. Take them durned glasses off so's I can see what my little girl looks like."

Tess smiled and removed her sunglasses. "It's just me." She held her hands out at her sides.

"Just you. That's for sure—just you who I haven't seen for nine whole months." Mary shook her finger under Tess's nose.

"I know. I'm sorry, Momma. It's been crazy, as usual."

"Your hair is different." Mary held her in place by both elbows, giving her the once-over. Tess's hair was cut in a shag that fell in disheveled layers well below the neck of her T-shirt in back, while in front it just covered her ears.

"They styled it for my next album cover."
"Who?"
"Cathy."
"Who's Cathy again?"

"Cathy Mack, my stylist—I've told you about Cathy."

Mary flapped a hand. "I guess you have, but you got so many people working for you I can't keep 'em straight. And land, girl, you're so skinny. Don't they feed you down there in Nashville?"

"I work at keeping thin, Momma, you know that—and you know it doesn't come naturally—so please don't start pushing food on me already, okay?"

Mary turned away and hobbled into the house. "Well, I should think, making the kind of money you do, that you could eat a little better."

Tess resisted rolling her eyes and stuck her sunglasses back on, following Mary inside. They went through a shallow living room that stretched across the entire front of the house, a west-facing room with bumpy stucco walls and well-used furniture, dominated by an upright piano. Three archways led off the opposite wall, the center one upstairs, the right one to the bathroom and Mary's bedroom, the left one to the kitchen at the rear of the house. Mary stomped through the left one, still talking.

"I thought country singers wore big hair."

"That's old, Momma. Things're changing in country."

"But you flattened all them pretty natural curls right out of it. I always loved them natural curls of yours."

"They want me to look up-to-date."

Mary's own hair could use some styling, Tess thought, studying a pinwheel of exposed skull on the back of her head. She'd given up coloring it and let it go natural, which proved to be a peachy gray. The remains of an old set clearly disclosed the need for an update. More important, however, was the pained gait with which she moved, lurching sharply to the right each time she put weight on that leg, using whatever furniture or walls were available for support.

"Are you *sure* you should be walking, Momma?"

"They'll have me off my feet plenty after the operation's over. Long as I can hobble around I'm going to."

She was a squat, squarish woman of seventy-four, wearing a disgusting old slacks set made of polyester knit that had begun to pill. The pants were solid lavender, the top had been white once, and was stamped with a cluster of pansies so faded their edges had lost distinction. The outfit had to be a good fifteen years old. Tess wondered if this was what her mother had worn when she went to tour the hospital today. She also wondered about the stylish silk trouser outfit she'd had shipped from Nordstrom's last fall when she'd been on tour in Seattle.

"The kitchen looks the same," she remarked while Mary turned on the water and began filling a coffeemaker.

"It's old but I like it this way."

The kitchen had white metal cupboards with brown Formica tops that were so worn they looked white in places. No matter how many times Tess had scolded Mary for not using a cutting board, she continued doing her chopping directly on the Formica to the left of the sink. The kitchen walls were papered in a ghastly orange floral, the two windows hung with orange floral tie-backs from a mail-order catalogue. There was a wall clock with a painting of a lake on its face, an electric stove with a chip in the porcelain where Judy had clunked it with a kettle one time when all three girls were fighting about who would make the popcorn. And beside the stove, on the dull brown Formica countertop, a homemade pecan pie loaded with about three hundred calories per slice.

Tess's eyes moved no further. "Oh, Momma, you didn't."

Mary turned around and saw what Tess was ogling. " 'Course I did. I couldn't let my little girl come home and not find her favorites."

What was it about being called her little girl that touched a nerve in Tess? She was thirty-five and had been gone from home since she'd graduated from high school. Her face and name were as familiar to most Americans as those of the president, and her income topped his many times over. She had accomplished it all with her own talent, creativity, and a business acumen worthy of Wall Street. But her mother insisted on referring to Tess as "her little girl." The few times Tess had corrected her, saying, "I'm not your little girl anymore," Mary had looked baffled and hurt. So Tess let it pass this time.

"Are you making that coffee for me?" she asked.

"Can't have pecan pie without coffee."

"I really don't drink coffee much any-

more, Momma . . . and I really shouldn't
eat the pie either."

Mary glanced over her shoulder. Her exuberance faded and she slowly shut off the
water. The baffled look had entered her
eyes again, that of one generation struggling to understand the next. "Oh . . .
well, then . . . shoot . . ." She glanced
down dubiously at the half-filled pot, then
turned on the tap and resumed filling it. "I'll
go ahead and cook some for myself then."

"Do you have any fruit, Mom?" Tess
went to the refrigerator and opened the
door.

"Fruit?" Mary asked, as if her daughter
had asked for pâté de foie gras.

"I eat a lot of fruit now and I could sure
use a piece. I haven't eaten since breakfast."

"I've got some canned peaches." Mary
opened a lower cupboard door and attempted to lean over stiffly.

"Yeah, that'll be great, but I can get 'em.
Here, why don't you sit down and let me?"

"It's no better when I sit. I'll do it. Why
don't you get your things out of the car and
take them upstairs?" Mary had found the
peaches and was taking a can opener from

a drawer. Tess reached into the drawer and covered her mother's hand.

" 'Cause I came home to take care of you, not the other way around. Now here, you give me that."

The peaches were packed in heavy syrup and had a rubbery skin surrounding mushy insides, but Tess took a fork and began eating them straight from the can, wandering around the kitchen, glancing at some notes that were pinned on a small bulletin board by the phone. The bulletin board itself had an ugly frame of molded plastic made to resemble spilled green peas. It held school pictures of her nieces and nephews, a reminder to check the long-distance bill to see if they'd charged a wrong number, and some grocery coupons cut out of magazines. Tide—twenty-five cents off. Once again Tess wondered what her mother did with the money she sent her. It was irritating that Mary would continue to use twenty-five-cent-off coupons when it was so damned unnecessary!

Mary opened the refrigerator and said, "I made your favorite hot dish—hamburger and Tater Tots. I suppose I could put it in the oven now but"—she checked the wall clock—"it's only four o'clock and it'll take an hour to cook. Five o'clock is too early to eat, so maybe we ought to wait a while and—"

"The peaches are fine for now, Momma. I know you don't usually eat till six."

She watched the concern fade from Mary's face once she was reassured the danger of altering the supper hour was passed. Tater Tot hot dish had been Tess's favorite when she was twelve years old. These days, beef was a once-a-week meat, and deep-fried Tater Tots never passed her lips. Not when she had a collection of cus- tom-made concert clothes in size seven that cost between eight and ten thousand dollars apiece. She took the can of peaches to the kitchen table and sat down. In the middle of the table a potted plant sat on the worst-looking plastic doily Tess had ever seen. It, like Mary's shirt, had been white once. It was now as yellow and curled as an old fish scale.

Mary poured herself a cup of coffee and sat, too, lowering herself gingerly to the chrome-legged chair with a cracked vinyl seat that was hidden beneath a tie-on cushion of brown-and-orange floral. She glanced at Tess's oversized white T-shirt that was silk-screened with four faces and a logo.

"What's that, then, 'Southern Smoke'?" she asked.

Tess glanced down at her chest. "Oh, that's the name of a band I know. They've been trying to break out, but so far it hasn't happened. I've been sort of dating one of the guitar players. This one . . . see?" Tess spread the shirt and pointed to a bearded face.

Mary squinted. "What's his name?"

"Burt Sheer."

"Burt Sheer, huh? How long you been seein' him?"

"Oh, just a couple of months."

"Is it serious?"

"In this business?" Tess laughed. "It better not be."

"Why not?"

"With his schedule on the road, plus me gone all over America singing a hundred and fifty concerts a year? Plus I'm cutting this new album right now that's taking an enormous amount of time, and doing promotions whenever and wherever the label thinks I should . . . well, anyway, I've seen

Burt exactly four times. And a couple of those times I had to argue with Jack because he thought I should go home and get some sleep instead of going to hear Burt's band at the Stockyard after I finished in the studio at ten P.M."

"What's the Stockyard?"

"A restaurant and club we go to."

"And who's Jack again?"

"Jack Greaves . . . my record producer."

"Oh, that's right." Tess watched the gleam of hope fade from her mother's eyes and knew Mary really did not see. She would never accept the fact that her youngest daughter had chosen a career over marriage and children. To a consummate mother like Mary McPhail that was tantamount to squandering your life.

"Which reminds me—I really should call Jack. He's laying down some harmony tracks on one of my new songs and I need to talk to him about it. It'll just take me a minute."

She called, using her credit card, from the wall phone at the end of the kitchen cabinets and reached Jack at Wildwood Studio, where she knew he'd be working.

"Hi, Jack!"

"Mac! Good to hear from you. You at your mother's?"

"Yes, sir. Got here safe and sound."

"How's she doing?"

"Middling."

"Well, now, you tell her I hope it all goes well for her."

"Thanks, I will. Hey, I listened to 'Tarnished Gold' all the way down, and the harmony on the word 'mistaken' still bothers me. I think it's got to be an E-flat instead of an E. When it becomes a minor it gets an edge that puts added pathos on the word itself." She sang the phrase, gesturing with her hand as if directing the quartet of canisters on the kitchen cupboard to sing along. "Know what I mean, Jack? . . . Can you get Carla back in there to record it again? . . . She still having trouble with her voice? . . . Well, ask her, will you? . . . Thanks, Jack, then Fed Ex it to me as soon as you've got it, but don't spend a lot of time mixing it till I've heard the new harmony, okay? You've got my mother's phone number and address, right? I won't be here tomorrow—tomorrow's the surgery—but I'll

call you from the hospital. Sure. Thanks,
Jack. 'Bye.''

When she'd hung up, her mother wore an
astonished expression. "You'd record
something again just because of a single
word?''

"It's done all the time. Sometimes we record an entire harmony track and never use
it at all. Last week Jack had a concert vio-
linist in the studio at my insistence, 'cause a
violin's got an entirely different sound from
a fiddle and I thought that this one song
should have a violin solo in one spot
where—''

The phone rang, interrupting, and Mary
began to push herself up. She winced and
Tess said, "I'll get it, Momma. I'm right
here.'' Tess reached for the wall phone and
answered, "Hello?''

"Oh . . . you're there.'' It was her sister
Judy, with little warmth in her voice. "I was
just calling to make sure.''

"I'm here. Got in about a half an hour
ago.''

"You drove, I hear.''

"How'd you hear?''

"People around town saw your license
plates.''

Tess turned her back on Mary and said more quietly, "I thought I should have my own car while I'm here. Four weeks is—" She stopped herself short: her mother could hear quite plainly.

Judy said it for her. "A long time . . . I know. I'm the one who took care of her last time, remember?"

For several seconds silent animosity crackled along the phone line while the two sisters relived the conversation in which Judy had ordered her younger sister home.

Finally Judy asked, "How's she feeling today? She had to go over to the hospital to have a pre-op check and go through some kind of little explanation and tour thing. I suppose it tired her out."

Tess turned to Mary. "Judy wants to know how you're feeling, Momma."

"Tell her I'm just fine. Nurse says my hemoglobin's normal and my lung capacity's good, so everything's set for tomorrow."

Tess repeated the message and Judy said, "Well, give her my love. Tell her I can't come over tonight but I'll be at the hospital before she goes into surgery in the morning. You have to have her there by six o'clock. Her surgery's at six-thirty. Did she tell you that?" Judy's voice snapped out the question.

"Don't worry, she'll be there."

"All right, then. Guess I'll see you there, too."

Mary began pushing off her chair again. "Just a minute, let me talk to her."

"Just a minute, Momma wants to talk to you."

Mary got up with great effort and made her way to the telephone. While she was speaking Tess moved away and stared out the double window beside the kitchen table. It looked out on the side yard, where some overgrown rhododendron bushes divided the property from the Anderson place next door.

"Hey, dear. Listen, thank you for picking up those groceries for me. I'll pay you when I see you. . . . No, no, no, you're not going to pay for my groceries! I'm fixin' to pay you back. I just appreciate your picking them up for me. How did Nicky do at his track meet? . . . Oh, isn't that wonderful. . . . And did Tricia find a dress for the prom? . . . Clear down there! Couldn't she find nothing in town? . . . Well, she'll look darling, I'm sure. You tell her I said to have a real good time and I'll be thinking of her Saturday night. . . . Okay, I will . . . yeah . . . yeah, 'bye."

Listening to Mary's end of the conversation, Tess felt light-years removed from her family. They shared a day-to-day flow of relationships and concerns that she had given up when she left home. Phone calls from Houston and Oklahoma City were not the same as groceries dropped off and put in a refrigerator, or grandchildren's lives bumping up against their grandmother's on a daily basis.

On the other hand the scope of their concerns seemed almost trivial to Tess when compared to her own. Had they sung at governors' mansions, or accepted awards on prime-time TV? Had they filled an auditorium with thirty thousand fans whose ticket fees meant the livelihoods of dozens of people, from studio technicians to DJs, stage hands to producers, all the way from L.A. to New York? Had they worried about meeting a deadline for delivering a finished album whose advertising, promo and shipping date had been determined even before all its song were written?

Prom dresses, track meets and groceries—none of them touched Tess's life anymore. And she wanted it that way.

Mary hung up and said, "I swear . . . Judy's got her hands full this week. She gave a wedding shower for Rachel on Tuesday, and prom is coming up this Saturday and every girl in school has made an appointment to have her hair fixed, so she's awful busy at the shop. Seems like Nicky's got some sporting event every night after school that she's got to try to run to, then on top of all that, Tricia insisted on drivin' clear over to Cape Girardeau to look for a prom dress. I keep telling Judy that sometimes she should just say no to those kids."

"Like you said no to us?" Tess replied.

Mary looked surprised. "Didn't I say no to you?"

"Couple of times that I can remember. Once when I wanted to get me a padded bra 'cause I had this huge crush on Kelvin Hazlitt, who was two years older than me and didn't know I was alive. I thought if I had some breasts like . . . well, you know"—Tess made two slings of her hands and bounced them at breast level—"like a pregnant rhinoceros, then Kelvin would ask me out. I'm still blamin' you 'cause he didn't.''

Mary chortled and hobbled toward her coffee cup. "Kelvin Hazlitt's been married three times already. Good thing I said no.''

"One other time you said no was when I wanted to get a tattoo.''

"A tattoo! Lord, I don't remember that.''

"Sure you do. Mindy got one, and I thought I needed everything Mindy had. By the way, what do you know about Mindy? I drove by her momma and daddy's house and couldn't help wondering where she is now.''

"Mindy's back. She and her husband have an appliance store here, and they've got two or three kids in school. One of 'em's in the same grade as one of Renee's, I think.''

While Mary went on talking, Tess put away her peaches in the fridge and dropped her fork into the sink. Through the window above it she had a clear view of Mrs. Kronek's backyard, across the alley. The block was dissected by that unpaved alley, and the two lots were laid out like mirror images of each other, one on each side. Houses, sidewalks, clotheslines, gardens and garages matched as perfectly as spots on a butterfly's wings. The garages were old, and single, and sat snugged up against the alley so tightly that their doors were perpendicular to it. While Tess was looking out, the garage door across the alley began to rise, then a car nosed up the alley, veered off and pulled into Mrs. Kronek's garage. A moment later a tall man in a business suit emerged, carrying a briefcase. He left the garage door open, glanced this way, then went up the sidewalk to Mrs. Kronek's back door.

"Who's that?" Tess asked.

Mary came over and took a look. "Why, that's Kenny Kronek, you remember him."

"Kenny Kronek?" Tess watched him climb the steps and enter the glassed-in back porch. He was tall and lean and dark haired, and the wind blew his tie sideways as he glanced over this way once more before the door slammed behind him. "You mean that dork who used to get the nose-bleeds in school all the time?"

"Tess, shame on you. Kenny Kronek is a nice boy."

"Oh, Momma, that's what you always said, because he was Lucille's boy, and she was your best friend. But you know as well as I do that he was a dork of the highest magnitude. Why, he couldn't walk a chalk line without tripping on it. And all those pimples! I can still smell the acne medication on him."

"Kenny took care of his mother till her dying day, and not every nice person in this world is coordinated, Tess. Besides that, he's a real good father and he takes real good care of the property since Lucille died, so I don't have a complaint in the world about him."

"You mean somebody actually *married* him?"

"Well, of course somebody married him. A girl he met in college. Stephanie. But they're divorced now."

"No wonder," Tess mumbled under her breath, turning away from the window.

"Tess," her mother scolded with a gentle glower.

"Well, he was always"—Tess's hands stirred the air as if to turn up the right word—"*looking* at me. You know what I mean?" She faked a shudder. "He was such a creep."

"I never thought so."

"Not you, but every girl in school, that's for sure."

"Oh, Tess, come on."

"Well, it's true. The only class we were ever in together was choir when I was a junior and he was a senior, and remember when we went to Choir Festival in St. Louis? We went on the bus, and Kenny came over and sat with me and I couldn't get rid of him. There he sat, with his pimples and his long, gawky neck with that Adam's apple that looked like a grapefruit in a sock, blushing so hard I thought he was going to have a nosebleed right on the spot. And his hair—mercy, Mother, remember how he used to comb his hair! So we're on this bus trip, and he comes over and sits with me and he tries to hold my hand!"

"Well, what's so wrong with that?"

"Mother, it was the seventies! Half the girls I knew were already sleeping with their boyfriends and Kenny Kronek—the nerd of all nerds—comes over and tries to work up the courage to hold my hand! I swear, all my friends teased me so bad I thought I'd die."

"You kids were so mean to him."

"Mom, there were kids you hung out with

and kids you didn't, and Kenny Kronek was definitely in the latter group."

"Still, you could have been a little nicer to him."

"No, I couldn't. Not to that nerd. All he had to do was look around at everybody else to see how idiotic he looked and try to improve himself. Only he never did. If he wanted to hang with us he could have worked a little harder at it."

Mary wasn't one to show her displeasure overtly, but there were signs—a tightening of a facial muscle, the persnickety way she picked up her coffee cup and carried it to the sink. Quietly she suggested, "Why don't you get your bags out of the car and park it back by the garage. It's probably better if you don't leave it on the street overnight, an expensive thing like that."

Tess knew when she was being chastised and it put a knot in her chest. What was it about her mother's displeasure that weighed heavier than that of others? Tess could handle herself out in the business and entertainment world like a pro, could make choices and decisions and lay down music that created respect—even awe—in those around her, but she hadn't been home one hour and already she felt the strictures of trying to return to a place she'd outgrown.

She drove around the south end of the block and headed up the alley past sheds and garages where she used to play hide-and-seek and kick-the-can when she was little, past backyard tulip trees and grapevines gone rambling over things they hadn't ought to ramble over. There were piles of blackened lumber and burning barrels that were used no more. Every place had a garden. The yards were green and old enough that their lot lines had become obscured by trees that had seeded themselves beside sheds, and by bushes that had ranged into the adjoining property. But here in Wintergreen, just above the bootheel of Missouri, where neighbors truly were neighbors and had been for twenty and thirty years, nobody cared about lines of demarcation.

Mary's garage was as old as the others and needed painting. Surprisingly, however, it had a new door. Nosing the car up to it and getting out, Tess glanced at the place across the alley. Everything painted, no ranging grapevines and not a piece of junk anywhere. Good for Saint Kenny, she thought sarcastically, grabbing her duffel bag and heading for the house. On the way through the backyard she noticed that her mother had somehow managed to put in a garden already. Tradition, this garden, no matter how unnecessary it was, and no matter how it must have hurt Mary's hip to get down on her hands and knees and plant it. Tess noticed that it was well established due to an unseasonably early spring, and supposed that during the next four weeks she'd end up having to care for it, which would positively ruin her nails! And her nails were one of her trademarks.

The back stoop was three steps high with a black iron handrail on one side only. Tess wondered how Mary would climb them after her surgery. Inside was a small landing with the basement door straight ahead, and the kitchen up a single step to the right. When Tess reached the house and bumped through the kitchen with her duffel bag, she called back over her shoulder, "Hey, Momma, you shouldn't have put in that garden this year with your hip so bad."

She was in the living room rounding the center arch when Mary called back, "Oh, I didn't put it in. Kenny did it for me this year."

Tess came up short and backed down the one step she'd climbed. She shot a look at the kitchen archway. All she could see was one chrome leg of the kitchen table and the window beyond it, and in her imagination, pimply Kenny Kronek planting her mother's tomatoes.

"He's got a rototiller," came Mary's voice, "and he offered, so I let him."

Saint Kenny the Rototiller, Tess thought wryly as she clumped upstairs.

Mary yelled, "And did you see my new garage door? He installed that for me, too."

Tess stopped in her tracks, resting the duffel bag on the step at her knee. The nerd installed the garage door, too? What was he after?

The upper story of the house was laid out shotgun style, its ceiling shaped like the roofline with a window at either end. The girls had called it "the barracks" when they were growing up, sleeping in three single beds whose headboards were pushed into the south roof angle. The stairs emerged onto the east end of the expanse with only a sturdy homemade railing to keep anyone from falling off the floor above. Straight ahead, at the top of the steps, was a window giving a bird's-eye view of Saint Kenny's yard. Tess whisked past it without giving it so much as a glance, executed a U-turn around the handrail and looked down the length of the room.

The beds hunkered along the left with a stack of drawers beside each one. On the far end a small dressing table stood beneath the window, and on the right, knee-hole closets filled the space beneath the eaves. She dropped her duffel on the farthest bed. They had earned their distance from the stairs by birth order; closest to the stairs and the downstairs bathroom was the oldest, Judy; middle bed was Renee's, and way over at the farthest end was Tess's, because she was the baby. She had always hated being referred to as the baby of the family, and felt a ripple of smug satisfaction at being the one who went off and did the best.

She stood looking around, then wandered to the dressing table where she had first written in her diary that she wanted to be a singer; where she had learned to put on makeup from Renee; and had sat staring out at the street with a puckered mouth when she'd been sent to her room as punishment. For what? It was hard to remember now, but there had been times. Times when she'd needed it, she supposed.

The top of the dressing table held an empty perfume bottle from Love's Baby Soft, and a framed photograph of Judy with two of her high school girlfriends; a pink glass dish containing a pearl button, a small ring, a cloth-covered ponytail holder and some dust. Dented into the top of the table, painted over in the years since, was the name Elvis, pressed there in ballpoint pen by Tess in 1977, the year he died and she graduated from high school. She'd grown up listening to Elvis and he had been her idol: if he could do it, she could do it. She brushed the word with her fingertips, as if it were a headstone, then switched on the familiar little lamp with the cheap flared plastic shade. She switched it off again and opened the single dressing-table drawer. Something went rolling and she reached inside and pulled it out: a tube of Bonne Bell root-beer-flavored Lip Smackers. She removed the cap and sniffed it. Nostalgia came rumbling like a tidal wave—being thirteen again and getting her first pair of panty hose; being fourteen and wearing these adolescent perfumes; being fifteen and going out on her first official dates with boys. She rubbed the Bonne Bell on her lips. It had turned sticky with age and she swiped it off with the side of one hand and dropped the tube back where it had been.

Bracing her palms on the tabletop she put her face near the window and glanced down at the street where she had watched for cars when her dates had come to pick her up. The trees in the front yard had grown. From up here she could see even more clearly the cracks in the sidewalk, the thin spots in the grass, the weeds. The sun was hovering just above the houses across the street where she used to babysit. On the lawn the dandelions were closing up as the afternoon waned.

And down below, her mother was calling, "Tess? Should I put the hot dish in now?"

She murmured to herself, "Yes, Momma, because the world will fall off its axis if it's not on the table at the crack of six." She pushed off the dressing table and called, "I'll do it, Momma! Just let me hang up some clothes first, okay?"

"Well . . . okay," Mary replied with grave doubt, then added, "but it's ten after five already and it really should bake for a full hour."

Tess couldn't help shaking her head. The normal schedule of a professional musician meant rising near noon, doing studio work from about two till nine, with a caterer bringing food in around six. On concert nights it meant performing between eight and eleven and eating supper around midnight; if you were playing clubs and doing a bus tour, packing up at one in the morning and eating your last meal of the day while you were rolling down the highway.

But Tess dutifully hollered down, "I'll be right there, Mom!"

Her mother had already put the hot dish in the oven but she let Tess set the table and get the rest of the meal ready. Mary's suggested accompaniments to the fat-filled Tater Tot hot dish were toast (with real butter and homemade raspberry jam), coffee (with cream and sugar, of course) and pecan pie with whipped cream (the real kind, not Cool Whip—add forty calories for the whipped cream, Tess thought).

A discreet inventory of the refrigerator turned up a head of cabbage but no lettuce, cheddar cheese but no cottage cheese, sour cream but no yogurt, and whole milk but no skim. Just what were these groceries Judy had dropped off anyway?

In the freezer, thank goodness, Tess found a bag of frozen broccoli. "Mom, do you mind if I cook this?" she asked.

Mary stared at her daughter as if her feelings were hurt. "There's vegetables in the hot dish."

Potatoes soaked in oil, plus rich cream of chicken soup.

"If you're saving it for something else—"

"No, no, go ahead and cook it!"

Tess did, but when the main dish was hot and bubbling it smelled so delicious and looked so tempting she dug into it like a soldier after a foot march. She guzzled the damned whole milk, too, because it was the only milk in the house, and had a half a piece of toast slathered with butter and jam. Mary smiled in satisfaction, watching her.

When their plates were clean, Mary began slicing a piece of pie. "I'll just cut you a small one."

"I can't, Momma, honest. It looks delicious, but I just can't."

"Oh, nonsense." Mary pulled Tess's plate over. "I made it just for you. What's one little piece of pie going to hurt? If you ask me, you look like a scarecrow. You could use a little meat on your bones."

"Please, Momma, no. I can't."

Mary slapped a wedge on Tess's plate anyway. "Just don't put any whipped cream on it, that way it won't be so fattening."

Tess was eating a single obligatory bite of pie when someone tapped on the back door and opened it without waiting for an answer.

"Mary?" he said and stepped inside, into the tiny back entry, no longer wearing a business suit but a red windbreaker, no longer carrying a briefcase but hefting a forty-pound sack of pellet salt on his left shoulder.

"Oh, Kenny, it's you," Mary said, going joyful in an instant.

"I brought your softener salt," he said, turning slowly beneath his burden and opening the basement door. "I'll take it right down."

"Oh, thanks a million, Kenny. Tess, get that light for him, would you, honey?"

"I got it!" he called as the basement light switched on. His footsteps thumped down, there was a pause while he slit open the bag, then the salt rattled into the plastic softener vat, and he came back up. Fast, as if jogging. "Got one more. Be right back."

When the door slammed Tess whispered, "He comes right into your house without knocking?"

"Oh, Tess, this is Wintergreen, not Nashville."

He was back in a minute with the second sack, carried it downstairs and emptied it into the water softener before returning to the main level. When he closed the basement door and climbed the single step into the kitchen, Tess stuck a second bite of pie into her mouth and fixed her eyes on her plate, as if he'd heard all the nasty things she'd said about him only minutes ago. She needn't have worried, for he gave her not so much as a glance. He shuffled to a stop beside Mary's chair, looking directly down on her, brushing off his hands and making his windbreaker whistle. "There. All filled. Anything else you need while I'm here?"

"I don't think so. That'll hold me for a while. Kenny, you remember Tess, don't you?"

He gave Tess a negligible nod that dis-

missed her as if she were still back in Nashville. It was brusque enough to be rude, and
accompanied by not so much as a single
word of greeting. She wasn't sure if he still
had pimples or not because she couldn't
find the wherewithal to raise her eyes.

While she went on eating her pie, Mary
said, "How much do I owe you, Kenny?"

He fished a receipt out of his jacket
pocket and handed it to her. "Seven-
eighty."

Mary said to Tess, "Honey, could you get
my purse? It's hanging on the closet door-
knob in my bedroom."

Tess went gratefully. In her wake she
heard Mary telling him what time Tess had
arrived, and him changing the subject, asking her if everything was set for tomorrow
morning. When Tess got back with the
purse, he stepped out of her way and said
nothing. Mary dug out the money and
handed it to him while Tess resumed her
chair.

"There you are. Seven dollars . . ." After
the bills she counted out some coins into
his palm. "And eighty cents."

"Thanks," he said, dropping the change
into a tight side pocket of his blue jeans and

reaching toward a rear pocket for his billfold. He had turned his shoulder on Tess
again, and a quick glance gave her a view
of his trim backside as the billfold slipped
out of sight. "So everything's all set for tomorrow?" he asked Mary. "Blood work
turned out fine? And you've got that walker
all polished up?"

"Yes, sir, I'm all set."

"Scared?" he inquired with an easy ca-
sualness.

"Not much. Been through it before, so I
know what to expect."

"So you don't need anything?"

"No. Tess is taking me to the hospital in
the morning at six o'clock. That is, if I can
get in that little car of hers. I don't know
what it's called but it cost more than this
house. Did you see it in the alley, Kenny?"

The room grew painfully silent. What
could Kenny do but answer, still avoiding a
direct glance at the younger woman.

"Yeah, Mary, I sure did."

"She drove all the way up from Nashville
just to take care of me."

When he turned to level his impersonal
gaze on Tess, what could she do but ac-
knowledge him?

"Hello, Kenny," she said colorlessly.

"Tess," he said, so coolly she wished he hadn't spoken at all. The dorky hairdo was gone and so were the pimples. He wasn't a bad-looking man, taller than she'd have guessed, brown eyed, dark haired, with conservative lines everywhere. But so cold to Tess. After giving her the requisite hello, he turned back to Mary and dropped to a squat beside her chair, resting his fingertips lightly on her knees. "Well, now listen, you . . ." While he went on encouraging Mary with warmth and deep caring, Tess escaped from the table, ostensibly to get the coffeepot, actually to hide her mortification at being ignored. Tess McPhail, who'd had her picture on the cover of *Time* magazine, and who'd been invited to sing at the White House, and whose appearance on a stage made fans scream and chant and sometimes get held back by police. Tess McPhail got snubbed by that nerd upperclassman, Kenny Kronek.

"I'll be thinking of you in the morning," he said quietly to Mary, "and I'll be up to see you as soon as you're feeling up to it. Casey says to tell you hi and good luck and she'll be coming up, too, when she can.

Now, you be good, and no dancing till the doctor tells you to, okay?"

Mary patted his hands and laughed. "My dancing days aren't over yet, Kenny, so you better keep your eye on me."

He laughed, too, and rose. "Good luck, Mary," he said quietly, then took her by both jaws, leaned over and kissed her forehead.

"Thanks, dear."

The kitchen was small. He turned to leave and found Tess in his way, the coffeepot clutched in her right hand, her eyes bulging with anger. "Excuse me," he said, and moved around her as if she were a stranger on an elevator.

When the screen door closed, she was left behind, blushing.

TWO

TESS MCPHAIL was unaccustomed to being treated like a tree stump. Where she moved, people paid attention. Fans loved her. Radio stations vied for her interviews. People in restaurants asked for her autograph. Her agent thought she was the greatest female talent he had represented in his career. Her producer said she had an ear for a hit and the talent to perform it that had elevated his status to that of star in his own right simply for having worked with her. She had the business and home telephone numbers of all the hierarchy from MCA Records, who picked up their phones the moment they learned she was on the other end of the line.

Yet if Kenny Kronek had been a dog with

a natural urge, he'd have raised his leg on her ankle.

The moment he left she slammed the coffeepot on the burner, spun to the table and began throwing some dishes into stacks. "Well!" she exploded, marching to the sink and whacking them down. "Since when did *he* become the man of the house?"

"Now, Tess, don't be ungrateful. There are lots of times when one of the kids can't get over here to help me, and Kenny is more than willing. I don't know what I'd do without him."

"I could *see* that."

"Why, Tess, what are you so upset about?"

"I'm not upset! But he comes right in here like he owns the place! And who's Casey?"

"His daughter, and will you stop throwing my dishes around?"

"I suppose she walks in here without knocking, too!"

The truth hit Mary. "Why, Tess, you're upset because he didn't pay any attention to you!"

"Oh, Mother . . . really. Give me a little credit."

"I give you all the credit in the world when you deserve it, but not when you criticize Kenny. And I said to quit throwing my dishes around. You're going to break them."

"If I do I'll buy you some new ones. Just look at these old pieces of junk anyway! They're all chipped and the gold color is worn right off the edges! Why don't you buy some new ones with the money I send you? Come to think of it, why don't you buy *any-thing* with the money I send you?"

"I like those old dishes. They've been around since your dad was alive, so please take some care."

"Mother, you shouldn't let a man just come walking into your house whenever he pleases!"

"Oh, Tess, just listen to yourself. He's my neighbor. What are you getting all worked up about? I knew his mother for forty years."

"He's rude."

"Not to me he's not."

"No, just to me!"

"Can you blame him? You just got done telling me how awful you used to treat him."

Tess made no reply. She turned on the

tap, filled the sink with soapy water and began washing the dishes, a job she ab-
horred. Five years ago she'd offered to
build her mother a new house with a dishwasher and air-conditioning and anything
she wanted! Five years! But would Mary say
yes? Of course not. Instead here was Tess,
washing dishes by hand and glaring out a
window at Kenny Kronek's house!

"All right! So he aggravated me, but the
man is a complete boor!"

Her mother found a dish towel hanging
inside a cupboard door and picked up a
wet plate. "I don't want to argue with you,
Tess. You never thought much of Kenny, I
don't expect that to change now. But he
has been good to me, and it makes me feel
good to know he's right across the alley
anytime I need him."

Tess took the towel and plate out of her
mother's hands. "I'll do the dishes. You go
do whatever you want to—lie down and
rest, read, get your things ready for tomorrow."

Mary glanced wistfully toward the living
room. "Well . . . the nurse *did* give me
some special soap that I'm supposed to

take a bath with tonight, and then again in the morning."

"Go ahead, take your bath while I clean up the kitchen. Do you need help with anything?"

"No . . . no, I can manage."

When Mary was gone, Tess gripped both ends of the dish towel and snapped it into a straight line, staring again out the window. *Four weeks,* she thought. *I'll be crazy before two.* A moment later the water could be heard running in the bathroom and Tess continued cleaning up the kitchen, trying to ignore the presence of the house across the alley and the fact that its owner had just snubbed her royally.

She could see his kitchen window through this one, and occasionally a head moving past it. The glass porch, which had been added to the back of the house in the sixties, was also lit up, though nobody was in it. Tess had dim memories of playing in it with Kenny when they were both toddlers and their mothers were having coffee together. More clearly she remembered balking at going there to play with him as she grew older.

She was nearly finished washing dishes

when the front door opened and a familiar female voice called, "Tess, you here?"

Renee. Tess's heart gladdened at the sound of her other sister's voice, even as she quashed the instinct to run toward her with a hug. Instead, she waited for Renee to appear in the kitchen doorway. Momentarily Renee did—a dark-haired, tall and classically pretty woman with a face composed of smooth lines, like a Walt Disney drawing of a princess. The middle of the three Mc-Phail girls, Renee was thirty-eight but looked thirty. She was dressed in a pastel blue skirt and blouse with a white sweater tied over her shoulders. Her collar-length auburn hair looked as if she'd been driving with her windows down.

"You *are* here!" she rejoiced, opening her arms and smiling broadly.

"Hi, you little shit."

Renee laughed, got Tess in a hug and rocked her like a bowling pin. "What do you mean, little shit?"

"You know what I mean, ordering me to come home and take care of Momma. I'm so mad at you I could choke you."

Renee found it amusing. "Well, if that's

what it took to get you home, I guess we did the right thing."

"You probably got me in a heap of trouble, you know that, don't you?"

"Oh, come on," Renee said despairingly.

"I've got a record contract and I'm supposed to be in a studio recording right now."

"And I'm supposed to be at home putting supper on the table for my family, but I've been off running down twenty-five potted violets for the tables at a wedding reception, and taste-testing Florentine chicken at a caterer's and trying to find anyone with a white horse-drawn carriage because Rachel insists they're going to arrive at the church in a carriage, and the only ones I can find in the whole country are black and look like they hauled Robert E. Lee through the battlefront."

"Do you know that I had to cancel seven appearances because of this?"

"What do you think we had to cancel the last time Momma had surgery?"

They were no longer hugging but leaning back taking each other's measure.

"But it's easier for you," Tess reasoned. "You live here."

"Try that argument on Judy and see how far it gets you."

"Judy. Ha! I won't have too much to say to Judy after the way she talked to me on the phone."

"She's disgusted with you, too. Has been for the last ten years because you never come home."

"What do you mean, I never come home? I come home!"

"Sure. Once a year or so when your schedule permits. Honey-pie, families deserve more than that."

"But you don't understand."

"Sure we do. You've got your priorities."

"Renee-ay!"

"Te-ess," her sister aped in the same singsong.

"I expected this out of Judy, but not out of you."

Renee said simply, "It's your turn, Tess, and you know it."

They were at a stalemate. Tess returned to the sink, pulled the plug and let the water drain. She squeezed out the dishcloth and swiped it over the faucets, then turned and gestured toward the bathroom, whispering, "She's gonna drive me nuts!"

Renee, too, kept her voice lowered. "It's only for four weeks, then I can help her once the wedding's over."

"But I don't live like this anymore . . . eating pecan pie and washing dishes by hand, for heaven's sake."

"For the next four weeks you do."

"She just doesn't understand, I have to keep in shape. It's part of my public image, and I can't go eating Tater Tot hot dish and pecan pie with whipped cream!"

Renee held Tess in place by her rolled-up T-shirt sleeves, looking straight into her amber eyes. "She's your mother. She loves you. It's how she shows it." She dropped her hands. "And how in the world would she know what you eat anymore? You're never around."

Apparently this was going to be a repeated refrain during Tess's time back home; she had difficulty stifling a retort, for none of her family had the vaguest idea of the immensity of the commitments she made and how many people were affected by them. They all thought she was merely caught up in fame, and that whenever she picked up a telephone or received an overnight package she was grandstanding. Any protestations to the contrary would fall on deaf ears.

"Is she in bed already?" Renee asked.

"No, she's taking a bath."

"Well, I'll go tap on her door and say hi and good-bye. I gotta get home. Just wanted to stop by and see if you got here okay."

Renee went through the living room into a small hall alcove where she tapped on the bathroom door with her car key.

"Momma? Hi, it's Renee, but I can't stay. Everything go okay today at your pre-op?"

"Just fine. Can't you wait till I get out?"

"Sorry, gotta get home and feed my family, but I'll be there in the morning before they wheel you in, okay?"

"Okay, dear. Thanks for stopping by."

"Anything you need?"

"Nothing I can think of. But if there is, Tess can get it for me, and Kenny offered, too."

"Okay, then, see you in the morning."

When Renee came back through the living room Tess was there with her hands in the pockets of her jeans and one shoulder propped against the kitchen archway.

"Kenny again," Tess said with a look of distaste that Renee missed.

"Thank heavens for Kenny. He treats her as if she's his own mother. We should all be plenty grateful to him. Well, listen . . . gotta run." Renee pecked Tess on the cheek. "See you in the morning, bright and early. She tell you what time she's got to be there?"

"She told me."

"Can you manage that?"

Tess rolled her gaze to the ceiling and mumbled, "I can't believe this."

"Okay, okay—just asking."

"I meet more schedules in one month than you and Judy will meet in your lifetime."

"Not at that time of day."

"Will you stop treating me like the baby of the family!"

"Okay, all right . . . I'm going. See you tomorrow."

Tess followed her sister and stood in the front vestibule watching her drive off in a blue van. Evening had fallen and the street was quiet. In the bathroom the tub started draining. The smell in the vestibule never seemed to change. It was one she associated with changeless places from her past—public libraries and churches and school buildings that still had wood floors. The floor in the vestibule was oak, the bound rug old and jute-backed, and the smell was stuffy, like the clothing of old people who don't go outside enough. The vestibule itself was a cramped cubicle with a door to outside and another to the living room, the kind that had been popular in another era before foyers had become integrated with living rooms. It had an antique mirror on the wall, and on the floor in one corner a tarnished brass container holding some old magazines. She stood there feeling disgruntled and misplaced, no longer comfortable in her mother's house and not fully understanding why, wishing she were in the studio in Nashville where she belonged and knew her function and purpose. Here, she felt cast upon a foreign shore. Her connection to it was gone, and she was being blamed for that, yet all she was guilty of was success.

Her mother came out of the bathroom dressed in a flowered cotton nightie and duster that snapped up the front.

"Tess? Is Renee gone?"

"Yes. She had to get home." Tess turned back into the living room where her mother was toweling her hair, releasing a strongly medicinal smell into the room. "Phew! What is that? It stinks."

"They just called it antibacterial soap."

"Can I comb your hair for you? I have my blow-dryer."

"No, thanks, honey. Got my brush right here. I have to use the soap again in the morning anyway—orders from the hospital."

The way Mary was moving Tess could tell she was in pain. "Is your hip worse, Momma?"

Mary put a hand to it and walked with a pronounced heel-slide, perching carefully on the overstuffed arm of a living room chair whose height made it easier to use than the seat. "It's hard getting in and out of the tub. Always makes it worse."

This time when Tess made her point she did so in much gentler tones than earlier when she was upset with Kenny Kronek. "Then why wouldn't you let me buy you a new house when I wanted to? You could have had a nice roomy shower instead of that cramped little tub."

Mary waved off her remark and tried to make herself comfortable on the arm of the chair, but could not.

"Mom, what can I do for you?"

"Get me a bed pillow and I'll stretch out on the sofa, then sit down and let's talk."

It took some time to get Mary reasonably comfortable on the sofa. When she was, she said, "Now tell me about the places you've been lately."

Tess began giving highlights of the last couple months. After years of traveling by bus she owned her own jet, so she could now perform a concert in California one day and be in Nashville recording the next. Since it was not cost-efficient to employ a mechanic and pilot for a single jet, she had bought five and opened a plane-leasing service to defray the costs. She had been telling her mother how well the two-year-old company was doing but after only a few minutes Mary's eyes grew heavy and got the intermittent glazed look of one who's trying to give the impression of alertness. Realizing her conversation wasn't getting through, Tess finally said, "Momma, you're tired. Let me help you to bed."

Mary stifled a yawn, and murmured,

"Mmm . . . guess you're right, honey. Have to be out by four-thirty anyway, so early-to-bed won't hurt."

Her mother's bedroom had changed only slightly more than the rest of the house. It had a new bedspread and matching curtains, but the furniture was the same, sitting in the identical spots it always had, and the carpet hadn't been replaced in all the years Tess could remember. On the chest of drawers her parents' wedding picture shared the space with the same wooden key- and change-holder that had held flotsam from the pockets of the daddy she barely remembered. He had died in an accident while driving a U.S. Mail truck when she was six. The three girls' portraits on the wall were the same ones that had been taken when they were all in elementary school and had hung on the pearlized beige-and-white wallpaper ever since.

What's wrong with me, Tess thought, that so little of this evokes nostalgia? Instead, it raised a mild revulsion for the stifling changelessness of her mother's life. How could Mary have lived all these years without replacing the carpet, let alone the man? She was an attractive woman, and a kind one, but she'd always said, "Nope. One man was enough for me. He was the only one I ever wanted." As far as Tess knew, her mother had never even dated after his death.

Tess drew up the covers when Mary lay down, and bent over her with a heavy sadness in her heart for all that her mother had missed.

"Mom, how come you never married again after Daddy died?" she asked.

"I didn't want to."

"All these years?"

"I had you girls, then the grandchildren. I know it's hard for you to understand, but I was happy. I *am* happy."

Tess tried to comprehend such unimaginative acceptance, but to her whose life was constantly filled with new faces and places, Mary's life seemed stultifying. When Tess would have straightened, Mary reached up and took her face in both hands.

"I know you came home against your will, dear. I'm sorry that Judy and Renee made you."

"No, Mom, I didn't, honest."

"Sure you did, but I don't hold any grudge against you for it. Who wants to stop everything to take care of a lame old woman?"

"Mom, don't be silly."

Mary went on as if Tess hadn't spoken. "But you know what I think? I think that the life you lead is wearing you out. That's why I let the girls force you into coming home, 'cause I think you needed it worse than I did."

"Mom, they didn't—"

Mary silenced her daughter with a touch on her lips. "No need to lie, Tess. I wasn't born yesterday. I said it's okay and it is. Will you make sure you get plenty of sleep yourself? We have to get going by four-thirty to be there by six, and that comes awful early. Now give me a kiss and turn out the lamp."

She kissed her mother's cheek and said, "Good night, Momma," and turned out the light.

"You can leave my door open just a crack. I like the light reminding me you're home again."

Settling her mother for the night, carefully leaving the door ajar, Tess felt a pang of disillusionment. *I'm not ready for this reversal of roles,* she thought, *as if I've become the mother and she's become the child.* The thought left her feeling trapped as she wandered restlessly around the living room, glancing at the piano, compressing one key soundlessly, wishing she could sit down and play. She leafed through some sheet music that had been left standing against the music rack, but Mary needed sleep, and the piano would keep her awake. In the kitchen only the stove light was on. Tess opened the refrigerator door, realized what she was doing, and closed it again, went to stare out the window over the sink at the lights coming from the house across the alley.

What was the matter with her? It had been an unsettling day, and there was more to come tomorrow, facing Judy and watching her mother be taken into surgery. She felt the stress at the base of her skull. She missed work already, missed the vital pulse of nonstop activity that marked her days, especially this time of day. Like every other professional musician she knew, her schedule of recording, promoting and performing had left her with the inner timetable of a coyote. Daytime she lay pretty low. Night-time, she howled.

But it was only nine P.M. in Wintergreen, with no howling to be done.

If she were at a concert venue right now she'd be performing. If she were in Nash-ville she'd be on Music Row in a glass box, wearing a headset, recording.

She picked up the kitchen phone, the only one in the house, and punched out four numbers before realizing the sound of her voice would carry and wake her mother. Hanging up again, she headed out to the car for her cellular phone. Passing the black square of turned earth where Kenny had planted her mother's garden, she relived her angry embarrassment at how he'd snubbed her.

So, what did she care? He was just some dorky neighbor she'd avoid while she was here and wouldn't have to bump into once she left.

The garden, however, halted her foot-steps. Picked out by moonlight, it was eas-ily distinguishable from the paler blue of lawn. It raised within Tess an inexplicable surge of exasperation. What did a seventy-four-year-old single woman with two bad hips and a millionaire daughter need with a garden in the first place?

Kronek's house was all lit up, upstairs and down, and his garage door was still up. Another car was parked on the apron—she hadn't seen it arrive—and she wondered whose it was. What did she care? The way the houses were situated, she'd be spending the next four weeks watching all the comings and goings over there, but what Kenny Kronek did with his home time was of absolutely no interest to her.

She took the phone back inside and closed up the house for the night before heading upstairs. There were Kronek's lights again as she reached the top of the steps and the unavoidable window. Irritated, she snapped down the shade and sat on her bed to call her agent, Peter Steinberg, in L.A., where it was only seven P.M.

"Hi, Peter."

"Mac," he said, "where are you?"

"In Wintergreen."

"Your mom come through the surgery okay?"

"It's not till tomorrow."

"Oh. Hope everything goes okay. Well, listen, I'm glad you called. . . ." He launched into updates on the cancellation penalties they were facing after canceling two of her venues for this month, and informed her the label executives had chosen a specific photographer they wanted to hire to shoot her next album photos and that they needed a firm title for the album ASAP so that final plans could be laid for Fan Fair—a week of meeting and greeting fans that was coming up in June. MCA intended to promote the new album there and the title *had* to be fixed soon. Also, word had been passed down from the promotions department at MCA that Tower Records in Nashville had requested an in-store autographing sometime during the week of Fan Fair. Was Tess interested in doing it?

When they'd finished their conversation she called her publicist, Charlotte Carson, and left a message on her answering machine about handling the invitation from Tower Records, instructing her to call them and answer yes. She told Charlotte to follow up the phone call with a personal letter and include a presigned publicity photo with it when she sent it to Tower. Also, could Charlotte please let the people at Putnam's know that she was definitely interested in being included in the calendar of country western singers they were planning to publish, but when did they need her photo? Could they wait until the new one was done?

Then she called her stylist, Cathy Mack, leaving another message about the photographer MCA wanted to use, assuring Cathy that Tess would want her to do hair and makeup on the cover photo, no matter who did the shooting. She'd talk to Cathy about it when she had more details.

Lastly, she called her secretary in Nashville and once again got an answering machine. "Hi, Kelly, it's me. Just thought I'd let you know I got here okay and I'm at my mom's house. Sorry I didn't get a chance to call before this, but you had my mobile number so I figured you'd get to me if anything important came up. Listen, Peter's been working on cancellations and he managed to get us out of Lubbock and Fort Worth, so take them off the schedule. There may be cancellation penalties, so check the contracts and let me know. Also, I forgot to let Ivy Britt know where I'll be for the next month, so please call her and tell her I want to see that song the minute she finishes writing it—we're on a deadline with the album and I still haven't picked the last two songs. Give her Mom's number and my mobile number. Tell her I really like her work and want to use her material again on this album, but I can't if she doesn't come through with it soon. Oh, yes, and MCA wants me to use some photographer they like. Will you get his name and address from them and a list of his credits? If you can get a couple samples of his work as well, that'd be nice. One more thing—the Minnesota State Fair invited me to perform there summer after next, but I need some numbers on attendance and specifically concert takes, both daytime and evening. Will you round them up for me and overnight them to me here? Well . . . guess that's all for tonight. Surgery is set for six-thirty tomorrow morning so I expect I'll be at the hospital all day long. I'll keep my cellular phone with me, so use that number if you have to. Okay, thanks for keeping things going at that end, Kelly, talk to you soon.''

When her business was done—a misno-
mer, for her business was never actually
done—she found her pajamas and went
downstairs to take a bath, tiptoeing on the
creaking stairway. In the bathroom, the water pipes seemed to sing like a boiling tea-
kettle, so she ran them at a dribble to keep
from waking Mary while the tub filled. It
took forever to get four inches of water. She
hated tubs, preferred showers.

Once in the water she lay back, studying
the pinkish-colored plastic tiles with swirls
of gray running through them like the lines
in Strawberry Revel ice cream. Right below
the shoulder-high top tier of tiles, a one-
inch strip of black belted the room. It was
absolutely hideous, so she closed her eyes
and thought about the album in progress.
She had eight solid songs on tape but ten
were requisite. Her producer, Jack, always
liked to record eleven, so they could scuttle
one if they wanted to. She needed three
more songs for this album. Finding good
material—that was the key to success in
this business. Nashville had fantastically
talented musicians, but they had to have
the song before they could do their work,
and there were a lot of successful singers

waiting to snatch up songs by the best songwriters.

So Tess had gotten into music publishing and hired a stable of twelve songwriters. She wasn't stupid, she knew that a performer's life is limited, and when her voice started to go the royalties from the publishing company would continue to bring in a magnificent income that would assure her a lifestyle of wealth and ease, no matter how old she lived to be.

But that still left the problem of which three songs she'd find to complete the album. Ivy Britt wrote good ones, but she was so slow. Sometimes it took her months to complete a song. Tess planned to spend some time at the piano writing while she was here. It was the perfect time, when business distractions were held at bay and her duties caring for Mary would leave her ample time to compose.

Maybe she'd write about coming back home and what it was like.

An opening line came into her head, and she hummed it.

One-way traffic crawlin' 'round a small-town square

She hummed the melody four times, then sang the words softly to the rhythm of the faucet dripping into her bathwater. It entered the world in 4/4 time, in major chords, as an upbeat ballad.

She thought of a second line.

Eighteen years've passed since she's been there . . .

And a third.

Been around the world, now she's coming back . . .

What rhymed with *back? Clack, flack, hack, attack, cognac.* Wrong syllable accented on *cognac. Track, attack, bric-a-brac . . .*

Tess opened her eyes and sat up to soap her washcloth, humming the verse and trying to come up with a last line. She tried a couple.

Feeling like she's somehow gotten off the track . . .
Trying to fit in here but she's lost the knack . . .

Neither of them pleased her, so she went on trying others. And so it went, the birth of a song. Some of them happened this way, an extension of what Tess was living, taking her experiences to a subliminal plane of creativity that spoke to her as if she had no part in the creating.

By the time she dried and powdered and put on her silk pajamas, she had the first three lines pegged and was impatient to get upstairs and write them down.

In her bedroom, she sat at her old dressing table and got the words on paper, wishing she could go down to the piano and pick out the chords she heard in her head. Unlike most country singers she had never played guitar. Piano was the instrument on which all three McPhail girls had been given lessons. She had tried guitar, but her fingers were too short and it ruined her fingernails, so she'd given it up. But often Tess envied the band members who could pick up their instruments on a bus or in a motel room and play, sing, or compose wherever they were.

At eleven o'clock she crawled into her old bed and turned out the light. At midnight she was still awake, energized by the song, kept awake further by the strange mattress that was far from comfortable.

The last time she looked at her clock it was 1:38 and she knew it would be hell rolling out at 4:30.

THREE

TESS SLEPT THROUGH HER ALARM and awakened with a start when her mother called up the stairs, "Tess? Time to get up, dear. It's five after five already."

Five after five . . . Lord o' mercy, did people actually get up at such a reprehensible hour?

"Okay, Mom, I'm awake," she croaked, and sat up unsteadily. A faint peachiness had begun tinting the east window shade. She scratched her head while peering at it with one eye squinted. Pulling herself to the edge of the bed by her heels, she tried to fix in her mind the fact that she really had to rise and get dressed. No time for a shower—oh, shoot, that's right, there was no shower, only a tub.

Her head felt like the surf was up at the

base of her skull. "Hey, Momma?" she called, shuffling to the railing and calling down. "Where we going again?"

"To Poplar Bluff." Wintergreen was too small to have a hospital of its own.

"Thirty minutes?"

"Thirty minutes, same as always."

Heading for the stairs, Tess passed the east window and pulled up the shade to verify that it really was the sun coming up. It was. In about twenty minutes or so it would splat up right over the top of Kenny Kronek's house. Grimacing, she jerked the shade back into place and grunted off in search of her toothbrush.

With little time for morning ablutions, she managed with only a quick splash and a smear of lipstick before dragging on jeans, cowboy boots, and a polo shirt over which she pulled a white sweat shirt with the word Boss plastered across the front in huge black letters. She spared time to hook on her earrings—she felt naked without earrings, no matter what kind of clothing she had on—then clattered back downstairs to see what she could do with her hair. While she was in the bathroom realizing the hair was hopeless on such short notice, Mary called from outside the door, "You just about set, Tess? We should be leaving."

"Yeah, just a sec."

In the end she finally rubber-banded it into a frowsy tail and pulled the tail through the hole of a bill cap that said *Azalea Trail 10K Run* across the top. Boy, did she look bad. But surgery schedules wouldn't wait, and her mother was hovering outside the bathroom door with her purse handle over her wrist.

Tess told her, "I'll take your suitcase out and put it in the car, then I'll come back to help you down the back steps. Now, you wait for me, okay?"

She returned to the house to find Mary in the kitchen with her hand on the light switch, surveying the room as if afraid she might never see it again. Her eyes moved in an affectionate sweep over her aged possessions: the stove on which she'd cooked for decades, the glass canisters shaped like vegetables with chips on the edges of their covers, the worn countertops, the garish wallpaper, the table with that ugly plastic doily getting uglier by the day.

On the doily sat the potted ivy. Mary's eyes stopped on it. "I watered my houseplants yesterday, so they should be okay."

"Everything will be just fine back here. I'll take care of everything."

"Judy brought milk and bread for you, and some hamburger she put in the freezer. Oh, and eggs! The eggs are fresh."

"Don't worry about me."

Still Mary hesitated, looking back at the room. Tess waited while her mother searched for other excuses to delay. A single word, uttered last night by Kenny Kronek, came back to Tess. "Scared?" he'd asked, hunkered down beside Mary's chair. At the time Tess had so much resented his presence and his familiarity with her mother that she'd disregarded the conversation. Now, watching Mary's hesitation, she realized she herself hadn't bothered wondering if her mother was scared to face this second surgery. It appeared she was.

"Come on, Mom," she urged gently. "We'd better go. I'll take care of everything, don't worry."

They left the house with the sun bending their long shadows against the back steps and up the wall beside the door. Watching her mother cling to the sturdy iron railing while painfully negotiating the three steps, Tess felt pity, and the greatest wave of love since she'd arrived home. She'd given little consideration to what her mother had been going through with the cartilage in her hips deteriorating. Principally, she'd thought, *It's a common surgery today. A lot of people have it. She'll pull through just fine like she did the first time.* Watching Mary's painful struggle from the house—the first time she'd observed her on steps—brought her condition into sharper focus. Tess took her momma's arm and helped her along the narrow back sidewalk toward the alley.

As they passed the newly planted garden, Mary said, "You'll water the garden, won't you, Tess?"

"Sure I will."

"The hoses are—" She tried to turn and point, but winced and shot a hand to her hip, trying not to gasp aloud.

"I'll find the hoses. Don't worry about it."

"If you don't know where anything is, just ask Kenny. The yard's going to need mowing before I get back, but maybe you can get Nicky to do it. He's pretty busy with his sports right now, so I don't know if he'll have time, but . . . well, you can ask him.

Otherwise, sometimes if Kenny sees it needs doing, he just comes over and does it without asking."

Oh, for Pete's sake! Was she getting sick of hearing about Kenny! Fat chance she'd ask that man anything.

They reached the Z and Tess opened the passenger door, but it was apparent from Mary's first effort that getting into the car was going to be too painful for her. The seat was low slung and would require her to bend too far.

"Mom, wait! It's . . ." Tess glanced at the closed garage door. "This is silly . . . can you stand here and wait while I get your car out? I think we'd better take it instead."

"I think so, too."

"Have you got the keys in your purse?"

"No, they're on the hook beside the door."

Tess ran back to the house and got them, but before getting Mary's car out of the garage she had to move her own. She maneuvered it backward into the cramped alley, left the engine running and got out.

Mary said, "Use the activator on my key chain. I've got a new automatic garage-door opener."

"You do? Wow! Way to go, Mom!"

"Kenny installed it for me."

Tess's exuberance soured. Saint Kenny the Garage Door Installer. What did the guy do, live over here?

The new garage door rolled up smoothly and Tess shimmied into the crowded building beside her mother's sensible five-year-old Ford Tempo, backed it out, got out to transfer Mary's suitcase . . . and found her mother smiling at Saint Kenny himself, who'd come walking over from across the alley. He was dressed in gray sweats and moccasins and hadn't showered or shaved yet. His brown hair stood in tufts as if shot with a pellet gun. His skin looked rough with morning whiskers. He didn't seem to care.

Tess stood beside her mother's car, motionless and ignored while her Z idled in a rich baritone.

"Morning, Mary," he said pleasantly.

"Good morning. What are you doing up so early?"

"Having coffee. Reading the paper. Saw you out here so I came to see you off. Got everything?"

"My suitcase is still in Tess's car. We

were going to take hers but mine is roomier."

"Want me to get it?"

"Well . . . sure, if you don't mind. She's trying to shuffle both of these cars here and . . ."

He went to the Z, opened the passenger door and extracted the suitcase from the cramped space behind the seats. He took it to Mary's car, opened the back door and shoved it inside, then opened the front door for her and helped her get in.

"Careful, now," he said while she hung on to the roof with one hand and gingerly fit herself inside.

"Oh, these old bones"—she gave a breathless chuckle—"just don't want to fold up so good anymore." When she was in she peered up at Kenny and said, "I was just telling Tess that if she wants to know where anything is she can ask you. The sprinklers and hose . . . oh, I forgot about gas for the mower. I think Nicky is going to have to mow while I'm gone, but he doesn't know you have to mix the gas with the oil otherwise it'll—"

"Don't worry about it. I'll see that it gets done."

---

eet
be so

nobody

ng helpful."
e can stay out

it did for him to
tiny ways. He's a

sk me! He just . . . just
e somebody's old junker!
ow much that car is worth?
ousand dollars, that's how
ne just couldn't wait to get in it,
Probably gonna run all over town
eople he drove it! Nobody but me
ver driven that car! Nobody! I don't
let valets park it!"

Mary was staring at her daughter in
dumbstruck surprise.

"Why, Tess . . ."

"Aw, hell, just forget it, Mom. He and I absolutely rub each other the wrong way."

"The gas can is—"

"I know where the gas can is, Mar̶ just worry about getting that new hi̶ reached in and squeezed her sh̶

" 'Bye, now, and good luck."

He slammed the door and for̶ time that morning looked over the̶ the car at Tess. He could keep hi̶ sion as deliberately flat as To̶ Jones. Contrarily, she waited to̶ greet her in any way at all. He di̶ let his eyes drop to the word B̶ chest, then sweep critically ove̶ and-turquoise earrings that shi̶ suspended raindrops at her ja̶ stepped back and waited for̶ and back the car up.

She threw herself into th̶ and slammed the door so̶ drums popped. She'd back̶ right! Right over his damned clumsy feet,̶ she could! Flinging an arm along the top of the seat, she shot backward only to discover, to her chagrin, that she had not backed her own car far enough out of the way. Another foot and she'd have hit it. Exasperated, she rammed the Ford into park and threw her door open.

glanced in the rearview mirror to find him ignoring her retreat while continuing to ogle her car.

She made a left turn onto Peach St̶ and her mother said, "You shouldn't̶ rude to Kenny, Tess."

"He was rude to me! And̶ touches my car! Nobody!"

"Why, Tess, he was just bei̶

"If he wants to help me, h̶

"I don't see what har̶ of my way!"

̶ move your car such̶ careful man."

"He didn't even̶ got in as if it we̶ Do you know h̶ Forty-two th̶ much! And̶ could hel̶ telling̶ has̶ ev̶

She ret̶ dow shade and to̶ great a burst of speed a̶ can muster. (Where was her three-̶ engine when she needed it?)

Reaching the north end of the alley, she

"Why, you've barely spoken to each other. How can you rub each other the wrong way?"

"Mom, I said forget it! Will you?" Tess realized she was yelling but was unable to stop herself.

After a perplexed pause Mary mumbled, "Well, all right . . . I just . . ." Her voice trailed off as she turned her face to the side window.

I shouldn't have yelled at her, Tess thought, *especially not today.* But sometimes she could be so dense! Prattling on about what a good boy Kenny was, totally ignoring the fact that he'd snubbed her for the second time, unaware of how unacceptable it was for him to touch a car worth that much money without permission. She could tell from the silence, and from the way Mary kept her face turned away, that she didn't believe she'd said anything wrong and was trying to figure out why she'd been snapped at.

"Momma?" Mary looked over with hurt in her eyes. Apologies had never come easy to Tess, and this one stayed locked in her mind. "Just forget it, okay?"

They drove on for a while but the silence

remained heavy. Outside the sun sat smack in the middle of Highway 160, forcing Tess to slip on her sunglasses. Things here looked the same as always. This was a poor county, Ripley, its chief income generated by transfer payments—Social Security, survivors' benefits, unemployment and welfare checks. Seemed as if half the residents of Ripley County lived in trailer houses. But the land was pretty. Red clay earth, green grass, lots of creeks, a few dogwoods on the fringes of the woods, big patches of yellow buttercups in bloom, rolling Ozark foothills, horse farms and little country churches about every five miles. They passed fields where biscuit-colored cows grazed, and a farm where goats stood on the tin roof of their shelter and a great whiskey-brown turkey fanned its tail and watched them pass. Farther along, they rumbled over the Little Black River, which ran full and brilliant as it was struck by the morning sun.

While they rode, Tess let the beautiful morning do what her absent apology should have done—take the edge off the tension in the car.

Finally she asked, "Want to hear my new song, Momma?"

Mary turned from her absorption with the view, eager to be in Tess's good graces again. "Of course I do."

The tape protruded from the deck, and Tess snapped it in.

Mary asked, "This the one with the bad note?"

"This is the one."

They rode toward the sunrise with Tess's voice singing about a marriage in jeopardy.

When the song ended Mary said, "Not a thing wrong that I could hear. That's very nice, honey. Will they be playing it on the radio soon?"

"Not till fall. There's another single— maybe two—they're going to release first before the album comes out."

"Has it got a title yet?"

"The album? No, we're still waffling on that. Jack wants me to call it *Water Under the Bridge,* which is the name of the first single, but the label executives say it makes me sound like *I'm* water under the bridge. So they don't want that. I kind of wanted to call it *Single Girl,* from an old Mary Travers song we revamped, but the MCA guys don't want to name it after a song that's been done before, no matter how old it is or

how different from our version, so I don't
know what's going to happen."

"*Single Girl* would be appropriate for you,
I suppose," Mary remarked.

Tess repressed a sigh of exasperation. "I
know you wish I'd get married, Momma, but
it's just not practical in my career. And besides, I haven't met anybody."

"Well, what about this Burt?"

They reached the intersection of Highway
67 and Tess turned left toward Poplar Bluff.
"I hardly know him. Don't push this, please,
Momma. I'm happy doing what I'm doing,
and until I'm not, marriage isn't something
I'm interested in."

"But you're thirty-five already."

"Meaning what? No children?"

"Well, it's something to think about."

"I'd make a terrible mother."

"No, you wouldn't. You've just never
given the idea a chance."

"Please, Mom . . ."

"Your sisters are good mothers. What
makes you think you wouldn't be?"

"Momma, I don't *want* to be!"

"Why, that's nonsense. Every woman
wants to be a mother."

Every woman did *not* want to be, but

there was no convincing Mary. She was of the old school who believed it was every female's mandate to give birth just because she was born with the right equipment. She probably believed that every homeless person deserved to be on the streets, and every person with the HIV virus was homosexual, too. Though she never raised her voice, there was a relentlessness in the quiet attitude that never changed, a stubbornness that warned, *Mind closed.* It was the same way at home about changing the house, cooking fatty foods, throwing away old clothes and planting a garden. Day two of Tess's stint back home, and four weeks were beginning to look longer and longer.

"Mom, I'm not going to argue anymore."

"Why, Tess, I'm not arguing," Mary claimed, in the same sweet voice that made Tess want to hook the seat belt across her mouth. "I'm just saying, it's not natural to stay single and not have babies. Turn left here. The hospital's on Pine."

By the time she pulled up beneath the porte cochere of Doctors Hospital, Tess was more than ready to get out of the car.

"Stay here, Mom. I'll get a wheelchair for you."

She drew in a humongous breath to calm her nerves as she headed into the brown brick building. *How can I love her and want to throttle her at the same time?*

Two women looked up from behind the reception desk. One was stocky, about thirty, with brittle brown hair and fat cheeks, wearing a snagged white sweater. Her name tag said Marla. The other was older, trimmer, with thinning salt-and-pepper hair and rimless glasses. Her name tag said Catherine.

"Good morning. I need a wheelchair for my mother. She's having surgery today."

The stocky woman gaped. "Why, you're . . . you're Tess McPhail, aren't you?"

"Yes, I am."

"Oh, my gosh, I love your music!"

"Thanks."

"I've got two of your albums."

"That's nice. Any chance of getting a wheelchair?"

"Oh! Of course."

Marla nearly broke her legs hurtling around the desk. As Tess strode toward the entrance Marla followed with the chair, her adulating eyes as wide as Judy Garland's when she was planning some musical shindig with Mickey Rooney.

"Got any new records coming out?"

"I'm working on an album now," Tess replied tersely, aware of how readily people who recognized her could become starstruck. The reactions were varied. Some became transfixed. Some acted as if they'd known her since childhood and had a right to pepper her with questions. Others became overly solicitous, ignoring everything else around them. Marla did all three.

"When's it coming out?"

"In the fall."

"Gosh, wait till I tell my mother. She's the one who introduced me to your music when—"

"Excuse me, but I'd like to introduce you to *my* mother, Mary McPhail."

"Oh, gosh, sure. So this is the mother of Butler County's most famous person. Well, you must be mighty proud!" Marla gushed as she helped Mary out of the car.

"Ripley County. We're from Wintergreen."

"I always heard you were from Poplar Bluff."

Tess was accustomed to people believing

they knew everything about her. She'd heard stories about people who became argumentative, insisting they were right when they were dead wrong. She found herself wishing that her mother hadn't bothered to correct the woman.

Though the attention was supposed to be focused on the patient, it more often shifted back to Tess, who accompanied her mother inside and saw her through the necessary computer work of registering. The older receptionist, Catherine, managed to act more professionally than Marla, but Tess suspected she'd alerted some of her friends on the hospital staff that a famous person was in admitting, for several people came and went during those minutes at the registration desk, dropping off papers, opening file drawers or using copy machines, their gazes seeking out Tess and lingering on her as they reluctantly moved off.

When registration was complete, Marla passed a paper over the counter and said, "Could I have your autograph, Mac? It's okay if I call you Mac, isn't it?"

"Me, too," Catherine added.

Tess quickly signed for both of them, flashed them a generic smile and reminded them, "Mother's surgery is set for six-thirty. Shouldn't we get going?"

In the surgery wing Mary was taken away to get prepped by staff members whose grins announced that they, too, had been informed of Tess's presence. She, meanwhile, was directed to a family lounge. It was located on the second floor and had a bank of windows overlooking a small garden area with park benches and a couple of picnic tables. The room was empty when Tess walked in. On a high wall bracket a television with its sound turned off flickered drearily through some morning newscast. The furniture was standard waiting-room fare—burnt orange sofa and brown armchairs, a round cafeteria table with stackable chairs. A small sink shared a wall alcove with an electric coffeemaker on which a red light glowed. Tess dropped her big gray bag on a chair and headed straight for it.

The coffee was steaming and fragrant. She filled a Styrofoam cup and lifted it to her lips. Turning, she encountered her sister Judy in the doorway.

The cup lowered slowly while the two sisters stared at each other and Tess remained where she was.

Judy offered no spontaneous exuberance, as Renee had. Instead, she let her purse strap slip from her shoulder and said, "Well . . ." as she advanced into the room with a touch of Roseanne Barr insolence in her slow waddle.

"Hello, Judy."

"I see you got her here on time."

"Well, that's a nice greeting."

"Too early in the morning for nice greetings." Judy's thongs slapped as she went to the coffee machine and filled a Styrofoam cup for herself. Watching her from behind, Tess thought, she's gained weight again. She was shaped like a hogshead and covered her mammoth curves with oversized tops that hid everything but her rather stubby lower legs. Today she wore a giant white T-shirt with a Mickey Mouse logo over a pair of faded black knee-length tights. She owned a beauty shop, so her hair was always kept dyed and styled, and she wore a modest amount of makeup, but the truth was, Judy was a very unattractive woman. Mary had always said, "Judy got her looks from Daddy's side of the family."

Smiling, her eyes seemed to get lost above her cheeks; unsmiling, she looked overly jowly. Her mouth was too small to be pretty, and she had, unfortunately, chosen to style her hair in a broom cut that accented how pudgy her face was.

For years Tess had held the conviction that the reason she and Judy didn't get along was because Judy was jealous.

As the older sister turned with a cup of coffee in her hand, the contrast between the two women pointed out the likelihood. Even thrown together as Tess was this morning, she was cute and thin in her skinny jeans. The unfussy fringe around her face gave a hint of the stylish haircut disguised by her cap. With nothing but lipstick for makeup her features broadcast the photogenic quality that had put her on the covers of dozens of magazines both in and out of the music trade—milky skin with a hint of freckles, almond eyes with auburn lashes and a pretty pair of lips. Her hands were eye-catching as well, her trademark nails nearly an inch long, painted persimmon and cultured to catch gazes. Judy lifted her cup with blunt fingers whose nails were cropped short and unpainted.

Given the marked difference in the two women's size and appearance, a stranger who walked in would never have guessed they were sisters.

Judy said, "The truth is, I really didn't think you'd come."

"The truth is, I didn't like how I was asked."

"I suppose nobody you work with gives *you* orders."

"You don't know the first thing about the people I work with or how we operate, because you never ask. You just make assumptions."

"That's right. And I *assumed* you'd do like you've been doing since you left Wintergreen, which is to leave every bit of Mother's care up to Renee and me and the guys."

"You could have *asked,* Judy."

"And what would you have said? That you had to go on tour in Texas, or that you had some rehearsals for some awards shows or whatever else is so God-almighty important that everything in the world should revolve around your schedule?"

"When did I ever say anything like that?"

"You didn't even come home for her birthday! Or last Christmas!"

"I sent her a birthday gift from Seattle, and last Christmas I was so exhausted I had only forty-eight hours off."

"She doesn't want gifts, don't you know that? All she wants is to see you now and then."

"You make it sound like I *never* come home."

"How long since you were here last time?"

"Judy, could we just . . ." Tess raised both hands as if pushing open a heavy plate-glass door. Her eyelids slammed closed, then opened again. "Shelve this and try to get along while I'm here? And the next time you need something from me, don't call and issue an imperial order. Just try asking, okay? I'm not sleeping in the farthest bed from the steps anymore, and I'm not your baby sister who's always getting into your diary and using your makeup. I'm all grown-up now and I don't take orders from you, okay?"

"Well, you did this time, didn't you . . . *Mac?*"

Nobody in the family called her Mac. To

them she had remained Tess, while Mac
had become her professional nickname. It
was the one her fans had coined, the one
they chanted as they waited for her to come
onstage, the one that was printed on the
shirts she sold at concerts, the one the nation recognized as they recognized only a
select group of other entertainers who'd
gone by single names—Elvis, Sting, Prince.

Mac.

While the word reverberated in the room,
a woman in a white uniform came to the
door and said, "Miss McPhail? I heard you
were in here. If it's not too much trouble,
may I have your autograph? I'll just leave
this on the table and you can drop it at the
nurses' station whenever. My name's Elly."
She was the ideal fan, in Tess's eyes, bringing respect along with good taste in her request. Tess loved the way she'd asked.
Leaving the room, the nurse said over her
shoulder, "Thanks a lot. You've got a super
voice."

It was more than Judy had ever said in
her life.

Tess sat down at the table, set her cup
aside and signed the paper while Judy
looked down her nose in silence.

As Tess finished, Renee showed up in the doorway. "Hey, you two, here's where you are! I just passed somebody in a uniform who says they want us down the hall before they take Momma in. Come on."

Tess got up and took off like a shot, passing Renee in the doorway.

"What's wrong with her?" Renee asked Judy.

"Same thing as always. Thinks she's too good for the rest of us."

"Judy! Do you have to be at her all the time? She just got here, for heaven's sake."

" 'Bout time, too," Judy grumbled as the two followed.

In the hall Mary was lying on a gurney, covered to the shoulders. By turns, her children bent over her, kissed her and hid their sibling animosities.

"We'll be right here when you wake up, Momma," Tess told her.

Renee added, "It's going to go just great, just like last time. Don't you worry."

"The kids and Ed all said to send you their love and to tell you they'd be up to visit," Judy said. "See you soon."

They watched the gurney roll away and stood motionless, three sisters in the middle of a hospital corridor experiencing some tempering of the discord among them as their concern was funneled toward the mother they all loved. She had looked defenseless, lying flat, her cheeks and jowls drawn backward by gravity, her hair smelling medicinal and looking tatty after back-to-back washings and no stylings. Hip replacement was certainly a common surgery in this day and age, but at seventy-four, who knew what could happen? She was getting set in her ways, occasionally forgetful, stubborn at times, and exasperating at others. But she was the reason they were sisters. She was the source of so many of their mutual childhood memories, the provider of sustenance and love that had been ever present in their lives. And for those few seconds while they stood watching her being rolled away into the care of strangers whose competence they were forced to trust, the trio bonded.

The doors swung shut behind the gurney and the squishy-soled white shoes and blue scrubs disappeared. A soft bell bonged on an overhead speaker. A feminine voice said quietly, "Doctor Diamond . . . Doctor Diamond." Then nothing more.

Renee sighed and turned to the others. "What do you say to a hot cup of coffee in the cafeteria?" She had been cast in the role of peacemaker for so many years it was natural for her to resume it now that they were together again. Taking their elbows, she forced them to walk with her. "Come on, now, you two, you're going to stop your squabbling."

There were perhaps a dozen people at various tables in the cafeteria, plus two workers behind the counter. One was in her fifties with a corkscrew home perm in her brown hair. She quit loading cartons of juice onto the stainless-steel cooler and did a double take when she saw Tess.

" 'Mornin'," she said.

"Good morning."

Behind the cash register another middle-aged woman with a poor complexion and outdated glasses took their money. When the three McPhails settled into their chairs it was obvious the two behind the counter were trying to decide if they were right about who Tess was. Tess deliberately sat down with her back to them.

Finally the one with the tight perm came over.

"Say, aren't you somebody I ought to know?"

Tess had been through this before. She knew the best way to handle it.

"I'm Tess McPhail."

"See, I told you, Blanche! It's her!" the woman trumpeted across the cafeteria. "I heard you were born and raised someplace around here. Say, you wouldn't mind signing an autograph for me, would you? I don't have any paper but you can use this." She pulled Tess's own napkin to the edge of the table. "My husband'll never believe me otherwise. Sorry, I don't have a pen, but you must have one in that great big bag of yours someplace, haven't you?"

Tess had hung her bag on the back of her chair. As she began to reach for it, a pen appeared from across the table.

Renee handed it over, telegraphing dry amusement in the set of her mouth and eyebrows.

Tess began to write. The fan said, "Would you make it to Delores? And say something about how good the food was in here or something like that, just so people will believe you really came in here and ate."

When she finished she handed the napkin to the woman who beamed at it and said, "Thanks, honey. Say, you sure are a little bit of a thing, and just as nice as you are cute. Thanks again." She gave Tess a whap on the back that hurt clear to the front, then went off examining the napkin and smiling.

When she was gone, Renee extended her open hand for the pen. Tess gave it to her and pushed back from the table.

"Excuse me," she said wryly. "Seems I need a new napkin."

As she returned with one, Renee began aping the fan Delores, using a pronounced Southern drawl. "Mah Gawd, it's Mac McPhail, and damned if she don't eat and use napkins just like othuh human bein's. Wha, Ah thought all she did was sing them country songs and get on awards shows and go to the bank with her money." Dropping the accent she added, "Lord-a-frighty, are they all like that?"

"Thank God, no. Some of them have brains in their heads."

"How often do you meet this kind?"

"Too often."

Renee started laughing behind her napkin. "I thought she was going to knock you right off your chair when she patted your back."

"That's better than the ones who want to hug you."

"Eek."

"Yeah. Eek."

"Mom told me about the one you found in your dressing room."

"That was scary."

"How'd he get in there?"

"Nobody knows for sure. There's always security when we're at a concert site, but somehow he got past it. I opened the door and there he was, smelling a bottle of my perfume. It was creepy."

"Momma was really spooked when she told me. She worries about you a lot when she knows you're out on the road."

"It's a lot safer now that we don't use the bus anymore, plus I'm usually with the guys from the band, and like I said, there's always security at the venue. There's really nothing to worry about."

"Till you find a man in your dressing room sniffing your perfume."

They exchanged sober looks, and Tess suggested, "Let's change the subject."

Throughout the entire cafeteria scene Judy had said nothing. She'd sat by as if the fans, the autographing and the story about the intruder had never happened. Her silent antipathy was a felt thing that colored the feelings among the three sisters as they ate their breakfasts.

Renee had ordered oatmeal.

Tess was eating a half a grapefruit and a toasted English muffin, dry.

Judy ate two doughnuts and a cup of hot chocolate.

Watching her, Tess thought, *Don't you have any more respect for your body than that? Three hundred calories apiece and you're pushing them down your fat neck in pairs.* Apparently Judy did not, for she polished off the first two doughnuts and went away to get a third.

Tess's eyes followed her to the counter.

"She should go on a diet."

"But as long as you're tinier than she is, she can disdain you for that as well as for your success, can't she?"

"You noticed."

"I've always noticed."

"Does she have to treat me like I'm some egomaniacal fan seeker? It's part of my business—an important part—and there are times when I hate it, but fans are my life-blood. She should know that."

"Deep down inside, I'm sure she does."

With a sad expression Tess studied her obese sister across the room. "You know something? She's never said one nice thing about what I do. It's like I don't even do it. She's never told me she bought a tape, or listened to a song on the radio—much less liked anything. Would it hurt her, for God's sake?"

"Judy's not a happy woman, Tess. Shh, here she comes."

Judy returned with an oversized cinnamon roll laced with sticky caramel and pecans. She set the plate down and used a two-handed tabletop press to lower her bulk to the chair.

Lifting the caramel roll, she looked up at the wall clock. "Well, Mom's about half done by now," she said, diverting attention from her addiction. And with that remark she also managed to continue her long-standing emotional embargo on her younger sister.

"Is she groggy?"

"Somewhat."

When the girls went in to visit Mary, they found her dozing with the head of her bed propped up. Sensing she was no longer alone, she opened her eyes and smiled wanly. They went to both sides of the bed and Renee spoke. "It's all done now. The doctor said it went just fine."

Mary nodded weakly. She had oxygen prongs in her nose, an IV drip going into her hand, and a catheter trailing from under the sheets. An adductor pillow held her legs apart beneath the sheets.

"So tired," she murmured, and her eyes drifted closed. They took turns touching her hands, kissing her cheek, smoothing the hair back from her forehead, but it was obvious Mary needed sleep more than anything. A nurse came in, smiled, and began taking her pulse. After writing it on a chart, she said, "She's going to sleep for a while. We can call you when she wakes up if you'd rather wait in the lounge."

So they returned to the lounge to sip more coffee and pass the hours taking turns checking on their mother. As the day progressed and the anaesthesia wore off,

Mary's discomfort grew. The nurses gave her pain pills and a light sedative. She was asleep and the girls were in the lounge late that afternoon when a teenage girl stuck her head around the doorway.

"Hi, everyone, how's it goin'?"

Judy looked up from her magazine. "Oh, hi, Casey."

Renee said, "Well, Casey, what are you doing here?"

"I was out riding my horse. How's Mary doin'?" She was dressed like a barrel racer who'd fallen on hard times—cuter than a bug's ear, with a loose blond French braid, a messy straw cowboy hat, faded shirt with pearl buttons, and blue jeans with enormous holes in the knees. When she advanced into the room, the smell of horses came with her.

"Pretty well, actually. The surgery went perfectly and she's been resting a lot."

"Well, hey! Sounds good!" She moved like an aging rodeo cowboy, with a graceless sway. "I don't believe we've ever met." She extended her hand to Tess. "I'm Casey Kronek. I live across the alley from your mom."

"Hello, Casey. I'm Tess."

"I know. Heck, everybody knows. I told my dad soon as I found out you were coming home, 'Hey, I gotta meet her!' And, I gotta tell you, I'm excited to be shaking your hand at last. So your mom, she's doin' okay, huh?"

"Just fine."

"I don't suppose people can see her yet."

"Tomorrow might be better. She's been sleeping a lot."

"Well, that's just as well, 'cause I stink." Casey looked down at her sorry jeans and sorrier cowboy boots.

Tess burst out laughing and said, "Yes, you do, actually."

"I was going out to ride my horse and it wasn't that much farther over here, so I figured I'd just sidetrack a little and see how Mary's doing. Your mom's one fine old babe. She's always been like a grandma to me, and I feel bad that she's got to go through so much pain and misery to get her hips fixed up." Abruptly she turned to Judy. "So, I hear Tricia's going to the prom with Brandon Sikes."

"Yes, he finally asked her."

"Boy, he's cute! And nice, too."

"She thinks so, too."

"Is she going to college next fall?"

"She's been accepted at SEMo, plans to be an elementary teacher. How about you?"

"Oh, gosh no!" Casey held up both palms. "No college for me, thank you! I haven't got the brains for that. Raising horses is more my style. Hey, Renee, we got the invitation to Rachel's wedding, and we'll be there for sure. It's pretty exciting, huh?"

"Yes, and not far off now. Less than a month."

"They gonna live here?"

"For a while."

"Bet you're relieved, huh? I mean, who'd want their kid to get married and then move off right away? I guess that'd be kind of a bummer."

"I'm glad they're staying, for a while anyway. You still singing with that little band?"

"Nope, we broke up. Couldn't find anyplace to get a gig around here, plus Dad said it was keeping me up too late at night and even if I *didn't* want to go to college, I had to finish high school. He said the band was getting in the way."

Renee turned to Tess. "Casey's just like you, Tess. Singing all the time."

"Shh!" Casey scolded. "She'll think I'm coming around here looking for her to help me get a break or something. She's prob'ly thinking, 'Help! Another one!'" Casey clasped her hands on her head, then dropped them. "I really just came to check on Mary. And to bring her this." She handed something to Renee. "It's a four-leaf clover. Found it out in the pasture. You give it to her and tell her Casey sends her love and I'll see her tomorrow or the next day, okay?"

"Sure will, Casey, and thanks for coming. She'll appreciate it, I know."

"Well . . ." Casey stood a minute longer, her index fingers hooked into the belt loops of her jeans. Abruptly she stuck out her hand to Tess. "Sure was nice to meet you, Miss McPhail . . . ah, Tess . . . Mac . . . I don't know for sure what to call you."

Tess could scarcely keep from wincing at the strength of the girl's handshake. Beyond her cute face, little about her was feminine, but it appeared she assumed the masculine body language on purpose.

"Around here everybody uses 'Tess'. Out there"—Tess gestured at the rest of the world—"it's Mac. Take your pick."

"Mac, then." Casey smiled and released Tess's hand, stepping back. "There is one thing I'd like to ask you if I could. Since we go to the Methodist church where your mom goes, and where you used to go— well, my dad directs the choir there and I heard you're going to be around for a while taking care of Mary, so do you think you could come and sing with us one Sunday? It'd really be awesome. I mean, just think of it—Tess McPhail and the Wintergreen First Methodist Church choir! We'd really have a packed house that day!"

The idea of standing in the choir loft and being directed by Kenny Kronek was about as appealing as chewing glass.

"Let me think about it, okay?"

"Sure. You think about it." Casey shrugged. "I suppose you get a hundred people a month asking you to do things for their groups—speeches and singing and signing autographs. I didn't mean to crowd you."

"You didn't crowd me. Public appearances are all part of my job, but I still want to think about it."

"Sure, I understand." Casey beamed straight at Tess, and a touch of high color painted a backdrop for the smattering of freckles on her cheeks. "Well, I better go. Nice to meetcha."

"Same here."

" 'Bye, Judy. 'Bye, Renee."

" 'Bye," they both said.

When she was gone, Tess remarked, "On top of everything else, Saint Kenny directs the church choir? Since when does he qualify?"

"He doesn't," Renee answered. "I guess all he's ever done was sing in the high school choir. But when Mrs. Atherton got sick, there was nobody to take over and Casey talked him into it. Since he already sang in the church choir and nobody else volunteered, he agreed to do it. That was about six months ago and nobody else has come forward yet, so he's still directing."

"How do they sound?"

"Pretty decent. They haven't been invited to back up Pavarotti or anything, but"—Renee shrugged—"decent."

Judy spoke up. "*Saint* Kenny?"

"Well, *isn't* he? Mother seems to have canonized him."

"He's very good to her."

"Very good to her! He might as well move right in! He plants her garden, fills her water softener, installs her new garage door! Hell, I'm surprised he didn't show up to do her hip replacement surgery this morning! I mean, every time I turn around I'm running into this guy. *What is going on?*"

Judy and Renee exchanged baffled glances.

"Maybe you'd better tell *us* what's going on," Renee responded. "The guy helps Mom—what's wrong with that?"

Judy added, "And we've known him our whole lives long, so, yes, what *is* wrong with that?"

Tess stood before her sisters caught in an unjustified bout of temper. How could she reveal—especially to Judy—that Kenny had set her off by ignoring her? If that didn't sound like a star with a bloated ego, what did?

"I send her money all the time. Plenty of money! What does she do with it? She could pay to have her garage door installed, and she could hire someone to mow her lawn, and have the Culligan man come and service her water softener, but instead she has Kenny Kronek do it. It just aggravates me, that's all! And you know what else hurts? The fact that I offered to buy her the house of her choice, a brand-new one so she wouldn't have to be replacing garage doors and everything else that's crumbling to pieces around the place. She could have a dishwasher, and a laundry room on the main floor, and an air conditioner and anything else she wanted, but she said no. For heaven's sake, have you taken a look at her kitchen cupboards lately? The Formica is worn right down to the underlayer in spots. And her front steps are tilting and the sidewalk is cracking apart. Her bedroom carpeting is as old as we are, and the tile in the bathroom is still that god-awful putrid stuff that was put on when the place was built. I send her nice clothes from really good stores when I'm out on tour, and she wears that lavender polyester slacks set that she probably bought fifteen years ago. I just don't understand her anymore."

When Tess quit speaking, a deep, thoughtful quiet spread through the room.

Judy and Renee exchanged discreet glances before the latter spoke quietly.

"She's getting old, Tess."

"Old! She's only seventy-four!"

"Old enough that she doesn't want change. She wants what's familiar."

"But that's absurd."

"Maybe to you, but not to her. There's a lifetime of memories in that house. Why would she want to move away from it?"

"All right, I'll concede that she probably wouldn't want to leave the house, but couldn't she update it a little?"

"You know what your trouble is?" Judy said. "You haven't been around to see her aging. You come home once a year or so and demand that she be the same as she always was, only she's not. Sure she gets stubborn, and sure she thinks that there's no use making changes at this late date, but if she's happy, leave her alone."

Tess stared at Judy. Then at Renee. "Is she right?"

"Basically."

"But does Mother have to look so shabby? Can't you get her to do something with her hair, Judy? You own a beauty shop."

"I've tried. She knows she can come in anytime for a style or a perm, whatever she needs, but it's always some excuse. Either her hips hurt or she has gardening to do."

"Oh, don't even *mention* gardening! That's the last thing on earth she needs is that garden!"

"It gives her great joy, her garden."

"It gives her hip aches, that's what it gives her."

"That, too, but you're not going to change her mind, so why try? She's had a garden her whole life long, and we all know she doesn't need to raise her own vegetables, but it makes her happy, so let her be."

"And while you're at it, let Kenny Kronek do what he wants for her," Renee added. "The truth is, he seems to be able to convince her to make changes when we can't. Jim told her I don't know how many times that she should have an automatic garage-door opener installed, because it hurt her hips when she bent down to reach the handle. He even offered to do it for her, but she always said no. Then one day she just announces that she's got one and Kenny put it in for her. I don't pretend to understand, but the two of them get along like peas in a pod, so I'm just grateful to have him around."

When Tess went into Mary's room for the last time that afternoon, she looked at her differently, trying to grasp the fact that she was aging, that at seventy-four she had a right to be getting a little feisty. Perhaps Judy was right. Perhaps coming home so seldom left Tess with the illusion that time was not marching on.

She pressed the four-leaf clover into Mary's hand. "That's from Casey Kronek. She came by to see how you are and said to give you this. She found it out in the pasture where she keeps her horse. Said to give you her love and tell you she'd be back to see you tomorrow."

"Oh, isn't that nice. That Casey's a sweet girl."

"Listen, Mom . . . I'm going to leave now but I'll be back tomorrow. Anything you want, you just let me know, and if you're uncomfortable during the night, you ask for a pain pill, will you?"

"I will."

"We're going to be going, too," the other girls said.

They took turns kissing her and left her looking drowsy and pale.

Outside, they took great gulps of the sweet air. They looked up at the blue spring sky. But they were all silent as they walked toward their cars. In the parking lot, Renee gave Tess a genuine good-bye hug, but Judy offered only a moue that passed for a kiss on the cheek but was not.

It felt like being released, driving away, even in Mary's old Ford Tempo. The spring day was glorious and had warmed up to eighty degrees. Creeping phlox and irises were blooming in front yards. Here and there, rhododendrons made a splash of color. Tess took her time, stopping at a Kroger supermarket and buying herself some fresh vegetables, low-fat salad dressing and boneless chicken breasts before heading back toward Wintergreen. Driving along the familiar roads, she found herself cataloging her mixed feelings about being home again.

There was something to be said for living away from family. Out there, in Nashville and beyond, she was clear of the daily reminders of her mother's health, of Judy's jealousy and all the other petty irritations that had cropped up in the twenty-four hours she'd been home. Being here had brought moments of nostalgia, but more often she became aware of how different she was from the girl who'd left. Her values and priorities had changed. Her pace had changed. Her acquaintanceship, scope and obligations. Was that necessarily bad? She didn't think so. What she had accomplished with her life had taken tremendous energy and commitment, so much, in fact, that on a day-to-day basis there was little room left in her mind for what she thought of as social trifles.

Judy's jealousy was a social trifle.

Mother's stubbornness was a social trifle.

When Tess was wrapped up in business she forgot about such things. At home, idle, they niggled and their importance in the overall scheme of life got blown out of proportion.

When she pulled up in the alley at five o'clock, another of those social trifles was waiting to irritate her: Kenny Kronek was mowing her mother's backyard, dressed in blue jeans, a white V-neck undershirt and a navy-and-red Cardinals baseball cap. He looked up but kept on mowing as she stopped in the alley and activated the garage door. Throughout the jockeying of cars, which took a while, he went on cutting swaths up and down the length of the yard, disappearing to the front, then reappearing in back. When her mother's car was tucked away and her own returned to the apron, Tess took her groceries and headed for the house. She and Kronek met head-on when she was halfway up the sidewalk.

Though they'd have rather snubbed each other, the woman they both loved had had surgery that day. They could hardly pass each other without mentioning it. He stopped and switched the motor to idle.

"How'd it go?" he asked, his weight on one hip, no smile on his mouth.

"Perfect," she snapped, as rudely as possible.

"And Mary?"

"Doctor says she's doing great. No complications at all. They'll be getting her up to stand tomorrow."

"Well, that's good news."

They both felt awkward, speaking with surface civility while wishing they need not.

"I met your daughter today," she told him.

He reached down, picked up a little stick from the grass in front of the grumbling mower and threw it into the garden. "She told me she might stop up there. I told her she should wait at least until tomorrow, till Mary was feeling a little better."

"She's quite refreshingly natural."

"Meaning she smelled like horses, right?"

Had he been anyone else, Tess would have laughed. Since he was Kenny, she forcibly refrained. "Some. But she apologized for it."

"She loves her horses." He still wouldn't look at her, but sent his gaze roving over the lawn and the backyard buildings, his weight once again on one hip in a stance she found cocky.

"She asked me to come and sing with your church choir."

He gave her a quarter of a glance and mumbled as if cursing under his breath, then scratched the back of his head under the cap, bouncing the red bill in front. "I told her not to bug you about it. I hope you don't think I put her up to it."

She remembered the crush he used to have on her in high school and said with enough sarcasm to nettle him, "Now, why would I think a thing like that?"

He squared the baseball cap on his head, gave her a drawn-back, deep, disgusted assessment from beneath its visor, then rolled away toward the mower, leading with one shoulder. "I gotta get back to work." He turned up the engine till it pounded their eardrums.

She leaned closer and shouted above the roar, "You didn't have to mow this lawn, you know! I was going to call my nephew!"

"No trouble!" he shouted back.

"I'll be happy to pay you!"

He gave her a look that cut her down to about the height of the grass. "Around here we don't pay each other for favors," then he added insolently, "*Ms. McPhail.*"

"I was born *around here,* in case you've forgotten! So don't take that tone with me, *Mister Kronek!*"

He let his gaze clip the edge of her face and offered, "Oh, excuse me . . . *Mac,* is it?"

"Tess will be fine, whenever you choose to come off your high horse long enough to speak to me!"

"Looks to me like I'm the one who got off his high horse first today!"

"But you sort of forgot who I was in the house last night, didn't you?"

"Bet that doesn't happen too often anymore, does it?"

"No. People are generally better-mannered than that!"

They were both still shouting.

"You know, you always *did* have an attitude."

"I do *not* have an *attitude!*"

He let out a snort and began pushing the mower away, calling back over his shoulder, "Look again . . . Mac!" He could say Mac with such an insulting tone she wanted to run up behind him and trip him! Instead, she stormed into the house and slammed the grocery bag down on the counter, wondering when in the last eighteen years she'd been this riled. All the while she used the bathroom, and changed into a cooler shirt, and opened up the windows in the stuffy loft, and put away her groceries in the refrigerator, the mower kept droning around the house, reminding her he was there, circling.

To distract herself, she decided to call

Jack Greaves, who informed her that Carla Niles was coming in to cut a new harmony track on "Tarnished Gold," and that he'd have it couriered to her tomorrow. She called Peter Steinberg, who ran some foreign sales figures by her and said Billy Ray Cyrus had called asking if she'd sing at a fund-raiser for a children's hospital in August. She called Kelly Mendoza and asked her to check their August calendar and get back to Cyrus; Kelly gave her a report on the day's mail and phone calls and said a fax had come in with the week's *Gavin Report* and that her current single, "Cattin'," had dropped one notch on the radio chart. Also, her custom-made boots had arrived from M. L. Leddy in Fort Worth. Would she like them sent down to Wintergreen?

While Tess was on the kitchen phone a car pulled up and parked behind Kronek's open garage door—the same car as yesterday, a white Dodge Neon. A woman got out and crossed the alley toward him. She was fortyish, wearing low-heeled pumps and a summer business suit of pale peach. As she approached him he stopped mowing and moved a couple steps in her direction. She was carrying a portfolio, which rested against her leg as the two of them talked. She pointed toward his house and continued casually gesturing while they discussed something. Kenny jabbed a thumb toward Mary's house and the woman glanced over briefly. Then she smiled and headed back across the alley while he returned to his mowing.

Who's that? Tess wondered, watching the woman disappear into the glass porch.

A half hour later Tess was washing a head of lettuce when she looked out the window and saw the woman, who had changed into slacks and a white blouse, carrying a tray out the back door to Kenny's picnic table. A moment later Casey followed with another tray. The woman hailed Kenny, who by this time had finished mowing Mary's yard and was halfway through with his own, and the three of them sat down to eat supper.

A *mistress*? Tess wondered. Could it be Saint Kenny actually led a life of promiscuity? Certainly the woman was more than a mere housekeeper, changing clothes the way she had and joining the family for supper. There was an unmistakable air of familiarity among the three of them as they sat down to share the meal.

Tess caught herself wondering and spun away from the window. Who cares, she thought, as she put a chicken breast on to poach, then went into the living room to do what she'd been eager to do all day long. Armed with a small tape recorder, staff paper and pencil, she sat down at the piano to work on the song idea she'd had last night.

The old upright piano was badly in need of tuning, but the easy action of the keys and its exceptional resonance surpassed many on which she'd played. This was one of her favorite parts of the work she did. Composing seemed like play, always had. At times she found it ludicrous that she should be paid for doing something that gave her such absolute pleasure. Yet the royalties from her original songs brought in hundreds of thousands of dollars a year. She'd always been imaginative, and the process of combining a theme, poetry, and music into one entity sometimes so captivated her that she didn't hear when she was being spoken to. During the years when she and the band had toured by bus she often wrote while they were rolling down the highway, setting down the words first, along with a basic melody line, to which she added chords by using a minia-ture two-octave electronic keyboard that she could hold on her lap and listen to through earphones. Sometimes her lead guitarist would work with her, especially on the more upbeat songs that would be gui-tar-driven.

The lines that had entered her head last night in the bathtub began to take concrete musical form. The words gained tune and rhythm.

One-way traffic crawlin' 'round a small-town square,
Eighteen years've passed since she's been there,
Been around the world, now she's coming back . . .

The last line of the verse kept eluding her. Ideas came, but she discarded them, one after another. She sang trial lines, picking out an accompaniment on the piano, but still liked none. She was wholly immersed in composing when a voice called from the open kitchen door, "Hey, Mac? It's me, Casey!" Tess was holding a chord with her left hand and committing it to paper with her right when Casey bounced into the room, uninvited.

"Hi!" the girl said brightly, bringing Tess around on the piano bench.

She stood jauntily in the middle of the room, smiling. Her stable gear was gone and in its place clean blue jeans with a yellow cotton T-shirt tucked into her slim waist. Having left behind her cowboy clothes, she seemed also to have abandoned the bowlegged cowpoke attitude that went with them. Instead, she had adopted a young Debbie Reynolds perkiness. Come to think of it, the tilt of her nose, the hair in a single French braid, the wide, interested eyes slightly resembled the young ingenue.

"Heard you playing," she said.

"Working on a song that came into my head last night while I was in the bathtub."

"You mean writing it?"

"Yup."

"What's it about?"

"It's about what it feels like to come back here after being gone so long. The people in this town, my mother, this house." Tess gestured. "How nothing changes, including some things that really need to." She went on explaining some of the feelings she'd had since she'd been back and how she was trying to encapsulate them in the song.

"Can I hear it?"

Tess chuckled and scratched her head to give herself time to think up an answer. "Well, I don't usually play my stuff for people until after it's copyrighted and recorded."

"Oh, you mean like I might steal it or something." Casey laughed, rolling up the left sleeve of her T-shirt. "Gee, that's a good one. You think I might be that good that I could actually do a thing like that? Not likely. Come on, let me hear it," she cajoled, flinging herself into an overstuffed chair and throwing a leg over its fat arm.

"It's not done yet."

"Who cares? Play what you've got."

Tess swung back to the piano, quite taken by the girl in spite of herself. She was approached by fans nearly every day, be it on the street, backstage or at public appearances. Most put her off either by displaying an overabundance of awe or prefacing their request for an autograph by admitting, "I don't own any of your records, but . . ." Casey Kronek did neither. She simply flopped down in a chair like a comfortable old buddy and said, "Come on, woman . . . cook." Why Tess did not bristle at the girl's familiarity she couldn't say, but there was a naturalness about Casey that fell just short of presumptuousness, and the proper amount of admiration held in reserve. The truth was, given Tess's busy life, she had few friends away from the music industry. This girl came on like one, and Tess bit.

"All right. This is what I've got so far."

She played the first three lines, tacked on the temporary fourth, then tried an optional fourth. It was easy to hear that neither worked.

"Play it again," Casey said.

Tess played and sang one more time.

One-way traffic crawlin' 'round a small-town square,
Eighteen years've passed since she's been there,
Been around the world, now she's coming back . . .

"Wider-eyed and noting what this small town lacks," Casey added in a corduroy contralto voice that was dead on tune.

"Can't return. Too much learned."

The last two lines Casey had tacked on created a haunting afterthought that would echo at the end of each verse. Tess got shivers. She heard the accompaniment in her head, picked it out on the keys, closing her eyes and holding the last chord as it scintillated off into silence like lazy smoke around their heads.

The room remained silent for ten seconds.

Then Tess said, "Perfect."

"It's what you were talking about, isn't it? Seeing the town's deficits through the eyes of somebody who used to live there."

"Exactly. I love the refrain idea. It all works."

Tess leaned forward and wrote the words and melody line on the staff paper. When she finished, she set the pencil down on the music rack, and said, "Let's do it again."

While she sang, Casey sat in the over-stuffed armchair with her left leg swinging, head thrown back, eyes closed, twisting the end of her braid around one finger and quietly adding harmony, almost as if to herself.

"You know what?" Tess said when they'd finished. "I just got shivers."

"Me, too."

"That's always a good sign. Plus, it sounds like you have a great voice. Why are you holding back?"

"Because it's your show."

"Hey, if you're gonna do it, do it. Wanna add harmony this time so I can hear it?"

Casey looked unsurprised. Tess liked that. "Sure."

They sang it again and Tess recognized a distinctively unique voice. It had a touch of grit and a touch of grime, as though it could rub the calluses off a working person's hands. It had a good musical ear behind it, but most importantly, a fearlessness. Not many seventeen-year-old girls Tess knew could sing side by side with someone of her renown without quailing. Casey did it with her leg still thrown over the chair arm and her eyes still closed.

When she opened them the country western star on the piano bench was looking back over her shoulder wearing a bemused expression. "So tell me . . . did you come in here to show me what you had?"

"Partly," the girl admitted.

"Well, I'm impressed. You could take the tread off of tires with all the gravel in that voice." Tess swung around and cupped her knees as she faced Casey. "I like it."

"Trouble is, it always sticks out."

"In a group, you mean."

"Uh-huh."

"Like a church choir."

"Uh-huh. Oh! Which reminds me! My dad didn't like me bothering you to sing with the choir. He said I'd been intrusive and or- dered me over here to apologize, that's the real reason why I'm here. So I'm sorry. I didn't mean to butt in to your private time at home, but I just didn't stop to think. Any- way, Dad said, 'You get over there across the alley and let her off the hook!' So here I am." Drawing forward to the edge of her chair, Casey let her hands dangle between her knees, and shrugged. "You ought to be able to come home and move around town in peace without people bugging you the way they do everywhere else you go."

"That what your dad said?"

"Uh-huh."

"Well . . ." Tess considered awhile, relaxing on the piano bench with her hands lining her thighs, the long perfect nails pointing at her knees. "I must say, that's a surprise." She cocked her head. "Tell me, is this choir any good?"

"Not much. But don't tell Dad I said so."

Tess laughed and said, "Oh, believe me, I won't."

"Their voices aren't so bad, but . . . I don't know. I'm probably not much of a judge. I just like to sing—country's my favorite, but it's not bad singing with the choir. It's not exactly a gig in a roadhouse, but it's singing, so I'm just glad Dad agreed to direct, otherwise we didn't know what we were going to do. You remember Mrs. Atherton?"

"Sure. Glasses, about so high, wavy black hair."

"Yeah, but it's gray now. She had bypass surgery, so I don't know if she'll ever come back and direct again."

"Hm, that's too bad." Tess got up and said, "Got some chicken poaching out here. I better go check it."

Casey followed her to the kitchen and leaned against the archway watching while

Tess lifted the lid, poked the chicken breast and found it tender. She put the lid back on, turned off the burner and got her salad fixings out of the refrigerator. While she tossed them with dressing, Casey inquired, "Have you got somebody who does this stuff for you when you're at home in Nashville?"

"What? You mean cooking?"

"Yeah."

"I have a housekeeper, and she'll do it if I ask her, but on days when I'm recording we're in the studio from midafternoon till about nine at night or so, and midway through the session a caterer brings food in. On the night of a concert I usually wait till after the concert to eat. I don't like singing on a full stomach."

"What's it like, being up there in front of all those people? I mean, it must be so awesome."

"It's the only thing I ever wanted to do. I love it."

"Yeah, I know what you mean. I've been singing since I was about three years old. First to my dolls, then to my mom and dad, then to anybody who'd listen."

"You, too?" Tess put her food on the ta-

ble and went to the silverware drawer.
"When I was little I was the same way."
She returned to the table with a fork and
knife, and Casey pushed away from the
doorway.

"Guess I'd better let you eat."

"No, listen, if you don't mind, neither do I.
Sit down and talk."

"Really?"

"I only cooked one piece of chicken, but
I've got a piece of pecan pie I can give
you."

"Mary's?"

"You bet."

"Hey, that sounds great."

When Tess made a motion to get it,
Casey ordered, "No, you sit down and eat.
I'll get it myself." She knew right where to
find a plate, fork and spatula. When the
wedge of pie was served up she said,
"Mary got any ice cream?"

"Sure. You know where."

Casey helped herself and brought her
dessert to the table.

"So what kind of place do you live in, in
Nashville?" she asked.

"I've got a house of my own, but I'm only

there about half the time. The rest of the time I'm playing concert dates."

"Is it bad, being gone so much?"

"It was worse when I traveled by bus. It was like being marooned together, living in such close quarters with the same people day after day. There were times when I'd get sick of the bus, sick of the people, sick of trying to remember what town we were in so I wouldn't make a mistake on some radio station. But I must like it. I keep on doing it. And it's much nicer since I own my own plane."

"Your own plane . . . wow! Mary told us when you bought it. I was *so impressed!*" Tess chuckled at the girl's unbridled candor. "So tell me what it's like when you're recording," Casey prompted.

Tess was still telling her when Kenny's voice came from outside the back door. "Casey, what are you still doing here bothering her?" Dark had fallen and the kitchen lights were on. The way the door was situated he had to gaze in at an angle to see the table where the pair sat, but he got a clear enough shot by putting his face to the screen.

Tess leaned forward to peer at him

around the far doorway. "She's no bother. I asked her to stay."

Casey said, "We're talking, Dad, that's all."

Uninvited, he stepped inside, into the tiny back entrance, a step lower than the kitchen. Pressing a hand on either side of the doorway, he poked his head into the room. "Casey, you come on, now. I told you to come straight back home."

"Can I finish my pie first?" she said with strained patience.

To Tess he said, "You sure she's not bothering you?"

"Let her finish."

"All right. Ten minutes," he replied, then pushed off the wall and disappeared.

When the screen door closed behind him, Casey said, "I don't know why he's breathing down my neck so bad today. He never does that."

Tess thought, *I don't know why a man who's antagonistic toward me would bother to come clear across the alley in the dark to tell his daughter to get home when he could have used the phone.*

"What does your dad do?" Tess asked.

"He's a CPA. He's got his own business

downtown just off the square about three doors down from the dress shop where Faith works."

"Faith?"

"Faith Oxbury, his girlfriend."

"She the one who was over there having supper with you tonight?"

"Mm-hmm." Casey licked the ice cream off her spoon. "She's over most nights for supper. Either that or we're at her house. They've been going together since forever."

Tess wondered how long forever meant, but she wasn't going to ask. Casey finished licking off her spoon, set it down and pushed back her plate. Propping one heel on an empty chair seat underneath the table, she slouched down and let her spine curl. "Daddy and Faith have been going together so long that people kind of treat them like they're already married. They play bridge together, and get invited to parties together, and if there's anything of mine going on at school, she usually comes with Dad. Heck, she even sends out Christmas cards with all of our names on them."

"Then why don't they get married?"

"I don't know. I asked him once and he said it's because she's a Catholic and if she

married a divorced man she couldn't re-
ceive the sacraments in her church anymore. But if you ask me that's a pretty lame
excuse not to marry a man you've been going with for eight years."

"Eight years. That's a long time."

"You know it. And I'll tell you something
else. They'd like me to think there's nothing
below the waist going on between them—I
mean, he pecks her on the cheek now and
then, and they'll hold hands sometimes, but
she never stays overnight at our house and
he never stays overnight at hers. But if they
think I buy that *charlotte russe* they're
stupider than they think I am."

"Charlotte russe?"

"Oh, it's just this name I've given it—we
made charlotte russe in home ec one
time—anyway, that's what I call it, this little
charade they play with me, like I'm still in
the sixth grade. But *nobody* goes together
that long without doing it." Casey brought
her observations up short, then shot a
straight look at Tess. "Do they?" she
asked, as if suddenly uncertain.

"Don't ask me."

"Well I don't think so. But you know
what? Underneath it all, I have to respect

him for caring enough about my respect for him not to want to jeopardize it. So we all pretend they're as platonic as siblings and she comes over and fixes supper and stays till nine or so, then he walks her to the car and says good night. And on Thursdays they play bridge, and once a week she comes over and irons his white shirts because he doesn't like the fold lines from the laundry, and once a week he goes over there and cuts her grass. And on Sunday she goes to her church and he goes to ours. But at least we all get along. Faith is real nice to me." Casey paused and took a deep breath. "Well . . ." She dropped her foot to the floor and slapped her knees. "My ten minutes are up and I have to get home." She got up and took her dirty dishes to the sink, followed by Tess. When she'd run water onto her plate she turned and said, "Thanks for letting me hear your song in progress, and for the pie, and for letting me ask you questions. Sorry if I got nosy, but I couldn't help myself. Could I give you a hug?"

Tess had just set her own dishes down when she found herself hugged hard and hugging back. While she was in Casey's clutches the girl pulled in a noisy breath, and exclaimed, "Ooo, you're just super! And I've always been blown away by the fact that you grew up right over here across the alley and made it as big as you did. I want to be just like you!"

With that, the impetuous girl hit for the door. " 'Night, Mac. Tell Mary I'll be up to see her tomorrow afternoon!"

FIVE

ON THE DAY FOLLOWING MARY'S SURGERY, Tess arrived at her bedside at midmorning and found she missed the company of her sisters, who failed to show up as promised. It was difficult watching her mother, whom she remembered as hale and hearty, now wearing support stockings, clinging to a walker and struggling to stand upright for a mere fifteen seconds.

Tess once again found herself sadly lacking in bedside technique. Without Judy and Renee, conversations with Mary tended to be brief and drift off into silences, or occasionally, run into brick walls. She told Mary about her visit from Casey, and how much she'd enjoyed the girl.

"She tells me she's sung with a band," Tess prompted.

"Yes, but I never heard them."

"Country?"

"I think so."

"She's got a really distinctive voice, a gruff contralto that sort of claws at you."

"Kenny made her quit doing that, though. He didn't like that bunch she was hanging around with, so don't encourage her."

"Kenny's got a real thing against country western singers, doesn't he?"

"Oh, Tess, are you still picking on him after all these years?"

That was one of the brick walls.

The day sent Tess's emotions vacillating.

A physical therapist named Virginia came in at midmorning and raised Mary's legs several times, drawing soft moans while Mary's eyelids closed tightly and twitched.

"You'll be helping her with her therapy at home," Virginia told Tess. "Would you like to try it now?"

"No! I mean . . . you go ahead. I'll help tomorrow." The idea of being the one to cause her mother pain caused a lightness in Tess's stomach. Who had done this for Momma the first time? Renee? Judy? Would they take turns this time or leave it all up to her once she got Momma home?

Midway through the day a nurse removed the oxygen prong from Mary's nose, which made her look so much less vulnerable. But the IV and catheter stayed, lashing her to the bed in her wrinkly regulation gown with the split up the back.

When Judy showed up around two P.M., Tess greeted her with overt enthusiasm, surprising even herself. Judy again remained cool to Tess, waddling over to the bed to give her affection to Mary instead. "Hey, Momma, how you doing today?"

"Not so good, I'm afraid. Lots of pain."

"Well, you know how it was last time. If you can just hang in there for the first couple of days, it gets better really quick after that." Somehow, it seemed to Tess, her sisters knew all the right things to say, whereas she felt awkward consoling her mother. "Renee's taking a day off today," Judy told Mary. "She's got some wedding stuff that she's got to do. She said she'll see you tomorrow. Anybody else been up to visit?"

At that moment a cacophony of chatter approached from down the hall and three people entered the room at once: Casey, her father—bearing a box of chocolates—

and a man in his mid-fifties wearing a short-sleeved summer shirt with a clerical collar.

Mary smiled when she saw him. "Reverend Giddings."

"Mary," he said fondly, taking her hand while hellos were exchanged around the room, the most enthusiastic from Casey to Mary. "I brought a whole greeting party! Look who I ran into in the hall!"

"Casey and Kenny . . . my goodness, this is nice."

They went to Mary and took turns kissing her while Casey sang, "Mary, Mary, quite contrary, how do your hip sockets grow?"

Mary caught Casey's spirit and replied, "With silver balls of some sort, I'm told," referring to the new ball-and-socket prosthesis she now wore in her right hip. Everyone laughed and Mary admitted, "All I know is it hurts like the dickens today."

"This should help." Casey took the candy from her father's hand and laid the box on Mary's stomach. "Your favorites—very, very extra-dark chocolates."

"Oh, my goodness, oh, yes, they *are* my favorites." She set to splitting the cellophane with a thumbnail while conversation enlivened the room. Casey oversaw the candy operation while Reverend Giddings passed along messages of goodwill from members of his congregation. In the general shifting of visitors Kenny somehow ended up standing near Judy and Tess at the foot of the bed.

"Well, Judy," he said, glancing down at her, "haven't seen you for a long time."

"Keeping out of mischief?" Judy asked.

"In this town?" he answered wryly. "Hard not to."

Assuming the typical male hospital visitor stance—feet planted and arms crossed—he glanced briefly at Tess and said, much quieter, "Hello, how're you today?"

He spoke civilly out of respect for Mary, and because the minister was in the room, but both of them felt awkward, standing side by side carrying on a conversation strictly for the benefit of others.

"Fine. A little tired. I'm not used to this schedule."

"I imagine you're used to working a little later at night."

"Most of the time."

Mary said, "Girls, look—dark chocolate. Would you like one?"

Tess answered, "No, thanks, Mom," but

Judy moved away to pick one from the proffered box.

"How about you, Kenny? Chocolate?"

"No, thanks, Mary. Bad for the waist-line."

Kenny and Tess stood apart from the others, an island of restraint in the room of six people, carrying on one of three conversations taking place simultaneously.

"Casey was pretty excited when she came home last night. I appreciate your taking time with her."

"I enjoyed her a lot."

"She told me you sang together."

"We did, a little."

"I suppose you know you lit a real fire under her."

"I think the fire was there before she came over to see me, so if you're upset about it—"

"Who says I'm upset about it?"

"Well, Momma said you didn't like her singing with her band."

"Bunch of potheads and school drop-outs, that's why. Heck, nothing short of a guillotine could keep Casey from singing."

"Do I hear my name over there?" Casey

came over and joined them. "What are you two talking about?"

"About last night," Tess said.

Casey's natural ebullience spilled out once again. "Last night was too cool! Best night of my life! Man, I couldn't even sleep when I got home!"

"I couldn't either. That song kept bothering me."

"You get a second verse down yet?"

"Mm . . ." Tess waggled a hand like a jet dipping its wings. "A bad one, maybe."

"I don't think you could write anything bad."

"Oh, listen, I've written some that were so bad my producer winced when he heard them."

"He the one who hears them first after you write them?"

"Usually."

"Why?"

"Well, because he's got a good ear and sound judgment. That's why I hired him."

"What if he likes it and you don't?"

"Actually, that's happened. He asked me to listen to a demo one time that I thought was a real dud. But I agreed to give it a try, and when we did I changed my mind. I found I liked it a lot better once the studio musicians put their touch on it. In the end it turned out to be one of my best-selling singles ever."

"Which one?"

" 'Branded.' "

"Oh, I like that one."

Kenny stood back, listening to his daughter and Tess as they seemed to forget everyone else was in the room. He was admittedly surprised by Tess's attention to Casey, given what he remembered of her in high school. Yesterday he had accused her of having an attitude, but it was nowhere in evidence today, with Casey. She talked with the girl just as she would with one of her own set in Nashville, as if the two of them were peers, and he had to admit, what they talked about was mighty darned interesting. He was aware, too, of Judy standing by taking it all in. She remained aloof, superior, eavesdropping on her sister but adding nothing, giving the impression she was above all the hero worship and hoopla surrounding Tess's fame. Tess talked about things the common radio listener was rarely privy to, and when the conversation had gone on for several minutes and inadvertently captured other ears in the room, Judy interrupted loudly, changing the subject and forcing everyone's attention to swerve away from Tess.

"Kenny, I hear you mowed Momma's lawn yesterday."

"Well . . ." He didn't want undue attention, particularly in front of Tess. "It was getting pretty shaggy."

Mary put in, "Oh, Kenny, that was so thoughtful of you. I told Tess to try to get Nicky over there to do it, but he must've been busy."

"It was no trouble," Kenny replied. "I had to do my own anyway."

To the room at large Mary said, "This boy always says it's no trouble, but I don't know what I'd do without him. I said as much to Tess the other day."

Reverend Giddings was the only one who hadn't spoken one-on-one with Tess. He chose that moment to approach her and extend his hand. "I don't believe I've ever had the pleasure of meeting you." He looked undernourished, fortyish, with thinning sandy hair and overlapped incisors that pushed out his top lip slightly. "I'm Sam Giddings. I've been minister at Wintergreen Methodist since Reverend Sperling retired."

"How do you do." Tess smiled at him. "Mother has talked about you."

"And *my* mother has talked about *you!* She's a big fan. So is my wife and most of my congregation. People around here are mighty proud of your success, young lady, and I confess I'm among them. I don't have a lot of spare time for listening to music, but I've put your tapes on a few times and had a thoroughly enjoyable time listening to them."

"Why, thank you."

"My wife is going to have her nose out of joint when she hears that I got to meet you. Of course, rumors get around, and Mary let it be known that you were coming home to take care of her. So this morning at breakfast my wife said to me, 'If you run into Mary's daughter at the hospital, why don't you see if you can get her to come and sing with the choir while she's here.'" He paused for effect, rocked back on his heels and glanced at Kenny. "I'm sure you know that Kenny here directs our adult choir, and Casey sings in it. I'll bet he'll find an extra hymnal for you if you'd be so kind as to join us one Sunday."

Damn that Casey, Kenny thought, cutting his eyes at her.

Casey threw both hands in the air like a cowboy with a gun in his back. "Don't look at me, Dad! I didn't say a word!"

"Reverend Giddings," Kenny began to explain, "Miss McPhail doesn't—"

"She likes to be called Mac," Casey interrupted.

"Mac . . ." he repeated with strained patience. "Yes . . . well, Mac has already been approached by my daughter, and it kind of put her on the spot. I'm sure that everywhere she goes she gets requests like this, and I don't think we should bother her while she's home."

"I can't imagine why using her voice to praise the Lord would be such an imposition. After all, He's responsible for her having it. The offer still stands, Ms. McPhail. Kenny here will give you a hymnal and I'll give you an introduction, and I'm sure the congregation would be most grateful. Matter of fact, a week from Sunday we just happen to be having our annual pledge drive, and a little incentive on our part might just swell the rolls and bring in a few more coins. If you'd agree to sing that day, we'd have enough time for the church secretary to type it up in this Sunday's bulletin, that you'll be on hand. Could help a lot with attendance. Now, what do you say?"

While Tess and Kenny were standing with their fillings showing, each embarrassed before the other, Mary spoke up.

"Well, of course she'll do it, won't you, Tess?"

Tess could have cheerfully gagged her mother with her own catheter tube. She gaped haplessly at Reverend Giddings, then at Kenny, then back at the minister. "Well . . . uh . . ." Her eyes connected with Kenny's and she offered him a feeble smile. He looked as uncomfortable as she. "I guess so, huh?" She gave an exaggerated shrug—"Why not?"—and let out a strained laugh that fooled no one.

Why not, indeed. There were at least five good reasons, which neither Tess nor Kenny could voice with the minister grinning and looking pleased with himself.

For the remainder of the visit they kept a goodly distance between them, as disenchanted with the situation as any two people could be.

Finally Reverend Giddings took his leave. The moment his back disappeared around the doorway, Casey decided to set the record straight about her involvement. "Hey, Mac! I never had anything to do with him asking you!" she declared. "You believe me, don't you?"

Every eye in the room was on Tess. She would have looked like a jerk to refuse to help, especially given how little time and effort it would take, and the nature of the cause. "Listen, I guess it won't kill me."

"But I wouldn't do that to you!" Casey insisted. "Not after you let me know you weren't too thrilled with the idea!"

From the bed, Mary spoke up. "But, Tess, why wouldn't you sing with the choir if you're going to church anyway?"

"Could we just drop it?" She raised both hands in surrender. "I'll do it. There. It's finished. No more discussion."

Though it was the end of the discussion, and Kenny and Casey left shortly thereafter, the whole scene continued to rankle Tess even after she left the hospital.

Driving home, she wondered whom to

believe. Certainly Casey seemed sincere in her disclaimer, and Kenny had appeared as discomfited as she herself by the minister's suggestion. She resisted giving him the benefit of the doubt, however, just because he was Kenny. What difference did it make now? It wouldn't be the first time she'd said yes to singing some benefit appearance she'd rather have skipped. So she faced the awful prospect of singing in Saint Kenny's choir, standing face to face with him while he directed her.

Damn Giddings anyway!

She was still disgruntled over it when she got home and went into the house to put her groceries away, check inside the front door for express packets and begin making phone calls. She washed some grapes and took a handful upstairs, confronted with the view of Kenny's house every damned time she turned around in this place. From the window at the head of the stairs to the one above her mother's kitchen sink, his house was constantly in her face.

It was hot upstairs. The afternoon temperature had reached eighty. She changed into a pair of cotton shorts and went back downstairs for more grapes. She was standing at the sink, plucking a few more from the clump when she noticed the wilted tomato plants.

Hell, she'd forgotten to water the garden yesterday.

Out she went, and into the service door of the garage to search out a yellow plastic fan-shaped nozzle. At the house she screwed it onto the coiled hose, and dragged the whole works across the narrow sidewalk to the garden. She had just started sprinkling when Kenny's porch door slammed and he came striding across his backyard toward her. Faith Oxbury's car was parked in front of his garage door, and Tess's Z was parked in front of Mary's. He swerved around both of them, heading toward Tess, who continued fanning the water across her mother's tomato plants.

"Just for the record," he said when he was ten feet from her, "I didn't have anything to do with Reverend Giddings's invitation! I didn't want to say so in front of your mother, though."

She let her eyes shift over him once. He was frowning, standing a body length away from her. He had changed out of his business suit and was wearing a white polo shirt

and khaki pants, ultratidy, as if he'd just finished showering and combing for the second time that day. His shirt collar was
turned up intentionally and he had trendy
Top-Siders on his feet.

She moved farther away from him, dragging the hose and waving the nozzle above
the carrots. "So you don't want me to sing
with the choir?"

"I didn't say that. I said I didn't put him
up to inviting you."

"I believe you," she said, refusing to
glance at him again.

He seemed nonplussed by her quick admission, and stood momentarily disarmed
before blurting out, grumpily, "We practice
on Tuesdays, though. If you intend to sing
with us you better sit in on next week's
practice."

She closed the thumb switch on the
sprinkler and threw it down on the grass.
"Look!" She marched over to confront him
at closer range, glaring up at his eyes. They
were brown and belligerent with a spiky set
of lashes that were perhaps his best feature. His mouth might not be bad if he ever
stopped crimping it up like a rooster's ass-
hole. But did he have to put on that *look*

and assume that domineering stance? She rammed her hands on her hips and thrust her nose forward. "You've been pissed off at me since the moment you walked into my mother's house and saw me there. You faked it real nice at the hospital today in front of the minister, but we both know something gives you an acid stomach every time we're in the same room together! So do you want me to sing with your choir or don't you? 'Cause it's no skin off my ass if I do or I don't! I mean, I don't need it, *Jake!* It's not my church and he's not my minister! But if you haven't got enough gumption to tell *him* you don't want me singing, then at least have the gumption to tell *me!* Because I don't intend to stand up in some choir loft and raise money for your church while I have to put up with your antagonism and your belittling attitude, so get rid of it, mister!"

"You're a fine one to talk about belittling attitudes!" he retorted with equal anger. "Yours stretches as far back as 1976, doesn't it?"

"Oh, so that's what this is about!"

"Y' damn right that's what this is about, and you know it!"

"How I treated you in high school?"

"You were cruel! You made a mockery of people's feelings!"

"Oh! And what about *my* feelings two days ago when I came home? You walk into my mother's house and treat me as if I just flossed in front of the Queen and your feelings were hurt? Why, you didn't even have the common courtesy to say hello to me!"

"And what kind of common courtesy did you show me when we were in high school? Do you think I didn't know how that gang of smart-asses you ran around with made fun of me?"

"Oh, Kenny, for God's sake, grow up. That was nineteen years ago. People change."

"Oh, yeah, and you really did! Roaring in here with your thirty-thousand-dollar car—"

"Forty."

"—and your vanity license plates, wearing a shirt that says Boss. Lady, you really impressed me."

"I wasn't out to *impress* you, *Kenneth*. The car is mine. I paid for it with my own money. Why shouldn't I drive it? And for your information, I bought the sweatshirt at a Springsteen concert."

"Oh. Well, excuse me! I guess I was wrong about how you used to poke fun at me back in high school, too!"

She gave him a short consideration and said, more calmly, "You carry a long grudge, Kenny."

"You deserve it, Tess," he replied, more calmly, too.

It was the first time he'd called her by her given name instead of Mac, with a sardonic twist. She backed off a little.

"All right, maybe I do, but did you have to be such a nerd?"

"See? Attitude! Didn't I tell you you have an attitude? You did then and you do now."

"Might I remind you of how you used to wear your hair? And how your glasses used to hang on your nose? Hey, tell me something. Do you still get nosebleeds?"

"No. Do you still think you're the best singer in the state of Missouri?"

"I know I am."

"And do you still send anonymous sappy and insincere valentines to guys you think have crushes on you, just to watch them squirm?"

"I never sent you valentines!"

"And I never had a crush on you. I hated you."

"You did not. You couldn't take your eyes off me."

"You thought every guy couldn't take his eyes off you. Probably most of them were just cross-eyed, though."

"Oho, very funny. What about that choir trip when you were a senior and I was a junior and you tried to hold my hand?"

"Hey, I wasn't trying to hold your hand, I was trying to cop a feel. I had a bet on with a bunch of my friends that I could feel you up."

"Kenneth Kronek! You are disgusting!"

"Well, that makes two of us. Kenny Kronek and the girl who stole his underwear and sent it back with a lipstick kiss on it, just to embarrass him. You were the one who did it, weren't you?"

"Guess."

"Who did you get to steal them out of the boys' locker room for you?"

"Guess."

"You got me in a lot of trouble, you little brat. That package came when I was at school and my mother opened it up."

"*All right, Lucille!*" Tess brandished a victorious fist in the air. "*Way to go!*"

"You were, without a doubt, the most reprehensible female in the entire high school."

"Oh, hey, what about Cindy Gallamore? She was more reprehensible than I was."

"Why? Because she got the lead in the school play that you wanted? Boy, that really bummed you out, didn't it?"

"She never quit rubbing it in. Never!"

"And I never quit applauding her for it."

"Does your sweet little daughter know you harbor all this hidden viciousness?"

"No, but she knows all about yours. I've told her."

"Oh, you have, huh?"

"She knows all about every rotten thing you ever did to me. How you teased me, and set me up, and wrote me notes starting 'Dear Kenny Crow Neck,'—C-R-O-W-N-E-C-K—and generally made my life miserable whenever you could."

"Yeah, but she still admires me, right?"

"That's right. So do you think you can haul your big ego over to church and give her some reason to?"

"If I do, are you going to treat me like an insect or are you going to be nice?"

"I'll think about it."

"Uh-huh," she said dryly.

They eyed each other warily for a few seconds, but the air had definitely cleared. They suddenly realized they were were sparring and enjoying it. They were very good at it, actually.

"Hey, you know what?" Tess said thoughtfully, tipping her head to one side a little.

"What?"

"For an ex-nerd, you sure are quick at repartee."

"Why, thank you, Tess. That's the nicest thing you've said to me since we were in rompers. I'm so relieved to know I've managed to elevate myself in your esteem."

They weren't actually grinning at each other, but they were tempted. It had been startlingly refreshing to air their grievances and see where it got them. They were still standing beside the garden with the watering forgotten, sending challenges with their eyes, when across the alley, the porch door opened and Faith called, "Kenny . . . are you out here?"

He tossed a glance over his shoulder, then locked eyes with Tess again. She bent down, picked up the hose, turned it on and sent the spray fanning across the rhubarb leaves.

"Better go," she said, smirking, "your girlfriend is calling."

He turned to do so. At his porch door Faith caught sight of them and waved exuberantly. It was obvious her exuberance was triggered more by her first glimpse of a Nashville superstar than by the man she was all but married to.

Tess put on her generic meet-the-fans smile and waved back. But as she watched Kenny's retreating back she couldn't help wondering what Faith was like and if the two of them had indeed been having an affair for eight years.

"Well, she's famous. I've never met a famous person before."

"Listen, Faith, you wouldn't like her any more than I do. She's mouthy and insincere and she thinks everybody should fall on their knees and murmur a mantra when she passes."

"I don't see how she can be that bad, coming from a mother like Mary."

"Well, believe me, she is. She hasn't changed a bit."

Faith walked into the kitchen ahead of him. "Still, she came home to take care of her mother. She must have a heart somewhere."

In the kitchen Casey was waiting to pounce on him. "Daddy, why can't I go over and talk to Mac? *You* did!"

"I'm not going to have you hanging around over there bothering her."

"I wasn't *bothering* her. She told you so today at the hospital."

"You are *not* going over there."

"Daddy!" Casey stamped her foot.

"Nope."

"But we're writing a song together!"

"*She's* writing the song. You keep out of there."

"Arrr! I could just *scream!*" She tried some histrionics, pretending to pull her own hair. "When I graduate, I'm going to be out of here so fast I'll leave a vacuum! And you know where I'm going? Straight to Nashville, that's where! Then there's no way you can keep me from seeing whoever I want!"

"Fine. When you graduate you can go wherever you want," he said calmly. "Tonight you're staying home."

She put her face smack in front of his and said, less dramatically, "Daddy, you are such a poop!"

He chuckled, and said, "That's about what she said. The two of you should have fun comparing notes on me when you go to Nashville. You smell like horses. Why don't you go up and take a bath?"

"Arrr!" She turned on her bootheel and clumped upstairs. A minute later her guitar started whanging as loud as she could make it whang, and she started singing some song he'd never heard, at the top of her lungs. But no bathwater began running.

He blew out a breath and muttered, "Teenagers."

Faith put her hand on Kenny's arm.

"She's not so bad. And you have to put

yourself in her place and understand her frustration—that there's an honest-to-goodness Nashville star right across the alley who has befriended her, and she's got to stay in this house as ordered. I'll bet you'd be frustrated, too. Just be careful, Kenny, that you don't rob her of an opportunity that could mean the world to her."

"What opportunity? You mean you think Tess wants her hanging around over there?"

"What *did* she say at the hospital?"

"Yes, but—"

"You dislike the woman so much that it could possibly be coloring how you're treating Casey."

"You think I should let her go over there?"

"Maybe. Maybe not. Just make sure you make a fair judgment. Now I'm going to go upstairs and see if I can soothe some ruffled feathers." She patted his arm before leaving the room with her customary unflappability.

Upstairs, she tapped on the closed door and asked, "Casey? May I come in?"

Casey stopped hammering her guitar. "I don't care."

Faith went in and shut the door, leaned back against it holding the knob at her spine. A guitar case lined in red velvet lay open on the floor. Casey sat on her desk chair, sulking, one cowboy boot resting on the overturned side of the other one, staring at her left thumbnail which was bent against the neck of the guitar.

"You know what, Faith?" the girl said. "I called Daddy a poop, but I really wanted to call him a shit."

Faith remained unruffled. "Good thing you didn't. You'd have hurt his feelings, and he's really not one, you know."

"I know," Casey admitted sheepishly.

"You really want to be a singer like Tess McPhail, don't you?"

Casey kept staring at her thumb. Finally she dropped her hand from the instrument and looked up at Faith. "Do you think I'm crazy?"

"Not at all. And maybe I'm not the best judge, but I think you're good enough."

"But Daddy doesn't, does he?"

Faith moved into the room and sat on the edge of the bed, crossing her knees and resting an elbow upon them. "Your dad might possibly be a little bit scared that you'll succeed. Did you ever think about that?"

"Why would he be scared of a thing like that?"

"Because it'll take you away from him. Because it's a hard lifestyle, being a successful performer. Because a lot of musicians use drugs and lead wild and ruinous lives—or so we're told. Take your pick."

"But he *knows* what my music means to me!"

"Mm-hmm," Faith said quietly. "And you know what you mean to him."

Casey quieted. "I know. He loves me. But I can't stay around here forever. What would I do in a town this size?"

"I don't think he expects you to stay. He's just fighting some of his own battles, getting used to the idea of you graduating next month and leaving, wherever you go."

"And I don't think Tess McPhail leads a wild and ruinous life, either. I think she works real hard at what she does."

"I'm sure you're right."

Casey and Faith had always gotten along together. Faith's placid personality seemed the perfect balance for Casey's excitable one. Faith had never criticized or badgered to get Casey to change her ways. Since she wasn't married to Kenny, she had no call to act like a parent; in giving Casey latitude, she had won her trust.

"Hey, Faith, can I ask you something?"

"Of course."

"When I'm gone, do you think you'll ever marry Daddy?"

Faith was still tipped forward with her inverted forearm draped across one knee. She fit the nail of her ring finger under the nail of her thumb and worked it around a little bit, studying it.

"I'd like to," she said, meeting Casey's eyes again. "But I just don't know."

"But you've been going together for so long."

"Maybe too long. We've each grown a little fond of our independence."

"You're scared. Is that what you're saying?"

"No, I wouldn't say scared. Wise, maybe."

"Is it because you're Catholic?"

"Well . . . partly."

"But you and Daddy see each other every day. What would be different if you were married?"

"I know this won't make much sense to you, but your dad and I have the best of both worlds. We have companionship, but at the same time we have our independence. I actually like going home to my little house and having nobody to answer to but myself."

"That's probably because I'm so noisy and sassy that you're glad to get away from me."

Faith smiled with genuine affection. "Not so noisy and sassy that I won't miss you too when you're gone."

"Has Daddy asked you—to marry him, I mean?"

Faith uncrossed her knees and dropped her hands to the edge of the mattress. "Not for a long time."

"Oh." The room grew quiet as Casey sat studying Faith and trying to make sense of her relationship with Kenny. Finally Casey laid her guitar in its case, snapped the lid closed and stood it in the corner against her bookcase. She didn't understand why Faith's answer left her feeling blue.

"Well," Faith said, taking a deep breath, "I guess it's about time I was leaving. Feeling any better?"

"Not really."

Faith rose and stood beside Casey's chair, a hand on her shoulder. "As fathers go, he's a pretty good one."

Casey nodded, her gaze fixed on the floor.

"Tell you what I suggest. Take a long, leisurely bath, and empty all of this out of your mind for a little while, and when you're done it'll all seem less crucial."

Casey nodded again.

"Want to have supper with us?" Faith invited nonchalantly.

That's what Casey liked about Faith. She understood that sometimes you had to be alone. "Naw. You go ahead without me."

"All right. But don't wait too long to talk to your dad again. The longer you wait, the harder it gets, okay?"

"Okay. And thanks, Faith."

Faith and Kenny ate alone that night, inside rather than out at the picnic table. After supper she ironed four shirts for him and watered his mother's old houseplants. She added spray starch to his grocery list and took out his garbage. When she left for home it was after eight-thirty and already dark. Kenny walked her to her car, which was parked in the alley, as usual. They went slowly, spiritlessly, into the sound of crickets and the dewy smell of the spring night, their moods still flat because of his disagreement with Casey. The porch light dimly illuminated the surface of the picnic table and laid its extended shadow on the damp grass at its feet. It ran a strip of reflection along the paint on the side of Faith's car as they walked around it and he opened her driver's door.

She turned before getting in. "I think you're going to have to let her try whatever it is she wants to try with her music."

He sighed long and deeply and said nothing. When he finally spoke, his frustration was apparent. "Why couldn't she have gone to college or trade school? Something she could fall back on!"

"She'd be miserable in college and she'd probably drop out anyway."

Kenny stood with one hand folded over the top of the open car door, staring at the toes of his shoes, which were illuminated by the dome light.

"I saw an interview with Henry Mancini once," Faith told him. "He said that his father had never thought music was a serious enough occupation, and even after he'd had many hits, even won Academy Awards, his father still wondered when he was going to get a real job. I always thought that was so sad."

Kenny said nothing, just kept his hand on the car door, his eyes downcast, nodding repeatedly.

"Well, I must go," Faith said. "Good night, dear." She kissed him on his cheek and he murmured "Mm" as if scarcely aware she'd done it.

She got in and he slammed the door for her. She rolled down the window while the engine churned to life. "Bridge at the Hollingsworths' tomorrow night," she reminded him.

"Yes, I remember."

As the car backed up and centered itself in the alley, he stood with his hands in his trouser pockets, following it with his eyes if not his thoughts. The headlights flashed across him and he raised his hand in an absentminded farewell.

When Faith's taillights disappeared, he stood for a long while, listening to the crickets, thinking about what she'd said regarding Henry Mancini. It was as close to chiding as he'd ever received from Faith. Good old Faith. What would he do without her? Especially after Casey graduated and moved away.

His gaze wandered across the alley to Mary's house. The downstairs lights were off and the single upstairs window below the roof peak was gold. Pretty early for a woman like that to be in bed, he thought. Where Faith's departure had scarcely registered, the nearness of Tess McPhail, a mere backyard away from him, smacked him with a sharp, masculine reaction, much like when he was in high school and hovered around the halls where he knew she'd be walking between classes. He stood looking up at her window recalling the exchange they'd had in the backyard a few hours ago, wondering how she could still manage to do this to him after all these years. By the time that encounter in the yard had ended they'd been flirting, hadn't they? Damned stupid, but that's exactly what they'd been doing. And why?

He'd made a happy, well-adjusted life for himself and Casey. He had exactly what he wanted—a nice little business that brought in enough money to afford him a comfortable life, a circle of long-time friends, one very special friend in Faith. All in all, a calm, secure, small-town life. Then *she* came back and things started changing. Not only could she still manage to get under his skin, she was getting under Casey's as well. No matter what Faith said, he didn't want his daughter hanging around with Tess Mc-Phail. Casey was too starstruck and impressionable to be molded by a woman like that. And as for himself, he'd better start acting like a committed man and being the kind of guy Faith deserved.

When he returned to the house Casey was in the kitchen, smearing peanut butter and jelly on a piece of toast. Her hair was clean and wet, and she was wearing a knee-length sleep shirt with a picture of Garfield the cat on the front. She licked the knife clean, holding the toast on the flat of her hand and watching him enter the room.

"Well . . ." he said, pausing just inside the door. "You took a bath."

"Uh-huh."

"Still mad at me?"

"Uh-uh. Faith and I had a talk."

He wandered a couple steps farther in. "Faith and I had a talk, too."

"What'd you two talk about?"

"You."

She finished licking off the knife and set it down. "Want a piece of toast? I made two."

"Actually, that sounds kind of good."

She handed him one and they rested their rear ends against the edge of the kitchen cabinets, munching.

"Our fights never last too long anyway, do they?" she ventured, balancing her toast on five fingertips, nibbling the crust.

"Nope."

"Daddy, if I go to Nashville after I graduate, can I still keep Rowdy so I can come home and ride him on weekends?"

"Costs a lot of money to board a horse. And how often do you think you'll get home? It's a five-hour drive."

"But would you go out and ride him sometimes so I don't have to get rid of him right away?"

"I guess I could do that."

She stopped eating her toast for a while and let it rest, forgotten, on her hand. He could nearly feel the wave of sadness wash over her as she thought about the changes ahead, the two of them separating, her living someplace else far away, leaving all the

people and things that were so familiar and
dear. He remembered her as a baby and
got sad himself, his memories as clear as if
they'd happened yesterday. He opened an
arm and she curled against him, tucking her
forehead beneath his jaw.

"Oh, Daddy, it's so hard growing up."

"Hard on parents, too."

"I'm going to miss you. And who's going
to take care of you?"

"Faith will still be around."

"Then will you marry her?"

"Well, I don't know. Maybe eventually."

"What kind of an answer is that?" She
drew back and looked up at him, perplexed,
her battle with tears forgotten. "Don't you
want to get married again?"

"I don't know. My life is all right the way it
is."

She studied him thoughtfully for a moment, then said, "Could I ask you something, Dad?"

"Couldn't you always?"

"You won't get mad?" She stuffed the
last bite of toast in her mouth.

"I don't usually. Why would I now?" He
polished off his toast, too.

"All right. Here it is." She brushed her

palms together as they continued leaning against the cabinet. "Does Faith put out?"

He choked on his toast and coughed twice. "What kind of a question is *that*?"

"Well, I was just wondering, that's all, 'cause you two are so . . . well, I don't know . . . comfortable together, I guess. I mean, it's like you've been married for fifty years. So naturally I wonder."

Kenny colored, and said, "Casey, you're impossible."

"That must mean you don't want to tell me." She glanced at him askance. "I figure she must. I mean, everybody does it at some time or another. It's okay. You can tell me and I won't be shocked. Then I'll tell you if I ever have. Deal?"

"Casey Kronek!"

"Well, don't you wonder? I mean, I'm seventeen already."

"Who would you have done a thing like that with? You've never even dated any boy seriously!"

"But what if I was curious? What if I just decided I wanted to know what it was like because all the other girls were talking about it?"

He frowned. "Did you?" Then a horrifying

thought struck him. "Casey, you're not pregnant, are you?"

She burst out laughing. "Oh, Daddy, you should see your face!"

"Well, you might think it's funny, but I don't."

"I was just testing you to see how shocked you'd be."

"Well, I was shocked, all right!"

"So you figure I'll be, too, if I find out you and Faith sleep together."

"You know perfectly well she's never stayed overnight in this house and neither have I stayed at hers."

"Oh, come on, Daddy, even I'm not naive enough to think it only happens at night, tucked under the covers."

"Well, I tell you what, smarty. What happens between Faith and me is none of your business, and it would be a breach of faith for me to talk about it with you, don't you think?"

"A breach of Faith . . . very clever, Daddy. Maybe you're the one who should be writing song words with Mac."

"Do we have to bring her up again?"

"Oh, I forgot. You don't like her because she used to tease you in high school."

"It's more than that. She's still got an attitude."

"No, she doesn't. Not when you approach her without thinking of her as a star,
but just as the girl who grew up next door."

"I'm not interested in *approaching* her at
all. As far as I'm concerned, the less our
paths cross, the better."

"Do you think she'll come and sing with
the choir though?"

"I don't know. I hope not. I was appalled
at Reverend Giddings asking her. Figured
she'd think I put him up to it."

"I saw you glaring at me as if I'd put him
up to it. Honest, I didn't have anything to do
with that. But wouldn't it be something if
she'd do it? Wow."

With a twist of sarcasm, Kenny mumbled
to himself, "Yeah . . . wow." Moments
later he was left behind while Casey wandered out of the room, daydreaming about
her idol and the possibility of singing in the
church choir with her.

Yeah, he thought ruefully, *that's all we
need around here.*

THE NEXT DAY when Tess went out to start her car she found a note stuck under the windshield wiper. It was written in pencil on a sheet of narrow-lined paper that had been torn out of a spiral notebook.

"Mac," it said, "I've got a verse two that I think will work. Try it out."

Mama's in the home place, never changed a lick,
House as worn and tattered as a derelict,
Same old clock a-tickin' on the faded kitchen wall,
Mama won't replace anything at all.
Mama's fine,
Can't change her mind.

Tess stood in the alley, reading the verse, singing it to herself.

She loved it! It worked so much better than the second verse she herself had concocted. How surprising that a seventeen-year-old girl had the insight to come up with something this good.

On her way to the hospital she dialed her producer, and said, "Jack, listen, I want you to save space on the album for one new song that I'm writing down here. It's not done yet, but it will be soon. I'm getting good help from a high school girl who lives right across the alley, and you won't believe it, Jack, but it's good. *She's* good."

"A high school girl! Tess, have you lost your mind?"

"I'm excited, Jack. She can write and she's got a voice."

"Tess," he said with exaggerated patience.

"I know, I know, but this one's special. She's bright and she's got talent to go with it. I want to encourage her and see what she's got. It's just one cut, Jack, okay? And if the song doesn't pan out the way I think it will, we'll use whatever you've got picked out from the demos."

He sighed—a man who'd lost the battle and knew it. "All right, Tess. What's it called?"

" 'Small Town Girl.' "

"A ballad?"

"Yes, upbeat. I'm working on the bridge, and if it turns out as good as the first two verses, the last verse will be easy. I'll let you know the minute it's finished."

"And you'll send a rough?"

"Of course, with piano accompaniment."

"Okay, Mac, you're the star. You know best."

"Jack, for the hundredth time, don't *say* that, as if I'm the only one responsible for making my records hits. You know you're indispensable to me."

He laughed, and said, "Okay, Mac. How's your mother?"

TESS'S MOTHER was progressing normally, which, in the case of hip replacement, meant slowly. By the third day her catheter had been removed and when Tess arrived, Virginia, the therapist, was in the room running Mary through a series of exercises to increase her blood circulation. Mary lay flat in bed, flexing her feet, squeezing her buttocks together and tightening her thigh muscles. But when she was instructed to use a towel as a sling to pull her recovering leg upward, things got more difficult. A male aide arrived to help Mary to her feet for her first attempt at using a walker. The process was slow, with Virginia showing her how to use a leg lifter to support her leg while swinging it off the bed, and instructing her

not to bend her hips more than ninety degrees.

"I know, I know," she said, "I've done
this before."

"All we're going to do is get you upright
first. There's no rush. Just sort of half sit,
half hang on the edge of the mattress and
don't put your weight on either foot."

When she had been swung around and
tipped upright, it was apparent she grew
dizzy. Her eyes closed and she gripped the
arms supporting her.

"Take your time. There's no rush." Virginia gave her a minute, then said, "Okay?"

Mary nodded twice in fast succession,
but her eyes remained closed and her nos-
trils flared.

Virginia instructed Tess, "Please pay attention, because your role will be to encourage and support. It'll help if you remind
her to go slow and be systematic. Now,
Mary, today we're going to do most of the
work getting you up, but at home you'll
push off the bed with both hands, right?
Stay inside the walker, make sure you don't
get your feet outside it or too far up in front
because it can tip over."

Mary nodded. When they got her up off the edge of the bed she reeled.

"Do you feel nauseated?"

"I'm . . . okay," she answered breathlessly.

"If you feel nauseated, let us know."

She nodded again and pulled in a sturdy breath through her nose.

"I know you've done this before, but just a reminder . . . all four feet of the walker need to be on the floor before you make your first step. The walker goes first, then your sore leg, then your good leg. Are you ready?"

Mary opened her eyes and nodded.

Tess was the worst possible nurse. She had always loved her mother, but moving along beside her during her first hesitant steps with the walker was traumatic. She discovered she was holding her breath, glancing from Mary's white knuckles to her grim face, from her moist forehead to the sheen of tears the patient couldn't keep from her determined eyes. Her legs looked like kegs, bound in those thick, flesh-colored PEDs. Everything about her seemed foreign, and Tess felt as if she never knew the right thing to say. Give her a crowd of ten thousand to entertain, but not one mother in pain.

"You're doing great, Mom," she tried, after Mary's first three steps, then overanxiously to Virginia, "Isn't she doing great?"

"Absolutely. There's no hurry, Mary. Take your time."

Tess repeated silently, *Take your time, take your time,* wishing she were anywhere but in that hospital room.

"Keep all your weight on the walker and don't look at your feet.

"Look up," Virginia instructed.

Mary went six feet that first time with the walker. Each step was arduous, a repeat of the pain suffered two years earlier, pain to which Tess had been oblivious until now. She was amazed by her mother's courage to face this a second time, knowing what she'd have to go through, and chagrined with herself for her chickenheartedness.

By the time the patient was returned to bed, it was hard to say who was more relieved, Mary or her daughter. Tess got Mary's adductor pillow and helped tuck it between her knees, covered her with the sheet, rolled up the towel she'd used to lift her leg, and put it in a bedside drawer. Mary looked worn and frail, and Tess again searched for a distraction to offer. Suddenly she remembered.

"Oh, I brought your mail!" she announced brightly, digging it out of her large gray bag. "Looks like you got some cards. Want me to open them for you?"

Mary lay with her eyes closed, her breathing labored. "In a minute."

Tess felt stupid for making the suggestion at the wrong moment. She would never be natural at this the way her sisters were. She bent down and felt awkward drying Mary's forehead with the sweep of a palm. She kissed Mary's forehead, and even that felt forced. "Of course. There's time for that later. You rest awhile first."

Mary nodded without opening her eyes and Tess was left to sit on a chair watching her and wishing she were someplace else.

Renee came later that morning and brought her daughter, Rachel, with her. They both seemed so natural at saying and doing the right thing. "How ya doing today, Momma?" Renee said, bending over the bed and kissing her mother. "Did they get you up to walk?"

"A little."

"And it was awful, I know. But this afternoon will be better and tomorrow better than that. Look who I brought."

Rachel stepped close. "Hi, Grandma."

"Rachel, darling." Mary rolled over and smiled wanly.

"Mom and I made you some cookies. The chocolate ones rolled in powdered sugar that you like so much."

"Top-of-the-Mountains?" She immediately brightened and made an effort to push herself up. "Where are they?"

While Renee uncovered the tin, Rachel found a chance to greet her aunt. "Hi, Aunt Tess, I haven't seen you yet."

"Hi, Rachel." They hugged a little stiffly: they scarcely knew each other. "How are the wedding plans coming?"

"Perfect. All we need is sun. I'm so glad you'll be home for it."

"Oh, Tess, look at these cookies," Mary said, already more animated since the two had arrived and brought the treats. "You've got to have one."

"No, thanks, Mom."

"Oh, what's one little cookie going to hurt?" Mary was looking into the tin as she spoke.

Renee said, "Mom, you know she doesn't eat this kind of stuff," and Mary stopped insisting.

The longer Tess was home the more she realized that her sisters were probably right, she was out of touch with her family. She couldn't have guessed that her mother preferred dark chocolate candy, or what kind of cookies were her favorite. She scarcely knew enough about Rachel to carry on a comfortable conversation. After the obligatory hug they found little to say, while Rachel and Renee found plenty to visit with Mary about.

Shortly after Renee and Rachel arrived, Faith Oxbury showed up, dressed in a pastel print dress, jewelry and pumps, bearing a big vase of irises.

"Hello there," she said cheerfully from the doorway. "Is there anyone in here with a brand-new hip?"

"Faith," they all chorused. "Hello!"

Tess straightened up and took notice of this woman whose car was parked across the alley most nights after work.

"Mary, dear, how are you? The nurses tell me that you've been up already and have taken a few steps. I'll bet you're glad it's over and all you have to do is file your insurance papers." She set down the flowers and kissed the patient's cheek. Then she stood at the bedside squeezing both Mary's hands, and looking right into her eyes. "I'm so glad the worst part is over for you. I can't tell you how many times I thought of you day before yesterday."

"Oh, thank you, Faith. That means so much to me."

"Kenny sends his best and tells me to give you a big kiss, so that's from him. And the irises, too. I picked them in his yard."

"They're absolutely gorgeous. Thank you again."

"And something from Casey, who says she'll try to come up tonight after supper." From her purse Faith extracted a card. "She made it."

Mary read it aloud.

> *"Certain people leave a glow,*
> *Love-dust everywhere they go,*
> *Smiles and cheer and happy-dom,*
> *Hurry home and sprinkle some."*

Everyone murmured appreciatively and the card got passed around. When it reached Tess she read the additional note Casey had put at the bottom. " 'Hospitals are best when you're getting out of them. Glad you're coming this way soon. Miss you! Love, Casey.' "

As Tess closed the card, Faith said, "Mary, I haven't met your other daughter yet, though I waved to her from the back step last night." She approached Tess and took both of her hands as she'd done to Mary earlier. "I'm Faith Oxbury."

Tess squeezed back. "Hi, Faith. I'm Tess."

"And you're every bit as pretty as your pictures."

Faith had the rare combination of sincerity and candor that struck the perfect chord with Tess. She recognized immediately what a genuinely kind woman she was. "Thank you."

"And as nice, if Casey can be believed."

Tess chuckled at Faith's directness. "Thank you again."

"She thinks you can walk on water. That's all we've heard around the house since you came home is Mac, Mac, Mac. You have that girl absolutely glowing."

"Well, I don't know why. I didn't do much."

"You respected her music, that was enough. I think you have a disciple for life."

Faith finally released Tess's hands.

Tess said, "So she told you she and I are writing a song together?"

"Told us! Why, that's all the girl can talk about! She's been up in her room playing her guitar and singing constantly since you got here."

"I didn't know she played guitar."

"Oh, yes. Since she was ten and her hands got big enough."

"Well, I'd like to hear her sometime." That was a statement Tess rarely made, but speaking the words today, she truly meant them. Undiscovered talents were always trying to get to her, perform for her, but most were not allowed. Yet Casey she welcomed, for reasons she had not clearly defined.

Faith was saying, "I'm sure all you'd have to do is say the word and she'd have it at your door. Her father is concerned that she's bothering you, though, coming across the alley too much."

"Oh, no, not at all. Will you tell her, by the way, that I like the second verse?"

"Second verse?"

"She'll understand."

Faith smiled. "I'll tell her."

Tess liked Faith Oxbury. There was nothing about her not to like. She was very genuine, charitable, kind to Mary, obviously as dear a friend to the entire family as Kenny was, and more than likely a wonderful influence on Casey.

What bothered Tess was that she found herself analyzing Faith not in light of all this, but in light of the fact that she was, from all apparent evidence, Kenny Kronek's long-time paramour.

SEVEN

AT SEVEN O'CLOCK that evening, Kenny and Faith had the house to themselves as they got ready for their weekly night of bridge. Casey had driven her rusty pickup over to Poplar Bluff to visit Mary at the hospital, and Faith had finished putting away the sandwich fixings from their quick supper. She closed the dishwasher, hung up the dishcloth underneath the sink and took a squirt of hand lotion from the bottle she kept on the windowsill. Rubbing it into her hands she passed through the living room to the only downstairs bedroom, the one she always used to change her clothes whenever she was here. It had been Kenny's parents' room, but after they were both gone, he'd never wanted to use it as his own. He always said, "It was theirs. It's where I remember the two of them being. I'm just as comfortable upstairs."

His mother had been a widow already when Kenny's wife, Stephanie, declared out of the clear blue sky that she didn't want to be married any longer and was leaving Casey and him and taking a trip to Paris, which she'd always wanted to see, and from there she didn't know where. All she knew was that living in this small town with its changelessness and dearth of culture was strangling her. She was sorry, but she simply had to go.

It was natural that Kenny, left in shock with a seven-year-old daughter, move back in with his mother, who took care of both of them until she had a stroke and lost the use of her left hand. Then the two of them took care of her until she had died two years ago. It had been a workable exchange and they'd gotten along extremely well.

Since her death, the house had remained largely unchanged. It had been Kenny's home for most of his life and he liked it as it was, even though it had only one bathroom, and that on the main floor next to his parents' old bedroom. The bathroom was a barn of a room, papered in yellow nosegays with a huge claw-foot tub and a lot of wasted space. It had a wide window that stretched from shoulder level down to ankle level—peculiar in a bathroom, Faith had always thought—but it looked out into a huge ornamental pear tree and had a white shutter on its lower half, so privacy was no problem. The room still held an antique washstand shaped like a small dresser in which Lucille had kept towels. On top of it, the attached towel bar still held two of Lucille's embroidered linen towels, which Faith washed and starched and ironed twice a year when they got dusty.

Faith was getting a washcloth out of the top drawer when Kenny came clumping downstairs and stopped in the bathroom doorway. He watched her as she wet the cloth and wiped off her face, peering in the mirror above the wall-hung sink. She was dressed in a pair of pleated beige trousers, beige flats and a white rayon blouse with pearl buttons and pleats down the front.

Circling wide around her eyes with the damp washcloth, she said, "I hope I don't get Midge Randolph for my partner tonight. She always plays for blood."

Kenny was thinking of something else. "I

had an interesting talk with Casey after you went home last night," he told her.

"About what?" she asked, taking a compact from a glass shelf above the sink and snapping it open.

"About a number of things. You and me mostly."

Faith rubbed powder on her face. "What about you and me?"

"She was wondering if we're ever going to get married."

Faith closed the compact and opened another. "Sounds like the same conversation I had with Casey," she said, applying rouge with a foam pad.

"Are we?" Kenny asked placidly.

"I don't know, Kenny. Are we?"

He wandered into the room, propped a hand on the towel bar of the dresser and let it take his weight. "We haven't talked about it for quite a while."

"I assumed you didn't want to talk about it."

"Well . . ." he said, and let the thought hang.

She put the rouge on the shelf.

"Well . . ." she said, using exactly the tone he had used.

"Casey thinks we should."

"Mmm . . ." She was applying rose lipstick; in the mirror he watched her open her lips and curl them against her teeth. When her lips were coated she took the time to rub them together and put the lipstick away before speaking again. "I suspect Casey's worried about your welfare and would like to know you'll be tied up with somebody for life after she's not here to watch over you anymore."

"That's about right. But I told her you'll still be here."

She smiled at him in the mirror. "Of course I will. Goodness, where else would I be after all this time?" She pulled a Kleenex from a box on the back of the toilet, blotted her lipstick and dropped it into a plastic wastebasket. She picked at a couple of curls around her face that had been pushed back by her powder puff, and began tucking her cosmetics into a small zippered case.

"Nothing's changed in the Catholic Church, and I know it means a lot to you, being able to go to Communion."

"Yes, it does. I'm . . . well . . . I'm

content if you are, keeping things the way they are."

"Fine with me." Kenny kept leaning on the towel bar, watching her as she smoothed a hand down her torso and re-tucked her blouse neatly into her waist-band. "Casey asked me something else last night."

"What was that?"

"She wanted to know if you put out."

Faith swung around and tried to stop her-self from laughing, but could not. A soft la-dylike snort escaped as she covered her lips.

"Oh, good gracious. What did you tell her?"

"I told her, 'On occasion.'"

"You did not."

Kenny dropped his hand from the towel bar and grinned, moving toward her, letting his head tip to one side. "No, I didn't, but if I remember right, you do put out now and then, don't you?"

"Kenneth," she chided, dropping her gaze like a blushing virgin.

He walked up against her and joined his hands on the shallows of her spine while she put her arms around his shoulders, leaning back and looking up at him.

"It's been a while," he said, "and we have the house to ourselves."

"I just freshened my makeup."

"We have twenty minutes before we have to leave for Laurie and Yale's."

She checked her watch over his shoulder. "Fifteen," she corrected. "But . . . well . . . all right."

They went up to Kenny's room, where Faith removed her slacks and pantyhose, and laid them neatly on a chair. He threw his trousers and shorts on the foot of the bed and said, "Why don't you come over here on the edge of the bed?"

Obediently she went where he suggested, and arranged herself in suitable fashion that would mess them both up the least. His shirttails got in the way and she held them aside. When he made overtures as if to incite her to orgasm, she said, "We don't have time, Kenny," and he obediently desisted. Reaching his own orgasm, he grunted softly. These were the only verbal exchanges they made during the coupling, although when it was over they smiled at each other. Then he kissed her for the first time that night, and she said, "We'll have to hurry because Laurie likes to get started on time."

When they left the house together, Faith was just as neat and tidy as she'd been at work that day.

AT NINE O'CLOCK that night Tess was just eating her supper—flatbread topped with herbed tomatoes and goat cheese, broiled. She was sitting at the kitchen table barefoot, in her baseball cap and a huge white Garth Brooks T-shirt, turning the pages of a JCPenney catalogue that had arrived in her mother's mail that day. The radio on top of the refrigerator was tuned to KKLR in Poplar Bluff and Trisha Yearwood was singing "Thinkin' about You."

Out in front of Kenny's house, Casey parked her pickup truck in its usual spot at the curb, walked around the south side of the building to the back porch door and called inside, "Hey, Dad, you home yet?" Getting no answer, she glanced across the alley. It was a warm spring evening with crickets singing and fruit trees blooming in the dark, giving the yards a faint sweet smell. Mary's kitchen light was on and the back door open: the invitation proved too much for Casey.

The sound of the radio wafted out as she bounded up the back steps and put her forehead to the screen. Peering sharply to her right she could see three empty chairs at the kitchen table. The view of Tess, sitting on the fourth, was bisected by the doorway into the room.

"Hi, Mac. It's me, Casey!"

Mac leaned forward and called, "Hey, Casey, come on in!"

Casey went in. "Just got back from visiting your mom. Saw your lights on."

"How is she?"

"They got her up to walk once while I was there." Casey winced as if watching Mary now. "Ouch."

"I know. But she's a tough one. Sit down. Want some flatbread?"

"What's flatbread?"

"This pale flat stuff without leavening. No fat. No fuss. Just broil some tomato and cheese on it, then put a little fresh basil on top and you got a meal. Here, have one."

Casey picked up a wedge and took a bite. "What's this white stuff?"

"Goat cheese."

Casey stopped chewing and looked sickly. "Goat cheese?"

"Never tasted goat cheese?" Tess took another piece herself. "It's good."

"Phew!" exclaimed Casey. "Tastes like their damn pen."

"Mm . . . the world's a big place. Lots of new things to taste out there."

"I bet." In spite of her complaint, Casey persevered and took a second bite. After all, if the great Tess McPhail ate goat cheese, Casey was going to, too. The fresh basil was a new and delectable taste, and before long she had finished her first piece. "It's not so bad if you keep at it. Can I have another one?"

"Sure, go ahead. I'll make more."

Tess got up to do so, and while the new pan was broiling, she brought Casey a Coke, and said, "Your second verse is good. I'm going to use it."

Casey looked stunned. "You're kidding!"

"No. I like it. I thought maybe since to-morrow's Saturday you could come over and we'll work on it some more, see if we can finish it together."

"Really? Me?"

"Really. You. But you know what? When it's published, you'll have to take credit as one of the writers."

"Oh, Mac, are you serious?"

"Of course. I called my producer and told him to save one slot on the new album for it. The quicker we finish it the better."

Casey locked her hands on top of her head and stretched out on her chair grinning up at the ceiling in rank ecstasy.

"Boy. My dad's not going to believe this. Nobody is. I can't believe you're gonna do this for me!"

"You're the one who's doing it."

Casey let out a whoop that lifted her heels, and Tess watched with pleasure.

"I gotta go out and take care of my horse first thing in the morning, but I'll be here after that."

"Great. But right now we eat." The new pan of flatbread was bubbly, and she carried it over to the table with a pot holder. "Let's celebrate our new association—co-writers."

Tess stretched out like Casey, both of them with their heels on the same chair. While they ate, Tess said, "I met Faith today. She's a nice lady."

"Yup. Faith and me, we get along like Ricky Skaggs and steel strings. Hey, you ever meet Ricky Skaggs?"

"Sure. Played at some state fairs with him a couple years ago."

"How 'bout Alan Jackson? You met him?"

"Sure. You ever heard of Freer, Texas?"

"Nope."

"Rattlesnake Roundup there every year. Looks like Alan Jackson and I might be there again this year."

While their impromptu dinner continued, Tess mesmerized the girl with stories about going on tours and doing concerts with the big names. They finished off all but one piece of flatbread and threw their crumpled napkins on the pan. Casey accidentally burped out loud and they laughed at her surprised expression. Travis Tritt and Marty Stuart came on the radio with an oldie, "The Whiskey Ain't Workin' Anymore," and they yowled along like a couple of beer swillers in a bar.

That's how Kenny found them.

IT WAS SHORTLY AFTER TEN when he pulled into his garage and closed the overhead door. From clear out in the alley he could hear their voices, and recognized Casey's immediately, singing at the top of her lungs. Was she over there *again*? The lights glowed in Mary's kitchen as he crossed the backyard and stopped at the bottom of the steps, listening.

They were bellowing fit to kill about needing one good honky-tonk angel, and someone was thumping a heel hard on the floor as Kenny climbed the steps and peered inside. He could see Casey's back and part of Tess's front. Casey was wearing jeans and her old cowboy boots; Tess, as far as he could see, wore nothing more than an oversized T-shirt. They were banging the tabletop with their drinks, and Mary's potted plant was quivering in time to the music.

The song ended and they yowled and clapped as if they were coming off a dance floor.

Tess said, "Girl, you and me are gonna get along just fine!"

Kenny knocked and called, "Is this a private party or can anyone join in?"

Tess tipped forward to see around the doorway.

Casey spun around on her chair. "Dad! What are you doing here?"

"I could hear you clear across the alley."

In an unusually happy and expansive mood, Tess said, "Come on in, Kenny. We're just eatin' goat cheese and stretching our vocal cords."

He opened the door and went in, stopping just inside the kitchen doorway, surveying the two of them. Tess had a tomato stain on her shirt and the table was littered with dirty dishes. It looked as though Casey had been here for a while.

"Sounds pretty raucous from out here. Who's eating goat cheese?"

"Me!" Casey declared proudly. "And it's good, too!"

"Here." Tess hooked a chair with a foot and sent it scooting backward. "Pull up a chair and try some."

He arranged himself on the chair across from her and studied the two of them, recalling that he'd ordered Casey to stay away from here, and realizing that an effective parent would follow through with a reprimand. Reprimands, however, were the farthest thing from his mind as he settled back and decided to enjoy himself.

Casey said, "Guess what, Dad. Mac likes the song I've been helping her write. She's going to record it on her next album, and she says I'll get credit as a co-writer! Isn't that right, Mac?"

"Yup. That's right."

"Really?" His gaze wandered from his daughter to Tess.

"That is, if you have no objections," Tess added.

"Wouldn't do me much good if I did, would it?"

"Probably not." Tess got up and stuck the remaining piece of flatbread in the microwave and got a can of Coca-Cola out of the refrigerator. When she clapped the soda down in front of Kenny his glance flicked up to her. "Thanks," he said, following with his eyes as she went back to the microwave to retrieve the warmed food. Her legs were bare and her T-shirt was hanging over braless breasts, small and uptilted. The soiled spot on her shirt brought her down to mortal level and prompted a smile, which he concealed as he drank. It had been a long time since he'd seen a woman act so ca-

sual about being half-dressed. He actually
didn't know what Faith wore to bed because he'd never spent a night with her.
One thing he knew is he'd never seen Faith
in any baseball cap. Tess's was pink and
said *Wailea* on the front. Her ponytail
looked pretty pathetic sprigging out through
the hole in the back like a skinny clump of
wire grass. For once she'd removed her
dangly silver-and-turquoise earrings, of
which he wasn't too fond. She looked better without them. Matter of fact, she looked
a little too good to him all the way around
tonight.

The goat cheese wasn't bad either,
though the crust was rather tough from being reheated. She returned to her chair and
became a major distraction, merely sitting
there. He had to force his attention back to
Casey, who went on talking. "Mac and I are
going to work on the song again tomorrow,
okay, Dad?"

"I guess so," he said noncommittally.

"Should we make it noon, Mac?"

Tess smiled at the girl's enthusiasm.

"Noon's good. Gives me time to visit
Mother in the morning."

"Gol, I'm so excited! Isn't she something,

Dad? I can't believe this is happening!"
Without pausing for breath Casey jumped
up and announced, "I gotta use the bathroom, okay?"

She knew right where it was and hurried
away without waiting for an answer, leaving
the other two in the fluorescent-lit kitchen,
trying to pretend disinterest in each other
and carry on a neutral conversation.

"Thanks for what you're doing for her,"
he said.

She waved his words away as if her help
were nothing, and surprised him by saying,
"You know, I was thinking . . . I really do
want to sing with your church choir after all.
You sure you don't care?"

He hid his surprise and answered, "No, I
don't care."

He sipped his Coca-Cola and watched
her over the can. She was used to being
watched. She could sit absolutely still beneath his regard and meet his eyes dead-
on, in spite of the undercurrents in the
room. Those undercurrents ranged clear
back to high school and became amplified
by the quasi-impropriety of a country music
megastar sashaying around in her sleep-

wear in front of a single man who'd once
had an enormous crush on her.

"Practice on Tuesday, right?" she said.

"That's right. Seven P.M. Would you want
to sing a solo?"

"That's up to you. I'm not after stealing
your choir's thunder."

"My choir's not that good. No thunder to
steal. If you want to do a solo, I'll pick out
some music."

"You decide."

A commercial came on the radio and
Kenny kept his gaze pinned on Tess for
several seconds. Then he cleared his throat
and sat up straighter, folding his forearms
on the table.

"So you met Faith today."

"Yes. She's very sweet."

"She said the same thing about you, actually."

"Did she?"

"Yes, she did."

"Don't believe her," Tess said with a grin.

"Don't worry," he replied, and an answering grin played on his lips.

Some seconds slipped by in which they
wondered if the challenge would forever be
between them, enjoying it at the moment.

Nothing would ever be easy between them—that much they knew—but the constant friction spiced up their encounters and made them think about each other after they parted. She dropped a hand to the JCPenney catalogue and absently flicked the corners with a long persimmon thumbnail. *Zzzt-zzt.*

"So what are you two? Engaged or what?" she asked.

"No. Friends."

"Oh, friends." She nodded as if giving that some thought. *Zzzt.* "For what? Eight years? Is that what Casey told me?"

"That's right."

"Mm." *Zzzt.* "Momma's mentioned Faith in her letters, of course."

"Of course."

"Momma loves her."

"And Faith thinks the world of your mother."

"Eight years is a long time." *Zzt.*

"For what?"

"Whatever."

"Friendships last like that in small towns. You ought to know that."

"So what happened to Casey's mother?" *Zzt.*

"She got tired of us and ran away to Paris."

"Got tired of you—just like that?"

"That's what she said."

"Wow. Bummer."

"Yeah, bummer."

Zzt. "So now you mistrust women, is that it?"

"Why do you say that?"

"Eight years with Faith and no wedding ring."

"By mutual consent."

"Ahh." *Zzt.*

He pointed at her thumbnail on the corner of the catalogue. "Would you mind not doing that anymore? It bothers me."

"Oh . . . sorry." She knit her fingers together loosely and rested them beneath her chin, her elegant trademark nails creating a striking contrast to her bill cap and clubbed hair. The room grew silent while she lightly stroked the underside of her chin with one knuckle. Finally she said, "Must've been hard on Casey, having her mother run away."

"She got along. My mother was alive then and filled in."

"But you and Casey are really close—I can tell that."

"I'd say so."

"And she's crazy about Faith. She told me so."

"Boy, you two have talked a lot. What did she tell you about me?"

"That you don't want her to grow up and be like me."

He said nothing, only watched her steadily, feeling no need to confirm or deny her statement, which she liked.

"It's understandable," she said. "The life doesn't leave much time for personal relationships."

"Meaning what? That you don't have any?"

"Are you asking if I have a boyfriend?"

"Well, you asked me about Faith."

She considered a moment before deciding she would answer him. "Yes, I do, as a matter of fact."

"Live-in or live-out?"

"Live-out. Way out. He's on the road right now, in Texas, and I'm here."

"And when you're both in Nashville?"

"That's only happened four times since I met him."

It was unclear why they were setting up boundaries. Perhaps both of them would have denied that's what was happening, but before they had a chance to assess their motives, Casey returned.

"You know what, Dad?" she was saying as she rounded the archway into the kitchen. Whatever she had to say was less important than her physical presence, which brought back their common sense. They kept it light after that and Casey had no idea what they'd been discussing while she was gone. Kenny and Casey left a short while later, and on the back step, Casey gave Tess another of her impulsive hugs.

"Thank you, Mac. You're making all my dreams come true."

"It's fun for me, too," Tess said, and it was true. Some who sought to befriend her left little impression at all; others she immediately took for opportunists seeking to use her in whatever way they could. Casey was different. She neither expected help with her career nor asked for it, but her vibrant personality, along with her talent, made it fun to help her anyway. She was a person with whom Tess could laugh and sing beer-drinking songs, and there were few friends

like that in Tess's life. She felt closer than
ever to the girl as they bade good night.

"See you tomorrow."

As Casey walked away with her father
Tess saw, against the distant porch lights,
that the two were holding hands. When they
were halfway to the alley she could hear the
murmur of their voices, but no distinct
words. She figured relatively few teenagers
held their parent's hand anymore. Would
she herself have done so at seventeen? Not
likely. But something within her was re-
newed watching them walk away.

As they walked home, Casey was saying,
"Do you see how nice she is?"

"I'll have to admit, she's very nice to
you."

"She was nice to you, too."

"It's just that I don't want you to get carried away with these dreams of glory and
then be disappointed."

"But Daddy, aren't you the one who always said I could do anything I set my mind
to do?"

"I said that, yes."

"Then why are you resisting my doing
this with her? Because you are, I can tell.
Even when you don't say so."

He sighed and offered no answer.

"Faith said you're scared that if I really decide to get into music I might succeed and it'll take me away from you."

"Faith might possibly be right. It's a scary lifestyle."

"Oh, Daddy," she said in gentle rebuke as they reached their own back steps and went inside.

Shutting out the lights and closing up the house for the night put an end to their discussion. Though it remained open-ended, Kenny felt himself growing more and more helpless to stop the contagious lure of fame and fortune that Tess McPhail represented for his daughter. Uncannily, she was beginning to represent a contagious lure for him as well. But one thing was sure: He wasn't going to act on it, for to do so would be to set his seal of approval on her in Casey's eyes, and he didn't want to do that. Faith was a consideration as well, for he felt committed to her whether they were married or not. Furthermore, there was self-preservation to consider. Tess would be gone back to the life of the rich and famous when Mary's hip was healed, and he was too smart to set himself up for another fall. It might be fun to sit and spar with her the way they'd done tonight, but any way you cut it, Tess McPhail was as off-limits now as she'd been nineteen years ago, and he knew it.

THE PHONE RANG downstairs in Mary's kitchen at twelve-thirty that night. Tess awakened with a start, surprised to find she'd already been sleeping for an hour. She turned on the bedside light and hurried downstairs, answering in the dark.

"Hello?"

"Tess?"

"Burt?"

"Finally got a chance to call you."

"Where are you?"

"Fort Worth. Billy Bob's. The boys are breaking down and I'm supposed to be helping them, but I decided to call you first."

"You sound tired."

"Just sick of the road. You know how it is. How's everything there? How'd it go with your Mom?"

"Okay, I guess. She's still in the hospital."

"When will she be home?"

"Day after tomorrow or the next day."

"So how you doing at nursing?"

"Terrible, I think. My sisters are much better at bedside stuff than I am."

He chuckled and let a beat pass before saying what was on his mind. "I was thinking about you tonight."

"Yeah?"

"We were doing 'I Swear' and the words made me remember the last time we were together." It was a romantic ballad about the kind of love that lasts a lifetime.

"Oh, Burt, that's sweet."

"Wonder if I'll ever have anything like that."

"That what you want?"

"I don't know. What about you?"

"No, I don't think so. Too hard when you do what we do."

"Yeah, that's for sure."

"I told my mother about you, though. Showed her your picture on my shirt."

"Oh, yeah? What'd she say?"

"She wanted to know if I might marry you. Ma clings to any straw."

"We could give Ma a thrill. How 'bout it? Want to?"

She could tell he was joking. "Oh, sure. Get serious, Burt."

"Yeah, I know what you mean." He sighed. "Well, anyway, I just needed a familiar voice tonight."

"I know what you mean. I've been there a thousand times myself. Where to next?"

"Someplace in Oklahoma. Can't even remember."

Somebody came by the phone and yelled something at him. He raised his voice and answered, "Yeah, yeah, I'll be right there!" To Tess he said, "Hey, listen, gotta go. Boys are giving me shit. Wanna get together next time we're both in Nashville?"

"Sure."

"Take you to the Stockyard for one of their luscious Cowboy steaks."

"Make it one of their fresh lobsters and it's a date." He chuckled and she added, "Hey, listen, call whenever you can, will you?"

"You got it. Miss you."

"Miss you, too, Burt."

" 'Bye, then."

" 'Bye."

After they hung up Tess stood in the dark kitchen, staring absently out the window, feeling the loneliness of being isolated from normality. Fine romance she and Burt could have. Seven hundred miles apart tonight, with the chance of crossing paths in Nashville five, maybe six times a year. She felt around for the drinking glass, ran the water and filled it. Drinking, she studied the outline of Kenny's house, its looming black roof peak haloed from beyond by a streetlight somewhere up on the corner. The windows were dark, everyone there asleep, secure in that small-town way that she had once known. Kenny would go to his office tomorrow, and would probably have supper with Faith tomorrow night, and afterward maybe play cards. Whatever their relationship was, they had companionship. Kenny had Casey, too, and Tess could understand his fear of losing her to this improbable life where commitments became strained by separation, fame and sometimes extreme wealth.

Ah, well . . . She sighed and turned from the window to go back upstairs.

When she was once again settled down in bed she lay awake thinking of Burt packing up his instruments, boarding a bus and trying to get a decent night's sleep while the driver pushed on up the highway to some city in Oklahoma.

She thought of Kenny in his familiar bed across the alley.

Of Burt and herself the couple of times they'd been together, trying to create some kind of relationship in a few rushed hours, knowing it took more than a couple of days every now and then to forge anything meaningful.

There'd been more meaning in the brief time she'd spent tonight with Casey and Kenny than in any relationship she'd had time to attempt in the last several years.

Burt again—rolling around with him on her living room floor because she liked him a lot and it felt good to do that sometimes with somebody you thought you could trust. Sex was something you generally did without when you were a star and single. Anything else was either dangerous or ill advised.

Oh, hell, why think about it?

Because of Burt's call, of course. But when she turned onto her stomach and tried to empty her mind so sleep could float in, it wasn't Burt she saw behind her closed eyelids, but Kenny Kronek.

TESS AND CASEY FINISHED THE SONG on Saturday afternoon. They sang it together so many times that they had every lick and dip down pat in their harmonies. Their vocal qualities were totally different—Tess's resonant and soprano, Casey's gritty and alto, but the combination created an arresting blend.

When Casey left at five o'clock, Tess had a rough demo tape of both their voices.

She called Jack Greaves and said, "The song is done. I'll express it to you on Monday so you get it Tuesday. When you listen to it, will you pay attention to the voice that's singing harmony? Tell me what you think of it."

"Okay," Jack said. "I'll let you know."

After the call to Jack she hung around the

kitchen feeling rootless: Saturday evening in a small town and everybody had plans. Casey was off to get together with some of her girlfriends. Renee and Jim were having dinner with their gourmet group. Judy . . . well, Tess didn't really want to be with Judy. So what was she going to do? Clean the house, since Mary was coming home tomorrow. It was a beautiful spring evening, however, and the prospect of housecleaning suddenly seemed like a gloomy occupation. If she were anywhere but here she'd be working, singing a concert or a club. She made herself a smoked-turkey-and-sprout sandwich and was standing by the kitchen sink eating it when she saw Kenny and Faith come out of his house and head for her car. So they had plans, too. They were all dressed up, she in a pink dress and he in a sport coat and tie. He opened the passenger door for her and for a split second Tess had a flashback of her daddy doing that for her momma. Kenny and Faith were probably going out to supper. What else would they be doing on a Saturday night? And why did their being together make her feel all the more alone? As Kenny walked around the rear of the car Tess wondered if he'd glance her way, but he didn't. He had his keys in his hand, searching for the right one, obviously with no interest in Tess Mc-Phail. He got in Faith's car, backed it up and the two of them drove away.

What was this heavy weight on Tess's chest? Disappointment? Because Kenny Kronek hadn't searched for her face in a window? She turned away, wondering what in the world was wrong with her. Was she so caught up in being idolized that she needed to make a conquest of him? *Again?*

Trying to drive the notion out of her mind, she dug into the housecleaning with a vengeance. She put clean sheets on her mother's bed, threw the soiled ones in the washer, dusted, vacuumed, scoured the bathroom, then followed all the instructions she'd gotten from the physical therapist, removing all the scatter rugs from the main floor, making sure no loose electrical cords were snaking into the traffic areas, tucking away any obstacles that might possibly catch the leg of a walker or the foot of a shuffling convalescent. She found the various recovery aids that Mary had told her to dig out: a bath bench, a long-handled sponge, a booster for the toilet seat, a long-handled shoehorn. From the basement she carried up a three-tiered rolling metal cart, washed it off and loaded it with chairside conveniences. It was already dark by the time she turned on the outside light and went out into the yard and picked some bridal wreath and tulips from the south side of the house, then did a horrible job of arranging them in a vase—Tess McPhail was accustomed to receiving flowers, not giving them. She threw away the awful yellowed plastic doily with the curled edges and set the bouquet in its place on a pretty scalloped-edged plate she found in a high cupboard.

Then she walked all through the house, inspecting her handiwork and realizing she was actually bone weary from the unaccustomed physical labor.

SOMETHING RARE AND WONDERFUL HAPPENED that night. Tess fell asleep on the sofa watching TV during the ten o'clock news. When she awakened it was deep night, the crickets were serenading outside, and she stumbled upstairs groggily to fall into bed and sleep like a lumberjack till dawn.

She awakened sheerly amazed at what she'd done.

The clock said 6:10, and she felt fabulous! So fabulous that she bounded up immediately, brushed her teeth, got some tea steeping and went out in the backyard to water her mother's garden.

This was a time of day Tess rarely saw. She stood on the back steps, tightening the belt of a short jade satin kimono, while enjoying the streaky explosion of colors in the eastern sky. It was a splendid daybreak! Vibrant heliotropes and oranges thrusting their fingers up, up into the paler light-washed sky overhead. She tipped back to look for the moon, but if it was still there it was on the other side of the house where she couldn't see it. The birdsong out here was downright impolite—mourning doves, sparrows, mockingbirds and robins all trying to outdo each other. She remained on the step for several minutes, listening, imbibing, appreciating the spectacle she so seldom saw. Everything was fresh, the grass jeweled with dew, the trees as still as oil paintings. The rowdy sun ascended high enough to place everything directly before it in a black hole. She squinted as it edged up above the garage roof and the ornamental pear tree in Kenny's yard—a magnificent orange ball whose radiance shut her eyes and finally forced her off the steps.

She went to the faucet, uncoiled the hose and dragged it across the crisp, wet grass to the garden, between the rows of beets and okra where she set the oscillating sprinkler, then padded back across the grainy dirt to rinse her feet clean with the dew on her way to turn on the tap at the house.

The spray hit more lawn than vegetables so she had to try again, running out between the rows when the sprinkler was at its nadir, then sprinting out of the way as it rebounded.

She was standing beside the garden watching the sprinkler when she heard a door slam softly across the alley.

She turned and looked.

And there stood Kenny on his back step sipping a mug of coffee and watching her. He was dressed as he'd been the day she'd taken her mother to the hospital, in gray sweatpants and a white T-shirt, only this time he was barefoot, and even from across two backyards his appearance telegraphed that he'd just gotten out of bed. Not even the distance could disguise the impression of hair still flattened from sleep and limbs not yet ready to hurry. He took a long pull from the mug, studying her with disconcerting directness, making no attempt to pretend he was doing anything else.

Finally he tipped the mug down and lifted a hand in silent greeting.

She raised hers, too, and felt a peculiar twist inside, a warning. *Not Saint Kenny,* she thought. *Don't even think it.*

But his watchfulness made her aware of her long bare legs and short silk wrap and the little she wore under it.

She turned back to the sprinkler, which still wasn't in the right spot. Once more she had to run out between the rows before she got it where she wanted it, high-stepping over the damp plants with her muddy feet and dirt-flecked legs while Kenny watched. The oscillator came back and slapped cold water across her rump. She yelped once and might have heard him laugh—she wasn't sure. Maybe it was just her imagination mingled with overt discomfort at cavorting in her sleepwear while he watched with his toes curled over the edge of the step.

Her feet got thick with mud. She worked them in the grass while standing in place, waiting out two oscillations of the sprinkler to make sure it was covering the garden right. Finally she turned her back on Kenny and made her way up the sidewalk, leaving wet footprints behind. On her way up the steps she felt his eyes still following, and, reaching the top, turned with the screen door half-open, to check. Sure enough—he stood as before, holding his coffee mug at chest height with both hands, not even pretending to disguise his interest. The sun had picked a path between the trees around his house and glanced off the roof of her car like a comet in her eyes. His face, to the right of the reflection, remained inscrutable. He did not move; did nothing more than watch her and make her heart dance as it had not in years, while she wondered foolishly if there had ever been a Sunday morning when Faith's car was parked behind his from the night before.

Silly woman, she thought, *that's none of your business.*

But when she turned and went inside her heart was still pounding.

AT TWENTY TO TEN SHE WAS HEADING UPSTAIRS to put on her own clothes for church when she saw Kenny and Casey come out of the house dressed in theirs. As they walked single file to the garage Tess realized what she was doing: noting the comings and goings of these people just like any other nosy neighbor.

She went to the ten o'clock service at First Methodist and heard Kenny's choir for the first time. They were passably good, and she could pick out Casey's voice as clearly as if she were singing alone. The choir loft was situated at the rear of the church, and she resisted the urge to crane around and look up there.

She recognized faces all around, and on this particular morning, it felt very fitting to be back again. Reverend Giddings announced from the pulpit that she'd be singing with the choir next Sunday, so everyone knew she was there in the congregation, and a good dozen people in her vicinity turned to smile at her. When the recessional hymn began, she piled into the aisle with everybody else, and people murmured kind remarks about her singing, and how nice it was to have her back home. Some touched her on the arm the way shy hometown folks will do. She smiled, and lifted her eyes to the choir loft, where Kenny had shucked his jacket and was directing in rolled-up white shirtsleeves. Casey caught her eye and waved unobtrusively.

Outside a steady procession of people came up to say hi, to offer congratulations on her successful career and ask if she would be doing any formal autographing while she was in town. Some she knew, some she didn't. Many people inquired after Mary, and wished her a speedy recovery. Judy's and Renee's families had gone to the earlier service, so Tess waited alone for the appearance of Casey and Kenny.

They came out when the crowd was thinning, and though Tess caught sight of both of them, her gaze remained on Kenny. He was resetting the collar of his suit jacket, and unless she was mistaken, searching the crowd for her. The moment their eyes met, his stopped moving and his hands sort of drifted down his lapels as if he forgot what he was doing.

He came directly to her, with Casey one step behind, and spoke anxiously.

"Well, what did you think?"

"Very respectable. I enjoyed the music a lot. I'm looking forward to practice on Tuesday."

"Hi, Mac," Casey said, and they hugged.

"Hi, sugar."

"I thought about our song all night long."

"Jack's going to call me on Tuesday the minute he hears it."

"Oh, great. Listen, some of my friends want to meet you. Would you mind?"

"No. Bring them over."

She brought up two girls who also sang in the choir. When Tess had given them several minutes of polite chitchat, the three girls drifted off, leaving her with Kenny.

"Casey's excited about the song you two finished," he said.

"So am I."

She expected him to express an opinion about her encouraging Casey, but none came. Still, the remarks seemed to leave a blank between them, and he quickly changed the subject, as if to keep her captive a few minutes longer on this beautiful Sunday morning with memories of day-break still lingering on their minds.

"So you're going to bring Mary home to-day."

"I've got the pillows all loaded in the backseat of her car."

"Well, I know she's mighty anxious to be back home."

"The truth is, so am I. It got a little lonely around there last night."

Neither of them made mention of the early-morning staring he'd done from his back step while she was jumping cabbage rows in her lingerie. They watched people getting in their cars at the curb and leaving, and realized they had nothing more to say but were lingering for the sake of lingering.

"Well . . ." she said, glancing at her watch. "I'd better be going. I can spring her anytime after noon."

"Yeah, I'd better find Casey, too. We left a ham cooking in the oven."

There was a parking lot at the rear of the church. When she turned toward it, he turned with her and strolled along at her side, his hands in his trouser pockets. They went around the side of the building past a crab apple tree that was blooming, their footsteps lagging, enjoying the sun on their heads and the simple act of strolling side by side through the lovely spring day. He walked her to Mary's Ford while thirty feet from it Casey and her friends stood talking near someone else's car.

" 'Bye, Mac!" she called, and they all exchanged waves.

Kenny opened the driver's door for Tess just as he had last night for Faith. He did it without hurry—a man who performed courtesies for women without conscious thought. Tess got in, stuck the key in the ignition, glanced up and said, "Thanks."

The day was so hot and still that the birds had stopped singing. The heat beat up from the blacktop parking lot and from the vinyl car seat as Tess found her sunglasses and slipped them on. In no particular hurry.

She started the engine. In no particular hurry.

Rolled down the window of the open door. In no particular hurry.

She glanced up at Kenny again but couldn't think of a thing to say. The stroll from the church to the car had felt as natural as slipping into the pew had felt earlier.

Much to her surprise, she found herself reluctant to leave him.

He acted as if he felt the same. He gave the car door a push with both hands, and said quietly, "See ya."

"Yeah, see ya," she replied, and realized, as she put the car in reverse and glanced in the rearview mirror, that the girls were standing there watching them.

SHE THOUGHT ABOUT HIM too much on her way to the hospital, about him and Casey and Mary, and how Mary loved them both, and about being back home, and this most peculiar lethargy that she was feeling this morning. It was easier to simply keep bumping into him than to avoid him, and each time she did, she lost a few more of her objections to him.

Sometimes it was more than bumping into each other. Like him with his coffee cup this morning. And her waiting till he came out of church after the service. These were not accidental encounters, they were planned.

To what avail?

Mary's car was like a kiln inside. Naturally, it had no air-conditioning, and Tess wondered again what she did with all the money she sent her. The tape protruded from the deck, and Tess snapped it in. She sighed, dried the sweat from beneath her nose with one finger and wished she could return to Nashville tonight. It'd probably be better for everyone involved, she thought, including Kenny Kronek.

SHE FOUND MARY bathed, dressed and eager to leave.

"Hi, Mom," she said, kissing Mary's cheek.

"Hi, honey."

"This is the day, huh?"

"At last. You got my car downstairs?"

"Right by the door."

"Well, then . . . let's bust me out."

A girl came in pushing a cart. "For the flowers," she explained, and left it. Tess started loading them up but Mary said, "Before you take them down, will you sign a couple autographs for some of the nurses who didn't get a chance to meet you? I told them you wouldn't mind."

Actually, Tess was in a hurry to get out of

there. A hospital was a dreary place on a beautiful spring afternoon, but she signed some papers anyway for the list of names Mary gave her, then finished loading up Mary's flowers. She was surprised to discover separate bouquets from Kenny and Casey, apart from the one Faith had picked and brought over herself. Every day Tess saw more clearly how their lives were intertwined with her mother's.

Getting Mary into the backseat at the hospital proved fairly easy with help there to assist her. Basically, Mary was instructed to do all the work herself, bearing her weight on her hands, which was safer than letting other people try to move her. When she was settled on the pillows with the windows rolled down, they headed home, Mary praising the weather, the beautiful day, and the joy of being released from the hospital. Then she said, "Kenny and Faith came to visit me again last night."

"They did? I saw them leave but I thought they were probably going out to dinner."

"They went to dinner afterwards. Do you know how many times he came up to see me?"

"How many?"

"Four. Isn't that something? Why, some of my own grandkids didn't get up to see me even once, and that boy comes up to visit me four times. That Kenny . . . I tell you . . . I don't know what I did to deserve him, but he's like the son I never had. I couldn't love him more if he was my very own, and that's the God's honest truth."

They stopped for a red light, and Tess said, "Momma, can I ask you something?" She tried to see Mary in the rearview mirror but could not. "Just exactly what is his relationship to Faith?"

"What do you mean?"

"You know what I mean, Momma. Are they lovers?"

"Tess, for heaven's sake. What kind of question is that?"

"Oh, come on, Momma, this is 1995. Unmarried people do have lovers."

"Well, I wouldn't presume to ask."

"You don't have to ask. All you have to do is look and see if her car is ever there in the morning."

"I don't pay any attention to things like that."

"Casey says they are."

"Well, Casey should button her lip! I can't believe they'd do anything like that around her. And why are you bringing it up anyway?"

"Just curious, that's all."

Mary said, "Oh, look, is that a pink dogwood in bloom over there?" and Tess understood, her mother didn't like anything less than complimentary being said about her precious neighbor.

When they pulled up in the alley at home, a surprise waited. Renee and Jim came out of the house waving hello and smiling. It was the first time Tess had seen Jim since she'd been home, and he had a bear hug for her, along with the greeting she'd come to expect over the years: "If it isn't old Tess-tickle. Hiya, sweetheart." They both laughed at the age-old joke. He had the most teasing smile Tess had ever seen, and crinkly eyes and not much hair. She liked him as much as she always had.

"Jim, you big bald brat. When are you going to stop calling me that?"

"Never. I'm going to tell the *National Enquirer* one of these days and they'll put it in a headline." He stood back and assessed her. "Jeez, you look good, kid." He braced his hands on his knees and looked through the open back door of the car. "Hi, Ma, how you doing in there? Need some help gettin' up those back steps?"

"Jimmy, Jimmy, Jimmy," she scolded, "will you stop calling Tess that awful name?"

Tess got the walker from the trunk and they all stood by rather helplessly, for there was little they could do except coach as Mary maneuvered herself out of the car, gripping the edge of the roof and moving by degrees. The walk to the house seemed a good half mile long in light of the slow progress Mary made with her walker, each forward movement measured and cautious. They hovered beside her and as they reached the back steps—three very high steps that had been homemade years ago—Kenny showed up, sprinting across the yards.

"Hey, wait for me!" he called.

There was a flurry of greetings and Kenny said to Jim, "Just like last time?"

"Just like last time, okay, Mary? We've got the program down." The two men took Mary's arms over their shoulders and lifted her bodily up the steps and into the house.

She ordered one of the girls to get her antique chair from the living room. The one with the high seat. When the girls asked if she shouldn't lie in bed and rest for a while, she replied, "Been away from my kitchen long enough, and I do believe that's coffee I smell. Nobody's going to stick me in the bedroom when my kids are here!" She carefully maneuvered herself onto the armchair and prepared to hold court.

Renee had, indeed, brewed a pot of coffee and she said that Judy and Ed were also on their way over. Judy showed up with a German chocolate cake and they all stayed to visit and snack. Ed's greeting for Tess was much less jovial than Jim's had been. He was a quiet man who repaired appliances and largely took orders from his wife, exerting his own form of retaliatory control by pinching pennies and making her account for every one she spent, even though she had a business of her own. The family characterized Ed by repeating the story of the time he had finally agreed to go to Hawaii, then refused to pay for a rental car and forever after claimed he didn't like Maui because there was nothing much there to do if you didn't know how to swim.

Ed greeted Tess with a hug that was chary of body contact, and said, "How are you?" then sat down to tell Kenny how many pounds of scrap copper he'd managed to pick up on the job, and how much it was worth per pound.

Within twenty minutes all three of Judy and Ed's kids showed up, too, and around three o'clock, the bride- and groom-to-be, Rachel and Brent Hill, along with Renee and Jim's other kid, Packer. Packer had earned his nickname at age three when he had gotten mad at his mother and declared he was leaving home, to which Renee obligingly replied, "Okay, sweetheart, you want me to help you pack?" She had helped him fill a duffel bag and load it on his red Radio Flyer wagon, then watched him trudge off down the driveway till he got to the curb and turned uncertainly with big crocodile tears in his eyes. Forever after, the family had called him Packer.

Amid the pouring of coffee and the serving of cake, the story got told again, and laughed about again, along with a few others. The cousins exchanged small talk about what was going on in their lives, and the adults did the same. It was small-town

U.S.A. on a Sunday afternoon, the traditional family gathering at Grandma's house, and Tess could see how her mother reveled in it. When someone remarked that they'd pretty much taken over her house, and asked if they were wearing her out and should they leave, she said, "Don't you dare!"

So they stayed, and Kenny with them.

The kitchen was crowded. Not everyone fit around the table. Kenny stood with his backside against the kitchen sink, and Tess stood with an arm propped against the living room archway. Sometimes, above the heads of the others, their gazes met, but they were careful not to be seen fixing on one another overly long.

Conversations overlapped. The fourth pot of coffee got perked. The phone rang and Kenny was the closest so he reached over and answered it without asking permission.

"Mary," he said, "it's Enid Copley. Do you want to talk?"

"I don't think I can get over there," she said from the other side of the table. "What does she want?"

He asked Enid what she wanted and reported, "Just wants to see if you're home yet and how you're doing."

"Tell her I'm doing okay and I'll call her tomorrow. Tell her all you kids are here."

When he'd hung up he refilled his cup, crossed his ankles and resumed his pose. As he settled back against the cabinets, his eyes met Tess's and this time they stayed. She had been watching him answer her mother's phone and refill his cup just as any of the others might have done. It struck her full force how he dovetailed into her family—not just into Mary's life, but into that of her extended family—with the nonchalance of one who need not think about it because his acceptance there is taken for granted. He knew them all, had known them for years. He liked them all and they all liked him. "Tell her all you kids are here," Mary had said, as if he were actually one of her own.

A little while later, he set down his empty cup and maneuvered through the thicket of chairs on his way to the bathroom. Tess was still leaning against the archway, blocking the way.

" 'Scuse me," he said, as he edged by her. She stepped back to make room for him, and he went through. When he returned a minute later, he stopped right behind her and she had the distinct impression he'd gone to the bathroom to get himself near her as unobtrusively as possible.

She glanced back over her shoulder and inquired quietly, "Where's Casey this afternoon?"—the first words she'd spoken directly to him since he'd been in the house.

"Out riding her horse."

With everybody else continuing to chatter in the kitchen their conversation went unnoticed.

"Horses and music," Tess observed, "those are her two big things."

"You've got that right."

He told her about the conversation he'd had with Casey about keeping her horse after she graduated, and asked, "Do you still ride?"

"I don't have time anymore. Lots of people around Nashville own horses, but not me. I live in town."

"Maybe you'd like to ride with Casey sometime while you're here."

"I thought she just had one horse."

"She does, but she boards him out at

Dexter Hickey's place, and Dexter's got enough of his own that they always need exercising. We can ride them whenever we want."

"Sounds tempting. Maybe when Momma gets more steady on her feet. Speaking of Momma . . ." She turned her back against the archway and crossed her arms, facing him. "I hear you went up to visit her again last night."

"Well . . ." His quick downward glance telegraphed modesty. "It was on our way to dinner." She had noticed before how he downplayed anything he did for Mary.

"Still, you stopped by." She paused before adding, "I guess I've never properly thanked you for all you've done for her."

"No thanks necessary. Mary's a great gal." He smiled at Mary through the archway, but she was busy enjoying her family.

"Faith's been awfully good to her, too."

"Yes . . . well . . . Faith is a good woman."

Of course Faith was a good woman. He wouldn't be tied up with her if she weren't. Tess knew that much by now. She couldn't stop herself from asking, "So where is Faith today?"

"At home. Sundays we save for ourselves."

So Kenny and Tess had cleared their con-
sciences, hadn't they? Sunday was
Kenny's day to do as he wished. It was his
and Faith's agreement. They were still wrestling with the idea when the back screen
door opened and Casey burst into the
room, still in her riding clothes.

"Hey, ya'll!" she greeted. "What am I
missing? Mary, you're home! Oh, cake!
Yum! Judy, did you make this?"

"Pee-ew, girl do you stink!" Renee said.
"Go take those boots off!"

Casey fit in as easily as Kenny did. She
put her boots on the back step, helped herself to cake and stood stocking footed, eating it and visiting with the cousins. Stuffing
the last bite into her mouth, she said, "Hey,
Mac, can we do our song for these guys?"

"What song?" somebody said, and the
next thing they knew they were all in the
living room, Mary resting on the sofa with a
pillow between her knees, the others sitting
on the furniture and the floor. The only one
who didn't come fully into the room was
Judy, who lingered behind Kenny in the

archway where it wouldn't be noticed if she failed to applaud.

Tess and Casey shared the piano bench with their backs to the group. But when they sang, everyone listened. And when they finished, everyone applauded. Except Judy. She had slipped away into the kitchen where she was cleaning up the cups and saucers. Kenny remained with his shoulder to the wall, arms crossed, but one forefinger lined his lower lip and the expression in his eyes was that of a man torn between celebration and suffocation as he watched and listened to Casey. He could hear, unquestionably, that his daughter had talent. But it would eventually take her down a road of which he disapproved, an eager disciple on the heels of her idol, of whom he was beginning to approve more and more.

When the song ended Tess sought his reaction first, glancing at him immediately, and in his frown she saw ahead to a time when all these undercurrents would become exposed and he would either blame or praise her for the part she'd played in Casey's future. There was more going on between them, too: there was this cat-and-mouse game they were playing with their unwanted attraction for each other, plus the words of the song itself, speaking about a woman reassessing her values and those of the people she loved.

Everyone started talking at once, the hubbub full of surprise and praise.

"Wow, that's good!" Packer said to Casey. "Are you gonna sing it with her?"

"I already did, on a demo tape."

"No, I mean like for real."

"No, she's got studio musicians who do that."

Kenny left the doorway and approached his daughter. He put a hand on her shoulder approvingly. "Is this what you've been working on behind your bedroom door when you were mad at me? Next thing I know I'll be hearing *you* on the radio." He hugged her. But he waited to say anything to Tess until he could do so away from other ears. All he said, quietly, was, "It's very good." Hardly effusive praise but it didn't need to be, for it erased the sting caused by Judy's flagrant jealousy.

When everyone left, the coffee cups and saucers were neatly washed and put away in the cupboards. The table was wiped off and the remaining wedge of German chocolate cake had been carried off by Judy when she went.

major cities of America, each headed by a
president in that town, and she had a person in her Nashville office who did nothing

NINE

WHEN EVERYONE WAS GONE, Mary lay down on
her bed to rest. Tess spent the time screen-
ing her fan mail and answering requests for
autographed copies of her CDs. Every week
at least a dozen fund-raisers wanted dona-
tions for their causes—city libraries, bat-
tered-women's shelters, schools and every
disease research facility known to man.
Most of them ran annual auctions, and Tess
sent a signed CD to every single one that
sent her a plea. Kelly had forwarded last
week's fan mail all in one batch, along with
a stock of CDs for Tess to sign, and a typed
letter to the representative of each group.
When she'd finished, she packed them all
into a postal express box to return to Kelly,
who would, in turn, send them on.

She also spent time answering special

fan mail. Though she had fan clubs in all the major cities of America, each headed by a president in that town, and she had a person in her Nashville office who did nothing but coordinate fan club activities, there were some of her fans who sent special gifts that needed personal answers. Others requested inspirational messages for relatives with cancer, or accident victims, or people whose tragic life stories were spilled out in heartbreaking detail, along with requests for something special from Tess because "she's your greatest fan, and a note from you would mean more than anything else in the world to her."

Such requests could not be denied, but the sheer volume of them became a drain on her time that she sometimes resented. She understood: she was luckier than most. She was rich and healthy and blessed in a thousand ways. But the requests never stopped. Nor did people seem to understand the protocol of sending a stamped, self-addressed return envelope when they wanted a reply. Some didn't even understand that it was ridiculous to expect her to fulfill their wishes, which were sometimes ludicrous.

Today's packet of letters included one from a woman who came right out and stated that she couldn't afford to buy CDs and would Tess send her her last two? Another woman invited her to come down to Coral Gables, Florida, to sing at a retirement home because all the ladies there just loved Tess's records, and they would just love to meet her; twelve letter writers wanted to know how she got started; two asked for the name of her agent; several wanted to know where they could buy Tess's past albums (had they never heard of asking in a record store?). One chewed her out for the lyrics on her new hit single, "Cattin'," because it condoned loose sex, which was immoral. An English teacher from Bloomer, Wisconsin, took her to task for all the double negatives in country lyrics in general.

There were, of course, many kind words in the fan mail, yet the negative ones left a longer-lasting aftertaste. It was just after Tess had been chewed out for the double negatives that Mary woke up complaining, "Why didn't you wake me? I missed the beginning of *Sixty Minutes*. I never miss *Sixty Minutes*."

"Well, you didn't tell me, Momma. How was I supposed to know?"

Perhaps Tess would have been more patient with her if it hadn't happened at that particular moment.

When Mary was settled on the sofa in front of the TV, she added, "And suppertime was at six, too. What are you making for supper?"

"Chicken breasts and rice."

"No potatoes?"

"No. Rice, I told you."

"But I always fix potatoes with chicken."

"This chicken is different. I marinated it and I'm going to broil it."

"It gets dry that way."

"Not if you don't overcook it."

"Broiling always makes it dry. I like mine fried."

"Mother, you don't fry marinated chicken, you broil it or grill it."

"Well, I don't have a grill, and besides, I never liked the flavor of charcoal anyway."

Tess sighed. Domesticity being her short suit, she was doing her best here.

"Do you want me to go to the store and buy you a piece of chicken so I can fry it?"

"The store's not open on Sunday night."

"Well, I could thaw one in the microwave then."

"Heavens, no. I wouldn't put you through all that trouble."

"But you just said—"

"No, I guess I'll have to eat mine however you're fixing yours."

But when Mary sat down to supper, distaste was written all over her face.

During the meal Tess attempted to broach the subject of Judy's jealousy and how it hurt her, but Mary said, "Don't be silly. Judy's not jealous. She was in the kitchen washing up the dishes while all the rest of us were having fun."

So THAT'S HOW IT WENT at mealtime, always disagreements about what Tess chose to put on the table, always differing opinions when they tried to talk. The yellowed plastic doily reappeared in the middle of the table and stayed. Tess couldn't believe her mother had retrieved it from the garbage, but there it was, looking as warped and discolored as ever.

Tess loved her mother, truly she did, but she was beginning to realize that as Mary aged she was becoming argumentative and persnickety about lots of things. She wanted to have her way. Maybe her hip was hurting, maybe she missed her privacy, maybe Tess wasn't the best cook in the world, but damn it, she was trying.

STARTING ON MONDAY they established a routine. Every day Tess helped her mother with physical therapy. Every day she watered the garden and fetched and carried, and did laundry and housecleaning and errands, none of which she enjoyed, and with much of which Mary found fault. Every day Kelly Mendoza sent an express packet that required Tess's attention, be it signatures, decisions, phone calls or simply reading. It became difficult to find a time when Tess could compose on the piano because during the mornings she was busy, and during the afternoons Mary watched soap operas on TV, and in the evenings there was prime time, followed by bedtime during which Tess hesitated to use the piano for fear of keeping Mary awake.

On Tuesday Jack Greaves called and said, "The new song is a winner and so is

the other voice. Is it that high school
girl's?"

"Yes. Her name is Casey Kronek. I
thought you'd like her."

"So what's on your mind, Tess?"

"I'll let you know."

ON TUESDAY NIGHT choir practice started at
seven-thirty. An hour beforehand, Tess
bathed, washed her hair, spritzed Jean-
Louis Scherrer eau de toilette on her neck
and behind her knees, dressed in a denim
skirt and white shirt, and hooked a pair of
silver discs in her ears. Tricia had been
commandeered into staying with her grandmother and arrived when Tess was putting
the finishing touches on her makeup. She
came and lounged against the bathroom
doorway. "Wow, Aunt Tess," she said, "you
look sensational."

"Thanks."

"Smell good, too."

"Some new perfume I just found last
month."

Tricia watched as Tess finished outlining
her lips with lip liner and began filling them
in with a lipstick brush.

"Going to a lot of trouble just for choir practice, aren't you?"

Tess checked the results in the mirror. Her makeup was perfect, her lip line crisp. "It's about maintaining an image. People expect you to look a certain way when they see you out in public."

It wasn't about that at all. It was about impressing Kenny Kronek, though Tess wasn't exactly admitting that to herself yet.

She walked out of the house with fifteen minutes to spare and was halfway to the alley when the man himself came out of his own house heading in the same direction. They caught sight of each other and felt a connection that kept their footsteps brisk and their gazes locked as they continued toward their cars, which were both sitting out.

"Hiya," she said jauntily, reaching her Z.

"Hiya," he answered, reaching his Plymouth.

She felt spunky and a little flirtatious and decided to test out her wiles on him. "I'm goin' to choir practice, where you goin'?"

He caught her mood and squinted at the clear violet sky. "Full moon. Thought I'd go out and bite a couple necks."

"You all alone?"

"Yes, ma'am," he drawled, opening his car door.

"Where's Casey?"

"Gone already. She picks up Brenda and Amy on the way." Those were the girls Tess had met after church on Sunday.

"Shame to take two cars when we're both going the same way. Wanna ride with me?"

He slammed his car door and crossed the alley. "You bet."

"You won't bite my neck, will you?"

"Might have to, to steal your car."

"Get in."

Inside the Z, they both buckled up and settled low in the leather seats, like riders in a bobsled. She started the engine and shifted into reverse.

"Boy, this *is* nice, and this time I mean it."

"Meaning you didn't the last time?"

"We both had attitudes that day, didn't we? The car's incredible, Tess."

"Thanks."

As the car rolled up the alley he ran his window down and cocked his head toward the throaty sound of the engine.

"Listen to that. Like a lion purring. Real leather, too," he noted, rubbing the edge of the seat.

"Absolutely."

"What'll she do?"

"I don't know. I've never opened 'er up." She tossed him a glance. "I wouldn't take you for a speeder."

"I'm not really, but sometimes a person gets the urge. 'Specially when there's a full moon." He sent her an arch glance. "Damn moon can make you do all kinds of things you shouldn't."

He seemed like a totally different man tonight, as if he, too, had been anticipating this get-together. It was easier than ever to spar with him.

"Hey, Kenny, know what?"

"What?"

"There's no full moon."

"There isn't?"

"There's no moon at all. It's not up yet. And if I'm not mistaken, when it shows it'll be about one half."

"Is that a fact? Must be something else that got into me then."

She gave him a second, longer glance. He was watching her from the corner of his eye, as if half-interested, relaxed in his seat. Everything about his pose was flirtatious and teasing. His clothing was a surprise. He was wearing pressed khaki trousers and a short-sleeved shirt in a bunch of wild summer colors featuring a ludicrous design of sunglasses and fish and seaweed. Very trendy and not at all the kind of thing she'd expect him to break out in. He was freshly shaved and smelled good, too. She'd noticed it as soon as he'd gotten in, and with the window rolled down the woodsy smell went grapevining all over.

"Pretty wild shirt," she told him, returning her eyes to the road.

"Damn right," he said smugly.

She gave the steering wheel a jerk, just to throw him off balance. He flew to the right, bounced off the door and grinned.

"Showoff," he said.

"But then I always was, wasn't I?"

He eyed her openly, not trying to hide it. "So what happened to the huge earrings tonight?"

"These were more reverent."

"Big improvement," he said.

"Thanks a lot," she said sarcastically.

"Hey, you know what? I read that about

you, that you have a very cutting sense of humor."

"Oh, so you read about me, huh?"

"Sometimes."

"That surprises me."

"Why wouldn't I? An old schoolmate. Hometown girl. Mary's daughter."

"The bane of your youth."

"That, too."

They arrived at First Methodist, a red-brick structure with a white bell tower and traditional ogive windows. She parked at the curb and they climbed the front steps together. Twilight was coming to a close as he opened the heavy wooden door for her and she stepped into the wine-hued dimness of the vestibule. Steps curved up to the choir loft from Tess's right. She climbed them without waiting for Kenny and stopped to look down at the nave, while in the dim recesses below he switched on lights that came on over her head. The sound of the switches echoed through the sanctified silence, followed by his footsteps on the wooden stairs. The church smelled exactly the way she remembered, of old wood and candle smoke and memories. It brought peace and a sense of suspended idleness; empty as it was tonight.

Kenny arrived and stopped beside her, looking down at the pews and altar, the familiar lines of the roof, windows and side pillars. Even the burgundy carpet down the center aisle seemed timeless.

"Churches never change," she said.

"No."

"We used to sit right down there." She pointed. "I remember coming to Sunday services when Daddy was still alive."

"I remember your dad. He used to call me sonny. 'Well, let me see if I've got any mail for you today, sonny,' he'd say, when I was way too young to get any. Then he'd hand me the letters for my mother and warn me not to drop any on my way into the house. Once when he came along the sidewalk with his great big leather mailbag I was sitting there trying to get my chain back on my bike, and he stopped and put down his mailbag and fixed it for me. Do you think mailmen still do that today?"

She smiled up at him. "I doubt it."

"Another time he was back by the burning barrel in the alley, breaking up a cardboard box, the kind that's from big bottles, like liquor bottles, you know? And he gave me the cardboard divider from the middle of it so I could play post office with it. I set it up on the front step to be the post office boxes, and I pretended my baseball cards were the mail I stuffed into them."

It was a nice moment, standing there remembering, their voices murmuring back to them in the quiet while the shadows grew darker in the space below. Whatever Kenny had been like as a boy, being with him now felt vastly nostalgic.

"Did you always go to this church?" she asked.

"Yes."

"I don't remember you here. I remember you in a lot of other places but not here."

"We used to sit down there." He, too, pointed.

A door opened downstairs—an intrusion as it clacked and echoed—followed by other footsteps ascending the stairs. A boy appeared, tall, gangly, with freckles and a red crew cut.

"Here's Josh," said Kenny. "Josh, come and meet Tess McPhail."

Josh Winkworth was a high school senior who played the organ and reacted with a blush when introduced to Tess. He had a long bony palm that was slightly damp when he shook her hand, and she could tell he was totally flustered to be meeting her.

Josh escaped to unlock the key cover on the organ and Kenny moved to the top tier of the choir loft, straightening the black metal music stands. "I don't know who's going to play the organ for us next year when Josh isn't here anymore. 'Course, by then I hope either Mrs. Atherton is back directing, or somebody else besides me." Tess moved along a lower tier, helping him with the stands. Voices sounded below and other choir members began arriving.

Casey and her friends made their appearance and Tess had the extreme pleasure of being able to tell her, "I talked to my producer, Jack Greaves, and he likes the song and wants to include it on the album."

"Are you serious?"

"Absolutely. You're going to be a published songwriter, one who gets royalties."

The squeals of excitement might have been the slightest bit out of line in the church, but giving Casey the thrill of her life gave Tess one of her own. Casey hugged her and thanked her while Brenda and Amy exclaimed, "Oh, Casey, wow! On a real album!"

Thirty-three people showed up for choir practice and Kenny performed a simple introduction.

"I know you all recognize Tess McPhail and know who she is, so make her feel comfortable by not asking her for her autograph tonight, okay?"

A ripple of laughter relaxed everyone and they got to work. Kenny warmed them up with the old warhorse of hymns, "Holy, Holy, Holy," and from the moment he raised his arms he became a different man. He became, in all respects, a leader, one who directed with animation and expressiveness. His choir liked him, and he them. They were not professionals. They were people who enjoyed singing, and it showed in how they responded to him.

For Tess, being directed by Kenny was not the trial she'd imagined when first asked. It was wholly pleasant, and blending her voice with the other thirty-three took her back to the Sundays of childhood when she did it regularly. She'd been placed with the sopranos, curved around on Kenny's right, while Casey stood with the altos on his left, and sometimes when they were singing, their glances caught and Tess had the feeling that destiny had brought her home for much more than caring for Mary. It had brought her here for Casey. And for Kenny, too? Heavens, what in the world was she thinking? It was exactly one week ago tonight that she had come back home and he'd walked into Momma's carrying that bag of salt. One week wasn't long enough to be having such fatalistic thoughts. But she'd admit that every time she was with him she saw a new facet of his personality, and what she saw she liked, more and more.

He had chosen mostly familiar hymns for the group as a whole. For Tess's solo he picked "Fairest Lord Jesus." She approved heartily, and so did the choir after they'd run through it. The beautiful old traditional hymn crowned their practice with a sense of celebration that was still intact as the session ended and they said good night. A woman near Mary's age was one of the last ones to leave. "I'm sure you don't remember me," she said on her way out, "but I'm Clara Ottinger. I've known your mother my whole life long. I remember when you were just a little shaver about so high, you used to stand up on the front steps in your yard and belt out songs to people who were driving by in their cars. I said then, 'That one's going to make a name for herself,' and you sure did. Well, good for you, honey." She squeezed Tess's arm. "We're sure proud to have you back."

Everyone was gone. It was ten after nine and the vestibule door resounded with an echo behind Mrs. Ottinger. In the choir loft, Kenny picked up a crumpled tissue that had been dropped on the floor and tossed it on top of the organ. He turned and met Tess's eyes across twenty feet of disarrayed chairs and music stands. Funny how their silences had gotten more comfortable tonight.

"They love you," he said.

"They love you, too," she replied.

Nightfall had painted the windows black and left the cavern below in darkness. Two inadequate ceiling lights hung by chains over the choir loft, tinting the hardwood floor gold but making shadows of Tess's and Kenny's eyes. There was a peculiar intimacy to the place, and their purpose there. Like last Sunday morning when he'd been

watching her from his back step, they recognized how their growing familiarity was
changing them.

He turned his attention to straightening
the chairs and music stands, moving along
the lower tier while Tess did the same along
an upper one. Somewhere in the middle,
they met, the job done.

"Thanks," he said.

"You're welcome."

They stood close, silence all around, captivated by each other but fighting it. He
turned and headed for the organ and she
followed, giant-stepping down to the lowest
level. He slid onto the bench and switched
off the gooseneck light that Josh had forgotten to turn off, then reached up for his
own music, which lay askew on top of the
organ. While he was tamping it together she
came up behind him.

"Kenny, I have to talk to you," she said
over his shoulder.

"Sure." He put the music in a flat pouch
and zipped it.

"About Casey."

"What about her?"

"May I?" she asked, indicating the organ
bench.

"Sure." He slid over and she slipped onto the bench beside him, joining her hands loosely in her lap. She took a moment, realizing that what she was about to say would have a major impact on his life as well as on his daughter's. She did not take it lightly.

"I want to take her to Nashville to sing harmony with me on 'Small Town Girl.' "

He sat so still she knew he didn't like it. But he looked into her eyes and gave himself time to adjust to what she'd just said.

"I figured this was coming."

"But I wouldn't ask her without asking you first."

He waited a long time before looking away and whispering, "Shit," forgetting where he was.

"You understand what I'm talking about . . . a recording session on a major label."

"Yes, I understand."

"It's what she wants, and she's good enough."

"I know. I realized that Sunday afternoon."

"I've already heard from my producer and he likes what he's heard on the demo."

She waited but he said no more, neither looked at her nor acknowledged what she'd said, but stared straight ahead at the empty wooden music holder on top of the organ.

She said, "Look, I know what you think of me and—"

He waved off her remark. "That was gone a long time ago, Tess, you know that."

"All right, then, what you thought of me, but if you think I'd let anything bad happen to her you're wrong. I'd be there. I'd look after her. I'd see to it that nobody took advantage of her."

"I know that, and I appreciate it. But what about her life?"

"You really think my life is so bad?"

"It's abnormal—no home to speak of, half the time traveling, no husband, no kids."

"It's rewarding when it's what you love to do."

He allowed himself a small explosion prompted by frustration. *"But it isn't what I want for her!"*

She let his outburst fade away before challenging him quietly. "The choice isn't yours, Kenny."

Tormented, he stared her down before breaking. His shoulders slumped slightly as he admitted, "I know that."

Though she understood what he was going through, she felt compelled to speak for Casey. "She'd get a chance to meet some studio musicians and maybe sing backup in some other sessions if nothing more. But Nashville's a small town. The word will spread fast that she's there as my protégée. Opportunities will happen for her after that. I want to give her that chance, Kenny."

She gave him time to think about it awhile. At length he spoke as if arguing with himself, in a quiet voice, watching his thumbnail absently dent a line in the leg of his trousers. "This is hard, you know. She's my only child and when you only have one you think about things like grandchildren and a place where you'll visit when you get old, and then you realize you're thinking selfishly and that you can't rely on others to make your happiness for you, but it's . . . it's hard letting go."

She laid her hand on his bare arm. "Of course it is."

He looked down at her hand, then covered it with his own, rubbing the back of it and toying with an oversized silver-and-turquoise Indian ring occupying the finger where most women wore a wedding ring.

Realizing what he was doing he withdrew his hand and she took hers back, too.

"When would she go?" he asked, meeting her eyes.

"As soon as school is out. The album's scheduled to come out in September. They've already released one single from it. We'd have to get into the studio and record our song in June so there'd be time for mixing and mastering and distribution."

"How long would she have to stay?"

"That's up to Casey. You can record a song in a single session. Sometimes it takes two, sometimes you actually get two songs done in one session. Just depends. If she comes, though, she can stay at my house until she finds a place of her own."

He stared at her, thinking.

"I know lots of people in Nashville," she reassured him, "at radio stations and at the Opry, all over town. She won't have any trouble finding a job. You know the story—there are big stars who started out as ushers at the Opry. Kris Kristofferson started that way." Still he looked unconvinced.

"Oh, Kenny . . ." She touched him again, then thought better of it. "If it hadn't been *with* me it would probably have been *without* me, and isn't it better that I'm there to see after her?''

He hooked his hands over the edge of the bench, hunched his shoulders and stared at his knees. She could almost read his mind.

''I suppose you're thinking, 'Why did Tess McPhail have to come back home?' ''

''Yeah,'' he said, ''that's exactly what I'm thinking.''

Their eyes met again and they sat absolutely still beside each other, realizing there was more than one reason for him to think that. Finally he straightened his shoulders, seemingly bone by bone. ''Come on,'' he said, sliding off the bench and tugging her after him. ''Take me for a ride in your shiny new car and make it up to me, okay?''

They walked downstairs together and she waited while he turned off the lights in the vestibule, then shoved the heavy door open and let some night glow show the way down the bank of steps to the street out front where her car waited. Lights shone from the windows of the houses around First Methodist, from a streetlamp a half block away, and from scattered stars.

The moon, however, was far from full.

"See?" she said, pointing up. "Half-moon. It's not full at all."

"Ahh . . . well, in that case, your neck is safe."

They got in and slammed the doors. When she'd started the engine she left her foot on the brake.

"So where do you want to go?" she asked.

"I thought we were going home."

"I thought you wanted a ride."

He studied the reflection of the dash lights in her eyes. "All right, then . . . go on up to the stop sign at the highway and turn right."

While she pulled away from the curb they both rolled their windows down and let the spring night rush around their heads. He lay back in the seat and closed his eyes. After a while he opened them and watched her as she drove. She was shorter than he, her seat pulled farther forward, so he could study her undetected. When necessary, he told her where to turn. The air scrolling around his head smelled of greening things and night damp, and farther out of town, of dusty gravel roads and pastures. Sometimes it smelled of her, some faint perfume he couldn't quite catch. She kept her speed around thirty-five so the night sounds could be heard—insects, and gravel hitting the undercarriage, and the wind patting their ears.

"I thought you *would* be a speeder," he said.

"I think you have a lot of misconceptions about me."

"No more than you have about me."

"You might be right. Anyway, why hurry? It's nice to get away from the house for a while."

"Mary tells me you two don't get along so well."

She glanced over. "When did she tell you that?"

"At the hospital."

"I think it's mainly age difference."

"My mother and I got that way, too, as she got older."

"I thought you two got along fabulously."

"As long as I bit my tongue."

"It's funny, isn't it," she mused, "how they can test your patience with the smallest things. You know that curled up, pitiful plastic doily the color of a pee ring that my mother keeps in the middle of her kitchen table? I threw it away while she was gone to the hospital. As soon as she comes back she sees it's gone and picks it out of the garbage and washes it and it's right back on the table. She probably had to lash herself onto her walker to keep from falling over while she did it, but she managed somehow while I wasn't looking."

He chuckled.

"And we argue all the time about what I'm going to cook for meals and how I'm going to cook it. You have to understand, I'm the world's worst cook to begin with."

"You don't like it?"

"*Nuh-uh!*" she said with great passion. "At home I have a housekeeper who does it for me or if I'm at the studio a caterer brings food in. Anytime I have to cook for myself it's chicken breast and salads. Who cooks at your house?"

"All three of us."

The reminder of Faith dropped between them like a mudslide. They rode awhile without talking, thinking about how their conversations always seemed to roll around to Faith.

Finally Tess said, "Could I ask you something?"

"About what?"

"You and Faith."

"No."

"But I—"

"No."

She shot him a sour glance, but he wouldn't look at her. She gripped the steering wheel tighter and decided she could be as stubborn as he. *Well, all right then, be that way. But I really don't have to ask, do I, Kenny? Because we both know that you sleep with her.*

Neither of them said anything further till he ordered, "Turn here."

They swung into a rutted driveway lidded by an aisle of trees that led to a cluster of buildings. One metal pole barn was larger than all the rest.

"Where are we?"

"At Dexter Hickey's. Pull up next to that fence." She did, and killed the engine. They got out and sauntered toward a chest-high wooden fence that appeared back-lit in the moonlight. Inside the paddock a half dozen horses stood close together. Roused from sleep, some lifted their heads while others slept on. Out of the cluster one dark shape separated and moved lazily, head hanging, hooves plopping softly on the battered earth as he approached them.

Kenny waited, his arms crossed on the fence, till the horse arrived and blew softly at his elbow. The white blaze on his face showed clearly against its darker hide. Kenny laid a hand between the horse's eyes and said, "This is Rowdy."

"Hi, Rowdy," she said quietly, waiting, letting the horse take her scent. He reached out his enormous head and put his whiskery nose to her hand. "You smell good," Tess said.

He didn't of course. He smelled like the paddock, fecund and equine, but it pleased Kenny that Tess was one of those who found horse scent friendly. Rowdy let her scratch his nose.

"How long has Casey had him?"

"Since she was thirteen. But she talked about having him since she was about five."

Rowdy's nose was velvet beneath her hand. She thought he'd probably fallen asleep again, for he stood motionless, breathing evenly in heavy warm gusts against her palm.

Tess asked, "Are you trying to make me feel bad for taking her away?"

"Maybe."

"Are you always this honest?"

"I try to be."

There was enough celestial light for each to see the other's eyes. On the fence rail their elbows nearly touched. Inside the pole barn another horse whickered. Behind them the engine ticked as it cooled. Above them the half-moon kept him from biting her neck.

Out of the blue she said something he never expected, said it sincerely, so that one more barrier crumbled. "I can see, Kenny, that you're a very good dad."

He'd been right earlier; the moon made people do crazy things, be it full or half. But much as he wanted to kiss her, it wouldn't be wise. There was his relationship with Faith to consider, and the temporary nature of Tess's stay here, and her fame and its demands, maybe even the risk that she might think her celebrity and wealth were the reasons he was coming on to her. Hell, who knew? Maybe they were. On second thought he didn't think so. This attraction went a long way back, clear back to the

stinging memories of groping for Tess Mc-
Phail on a school bus on a choir trip, all
those years ago, and being laughed at for it.
Kissing her would be the height of folly, but
he kept standing there thinking about it.

The moon might have had its way if
Rowdy hadn't whickered then and shaken
his big head, startling them.

They drew back from the fence, and Tess
said, "Do I have your permission to ask
Casey, then?"

He expelled an uncertain breath before
answering, "Yes."

And they returned to the car like two sensible people.

Small Town Girl   297

TEN

THEY DROVE HOME through the piquant spring night realizing it would be most prudent if for the remainder of her time here they'd limit their encounters to waving hello across the alley. She considered saying so, then switched on the radio so they need not speak at all.

Halfway back to town one of her own songs came on. It was "Cattin'."

He reached over and turned the volume up.

She reached over and turned it down.

"What did you do that for?" he said.

"You don't have to turn it up just because it's me."

"I turned it up because I like it." He cranked the volume again and one of his knees started wobbling in time to the music.

She gave him an arch glance. "It's immoral, you know."

"What is?"

"That song."

He burst out laughing—a long, loud, lusty laugh with nothing held back. After he got done she ended up telling him all about the letter she'd gotten from the irate listener who called the words "filthy," about the preposterous demands her fans sometimes made on her, and the frustration of becoming so famous that people think they own a piece of you and can tell you how to conduct your business. She also confessed her guilt for having these feelings because her fans were her lifeblood, and without them she'd be nowhere.

"I suspect what you're feeling is probably universal among the very famous," he said. "Don't worry about it so much. Fans are like any other people, some are nice and some aren't. Some are reasonable and some aren't. It's the same in any business."

They reached town so fast she couldn't believe it, talking all the way. When they pulled up in the alley she shut off the engine but neither of them moved. It was suddenly very quiet without the radio.

"The trouble is, Kenny, you're too easy to talk to."

"That's trouble?"

"You know what I mean. I don't remember you being this easy to talk to when we were in high school."

"Same here. I remember you being a stuck-up snob."

She considered awhile. "Maybe we're both getting over some misconceptions."

They could look at each other now for great lengths of time while silence fell between them and underscored their changing attitudes toward each other and their marked reluctance to part. But both of their houses had lights on, and this lingering was getting them nowhere. He glanced at her house. She glanced at his. She was supposed to give Tricia a ride home, and he ought to go in and give Faith a good-night call, which he usually did on the evenings he didn't see her.

"Looks like Casey's still up," she noted.

"And your mother, too."

"Tricia, too. She's taking care of Momma."

"You have to take her home?"

"Yes . . . and I'd better get going. It's a school night."

"Well . . ." he said, reaching for his door handle, looking back at her. "Thanks for the ride."

"Anytime."

They smiled at each other in the semidark while the half-moon shone in the back window and the shadows of the trees patterned the garage roofs. There was no further reason to linger. They got out of the car, slammed the doors and stood in the warm night on either side of the Z.

"Good night," he said over the car roof.

"Good night."

It took a while before either of them moved. He finally turned and walked across the alley slowly, and she watched him become a black cutout against his distant porch light.

"Hey, Kenny?" she called, wishing to detain him awhile longer. He turned, stopped. She could tell he really didn't want to go in the house yet. "I really did enjoy talking with you tonight."

"I enjoyed it, too."

"Especially the stuff about my dad. Thanks for that."

"No need to thank me. He was a part of my childhood, too."

"In Nashville all my friends are music related. Seems like all we talk about is music. But back here it's . . . well, it's good to reminisce a little."

"Yes, well . . ." He thought of how much she'd changed in these few short days at home, and how much his opinion of her had changed as well. He wondered what her reaction would be if he simply walked back to her side of the alley and kissed her. But it struck him afresh who she was, and who he was, and that he was on his way inside to call Faith and say good night.

"Good night again," he called, doing the right thing. "See you Sunday."

"Yeah, see you Sunday."

AFTER TESS HAD TAKEN TRICIA HOME and prepared for bed she turned out the light and stood for a few minutes at the window overlooking the backyard. Across the alley one upstairs light was on in the bedroom that used to be his when he was a child. Did he still use that room? Or was it Casey's now? What was the point of wondering? Yet she did, even after she got into bed and lay in the dark going over this evening and how very, very enjoyable it had been. Singing with him, driving with him, petting the horse with him, talking about the old days. It was true what she'd told him when he was walking back to his house, every friend she had now was somehow connected to the music industry. None of them had known her as a child, none could share recollections of her past, yet Kenny even remembered her father. How precious his story had been and how very connected it made her feel, as if this place would always be here for her, with its living family as well as its dead. This then was nostalgia making its impact, and in her lucid moments she realized it was temporary and would fade as soon as she returned to Nashville. But in her less guarded moments, it—and Kenny Kronek, too—made her question where she belonged.

IN THE BRIGHT LIGHT OF MORNING she knew exactly where she belonged. The daily express packet arrived from Kelly Mendoza and it was back to business, in between housekeeping duties. She called Jack Greaves and told him, "I'm going to ask Casey Kronek to sing backup on 'Small Town Girl.' Okay with you?"

"I think your voices are a perfect blend."

"Thanks, Jack. This means a lot to me."

"Not nearly as much as it means to Casey Kronek, I'll bet."

"Listen, put it on the schedule for the first week of June."

"Will do."

She went to find Mary and tell her. Mary was resting in bed with her eyes closed and a cup of coffee balanced on her stomach, as if she'd just dozed off. As Tess stopped in the doorway a floorboard creaked and Mary awakened with a start. Her hands jerked and the coffee sloshed onto the sheets.

"Oh, Tess . . . oh, dear, look what I've done. The sheets."

"That's okay, Momma, I can change them." She went in and took the cup from

Mary, setting it aside. "I came to tell you something exciting."

"What's that?"

"I'm going to ask Casey to sing backup on the song we wrote together."

"You mean on the real record?"

She no longer tried to correct Mary when she referred to tapes and CDs as records. "Yes. I just talked to Jack about it."

"But Kenny isn't going to like it."

"I got his permission last night."

"You did?"

"I wouldn't ask Casey without it."

Mary thought a moment. "Well, in that case then, my, this is going to be something, isn't it? Casey's going to flip when you tell her."

"You know what, Momma?" Tess sat on the edge of the bed with the air of a girl sharing confidences. "It's really exciting to find somebody with talent like hers, and to be able to give her a start. And everything's so perfect, the two of us having written the song together; the old, established star taking the young one under her wing when we're both from the same small town. It'll make great press, and besides that, Casey and I are going to have fun together, I can tell."

Mary squeezed the back of Tess's hand. "It's real nice of you to do this for her, honey."

"I think I'm going to get as much out of it as she is."

It was one of the more contented moments Tess had shared with Mary since coming home. They sat holding hands for a moment, enjoying each other while Tess mused, "Maybe someday we'll be in concert together and you can come and hear us both."

"Wouldn't that be something."

Mary had been to several of Tess's concerts during her career, but the plane rides were getting harder on her. She hadn't heard Tess live in six years.

"Well . . ." Tess said, realizing there were things to do. "Better get these sheets in the washer, huh? Up and out of there, Momma, unless you want to get thrown in with them."

The rapport between them was too good to last. A half hour later when the sheets were washed, Tess went downstairs and put them in the dryer. She came back up to find Mary waiting in the kitchen with her walker.

"You didn't throw them in the dryer, did you?" she said anxiously as Tess came around the corner.

Tess halted, nonplussed. "Well . . . yes . . . I did."

"Sheets get wrinkled in the dryer. I want them hung on the line."

"What will it hurt this once?"

"I never put my sheets in the dryer."

"Momma," Tess said, exasperated.

"They smell stale and the hems get all crinkled up."

"I dried them in the dryer on Saturday."

"I know, and they were *all wrinkled*. Hang them outside."

Tess's mouth took on a stubborn set. "I don't know how."

"Well, it's time you learn."

Tess wanted to shout, "Why? It's an obsolete method and I'll never use it again!"

"Besides," Mary added, "there's no sense burning up electricity on a nice day like this."

Tess would have gladly paid the damned electric bill, but saying so would only prolong the argument. Mary turned away and stumped to a high kitchen stool, ordering, "Put them in the clothes basket and bring them up here and I'll show you how."

Tess stomped back downstairs, the affable mood of earlier soured. In Nashville she had a housekeeper who took care of laundry for her, yet here she was doing it for her mother, and she thought she was doing pretty well, considering her lack of experience. Couldn't Mary accept things done just a little differently for the two and a half weeks that were left?

Mary was sitting on the stool waiting to deliver the useless instructions when Tess brought the laundry basket up and dropped it down beside her, then stood there with her mouth puckered like a dried mushroom. Mary stretched the edges of the sheets, got them doubled together and gathered into three peaks. "Here, hold it this way. It's all ready for the clothespins. Then just do the second one the same way, only match the four corner seams."

Outside, the first sheet went up with no trouble. The second one—the fitted one—was like wrestling a python. It was midmorning and Tess hoped to God nobody was home at Kenny's house watching out the window while she made a nincompoop of herself. Around here there were probably women who still didn't own an electric dryer, while she didn't even know how to hang a sheet.

She was in a full-fledged snit by the time she finished and clumped back to the house. Mary had been watching through the window and said, "You stick the corners together first, and *then* hang them."

Tess wanted to shout, "When I get out of here I'm never going to hang another sheet for the rest of my life, so bug off, Mother!" She bit her tongue instead and decided the best way to handle her anger was to get out of the house for a while.

"I'm going up to Stillman's Market. What do you want for supper?"

"Well, we haven't had beef roast in quite a while. That's easy."

Fatty beef roast. What else had she expected?

Tess swung by Renee's house hoping to unload some of her pent-up frustrations, but Renee was distracted by wedding preparations and her phone kept ringing. Finally Tess left, and on her way out the door Renee gave her a hug, and said, "She doesn't mean to get on your nerves so badly. It's just that she's not used to having other people around doing things their way. She's lived alone a long time."

"I know," Tess conceded, and though her visit with Renee had been brief, it had helped.

A short while later she was selecting green grapes at Stillman's Market when she turned around and collided with a shopping cart.

"Oh, excuse me."

"Tess?" a familiar voice said. "Oh, my gosh, it's you! I heard you were back!"

"Mindy Alverson!"

"It's Mindy Petroski now."

"Mindy Petroski, of course, I knew that, but you'll always be Alverson to me. It is *so good* to *see* you!"

They hugged hard and rocked like bell buoys, bumping their shopping carts together and making them chime. Finally Mindy gripped Tess's arms and set her back to get a better look.

"Hey, you look fabulous, Tess!"

"So do you." Mindy was still dishwater blond, still wearing jeans, still needed heavier tweezing between the eyebrows.

Her hips had spread and her breasts had drooped, but she didn't seem to care. "Momma says you live here now, and you and your husband own the appliance store."

"Right around the corner from the town square where Moore's Plumbing used to be."

"Oh, sure, I know where that is. And you have kids."

"Three." Mindy stretched out her T-shirt. It said, Moms Rule When Their Kids Let Them.

They stood in the aisle catching up. Mindy's parents had sold the house and lived out on Lake Wappapello. Her husband liked to fish, so they spent a lot of time out there. Of the classmates from high school only a couple lived around here anymore.

"Speaking of kids from high school though," Mindy said, "it's all over town that you've been singing with Kenny Kronek's church choir."

"News travels fast."

"When it's about Wintergreen's most famous graduate, of course it does."

"How did you find out?"

"We play bridge with Kenny and Faith."

"Ah, Kenny and Faith. So you're good friends with them."

"Pretty good. He does the taxes for our business, and he and I have worked on a couple of civic committees together. Kenny's one of those guys who takes on the volunteer duties that nobody else wants to do. That's how he became the choir director."

"So I've heard."

"If you need somebody to organize a Fourth of July parade, or a Lion's Club pancake breakfast, all you have to do is ask Kenny. He knows everybody in town."

"Surprising how people change after high school."

"Oh, Tess, remember how mean we used to be to him? Weren't we just awful?"

"I guess we were."

"And he's such a nice man, really he is."

"My mother certainly thinks so. He's over there helping her all the time."

"Sounds like Kenny."

Tess put some watermelon into her cart and asked, "So how does Faith fit into the picture?"

"Faith? Oh, they've been going together forever."

"Funny they don't marry."

"I think he got stung pretty badly the first time—you know about his wife walking out on him?"

"Yes, I've heard."

"My guess is he'll never get married again, not to Faith or anybody else."

They visited awhile longer, and though Tess was infinitely curious about the degree of intimacy between Kenny and Faith, she could hardly inquire about it in the aisle of the supermarket without starting the whole town talking. Furthermore, it was none of her business. If Kenny had wanted her to know, he would have answered her last night. Instead, he'd cut her off and changed the subject. When she said good-bye to Mindy, Mindy said, "You'll still be here for the wedding, won't you?"

"You mean Rachel and Brent's? Of course."

"Great! Well, we'll see you there."

And so Tess got a new take on Kenny Kronek. He was liked, respected, even praised by the townspeople, and nobody seemed to think it odd that he'd never married Faith Oxbury.

At the end of that afternoon Tess was

plucking the sheets off the clothesline when Faith pulled into the alley and got out of her car carrying a grocery sack.

"Hi, Tess!" she hailed, and came right over.

"Hi, Faith."

"How did the choir practice go last night?"

"Went great. I really enjoyed it."

"Kenny says you're so good he feels ill matched to your talent."

Tess couldn't have been more surprised. "He said that?"

"Oh, he's quite in awe of you and your fame."

How peculiar that Faith should say a thing like that. He'd never given the slightest inkling he felt that way.

"While I'm here I'm just another singer in the Sunday choir."

"Not to him you're not. He's having trouble sleeping at night, worrying about how you got roped into doing this, and afraid his choir isn't good enough for you. I talked to him on the phone today and he was just a little bit grouchy. He said he didn't sleep much at all last night."

"Well . . . I'm sorry." She glanced over

at his old bedroom window. "Tell him . . ." *Tell him I think the reason he didn't sleep last night was something else entirely, just like it was for me.* "Tell him while I'm here he should forget who I am and treat me just like everyone else."

"See? That's what I told him, that you're so down to earth he's worrying himself sick for nothing. I'll tell him exactly what you said. Well . . ." She hefted the brown paper bag higher on her hip. "Better get home and get these pork chops in the oven." Tess noticed that Faith called Kenny's house "home." She headed toward it, then stopped in the alley and called, "Oh, I almost forgot to ask, how's Mary today?"

Driving me crazy. "The walking's going better."

"That's just great. Well, you tell her I said hi, and call if she needs anything."

"I will."

IT SEEMED as if everywhere she went around this town people spoke to her about Kenny. Either that, or she was running into him, until the man was on her mind constantly. So was it necessity or curiosity that drove her to his back door that evening at six forty-five when she'd put away the leftover roast beef and finished the dishes at home? Though she told herself she was going over to talk to Casey, she could have telephoned just as easily. Instead, when the dishes were put away and Mary was settled before the TV, Tess went into the bathroom, freshened her lipstick, shook her hair and crossed the alley to visit the Kronek house for the first time in eighteen years.

It was hot on Kenny's back step. She knocked and waited. The wind and sun got trapped in the L where the porch met the house, and she felt beads of sweat trail down the valley between her breasts. She tried not to peer into the porch, but who can stand beside a glass wall and resist? Where his mother used to dry her gladiola bulbs in the autumn and hang clothes on rainy days, a sitting area had been created with bent-willow chairs and plants. It looked very cozy. She wondered if the change was Faith's doing.

Suddenly Casey appeared. "Hey, Mac, what a surprise!" She threw open the door and held it with the toe of one cowboy boot.

"Come on in!" She turned around and led the way, yelling, "Hey, you guys, it's Mac!"

Tess realized the moment she stepped inside that she'd made a grave error in timing. The aroma of baked pork chops warned her that they were still eating their supper.

She followed Casey nevertheless, and when they entered the kitchen, there they sat, Kenny and Faith, at their meal, a picture of perfect domestic bliss. An array of old-fashioned foods was spread on the table before them: pork chops, mashed potatoes, gravy, buttered hominy and a cucumber salad with dill sprinkled on top, probably the way Kenny's mother had fixed it. They had just filled their plates and sat with their forks poised, staring at Tess. Casey returned to her chair. "Come on in and sit down. Want a glass of iced tea?"

"Oh, no . . . I'm sorry. I thought you all would be done eating. I'll . . . I'll come back later."

Faith immediately rose, the picture of unruffled grace. "No, no! Please . . . come in, Tess. We're running a little late because Kenny had a meeting after work today, but do sit down, I'll get you some tea."

Kenny rose and said, "I'll get it. You sit down, Faith."

Casey said, "I'll get it. You both sit down."

In her entire life Tess had never felt more of an imposter. Given what had passed between her and Kenny last night she was sure he could divine that part of her reason for coming here was curiosity. Now that she was here, eavesdropping on his domestic setup, she felt like a fool.

If he sensed her ulterior motive, he hid it well, recovered from his surprise and said politely, "Please . . . sit down, Tess."

Casey made the point moot by putting a glass of iced tea at the empty place, then sitting back down and resuming her meal.

Tess sat, and said, "Thanks, Casey."

She saw at a glance how Faith suited him. They might take turns cooking over here, but this was her production, and the way it looked, his mother might not even be dead. This was exactly the kind of meal Lucille would have prepared, probably even the kind of clothes she'd have worn. Faith had changed into pastel green cotton slacks and a crisp green-and-white print blouse. She looked as fresh and old-fashioned as her own cucumber salad. Even the kitchen had remained unchanged. Same white walls, same blue plastic clock, same Formica-topped table. Different curtains, but the same style hung on the same brass café rods. Tess even recognized the dishes they were eating from. When her gaze had roved around the room it returned to the table where Kenny and Faith made halting stabs at returning to their meal. She decided since she had ruined their peaceful meal, she might as well go the rest of the way.

"I really came over to talk to Casey."

Casey was cutting a pork chop, the only person at ease in the room. "Sure. What's up?"

"I want you to come to Nashville and sing backup for me when I record 'Small Town Girl.' "

Casey's eyes grew as big and brown as horse chestnuts. The fork and knife fell from her fingers and clattered to her plate. "Oh, my Lord," she whispered. She covered her mouth and nose with both hands. "Oh, my Loooord."

Faith looked back and forth uncertainly

between Tess and Casey, and whispered, "Oh, my goodness."

Kenny set down his silverware silently, watching his daughter's eyes fill with tears. Without another word Casey rose and went around the table to Tess. "Come here," she whispered thickly.

Tess rose and stepped into Casey's embrace. It was more than an embrace, it was gratitude and speechlessness and an inability to express her stunned joy any other way than to stand there clinging to her idol while stardust seemed to be falling from above. Something magnificent happened inside Tess while the girl hugged her. *This must be what it feels like to be a mother,* she thought, *to have someone love you unconditionally because they need you and respect you and hold you up as a role model.* Her heart was absolutely clubbing with happiness.

"You mean it, don't you?" Casey finally managed, stepping back to look into Tess's face.

"Yes, I mean it. I've already talked to my producer and he's setting up a recording session for the first week of June, right after you graduate. I talked to your father about it last night and he's agreed to let you come and stay with me until you can find a place of your own in Nashville."

Casey turned to Kenny, amazed, her face streaming tears. "You did? Oh, Daddy, did you really? I love you so much!" She flung herself against him and gave him the same unfettered stranglehold she'd bestowed on Tess. "Thank you, thank you!" She kissed him flat on the mouth, then bounded away as the initial shock turned into excitement. "Oh, my gosh, I can't believe it! I'm going to Nashville!" She grabbed Faith's face and kissed her, a fast smack, square on the mouth. "I'm going to Nashville, Faith! *Nashville!* I'm going to sing with Mac on a record!" She began bouncing around the room like a bumper car. "I've got to call Brenda and tell her. And Amy! No, wait a minute, I'd better sit down for a minute . . . my stomach feels funny." She dropped to her chair and grabbed her belly, shut her eyes, sucked in a breath and put a hand on her chest. "Oh, my God," she whispered again, "Nashville."

While Faith enjoyed Casey's reaction, Tess glanced over at Kenny on her right. He was wearing a smile with the most bittersweet edge she had ever seen. "I think you've made my daughter somewhat happy," he said in dry understatement.

Everyone laughed and Faith refilled tea glasses. "I think this calls for a toast."

The four of them touched the rims of their thick amber tumblers while Faith said, "To Wintergreen's next star."

Kenny added quietly, "And to Tess for making it possible."

His eyes met hers over the rims of their glasses as they drank, but their gazes dropped discreetly before the others. In that moment, however, she understood what it took for him to add those words and she admired him for giving Casey her freedom against so many of his own reservations.

When they lowered their glasses, another awkward moment passed, with Kenny and Tess trying to avoid eye contact with each other. "Well," she said, filling the void, "I've certainly managed to ruin your supper, haven't I?"

"Ruin it!" Casey yelped. "Are you kidding?"

Kenny pushed away his plate, and said, "We can eat anytime."

Faith added, "That's for sure, but will you stay for some blueberry cobbler, Tess?"

"Oh, yes, please," Casey added. "You can't desert me now. I've got a million things I want to ask you!"

Tess stayed for cobbler, pushing aside the ice cream and eating mainly the berries. Sometimes she and Kenny exchanged unavoidable glances, but they both did a convincing job of hiding any inchoate feelings.

When the meal was finally finished, Casey insisted Tess come up to her room and listen to a song she'd been working on with her guitar. Not that she expected Tess to record it, she explained, but would she come up and listen anyway, because if Casey was going to Nashville she might as well find out right now if she had more than one song in her or if she was going to be just a one-song composer.

Tess spent a half hour in Casey's room, and during that time she learned that the girl definitely had more than one song in her. She also discovered that Kenny still used his old upstairs bedroom, and that the one downstairs was called "Faith's room." Casey called it that as they passed it on their way upstairs. "That's Faith's room," she said offhandedly. Then at the top of the steps, "And that's Dad's. This is mine."

When Tess left, via the kitchen, Kenny and Faith were just finishing up the supper dishes. She was washing and he was drying.

"Well, guess I'll be getting back home. I've left Casey composing upstairs. By the end of the night she'll probably have enough new material to fill two albums of her own."

Faith turned off the water and Kenny laid down his dish towel on the countertop.

"I'll see you out," he said.

"Oh, no, you don't have to bother."

"It's no bother."

They went out through the porch, leaving Faith tidying the kitchen. The door slammed behind them and he followed Tess toward the alley. They walked more slowly than advisable, given that his girlfriend was in the house behind them, and the evening light ample beneath the marbled gold sky.

"Well, it's done now," he said. "She's going to Nashville."

"Why do I feel like I've dealt you a low blow?"

"I'll get over it."

Tess was conscious of his body heat warming her left shoulder blade and the fact that in all likelihood Faith was watching them through the window beside the kitchen table.

"If it's any consolation, I know how hard this is for you, and I admire you for how you're handling yourself."

"It's not much consolation. I'd prefer she do anything else."

"Yes, I know that. I'll do my best for her, Kenny, I promise you. Thanks for letting her go."

They had reached the alley. When she turned to face him she made sure there was plenty of space between them. Her shoulder blade felt suddenly cold. He stood his distance, with his hands in his back pockets, as if in an effort to keep them off her.

"Faith is really quite wonderful," she said with utter sincerity.

"Yes, she is."

"The two of you look like you're very well suited."

"That what you came over for, to see how we're suited?"

She wasn't sure how to answer, and finally chose ambiguity. "What if I said yes?"

"Then I'd probably ask what the hell you're after."

"And I'd probably answer, I don't know, Kenny. And that's the honest truth. I don't know."

He searched her eyes while she worried about Faith watching from the house and found herself listing the things she'd grown to like about him. Somewhere in the yard a robin was repeating his one-note song the way they'll do when a sprinkler is going. And in the house on Tess's side of the alley two main floor windows faced this direction. Kenny gripped himself through his back pockets while the tension built between them, and finally he released an immense gust of breath and let his head hang. "Jesus, why do I feel like I'm back on that school bus again?"

The time was getting long. Certainly Faith would be wondering what was keeping him.

"Listen, you'd better go back in."

"Yeah, I'd better go back in," he said with a note of irony, lifting his head again.

But neither of them moved.

Just like last night in the car, their reluctance to part kept them anchored face-to-face a moment longer.

Finally he whispered, "What are you trying to do to me, Tess?"

They both knew that her relationship to
Casey connected her to him as well. There
were bound to be times in the future when
he would come to Nashville to see his
daughter.

She took a decisive step backward. "I
have to go," she said. "I'll stay on my side
of the alley from now on. I'm sorry, Kenny."

When she turned she discovered she was
backed up against Faith's car and had to
swerve around the tail end of it to cross the
alley.

ELEVEN

THE WEEK WANED. Casey came over every
day after school but Tess avoided Kenny
and the backyard when she knew he was
around. She helped Mary with her physical
therapy and they seemed to argue about
everything. Burt called on Friday from
Omaha. Southern Smoke had played Still-
water, Oklahoma, Wichita, Kansas, and
would end up back in Nashville the same
week Tess returned. The two of them set a
date at the Stockyard Café on Tuesday of
the week they got back home.

On Sunday Mary announced she wanted
to go to church and hear Tess sing. She'd
been stuck in the house for a whole week
and it was time she got out.

Tess was loading up her wheelchair when
Kenny came out of his house and called,

"Wait! I'll help you with that!" He was all dressed for church and looking hunky enough to set her heart beating at a faster clip.

"I thought you were gone already," she said as he lifted the wheelchair effortlessly into the trunk.

"No. I always leave at twenty to." He slammed the trunk and brushed his palms together, avoiding her eyes. Instead he looked at the house. "Do you need any help getting her in the car?"

"No, she'll do it herself."

"All right, then. See you there." Heading for his garage, he whistled shrilly through his teeth and Casey came flying out the back door. "Hurry up!" he yelled. "We're going to be late!"

Casey shouted a greeting as she ran— "Hey, Mac!"—and a minute later they were gone.

So, she thought. *Mister Iceman. He couldn't resist running out when he saw me, but he didn't like himself for doing it, so he took it out on me.*

———

TWENTY MINUTES LATER she was singing "Holy, Holy, Holy" while he directed. It sent shivers up her spine and broke down the icy barrier he'd placed between them. Their eyes met too often, and locked too intently for them to remain aloof to one another. They learned, both of them, that sharing a worship service with someone on this level draws you closer, whether you want that to happen or not.

By the time she sang "Beautiful Savior" he had removed his suit jacket, loosened his tie and rolled up his white sleeves. Something phenomenal happened between them when she sang her solo. Something irreversible.

In the vestibule after the service she was mobbed. Word had spread that she was singing there today and the congregation had swelled beyond anything the church had ever seen, augmented by many who were regulars at other churches around town. Everyone praised Tess, asked if she was singing at her niece's wedding (she was not), and wanted to know if it was true that Casey Kronek was going to sing on one of her records. Answering that question was fun. Casey stuck by her, even after

Tess had joined the rest of her family, who had rolled Mary down the ramp to the broad flat front step where the entire troop had gathered. Though some preferred the earlier service, they had all come for the later one today, and she was touched by their show of support. Nieces, nephews, brothers-in-law and sisters all had hugs and pride in their eyes. Except Judy, who seemed willing to bask in the reflected glow of having a famous sibling, but still could not bring herself to offer a compliment. Instead, she hung on the fringe of the family while Reverend Giddings approached and engaged Tess in a prolonged handclasp. He was grinning so broadly his eyes nearly disappeared.

"I cannot thank you enough, young lady. Splendid job. Splendid! You certainly brought them in." He leaned closer and spoke in an undertone. "And unless I miss my guess there are some pretty empty churches around town this morning." After a final hard squeeze he released her hand and said to someone behind her, "Very nice job, Kenny, and a particularly fine choice of music." She had not known he was there, and turned to watch Reverend Giddings shake his hand and clasp his arm. Again the minister lowered his voice, including them both in his confidence. "The ushers tell me the collection plate was overflowing, which bodes well for the annual pledges. Thank you both again."

Though surrounded by a sea of familiar faces, Kenny and Tess became attuned only to each other. They stood in the sunlight close enough to pick out the shadings in each other's eyes, the black flecks in her amber ones, the green ring within his brown. He had reclaimed his suit jacket but his tie remained loosened and his collar button freed. She wore a thin skirt and blouse of brick-colored silk that fluttered in the breeze. They stood so close it sometimes touched the legs of his trousers. At her throat hung a tiny gold rose on a chain, and on her ears tinier rosebuds, jewelry she thought he'd prefer. She was carrying a white clutch purse too small to hold sunglasses. She lifted it to shield her eyes and he stepped over to create a shadow. It was his day away from Faith, a day he did as he wished.

"This was probably the best Sunday I've had since I started directing," he told Tess.

"Why?"

"You."

She hadn't expected his directness. It loosened her resolve as well.

"Something got me . . . here." She laid a wrist across her heart.

"I could tell."

"Something got you, too, didn't it?"

"Yes. Something got me, too," he confided.

"It's how it used to be when I was little . . . the music, my family, the familiar church . . . I don't know."

"I understand now more than ever why you've succeeded the way you have. You have charisma."

"You didn't seem to think so this morning when we met in the alley."

"Oh, that."

"I thought you were mad at me."

"I'm sorry about that. I get moody sometimes."

"Don't do that again, okay? Don't get icy like that."

"I'm sorry. I thought it would be best, considering . . . well . . ." He stopped himself short of saying "Faith."

"We can meet in the alley and say hello without hurting each other, can't we?"

"You're right. It won't happen again." Without warning he did what he could not do when they were alone. He took her in a quick embrace and kissed her temple. "I'm sorry," he told her quietly. She had the swift sensation of bumping against his body, of sandalwood scent on his skin, of the touch of his lips at her ear. "Thank you for singing today. I'll never forget it, Tess."

As quickly as he'd taken her, he set her free. Casey appeared and put an arm around each of them. "Hey, Tess, you want to go horseback riding this afternoon? Perfect day for it."

Linked by the girl, they stood in a trio while Tess tried to hide the fact that she was rattled.

"Gosh, I don't know if I should leave Momma alone."

"Can't somebody else stay with her for a few hours? You need a break now and then, too." Before Tess could answer, Casey spun away and nabbed the first family member she encountered. It was Renee.

"Hey, Renee, can somebody stay with

your momma this afternoon so Tess can go horseback riding with me?"

"Sure. I can," Renee replied. "What time are you leaving?"

Apart from the others Tess asked Kenny, "Are you going, too?"

His eyes came to her and lingered, but he cleared his throat and answered, "No. Better not."

She hid her disappointment as Casey returned, insisting, "What time do you want to leave?"

"Whenever you want to."

"One o'clock? I need to be back in town by four or so."

The plan was set.

THEY TOOK CASEY'S PICKUP, which was so old it had rear wheel wells that stuck out like a bulldog's shoulders. Every time they went over a bump, dust rose from the junk littering the dash. But the radio worked, and they either sang country songs or talked about them all the way out to Dexter Hickey's.

The place looked different by daylight. The white fence needed painting and the yard needed mowing, but the surrounding countryside was breathtaking. The ranch was framed by a great stretch of undulating grassland dotted by apple trees that had been cropped low by the horses. Wild buttercups bloomed in patches of yellow across the verdant pasture. To the west, north, and east trees rimmed the valley and rusty red trails, worn by the horses, snaked into the woods from one hub, like mountain highways on a map.

Inside, the stable was clean and the tack room orderly. Dexter had left a mare named Sunflower in a box stall for Tess with instructions to turn her out after they were done riding.

Casey asked, "You know how to saddle a horse?"

"It's been a while."

"No problem. I'll do it."

When Sunflower and Rowdy were saddled, the women mounted up and walked the horses down the length of the barn, the syncopated hoofbeats clacking on the concrete until they reached an earthen ramp leading outdoors.

In the sun the horses' hides gleamed and the heat from their bodies lifted their scent.

Casey led the way along the fence to one of the worn trails that headed toward the rippling woods.

She turned in the saddle and asked, "How does it feel?"

"Like I'm going to hurt tomorrow. I'm not used to it."

"We'll take it slow at first."

"Fine."

Casey was a natural on horseback; she dressed and rode like a saddle tramp, in old jeans, worn cowboy boots, a faded plaid shirt and a stained cowboy hat. She sat her horse straight as a picket with one hand on her thigh.

Tess, on the other hand, dressed and rode like a tenderfoot. She wore jeans and a lopped off T-shirt, shiny cowboy boots, a baseball cap and her oversized sunglasses. She rode as if unsure this was a good idea.

When they reached the spread of buttercups Casey yelled back, "Hey, Tess, guess what. I got a date tonight."

"Good for you. Anybody special?"

"Nope. Just a boy I had a crush on last year, called and asked if I wanted to ride into Poplar Bluff and go to a movie. Seems like all of a sudden I'm hot stuff since I'm going to be recording with you. I thought about saying no, just to get even with him for ignoring me last year, but then I thought, what the heck. A date's a date.''

"I didn't have much time for boys when I was in high school either.''

"I know you didn't have much time for my dad.''

When Tess made no reply, Casey dropped her chin and looked back over her shoulder, giving Tess a shot of the underside of her hat brim and her teasing eyes. Finally she asked, ''Want to try trotting awhile?''

"Why not.''

She kicked Rowdy into a trot and Sunflower followed suit. After fifty yards they picked up to an easy canter that took them up the rim of the valley into the woods, where Casey reined in and was waiting at a standstill, head-on, when Tess reached her and reined in, too.

"You doing okay?'' Casey asked. She gauged Tess's inexperience well and wasn't pushing it.

"So far, so good.''

The horses both shook their heads, sending their manes flopping and their harnesses jingling.

"We'll let them rest for a while." Casey patted Rowdy's shoulder, then sat silently, looking up at the trees. After a while she slung a leg around the pommel and braced her hands on the horse's rump, still studying the green canopy above them. Some cottonwoods rustled and a nearby pine gave off a scent of dry needles. The horses dipped their heads to crop grass.

Out of the blue Casey asked, "So what's going on between you and my dad?"

Tess did a poor job of hiding her surprise. "Nothing."

"I thought I caught some undercurrents at our table the other night, and on the church steps this morning I interrupted something. I could tell."

"No. Nothing."

"He was whispering and you were blushing."

"In front of all those people? You think we'd carry on some kind of flirtation with half of the town gawking at us? That wouldn't be too bright."

"Well, what was going on then? He was hugging you."

"He was thanking me for singing today."

"Oh, is that all," Casey said dryly. Again she looked up into the trees as if the subject were forgotten, then abruptly she added, "Well, he's a good man. You could do worse." She swung her leg off the horse's neck and picked up the reins as if to move on.

Tess said, "He's committed to Faith and I'm going back to Nashville in two weeks."

"That doesn't mean something can't be going on. And just in case it is, I want you to know it's perfectly okay with me. I think it'd be wild to have you and Dad carry on a real steamy love affair. I'll bet you could show him a thing or two."

"Casey!"

"Well, Faith is okay, but I'll bet kissing her would be like kissing somebody in a coma."

"Does your dad know you talk about her like this?"

"Heck, no. Got to keep the old charlotte russe going."

Against her better judgment, Tess laughed. Casey was turning her horse deeper into the woods when she glanced out toward the meadow and said, "Well, well . . . look who's coming."

Tess craned around in her saddle and saw Kenny riding toward them. His mount was a bay stallion, and he rode him at a trot, the reins in one gloved hand and his curled straw hat brim pulled low over his eyes. He caught sight of them in the shade and kicked the bay into an easy canter. Though his face was unreadable at this distance, his posture radiated absolute purpose as he headed toward them. He rode like a man to whom doing so is second nature, dressed in blue jeans and a spotless white T-shirt, which the wind pressed against his chest and rippled across his ribs.

Reaching them, he reined to a stop, and said, "I changed my mind. It got lonesome at home." He barely had a glance for his daughter but studied Tess from beneath his hat brim with eyes that gave away more than he wanted.

Casey was grinning. "I was just saying to Tess—"

"Casey!" Tess shot her a warning glare.

"Nothing," she finished, turning her horse up the trail. "Glad you came, Dad.

We're taking it easy 'cause Tess isn't used to it."

They rode for another hour and a half, talking little, enjoying nature and the beautiful spring day. Casey and Kenny kept Tess between them, and the horses behaved beautifully. Near four o'clock when they were heading back toward the paddock, thunderheads had built up in the southwest and the breeze had cooled.

"Gonna get some rain," Kenny said.

"The garden could use it," Tess replied, a reply that would not have occurred to her two weeks ago.

Casey only grinned back at them over her shoulder. *Discussing the weather like a couple of old farmers. You don't fool me.*

They each undressed their own horse, but Kenny came over and helped Tess remove her saddle. She watched him carry it through the door of the tack room and throw it over a sawhorse, his sturdy arms taking on definition as he moved and twisted. His back was as tapered as a turnip, his T-shirt still tucked in neatly at the waist. She fixed her eyes on the spot where it disappeared into the denim waistband of his jeans.

He turned and caught her staring, and she returned to the business of taking care of Sunflower, who was crosstied in the aisle between the box stalls.

Kenny came back and asked casually, "Want to ride back to town with me, Tess?"

She looked first at Casey, then at him. "Oh, I don't think I'd bet—"

"It's okay," Casey put in. "Go with him. I gotta stop and put gas in my truck anyway, and besides, I'm in a hurry. I'm not even going to take time to curry Rowdy. Gotta get home and get ready for my date." She led Rowdy to the door and turned him out into the paddock, then came back, lifting a hand as she passed. "Hey, you two have fun. See you in the morning, Dad. I probably won't get in till after eleven 'cause we're driving clear over to Poplar Bluff to a movie."

"Okay. Be careful."

A minute later Tess and Kenny heard the sound of her truck starting and rumbling away. They rubbed down their horses in silence, conscious of each other as they moved around the animals. He set down his brush and came to her. "That's good. I'll take her out." He led Sunflower to the door where he turned her out before doing the same with his horse, then took their brushes and halters to the tack room and returned to the doorway, pulling off his gloves.

"If you want to wash your hands there's a sink in here."

"Oh . . . thanks."

They stood side by side lathering at a black rubber sink with an oversized cube of bumpy yellow soap that smelled like petroleum. She watched his square capable hands and his hairy arms as he ran soap to the elbow and rinsed like a doctor before surgery. He watched her fair, freckled arms and perfect persimmon nails as she rubbed her delicate hands together, rinsed once avoiding her expensive watch, checked her nails for chips, then rinsed again.

He snagged a rough blue towel from an iron hook on the wall and they each used one end. They accidentally looked up once while drying their hands, then quickly down again. When they finished he slung the towel over the hook and picked up his gloves.

"Let's go."

His car was as clean as Casey's truck

was filthy. He drove with no particular hurry, the windows down and the wind blowing in while the sky grew darker and the pines beside the road started bending. Tess removed her sunglasses and hung them from the neck of her T-shirt.

He glanced over, then back at the gravel road.

"You hungry?" he asked.

"Famished."

"How 'bout if a country boy from Wintergreen takes you out to dinner?"

"Dressed like this?"

He turned his head and gave her a lazy grin. "I know just the place."

He took her to the Sonic Drive-in, and they parked under the long metal awning, between an old couple who were having root beer floats, on their left, and fifteen empty spaces on the right. The menu and speaker were on his side. He rested his elbow on the window ledge and pinched his lower lip as he looked it over. "What do you want?"

"I can't see the menu." She unsnapped her seat belt and slid over, one hand on the wheel, the other on his headrest. While she ducked her head and searched the menu, he kept studying it as well. Their hat brims were six inches apart.

She said, "Is that you who smells like gasoline, or is that me?"

He laughed and turned his head, reducing the six inches to four. "Gasoline and horses, a mighty tempting combination, isn't it?"

She drew her mouth into a smirk, and said quietly, "Mighty tempting."

"So?"

"Burger in a basket."

"All right. Then get over there on your side if you know what's good for you."

She slid back to her side, turned her shoulder blades against the door and pulled a knee up on the seat while he pushed the call button and gave their order.

When he finished, he angled himself in the corner and looked back at her, the brim of his straw hat tipped so low it hid his eyebrows. Thunder rumbled off toward the southwest, but they scarcely paid attention. They had immersed themselves in the illusion that they were teen-agers again—the car, the drive-in, their flirtatious poses. They let themselves become willing victims of the mood they had created—unwisely perhaps—but for these few unfettered hours on a Sunday afternoon they threw wisdom to the wind.

Finally Tess said, "Casey asked me today what's going on between you and me."

"What did you tell her?"

"The truth. Nothing." She picked a piece of horsehair off her jeans and flicked it on the floor. "Then she said it's okay if we start something."

"She said that, did she?"

Tess gave the faintest shrug. "You know Casey."

"Yeah, I know Casey."

They thought about it for a while before Tess said, "Of course, we both know that's not a good idea."

"Of course."

"After all, there's Faith."

"Yes, of course, Faith."

"And I'm going back to Nashville in two weeks."

"Where you belong," he added.

"Where I belong."

"And I'm just a small-town accountant with"—he gestured at their surroundings—"nothing to offer but an occasional burger in a basket at the Sonic Drive-in and a mediocre choir to back you up on Sundays."

They either had to give in and kiss each other or die wanting to. The carhop saved them from either catastrophe by delivering their tray.

"Could you roll up the window some?" she said, and, when he had, she hung the tray. "Ten dollars and seventy cents, please." He dug the money out of his pocket. Tess enjoyed watching him lever himself off the seat and dig for change in the front and his billfold in the back, his stomach going flatter inside his T-shirt.

"You know what?" Tess said when he was reaching for their food. "This is the first date I've had in two years. More than two years."

He passed her a red plastic basket.

"What about the singer back in Nashville?"

"No, I mean a date, where I go out with a man and he buys me dinner and takes me home. I find I can't do that anymore."

"Too rich? Too famous?"

"Both. You don't know what people are after you for."

A shiny new pickup with three teenagers

pulled in on their right. It had a chrome roll bar, a royal blue cab, and a radio booming like the South Pacific in World War II. When it silenced, Kenny asked, "That what you think about me? That I'm after something?"

"No. I think you're just an accident."

"Oh, that's flattering."

"You know what I mean."

"Well, it's nice not to be lumped with the groupies."

"In Nashville we call them germs." She pronounced it with a hard G.

"Germs?"

"Comes from groupies and germs. But, believe me, you're not one of them."

The burgers were juicy and delicious and they gave up flirting to sink their teeth in, dipping their french fries in ketchup and munching pickles. She couldn't finish hers, and when she laid it down he asked, "You all done?"

"Yes. You want it?"

He laid claim to her burger and while he was polishing it off she wiped her mouth on a paper napkin and glanced at the blue pickup.

"Oh-oh," she said, "I think I've been spotted." Three faces with bad skin were smiling her way and gaping. "You all done?" Kenny jammed the rest of her burger in his mouth and she said, "Let's go."

He tapped on the horn and the carhop came out to collect their tray.

The rain began as they backed out of their parking spot. They rolled up their windows and he switched on the wipers and turned left onto Main Street. They cruised its deserted length at fifteen miles an hour, neither of them anxious to get home. The town had one traffic light. Luckily, it was red, which gave them more time. They stared at the rain streaming down the windshield, looking like fruit juice in the reflected glow of the traffic light. On the car roof it began pattering louder as they waited for the light to change and resisted every bodily instinct that had been badgering them all afternoon. She looked at Kenny. He looked at her. The light turned green and they moved on.

Tess said, "Faith is probably going to find out you were with me."

"You know, I get a little tired of you bringing up Faith all the time."

"Sorry," she said meekly, and looked out her side window. After that he got silent as a sphynx, the way he'd been in the alley this morning before church.

They drove around the town square, then headed north on Sycamore. The rain began pounding down even harder and he increased the tempo of the wipers. The air felt clammy and tense as home got closer and closer. When they were approaching the south end of their alley she said, "Thought you said you weren't going to do that anymore."

"Do what?"

"Ice up on me."

It was his turn to be meek. "Sorry."

He turned into the alley and the trees formed churning blurs in the wind-whipped storm. The headlights rocked against wet garage walls that pressed close on both sides. He reached his own garage and pulled up before it, activated the door and would have driven inside, but she said, "Leave it out here. I like the storm."

With only a glance at her he complied, killing the lights, wipers and engine. They sat with the rain battering the roof, sealed inside the humid, dark car. Thunder and lightning created havoc around them.

"Well, here we are," he said.

Tess peered at the lights in her mother's kitchen window. "Renee is probably ready to kill me for being gone so long."

"You gonna run through this?" he said.

"No, I'll wait a minute."

He glanced at the dark windows of his house. "The kids probably got caught in this on their way to Poplar Bluff."

"They'll be okay."

More rain, more lightning, more thunder, and the two of them unable to think of more to say. The windows began fogging over from their breath and their clothes seemed to cling to their skin. Though it was only six P.M. the world was murky and obscure beneath the roiling clouds. Nobody in the house could see a thing that was going on out here, and both people in the car knew it. Suddenly Tess's frustration boiled over.

"Look, Kenny, this is ridiculous! I'm a full-grown adult and I'm playing games with you like a kid. Just don't tell Faith I did this, all right?"

She reared up on one knee, dropped sideways, braced a hand on the driver's door, and kissed him. Angled beneath his straw hat, she found his mouth with her own and stayed a while, forcing the issue they'd both been sidestepping since . . . since when? Hard to remember when the compulsion first arrived. Sometime between the night of her arrival when he'd snubbed her and the night of choir practice when he'd ridden in her car. She'd caught him so off guard that he'd actually pulled back. She used it to her advantage and took a fair bit of time having her way with him while he was still wondering what his sense of honor would allow him to do. It was a good kiss, and honest, a two-way exchange, and when it ended he had both hands around her ribs under the lopped-off T-shirt to keep her from falling completely against him.

She drew back a mere inch. His breath came fast and his lips were open in surprise. She smiled in the dark, and told him, "That's for the time I teased you on the school bus." Her pose was awkward, his hands on her rib cage warm and spanning two-thirds of her girth. "Consider this completely my doing," she added. "I absolve

you from all guilt, my dear Saint Kenny.
Thanks for a wonderful day."

   She kissed him again, quickly, got out
and ran through the cold, driving rain to the
house.

TWELVE

INSIDE THE HOUSE Mary and Renee were watching *60 Minutes.* Tess came charging in the back door, dripping. "Hey, will somebody bring me a towel, please?"

Renee showed up a moment later and tossed her one.

"About time you got here. We were getting worried."

"Sorry. I should have called." She threw off her cap, mopped the ends of her wet hair and sponged her soaked T-shirt.

"You weren't out riding all this time. Not in the thunder and lightning."

"No. I went to the Sonic Drive-in with Kenny."

"With Kenny. Well." Tess sat on a step and pulled off her boots while Renee studied the top of her red hair. "I thought you went riding with Casey. I didn't know he was going along."

Tess stood up, damp but no longer dripping, and set her boots against the wall. "Hey, listen, are you in a hurry to get home or could I talk to you for a minute?"

"I can stay awhile longer."

Tess led the way across the kitchen and said quietly, so Mary couldn't hear, "Come upstairs with me." In the living room Mary said, "You're back, did you have a good time?" and returned to her show.

"Sure did."

Upstairs Tess stripped off her wet clothes while Renee sat cross-legged on her old bed. "Just like when were girls," she said. "So what's going on?"

Tess threw on a cotton pullover, pulled the rubber band out of her hair and sat at the vanity table, facing Renee, combing her wet bangs straight back, flat to her head. "It's bizarre," she told Renee. "You aren't going to believe it."

"Something with you and Kenny, obviously."

Tess looked down at the comb in her hands and said, "Talk some sense into me, will you?"

"Maybe you'd better tell me what's going on first."

"I kissed him about five minutes ago in his car. He wouldn't kiss me so I finally kissed him. Pretty stupid, huh?"

"That's all. Just a kiss?"

"Yes. But, Renee, something has happened to me in these couple weeks I've been home. I'm bumping into him all the time and he turns out to be about the nicest guy I've met in years, and all of you treat him like he's your brother, and he treats Momma like he's her son, and then Casey gets into the picture and I'm just crazy about that girl, and I see what a good father he is, and the next thing you know we're going to choir practice together, and this afternoon he shows up at Dexter Hickey's and I start acting like a lovesick teenager. Renee, that's not like me."

Renee digested this for a moment. "Is he the reason you're taking Casey to Nashville?"

"No! Renee, what do you take me for?"

"You're sure?"

"Of course I'm sure. The thing with Casey started before I even said two words to Kenny."

Renee took stock of her sister, weighing the situation for some time before speaking again.

"What about Faith?"

"He won't tell me anything about their relationship."

Renee's face looked as if she'd given this plenty of thought on her own. "They're intimate, I'm sure. They just don't flaunt it, so people around here accept it." Tess stared at her sister, unhappy to have her suspicion corroborated. "You've got to be careful, Tess. You can't toy with people's feelings."

"I'm not toying."

"Aren't you?"

"No!"

"Then what's going to come of it? You'll head back to Nashville and leave him behind, and if you've spoiled what's between him and Faith, he'll end up the loser. Maybe you've lost sight of just how big a star you are, and just how impressed a man could be with your attention."

"I haven't. I've thought about that."

"And Kenny had a crush on you in high school. He's got no defenses against you, Tess."

Tess stared at her comb while the curls

around her face began drying and coiling free. She thought about the perfect day she'd had with Kenny, starting with church this morning until they sat in the sexually charged atmosphere of his car in the rain. Any other woman would simply be able to do what she had done and not require confession afterward.

"You know what, Renee? Sometimes it can be mighty lonely being Tess McPhail."

"I'm sure it can, but pick on someone else besides Kenny."

"Who? The germs who hang around by the stage door? The guys in the music industry who are probably after me to further their own careers? Some other big star who'll be out on the road the few times when I'm not? The guys in the band?" She laughed ruefully. "Good way to lose a good band member."

"You chose it, Tess, I didn't."

Tess sighed, half swiveled and threw her comb on the vanity.

Renee studied her and caught a hint of defensiveness. "What about this guy from this other band that Momma said you're dating? She says he's called you a couple times since you've been here."

"Burt. Yeah, he's called. I made a date with him to get together in Nashville as soon as we both get back. I thought if I had that to look forward to it might distract me from Kenny."

"But it hasn't. So you made a play for him tonight."

"I didn't make—" Tess stopped herself, realizing how false she sounded. She jumped up from the stool and crossed the room to the rough railing around the stairwell. Leaning against it she could see out the window through the driving rain to the blurred lights from Kenny's house. His bedroom lights came on.

Behind her Renee said, "You wanted me to talk some sense into you, well, here it is. For the rest of the time you're home, stay away from Kenny. Leave him to Faith and you'll thank yourself later." She rose from the bed and approached her sister, placing her hands on Tess's shoulders. "Okay?" she asked.

Tess nodded glumly.

"Hey . . . come here." Renee turned her around and hugged her. "You mad at me now for saying what I think?"

"No." They rocked for a while, clenched

together, and Tess began crying. "Oh, why did I have to come back home and get my priorities all screwed up? I love what I do! And most of the time I never even think about what I've given up!"

"But sometimes that big old S word rears its head and starts making demands, huh?"

In spite of her tearfulness Tess chuckled and pulled back, drying her face with her hands. "Oh, damn it. And damn you for dragging me back here."

Renee said with humor, "Well, I never thought you'd get the hots for Kenny Kronek." She went and got a tissue from the vanity and handed it to Tess, who blew her nose.

"I don't have the hots for Kenny Kronek." Renee gave her a scolding look. "Well, all right, maybe I do, but if Faith's got first dibs on him, I'll be a good girl and keep my distance, and if he comes to Nashville to visit Casey I'll . . . I'll . . ."

"You'll what?"

Tess crumpled. "Hell, I don't know what I'll do."

"You know, Tess, there's one thing we're overlooking."

"What's that?"

"Kenny himself. If he's the kind of man I think he is, he'd never two-time Faith. You said yourself he refused to kiss you."

Tess thought for a moment, then said, "You're right. And you know what? That's one of the reasons I think so much of him."

TESS ACCEPTED RENEE'S ADMONITION and took it to heart. She decided she'd been wrong trying to provoke Kenny into kissing her, and made a resolution that she would do everything in her power to avoid him from now on.

On Monday, in spite of aching everywhere, she mowed the lawn in the midday heat to avoid doing it when he was home. That evening Casey called, and said, "So how'd it go with Dad?"

"Why don't you ask him?"

"I did, but he's in one of his wounded-boar moods and all he did was snap at me."

Wounded boar? Tess figured Kenny had probably come up with the same conclusion as she; that it was better if they avoid each other.

"Well, nothing happened," Tess lied.

"Oh, shoot. Well, I'll keep hoping."

She saw him, naturally, coming and going from his house, but she stayed inside whenever he appeared in the backyard. Sometimes he'd glance at Mary's house as if hoping Tess would appear in the doorway, but she stayed hidden from sight.

On Tuesday evening, by mere chance, four of Mary's friends came visiting, one right after the other, and Tess was kept busy brewing coffee and visiting. But her mind kept veering to choir practice where she'd been a week ago. She had seen Kenny leave at seven-fifteen and pause beside his garage and look this way, but in the end he had gone without coming to ask if she was going along.

On Wednesday evening Mary said she needed some fresh air and insisted on taking her evening walk outside. She managed to make her arduous way down the front steps on her crutches, then, with Tess at her side, headed down the block. It was a pretty evening. The mourning doves were calling softly from the telephone wires on the street, and Mary's neighbors came out to wish her well when they saw her passing. She and Tess were a block away from home when Kenny came driving by, swerved over to the curb and stopped. He leaned across the empty passenger seat and called out the open window, "Walking pretty good there, Mary!"

"Practicing for walking down that aisle at Rachel's wedding. You can roll me *out* of that church in my wheelchair, but I'm *walking* in, by gum."

A beat passed while Kenny and Tess exchanged glances, then he said, belatedly, "Hello, Tess. Missed you at choir practice last night."

"Sorry. I was busy."

"I take that to mean you're only singing the one Sunday."

"I think so."

"Well . . . that's disappointing. People were asking."

He paused another moment, then said, "Well . . . Faith's got a dead shrub that needs replacing so I'd better get over there. See you around." Without another glance at Tess he slid over, put the car in gear and drove away.

She felt just awful watching him go—the lump in the chest, the emptiness in the heart, the longing to follow him and say,

Let's talk about this. But what was there to talk about? Their situation was hopeless and they both knew it.

On Sunday she went to the earlier church service in order to avoid singing in the choir. Shortly before noon Casey called and said, "Hey, where *were* you?"

"I went to the earlier service with Rachel's family."

"But we thought you'd come and sing with the choir again!"

"No, I missed practice."

"But Dad wouldn't have benched you for missing practice! My gosh, you're Tess McPhail!"

"Listen, Casey . . ." Tess's voice held a plea for understanding. "It . . . it just worked out best this way, okay?"

"Oh." And after a pause, meekly, "Okay . . . I guess. Hey, did something go wrong between you and Dad last Sunday?"

"No, nothing."

"Oh, good. Well, listen, you want to go riding again today?"

"No, I don't think so, Casey. I've got things to do here."

"Oh. Well . . . okay. But when will I see you again?"

"Stop in anytime. Otherwise, next Saturday at the wedding, for sure."

"Okay. Well, hey, take it easy, and say hi to Mary."

Casey popped in a couple times that week, reporting that Kenny had been difficult to live with. Casey said she thought he must've had a fight with Faith, although to the best of her knowledge, they never fought.

For six days Tess glimpsed him only through windows, but every time she thought about Saturday, when she would see him at the wedding, a queer tightness caught her just beneath the heart and she'd find her hands idle.

IT HAD BEEN OVER THREE WEEKS SINCE MARY'S SURGERY. She got stronger. She felt increasingly better. Feeling better, she seemed to argue less. By Thursday Tess thought it was time to broach the subject that had been on her mind since the night she arrived.

Mary had wanted to eat supper in the living room in front of the evening news, so Tess had set them up on a Duncan Phyfe occasional table that she hauled over in front of Mary's chair, bringing in a kitchen chair for herself. They'd finally had a meal with no clashes. Tess had found something that pleased them both, a taco salad in which she'd cut down the fatty ingredients in her own and added more of them to Mary's. The news was over and they were finishing up their meal when Tess said, "Mom, I've arranged a surprise for you."

"For me?" Mary said, surprised already.

"On Saturday morning at eight o'clock a hairdresser named Niki is coming to fix your hair for the wedding and she'll do anything you want. Color it, perm it, cut it—anything."

Mary looked amazed. "Right here at home?"

"That's right."

"Why, I never heard of such a thing."

"It can be done. I thought you'd like to get it fixed for the wedding."

"This Niki—she's not from Judy's shop?"

"No, she's not. Judy and her girls are doing all the bridal party that morning so they'll be busy. But she said Niki will do a good job for you."

"Well . . . my goodness." Mary continued to look amazed.

"That's all right with you then?"

"Well, sure!" she said enthusiastically.

"And, Momma, there's one other thing I wanted to ask you about." This issue was perhaps even more delicate than the hair, but if she didn't bring it up, who would? "You know that pretty green silk trouser suit I sent you last year from Seattle? Have you worn it yet?"

"I tried it on."

"But you haven't worn it."

"Well, it's . . . it's awfully expensive—I could see that."

"Why don't you wear it for the wedding? It would be perfect, since your legs have to be wrapped in those ugly stockings all the time. What do you say, Momma?"

"I was going to wear this other pants suit that I got last spring. It's perfectly good and I've only worn it a few times."

Tess's first reaction was anger, and she got up and started stacking their dirty dishes, trying to swallow a little lump of hurt that had grown into a stone in her throat. She had a pyramid of dirty dishes in her hands before she changed her mind, set them back down and dropped to one knee beside Mary's chair. "Mom, I need to tell you something that I'm not sure you'll understand, but . . ." Taking Mary's hand in both of her own she looked up into her mother's aging brown eyes. "Listen, Momma, I don't know how else to say this. I'm rich. May I say it without sounding like I'm blowing my own horn? It's a fact of life now. I'm very, very rich, and it gives me great pleasure to send you things. Nice things from stores you never get to see because you don't get the chance to travel like I do. But it hurts my feelings when you won't even try to use them."

"Oh, dear . . . well, I . . . I guess I never thought of that. I just always think those things are too grand for Wintergreen, Missouri."

"I'm not sending them for Wintergreen, I'm sending them for you."

Mary sat awhile, looking somber and somewhat stricken. Finally she glanced away, then back at her daughter.

"Well, since you're being honest, let me be honest, too. Sometimes when you send things I think it's because you know you should come to see me yourself, but you're too busy to take the time. Maybe that's why I sometimes don't use them. Because if the truth be told, I'd rather have you than all the fancy presents in the world."

Mary's words stung sharply for they were true, and Tess at last admitted it. How many times had she been charging through some store in a far-off city and spied something for Mary, but while she was waiting for her credit card to be processed a guilty thought would come niggling: *You should go see her instead.* But it was so much easier to send gifts. It infringed so much less on her busy work schedule.

There were people in this world who had no mothers, who would count themselves blessed to have a loving one like this, yet Tess not only saw Mary less often than she should, she found fault with her vagaries and took issue with petty aggravations that love should overlook. Now here she was, looking up into Mary's face, which appeared decidedly older at this moment. The impression of age was amplified by the limitations put upon her by the new hip, for she sat on the stiff chair with her knees spread and her ankles uncrossed. Her crutches waited at arms' reach and her face was swagged with sadness. Tess could see in the line of Mary's jowls and in the pattern of creases around her eyes and mouth the stamp her own aging would leave upon her face. An unwanted image came, of the day when Tess would be Mary's age, and Mary would be gone. Who knew how many more years they had?

"I'm sorry, Mom," Tess said softly. "I'll try to do better."

Mary reached out and put a hand on Tess's hair. "You know how proud I am of you, don't you, dear?"

Tess nodded with tears in her eyes.

"And I know what it took for you to get where you are. But, Tess, we're your family, and you only get one of those."

"I know," Tess whispered, choked.

They remained in that tableau, each accepting what the other had said, Mary on the stiff, high chair, Tess kneeling to her, the dinner remains spread on the old-fashioned parlor table while the low sun streamed in from the west. Outside, a dog began barking and somebody whistled, silencing him. The details of that moment would come back to both women in the days to come, for they had not felt closer since Tess graduated from high school and loaded up her car to head for Nashville.

"Now I'll tell you what you do," Mary said, forcing brightness into her voice. "You go in my closet and you find that pretty slacks suit that you sent me, and get it ironed up for Saturday, and when this Niki finishes my hair, I'll put it on and do you girls proud at that wedding. How's that?"

Tess stretched up and kissed her mother's cheek. "Thanks, Mom," she said, and smiled.

TESS CALLED RENEE later that night after Mary was in bed sound asleep.

"I got Momma to agree to leave her old polyester pants suit in the closet."

"Oh, Tess, did you really? You're a miracle worker!"

"She's wearing the one I sent her from Seattle last year."

"Super! It's so beautiful and Rachel will really be happy to hear this. Tess, I owe you one."

"That's not all."

"Don't tell me she's having her hair done!"

"That's what I'm telling you. Right here at

home. I hired someone to come in and do it."

Without a wisp of jealousy, Renee remarked, "It must be fun to have enough money to be able to do things like that."

"It is." There were few people Tess could talk to about money. She loved Renee even more for accepting this difference between them.

Renee said, "I have to say, on Judy's behalf, that she tried. I can't tell you how many times she's told Momma to come into the shop whenever she wants, but Momma's so proud. She's afraid she'll go and have her hair fixed, then Judy won't charge her. Well, whatever you said to change her mind, thanks."

"Sure. Listen . . . about the wedding, when do you want her at the church for pictures?"

"The wedding starts at five, so, four o'clock, I think. The photographer wants the rest of us there by three, but I told him to plan on taking all the ones with the grandparents last, so she doesn't have to be there any earlier than necessary. Do you think she'll be okay till we get through dinner?"

"She'll be fine. She insists on walking in with her crutches, but we're taking her wheelchair, too, and whenever she wants to come home I'll bring her. She's really done a remarkable job with her physical therapy. Never a complaint, no matter how it hurts. She's so determined."

"Well . . . this is a different Tess from the one who said the first day that Momma was going to drive her nuts."

"I guess I just expected too much of her. And you're right. She is getting old. I believe I'm finally accepting that."

"So tell me . . . do you still resent the fact that Judy and I railroaded you into coming home to take care of her?"

"No, not anymore. At this point I think my record producer resents it more than I do."

"Well, listen, kid, it's late and tomorrow's going to be crazy."

"Sorry I kept you so long."

"One more thing. Have you been staying away from Kenny like I advised?"

"Absolutely away."

"Good. See you at the wedding. I'll be glad when it's over and my life gets back to normal."

THE WEATHER ON SATURDAY couldn't have been more ideal. Eighty-three degrees and sunny when Tess was getting dressed. She'd bought a new outfit at Barney's in New York, a midnight blue sheath, utterly simple, and matching sling-back faille pumps with a faint peppering of miniature blue rhinestones on the toes. At her neck she hung a platinum chain with a diamond-covered orb the size of a marble. On her ears were small sickle moons, also covered with real diamonds. Though she had carefully refrained from wearing anything that smacked of wealth or glamour since she'd been home, the wedding, she decided, was an occasion when a little glitz was permitted.

The sheath fit more snugly than when she'd tried it on in New York. She sucked in her breath and pressed her belly. No more burgers and fries at the Sonic Drive-in, and you'd better start jogging every day or you'll be up a size before you know it.

When she walked into Mary's bedroom, Mary stared.

"Something wrong?" Tess asked, glancing down.

"You've been running around here so long in your blue jeans and T-shirts that I forgot you're actually a big-time star. My lord in heaven but you're beautiful, child."

"Oh, Momma . . ."

"No, you are. A regular sight for sore eyes. Are those real diamonds?"

Tess touched her ear. "Are they too much?"

"Ha. You just wear them. You earned them."

"Thanks, Momma." The praise touched Tess deeply, especially Mary's approval of the diamonds when Mary herself had never had any of her own beyond her worn wedding ring. Perhaps it was the prerogative of all mothers to want the best for their children but expect none of it for themselves.

"You'll have every man in the place eyeing you. And half the women, too."

"Well, what about you? Wait till we get that suit on you—you'll see."

The suit was the color of light through a glass of crème de menthe and closed up the front with four satin frogs. Getting it on Mary took some effort, but together they managed. When the trousers were in place and the jacket was buttoned, Tess said, "I want to put some mascara on you, okay? Wait while I go get the kitchen stool."

There was an old-fashioned dressing table in Mary's bedroom, part of the original bedroom set, but the stool for it was far too low. Tess went into the kitchen and got the white metal step stool and returned with it to the bedroom.

"Oh, Tess, you don't have to go through all that work for me," her mother scolded.

"No, we're going to do this right. Come over here and sit down."

When Mary was seated before her mirror, Tess powdered her cheeks, brushed them with faint coral blusher and used a little color stick around her eyes. She had her blink across the mascara wand, then used lip liner and applied lipstick with a brush. Niki had done a commendable job, giving Mary a flattering hairstyle that took five years off her age. Her peachy gray hair lay in soft waves tipped up at the ends above her ears.

"Now earrings. I have just the perfect ones." Tess produced a small box of pale aqua, also purchased in New York, and handed it to her mother. When Mary read the single word embossed on the cover she lifted disbelieving eyes to Tess in the mirror.

"Tiffany? Oh, Tess, what have you gone and done?"

"Open it. Happy Mother's Day a little early."

Inside the aqua box was another of black velvet. Mary lifted the lid to reveal a pair of teardrop earrings of emeralds surrounded by diamonds. Her eyes immediately began to well with tears.

"Oh, Tess . . ."

Standing behind Mary, Tess chafed her mother's upper arms and smiled at her in the mirror. "Mustn't ruin your new makeup job. Go ahead, put them on."

"But, Tess . . . these are—"

"Yes, I know. But I can afford them, Momma, and since you won't let me build you a new house you'll have to take these instead."

Mary's hands trembled with excitement as she lifted the gems to her ears. When the earrings were in place she stared at her reflection, her breath caught in her throat. She put a hand to her fluttering heart and whispered, "My word."

Tess bent down, put her head beside her mother's and they studied their twin reflections in the mirror. "You're beautiful, too, Momma." At Mary's ears the jewels caught the light from the small dressing table lamps and strewed it across the walls. But the change was wrought by more than the gems. It was everything—the fresh hairdo, the makeup, the elegant cut of the brushed silk and the glittering eyes of a seventy-four-year-old woman who found few occasions in her life that called for dressing up this much anymore. Tess felt the immense satisfaction of watching her mother believe she was beautiful again.

Mary McPhail looked in the mirror and lit up with pleasure. "Thank you, Tess." With their heads on the same level she reached up and touched Tess's jaw lovingly, and Tess smiled at her one last time in the mirror.

"You're welcome. Now let's go knock 'em dead, eh, Ma?" Mary laughed, and Tess said, "I'm going to go switch the cars around and put your wheelchair in the trunk. Wait till I come back before you use those crutches on the back steps, okay?"

"Okay."

She left her mother gazing at herself in the mirror and whispering, "My word, I can't believe this."

Tess hauled the folded wheelchair down the steps and pushed it down the bumpy back sidewalk. As she reached the car a couple of boys wearing bill caps backward on their heads came down the alley toward her, one of them bouncing a basketball. They slowed when they saw her unlocking the Z.

"That your car?" one of them asked.

"Yes, it is."

"Cool."

"Thanks."

"You that country singer?"

"Yes, I am."

"Coo-wull!"

They hung around to watch her get in, start the engine and back the car up, then continued on their way up the alley, playing catch with the basketball. She got Mary's car out, put hers away, opened her mother's trunk and was getting ready to lift the wheelchair when Kenny opened his porch door and yelled, "Hey, Tess, wait! I'll give you a hand with that!"

He strode down the length of his backyard suited up for the wedding in a navy pin-striped suit while she waited beside the open trunk with the folded wheelchair. "You're a lifesaver, Kenny. This thing's heavy." He stowed the chair and slammed the trunk.

"There." He turned, brushing his palms together.

"Thanks."

"Can't have you getting . . ." His eyes went down to her glistening toes and back up while his palms brushed slower and finally stopped. He never did finish the sentence.

"Nice dress," he said, more quietly.

"Thanks. Nice suit. And that's a Norman Rockwell print on your tie, isn't it?"

He glanced down. "Yes . . . thanks."

It took a while before either of them spoke again.

He certainly hadn't bought his clothes in Wintergreen, nor had he any idea how his appearance made her blood rush. He knew how to tie a tie and match a tie to a suit and a suit to his body, and he knew how to fix his gaze upon a woman in a way that made her aware of all these things, deep down on a visceral level where she didn't want to be aware.

But if she was aware, he was, too, of his gut-deep sexual attraction to her, and of hers for him. In her silk, jewels and makeup, she stood before him for the first time as the woman he'd seen on the covers of magazines and on country awards shows on TV. Her dress with its simple lines made her look youthful and innocent. It did not cling, but flowed over her bones like the wind over her Z. Its neckline showed the barest hint of collarbones, its hem sliced her modestly at the knee. The diamonds at her ears glinted in the sunlight, and the orb that hung between her breasts looked the more stunning for resting against the rich, deep blue of the silk.

They realized they'd been staring.

Their glances shied away.

"Well," she said, "I'd better get back up to the house. Momma is waiting."

"Does she need any help?"

"No, I don't think so. All I can do is hold the door for her, but she's got to negotiate the steps by herself."

In spite of her refusal, when she headed

to the house he followed, watching her from behind.

Her hosiery was the sheerest midnight blue. Her heels were high and accented the curve of her legs. As she walked he caught glimpses of the rhinestones on her toes, and snatches of an expensive perfume that he recognized from the night they'd ridden to choir practice together. A breeze pushed her dress from the left and he felt himself threatened by the certainty that before she went back to Nashville they would continue what she'd started in the car that night in the rainstorm.

They reached the house and Tess went inside while he waited on the step. Momentarily she reappeared, coming out first to hold the screen door open for Mary, who stumped over the threshold on crutches and paused, smiling, pleased.

From three steps below her Kenny took one look and exclaimed, "Lord o' mercy, look at you!" His admiration was so genuine it made a blank of his face.

"Hi, Kenny," the old woman said almost girlishly.

He smiled so broadly that Tess wanted to kiss him. If Mary could have spun in a circle she would have done so. As it was, she clung to her crutches while he gaped. "Tess took me over. What do you think?"

"I think if I were twenty years older I'd fall head over heels in love! Come to think of it, I might anyway."

Kenny rained all his admiration on Mary, who, unmistakably, blushed. She looked like a woman reborn as she headed down the steps with Tess hovering solicitously. One on either side of Mary, she and Kenny escorted her to the car. He opened the back door and waited patiently while she fitted herself inside. When she was arranged on her pillows, he put the crutches on the floor and slammed the door, then walked Tess around to the driver's side and opened the door for her, watching as her legs folded and swung out of sight.

Holding the door open, he asked, "Will you be okay getting her into the church?"

"I'll be fine, thanks."

She looked up and for a moment they became enmeshed in the illusion they were husband and wife, helping Mary as they had, loving her as they did, loved by her as they were. Even the way he'd escorted Tess to her side and was waiting to slam the door, enhanced the illusion. They realized they were pretending, and he came to his senses first. "Well . . . I'd better go see if I can light a fire under Casey. You know how girls are when they're dressing up. See you later."

He slammed the door and she admitted to herself that no matter what she'd promised Renee, she and Kenny were treading a fine line between common sense and a move that would create impending disorder in their lives. It seemed highly likely that before this night was out, they would set that disorder in motion.

Small Town Girl   375

THIRTEEN

KENNY AND TESS SAT on the same side of the aisle but she was ushered up front with the other family members. He was seated a few rows back. The wedding was typical small-town: the organ was too loud, the singer projected in a piercing soprano, the four-year-old ring bearer veered off the center aisle when he saw his mother, and a baby fussed intermittently from one of the back pews.

Mary walked up the aisle on her crutches, then sat in her wheelchair with the footrests lowered to their limits. Afterward Ed pushed her out of the church, while Tess followed with Judy.

The bride received less scrutiny than Tess. For Tess, occasions like this were uncomfortable yet heady: people staring as she passed, whispering to those beside them; avid fans beaming overtly, hoping she'd smile their way while she kept her eyes fixed on the exit doors. The exception was when she passed Kenny. He, Casey and Faith shared one pew like a regular all-American family. Casey waggled her fingers when Tess walked past. Faith smiled. Kenny only watched her with those disconcerting brown eyes that had admired her in the alley less than two hours before.

Mary was part of the receiving line in the vestibule, leaving Tess free to join the crowd outside. The wind had come up to relieve the afternoon heat, and great white cloud puffs scuttled along the blue backdrop. A black carriage and two Appaloosa horses waited at the curb. Judy fell away to visit with someone she knew. Even those who pretended not to be staring at Tess were. But not one soul approached.

Not until Casey came out of church. She made a beeline straight for Tess, exclaiming, "Wow, you look awesome, woman! Where'd you get that dress? And those *shoes!*"

"Casey, am I glad to see you."

"What's wrong?"

Tess leaned close and lowered her voice. "I was feeling like a turd in the punchbowl. Everybody looking but nobody coming close."

Casey giggled and glanced around to find many people standing off, watching the two of them.

"They're probably scared. Hey, these clothes . . . *woman!* You can't find anything like that in Wintergreen."

"The dress came from Barney's in New York. The shoes are from Nordstrom's in Seattle."

"Kill*er!*" Casey came close, and whispered, "Don't tell Faith, but I think Dad was staring at you all through the service."

"I doubt it."

"He was, too, but I bet you're used to guys doing that, aren't you?"

"I'd be lying if I said no, but some situations are more comfortable than others. This one isn't. Stick around, okay?"

Faith approached and commandeered both of Tess's hands. "Well, hello, Tess. Heavens, you look stunning."

"Thank you. Doesn't everybody?"

Kenny was right behind Faith, attempting to pretend polite indifference to Tess. Their glances settled elsewhere. "Wasn't it a nice ceremony?" Faith prattled on. "I thought for sure you'd sing today."

"Rachel asked me to but I told her I just wanted to be a regular guest this time."

"I'm sure she was disappointed."

"She was very gracious about it."

They made small talk until Judy rejoined them, along with Judy's daughter, Tricia, who brought a tall, thin, pretty girl with hazel eyes. "Aunt Tess? My friend Allison wants to meet you. She's a big fan of yours."

Tess shook the girl's trembling, damp hand. "Hello, Allison."

She was one of the shy ones, blushing furiously, trying hard not to show her braces. In the end she failed and a set of blaze-pink hardware flashed clearly behind her wide smile. She stammered what thousands of others before her had stammered, things like "Gosh, I can't believe I'm really meeting you," and "You're so pretty," and "I couldn't believe you were really Trish's aunt." All the while Judy stood by, observing with the same uppitiness as that day at the hospital. Kenny stood back observing, too, behind Faith, making Tess self-conscious in a whole new peculiar way that made her proud of being a star but wishing that today she were not. For this one day she wished she were just a nondescript girl free to flirt with a guy who sort of turned her on. Instead, every move she made was watched by dozens.

The crowd around her grew, cutting her off from her family and taking snapshots without asking if she minded. Someone requested an autograph and she murmured, "Not right now. The bride and groom will be coming out soon." An overweight woman in a polka-dot dress barreled over, and blared, "Mac McPhail, my *Gawd,* it's really you! Oh, honey, could I shake your hand?" As if that were not enough, she insisted on giving Tess a hug. Hugs often left makeup on her shoulder and flattened one side of her hair. Of all the fan responses she disliked, getting hugged was the most invasive. Over the fat woman's shoulder she caught Kenny's eye and shot him an expression of hopeless resignation, to which he replied with a sympathetic wince. After that she didn't see him again. The crowd circled, and—like it or not—she found herself the center of attention.

When the last of the wedding guests spilled from church, she caught sight of Kenny wheeling Mary down the ramp leading from the side door of the vestibule. The bride and groom emerged into the wind, which made a parachute of her veil. She clapped a hand to her head to hold it on while birdseed flew and the church bells clamored overhead. Then Casey appeared at Tess's side.

"Dad's taking your mom to her car. He says take your time."

"What happened to Ed?"

"Tricia had to pour punch so he had to take her ahead to the reception hall."

"Where's Faith?"

"She's right over there talking to her sister. Listen, I'm taking off. See you at the reception!"

She was gone with her friends and minutes later Tess moved toward the parking lot where she found Kenny standing beside Mary's car waiting for her. Mary was already installed in the backseat with the door still open. It was a relief to speak to him directly at last.

"Thanks for taking over my job."

"I could see you were a little busy." His

grin told her he was referring to the woman in the polka-dot dress. "She didn't crush you, did she?"

"Not quite. Did she leave any makeup on my dress?"

He took advantage of her question to touch her for the first time: his fingertips brushed the blue silk at her collarbone. "None that I can see."

"Who is she anyway?"

"Lenore Jeeters. She's on the city council."

From the backseat Mary spoke up. "A loud-mouthed sow who could do the play-by-play at the Super Bowl without a microphone. She's always trying to get me to talk you into coming back home for fund-raisers, Tess. I wouldn't give her the satisfaction, even if I thought you'd say yes, which I know you wouldn't."

Tess leaned down and smiled into the car. "Thanks, Momma. I owe you one. How you doing? You getting tired?"

"Doing just fine, but I sure could use some supper. Wouldn't mind if you'd get me to that reception before I faint dead away."

Kenny slammed the car door and for the

moment he and Tess became an island again, cut off from Mary, feeling that surflike push-pull of an attraction that was inadvisable. "I mean it, Kenny. Thanks for seeing after Momma . . . again and again and again." She took her turn at touching him . . . on the sleeve, letting her hand trail down as she moved away. Their fingers joined in passing—a quick, private pressing of flesh, then Tess continued around the car.

The reception was held out in the country at a place called Current River Cove, which years ago had been a roller rink, then an onion-storage shed before someone had bought it and knocked four long windows in the wall, hung a wide deck on the side facing the river, installed a kitchen and turned it into the most roomy reception hall in Ripley County. It was carpeted in ghastly indoor/outdoor olefin with more colors than an oil slick, furnished with Formica tables and stackable chairs, and it smelled like a generic school lunchroom when the wedding party arrived. A band was setting up in one corner and their filler tape amplified a mixed bag of country music across the hall.

Over two hundred guests milled and mingled, waiting for the arrival of the bride and groom. Though they had for the most part kept their distance from Tess on the church steps, the presence of cocktails seemed to signal that it was now all right to approach her and make small talk. It seemed to Tess as if she spoke to every one of them during the half hour before dinner was served. All except Kenny Kronek, who visited with everybody else in the place and must have decided once again to keep some distance between himself and Tess. But Tess seemed to have developed some sensory radar that kept her aware of where he was every minute.

Nearly every person asked her why she hadn't sung at the wedding and if she was going to do so at the dance.

"No," she replied again and again. "I'm a guest here today. The bride and the groom are the stars." There had been hundreds of similar situations during the course of her career, and she had learned well how to avoid upstaging the guests of honor without alienating her fans.

When the bride and groom arrived and dinner was served, Tess and Mary sat at a round table for eight, joined by Judy and

Ed, and Tricia, who was done tending the punch bowl. No sooner were they seated than Faith Oxbury approached, and asked, "Are these seats taken?"

"No," Judy answered. "Sit down. My other two kids were ushers so they're seated at the head table."

"Do you mind?" Faith asked Tess politely.

Mind? Sharing a table with Kenny? Unwise, perhaps, but what else could Tess answer? "No. Not at all. I wanted to talk to Casey anyway."

"Oh, good. I'll go get Kenny." While she was gone Casey arrived, breathless, and took the chair right next to Tess. "Boy, I've been talking to some of the members of the band. Are they gonna be good!"

"Do you know them?"

"Two of them. We used to do a little messing around together with guitars."

While they visited, Faith returned with Kenny in tow, and the two of them took the remaining chairs directly across from Tess, filling out the table. With everybody knowing everybody else, the conversation bounced around and changed subjects often.

Dinner turned out to be a tasty combination of chicken and herbed cheese rolled around asparagus and baked in puff pastry with a light tarragon cream sauce. The wines were excellent—a peppery pinot noir and a fruity zinfandel that were passed around and poured and toasted with and laughed over. And in the case of Tess and Kenny, used as a shield to deflect gazes that tended to get tangled up a little too often.

It was Faith who mentioned Mary's earrings and peered at them more closely.

Mary touched one and divulged, "They're real. Tess gave them to me this afternoon." Six people admired them and yodeled praise. The seventh pursed her lips and nudged her husband's elbow. "Give me some more of that wine, Ed."

Mary said, "Yeah, give me some more, too, Ed."

"You're on medication, Momma," Judy chided. "You're not supposed to be drinking alcohol."

"Tell you what, Judy. You get two new hips and sit at your granddaughter's wedding and see if you don't want to celebrate a little bit. I didn't take my pills this morning, and a couple of glasses of wine aren't going to kill me. Fill 'er up, Ed."

Everyone became more jovial except Judy.

In the middle of the meal Tricia brought up the fact that Tess was taking Casey to Nashville and that everyone in town was buzzing about it.

"Isn't she wonderful?" Casey beamed at Tess, dazzled and slightly giddy: she'd been sneaking sips of wine. "She's making all my dreams come true."

Tess said, "It's not a record contract, Casey, it's only singing backup on a single cut."

"I know, but Nashville, Mac! It's what I've dreamed about my whole life long!"

Mary had finished her second glass of wine and was looking well pleased with everything. Ed, also under some alcoholic influence, grinned and said, "Nice going, Casey. You've got a class act to follow in Tess here."

Faith said, "I think it would be appropriate to make a toast to our up-and-coming star." They all raised their glasses, Judy, too, unable to do otherwise without looking like a jerk. But the moment the toast ended she slipped from her chair and escaped to the ladies' room.

Tess watched her go, laid down her napkin and said calmly, "Excuse me, please. I have to talk to Judy."

Once inside the ladies' bathroom she locked the door. The room had three gray-painted stalls and a vanity with two sinks. Judy had thrown her handbag on a counter between them and was stabbing at her hair. Tess set down her own beaded handbag and faced Judy's profile rather than her reflection in the mirror.

"All right, Judy, let's talk about it."

"Leave me alone."

"No. Because I can't stand this anymore."

"Stand what?"

"Your jealousy. I've been home for three weeks and every single time I've seen you, something has managed to get your goat. Either it's somebody asking for my autograph, or somebody asking me to perform, or something I gave Momma."

"You love to throw it in our faces, don't you?" Judy accused. Abruptly her voice became mimicking. "Look at me, the rich, famous star coming back home to show the peons just how drudging their lives are!''

"Damn it, Judy, that's not fair! I have never flaunted my fame or my money around you and you know it!''

"Start with your car, and those clothes you're wearing today, and your *mobile phone.*'' She made the words sound reprehensible. "Yuppie country star cruises into town talking on her phone, impressing young girls who have dreams of being a star, too.''

"I do my business by long distance. And you bought new clothes for the wedding, didn't you?'' Judy refused to answer. "All right, then, so did I. And as for Casey, I wouldn't have paid her two cents' worth of attention if she didn't have talent. But she does, and if I can help her develop it, why shouldn't I?''

"You made sure you announced it where everyone would know how *magnanimous* you are, didn't you?''

"I didn't *announce* it. I told Casey a week ago at her own house, in private. Somebody else brought it up tonight, and somebody else made the toast. But you could barely stand to lift your glass with the oth-

ers, could you? You can't even be happy for
Casey. And at Momma's house the day she
came home from the hospital, when everybody asked us to sing, what should I have
said? No? Because my sister Judy can't
stand it? She's going to go in the kitchen
and sulk? That's what you did, Judy, and it
hurt me. It always hurts me when you treat
me as if what I do for a living is something I
should be apologizing for. Do you know
that you've never once said, 'Congratulations, Tess' or 'Nice song, Tess,' or 'Bought
your tape, Tess'? Nothing. As if what I do
doesn't even exist. Instead, when anybody
else offers me any kind of attention you just
curdle up inside. But this is what I *do,*
Judy." She leaned forward earnestly, one
hand on the vanity top. "I sing. I sign autographs. I wear glitzy clothes and get photo-
graphed for magazine covers because it's
part of my work. And when I have the
chance to discover new talent and bring it
to Nashville, I'm going to do it. Should I pretend none of that is true whenever I'm
around you? And should I drive a rusted-
out used car for you, too? And not give
Momma nice things because it pisses you
off? Look, she isn't going to be around for-

ever, and if I want to buy her emeralds, I will! And if I want to take Casey to Nashville, I will! And if you can't accept that, then I pity you. Because the people who really love me are glad for me, *and* for my success, *and* for my fame, because they know I worked damned hard for it."

Someone tried the door.

Judy picked up her purse, but Tess grabbed her arm.

"Let me go." Judy tried to pull away, refusing to meet Tess's eyes.

"In a minute. I'm going to tell you something first. If you were happier with yourself you'd be happier with others as well. Think about it."

The woman outside banged on the door. "Hey, who's in there?"

Judy yanked her arm free and glared at her younger sister. "Why don't you just go back where you came from?" she said venomously. "The rest of us can take care of Momma and do a lot better job of it, too."

The lock clacked open and the door slammed against the tile wall as Judy stormed out.

Tess stayed behind, struggling to compose herself. Though she was trembling

and tears were threatening, she smiled
falsely at the pair of women who came in
looking curiously at her. When they saw
who it was they decided not to go into the
stalls, but to fuss first at the mirror. Tess
withdrew a lipstick and powder from her
bag and put them to use. Her cheeks held
blotches of bright pink while an unflattering
flush had mottled her neck.

"I really like your shoes," one of the
women said.

"Thank you."

"Are you going to sing with the band tonight?" the other asked.

"No, I'm sorry, I'm not."

"Oh, shoot."

She tucked away her makeup, snapped
her handbag shut and hid anything personal from these strangers. Her smile said
Sorry to disappoint you, while she offered
her customary response to this common request. "You can hear me anytime on the
MCA label."

By the time Tess returned to the table the
band had started playing and Judy and Ed
were gone. So was everyone else except
Mary, who inquired, "What went on in the
ladies' room anyway? Judy nearly pulled

Ed's arm out of his socket getting him out of here."

"I told her what I thought of her jealousy, and Momma, so help me, if you claim one more time that Judy isn't jealous, I'm going to take your wine away, which is probably what I should do anyway!"

"You're too late. Kenny and Faith already cut me off."

"Where are they?"

"Dancing. Everybody is. They all suddenly decided to get up and go out on the dance floor when Judy came roaring out of that bathroom like a wounded rhinoceros and hauled her family home. What is it about weddings that starts so many family feuds?"

Angry tears sprouted in Tess's eyes. "Momma, I just wasn't going to take any more of Judy's shit. She's your daughter, too, and I know you love her, and I'm not asking you to do anything else, but I've been hurt by her so many times, and it's all because she's got such low self-esteem that she can't handle any aspect of my success. It's all *right* for Judy to get up and leave the room when anybody treats me like a star, but it's *not* all right for me to call her on it, because that makes me egotistical! Well, I took it, Momma, without saying a word, but no more! Tonight she cut you off when you were excited about your earrings, then she did the same thing to Casey when she was excited about going to Nashville. Now, I ask you, who is small and who isn't?"

Mary sighed and rubbed the back of Tess's fist on the tabletop. "I've been thinking about it since the first Sunday you were home when all you kids were at the house together, and I know you're right. She left the living room as soon as you and Casey started singing. And I've seen other evidence that I just didn't want to believe. Judy's awful good to me, you know."

"Of course she is, Momma, but this isn't about whether or not she's good to you."

"No . . . no, it isn't."

"You know what would help her a lot? If she got on a good weight-loss program and started taking more pride in her appearance."

"I know, but who's going to tell her so?"

"Not me."

"Not me, either."

"I came as close to telling her as I ever will, five minutes ago in the bathroom."

"She looked nice tonight," Mary said wistfully.

"She looked very nice tonight. But she'd look better if she lost some weight."

Renee interrupted at that moment, arriving breathless from the dance floor and bracing both hands on the tabletop. She looked particularly radiant in an apricot dress with a lace bodice and a sheer skirt. "What happened to Judy and Ed?" she inquired.

Tess confessed, "My fault. I got into it with Judy in the bathroom about you know what."

"So she stomped off home?"

"And took Ed and Tricia, too. I'm sorry, Renee."

Renee straightened up, lifted the hair off her hot neck, and said, "Hey, you know what? It's Judy's problem, not ours. And I'm not going to let her spoil my daughter's wedding for me. Now, listen . . . the bride and groom sent me over to talk to you. They're getting so many requests from their guests that they told me to ask if you'll sing just one song with the band. They said to tell you that if you say yes they'll give you their firstborn."

"Just what I need is a firstborn."

"What do you say?"

"I've been telling everyone all night long that I'm not singing."

"Not even at the bride and groom's request? It would mean so much to them, Tess. Come on," she cajoled.

Tess glanced at the dance floor. Rachel and Brent were half dancing, watching Tess with hopeful expressions on their faces. Tess knew that if she sang it would make their wedding the talk of the very limited social season in Ripley County.

Renee said, "I suspect part of the reason you didn't want to sing was Judy. Now that she's out of the way, what other excuse have you got?"

"You sure it's all right with the band?"

"Are you kidding? What band wouldn't want to say they backed up Tess McPhail?"

"All right. Just one song."

Renee gave the bride and groom a thumbs-up, and they hugged in jubilation, then Rachel blew Tess a kiss and went to the foot of the stage and spoke to the lead guitarist while he continued to play.

At the next song break the band immediately announced, "Everyone knows we have a famous Nashville star with us tonight. She's the bride's aunt, and she's agreed to come up and do a song with us. Hey, everybody, let's make her welcome . . . Tess McPhail!"

The crowd parted for her, and she went up on the stage with a confident stride, cueing the band on the way. "Can you give me 'Cattin' ' in G?"

The drummer said, "You got it, Mac," and gave them a four-beat cue on the rim of his snare.

When the rhythm broke and she grabbed the mike she took two hundred hearts captive on the spot. They applauded so loudly they drowned out the first twelve bars of the music, then spontaneously resumed dancing, their faces lifted to her all the while.

She gave Wintergreen something to talk about for the next ten years, planting her glittering high heels as far apart as her straight dress would allow, keeping rhythm with her right knee and sending blue jets shooting from her sequins. She forgot about Judy and became one with her audience, giving them a performance filled with energy and rhythm. "Cattin'" had a rock beat and slightly naughty words. She used her hands and long flashing nails like a sorcerer to put her audience under her spell. She had an innate sense of drama and played the crowd like an actress, using eye contact and a hint of flirtatiousness to make each listener believe she was singing exclusively for her or him.

Suddenly Kenny was below her, dancing with Casey, both of them smiling up at her, having fun.

She pointed at Casey. ". . . gonna dress in satin . . ."

And at Kenny. ". . . gonna go out cattin' with youuuuu."

She winked and he laughed, then her attention shifted smoothly to others in the crowd. She knew how to make her eyes glitter with promise and how to hold a hand mike so that the men imagined it was they, close to her lips, and the women imagined they were as alluring and confident as Tess McPhail. There were songs she sang to women; this was not one of them, but the women in the audience didn't seem to care. When the song ended they applauded as enthusiastically as the men. Casey stuck her fingers between her teeth and whistled like a cattle drover. Renee yelled, *"All right, sis!"* The bride and groom clapped and accepted remarks from those around them while a general chant went up.

"Mac! Mac! Mac!"

It pulsed through the room.

Taking her bow, Tess made sure she caught her mother's eye. Mary was applauding proudly from her wheelchair by the dinner table, and Tess felt particularly warmed by the pride she sensed radiating from Mary. Scanning the faces below, she caught impressions of townspeople she'd forgotten—ex-teachers, store owners, Renee's and Judy's friends, long-time neighbors, people from church, everyone still applauding, calling for more. The bride and groom made their way to the foot of the stage, their faces lifted. "Please do one more, Aunt Tess . . . please!" Rachel begged.

She sang one more, a slow one for the newly married couple.

"I've never recorded this song," she announced, "but I've always loved it, especially at weddings. Rachel and Brent, this one's for you."

She sang a moving rendition of "Could I Have This Dance for the Rest of My Life" and watched the swirl of partners gliding past. Renee waltzed by with Jim. The groom had his bride. Packer had one of the bridesmaids. Mindy Alverson Petroski was with her husband, the appliance store owner. And Kenny danced by with Faith.

They'd have kept Tess on the stage even longer, but after the second song she thanked the band, gave a farewell flourish and replaced the mike on the stand.

A dozen people complimented her on her way back to the table, and more came after she got there. Mary was flushed with pride, and said, "Honey, you sure knocked 'em dead. I don't know where you got a voice like that, but it sure wasn't from me." People were very kind, coming by one after the other to thank her for singing and to offer the usual platitudes.

Enid Copley and a bunch of Mary's friends came and Mary found herself the center of attention, the mother of the girl who did good.

But a phenomenon happened that sometimes occurred after Tess had sung. Once she'd done so she became such a superstar that the people, fearful of offending her, kept their distance. They came by, said something quickly so they could claim they'd spoken to her, then hustled away, leaving her lonely in the crowd. Casey was in another part of the hall, hanging out with the kids her age. Renee and Jim were having the time of their lives. If Ed were here, she might have danced with him, but he was gone. Nobody was going to ask the famous Tess McPhail to dance, so she was left with Mary, who never lacked for company.

Two teenage girls approached and shyly asked if Tess would sign a paper napkin, which she did. Mrs. Perry, who'd lived across the street when Tess was little, turned from Mary to remind Tess how she had loved the English toffee she used to make at Christmastime, and how Tess had once abashed Mary by knocking on Mrs. Perry's door and asking if she could have some. It was an old story that had been repeated every time she'd run into Mrs. Perry since she was in elementary school. They talked about the Perry kids, where they were now, what they did for a living, then the woman rejoined the older group.

"Mom, you let me know when you're ready to go home," Tess said.

"Pretty soon," Mary replied, but she and Enid Copley and Mrs. Perry and the others were still deep in conversation.

One song ended, another began, and Kenny came off the dance floor alone, snagged the chair next to Tess and dropped onto it, facing her. He looked warm from dancing. His suit coat hung open and he had loosened his tie and freed his collar button. He reached for his glass, took a drink, propped an elbow on the table and said, "Great wedding."

"You look like you're having fun."

"I am."

"Where did you leave Faith?"

"Dancing with her brother-in-law. How come you're not dancing?"

"Nobody asked me."

He glanced around, let his eyes return to her, and said, "Well, we can't have that, can we? Would you like to dance?"

"I'd love it."

He took her hand and walked her onto the dance floor. The band was playing "The Chair" as she swung lightly into his arms in the traditional waltz pose.

"Thanks for rescuing me," she said at his ear.

"What's wrong with the guys around here anyway?"

"They get a little spooked by me. Happens all the time. You're a good dancer."

"Thanks. So are you. And a helluva terrific singer. They all loved you."

"Thanks. I was watching you with Casey from the stage. It's nice to see a father and daughter having fun like that."

"I'm going to miss her when she goes to Nashville."

"I know you will."

"But, Lord, Tess, you've made her so happy. You know that, don't you?" He leaned back so he could see her face.

"Makes me happy, too."

"Thanks for all you're doing for her."

"That's got to be hard for you to say."

"It's one of those stepping-stones a parent faces. Maybe I've grown up a little bit since you came home."

They spent some pleasurable moments gazing at close range, flirting silently in plain sight of two hundred people. When it became too obvious, he tightened his arm till their bodies brushed, and her temple rested against his jaw. She recognized the smell of his cologne coming off his warm skin and thought about Renee's admonition to stay away from him. But it felt right, shuffling around the rim of the dimly lit floor in his arms. She had few opportunities to dance anymore. Ironically, creating the music to which others danced robbed her of the chance to enjoy it this way.

"I have something to thank you for, too," she told him. "What you said to my mother when you came to the door to get her this afternoon. I'd told her the same thing, but coming from a man, it meant more."

He glanced Mary's way through the crowd. "She does look great, doesn't she?"

"See? That's what I mean—your response was so genuine that it lit her up like a Christmas tree. She's seventy-four years old, and her hips have been replaced and her face is getting jowly and her hair is getting thin, but when you came to the door and caught your breath you made her feel beautiful."

"Actually, I think you did that, with the makeup and the hair and the jewelry. Those earrings are pretty special, Tess."

"So's my momma."

He cinched her tighter around the waist as if to say, I'm glad you know that at last, and executed a neat turn. She stayed right with him, cushioned by his legs and midsection, and they began to feel the particular exhilaration of two dancers who are equal to one another and enjoying the physical contact.

"Hey, Kenny?" she said just below his ear.

"Hm?"

"I thought you used to be the clumsiest klutz in the whole school. What happened?"

He laughed and smiled against her hair. "Keep up that smooth talk and I just might let you have your way with me."

He had wrapped her up so tightly that she'd have known if he had a nickel in his pocket.

"Did we ever dance in high school?" she asked.

"I don't think so. You'd never have let me get this close to you."

"Mm . . . too bad," she murmured.

He leaned back to see her face. They got reckless and let their eyes and smiles say a lot, and the conjunction of their bodies say the rest. A woman knows when her dance partner is thinking about more than dancing, and a man knows when her thoughts are taking the same track. Kenny and Tess both knew.

"Would those be moons on your ears?" he asked, grinning, as the diamonds scattered light onto his shoulders.

"Yes, but they're not full."

"I think I've discovered something," he told her.

"What's that?"

"It takes much less than a full moon to make people do crazy things." He moved close again and started humming with the music. She smiled, enjoying the novelty.

"Feature that, would you . . . a man singing to me."

"I'm probably the one man you know who isn't intimidated by your success. If I feel like singing I'm going to sing."

"Me, too."

They finished the dance singing in each other's ears, keeping up the surface playfulness to make light of the all-too-remarkable enjoyment of the contact down below.

When the song ended they separated immediately, knowing people around them were probably gawking. They always gawked at Mac McPhail. She turned as if to lead the way off the floor, but he caught her hand and said, "Stay, Tess . . . one more."

She didn't bother saying yes, only moved up close to his side, hiding their joined hands until the next song started.

The tempo changed. The band played George Strait's "Adalida" and Tess and Kenny smiled and laughed a lot in celebration of how well they did together.

Once she yelled, above the music, "I'm having so much fun!"

He yelled back, "So am I!"

When the song ended they were flushed and hot, returning to Mary's table.

"Well, you two look like you've done that before."

"Not together," Tess said.

Enid Copley and the rest of the bunch were gone. Mary's wineglass was empty and her small purse was resting on her lap. "I know it's early, but I'm afraid I've got to go home, Tess. I sure hate to take you away from the dance, but you can come back can't you?"

"Of course I can. I'll take you right away."

Kenny said, "I'll come along and help."

Tess carefully refrained from looking at him, but she knew he had more than one reason for offering. Lovers will find a way. They had found theirs.

"Oh, thank you, Kenny," Mary was saying. "That would be nice. She's got that beautiful dress on and this darn contraption is so heavy." She meant the wheelchair.

"Just let me tell Faith I'm going, okay? Be right back."

Tess wheeled Mary near the exit and they waited while Kenny found Faith. Faith looked over and waved good night to Mary and Tess. A moment later he joined them and took charge of pushing Mary outside. When she and the wheelchair were tucked into her Ford, Kenny asked, "Would you like me to drive?"

"Actually, yes," Tess said, and gave him the keys. "I've had a little more to drink than I probably should have. If I got stopped and the tabloids picked it up . . . well, you know."

It took fifteen minutes to drive back to town, and another fifteen for Tess to help Mary get settled into bed. While she did,

Kenny waited in the kitchen, familiar with the house and comfortable in the dusky room lit by only one small pin-up lamp near the kitchen stove. He listened to the women's voices, drank a glass of water at the sink, sat down in the shadows at the kitchen table and waited patiently for Tess and the encounter they'd been anticipating all day. Ever since he'd seen her in that blue dress in the alley he'd known it would happen, that they'd somehow find the private moment that would allow it.

She entered the kitchen and he rose from his chair and spoke quietly. "Get her all settled down?"

"Yes."

Mary called from the bedroom, "Good night, Kenny! Thanks for helping out!"

"Good night, Mary," he called back.

He looked down at Tess and they thought about returning to the dance. Thought about what they really wanted to do. His tie was rolled up in his pocket, his top two shirt buttons were open as they stood close, wondering who'd make the first move, certain by now it would be made.

"Want that light out?" he asked.

"No, leave it on for me later."

He stepped back and let her lead the way outside. The backyard was dark. Even Kenny's backyard was dark. They had left in broad daylight and nobody had thought to turn on the outside lights. Tess preceded him down the back steps, one hand riding the cool metal handrail, her high heels tapping out an unhurried beat. His footsteps, more blunt, followed along the narrow sidewalk until they were halfway to the alley.

"Tess, wait," he said, and snagged her arm.

The single, willful touch was all the invitation she needed. She swung about, swift and sure of what she wanted, and wrapped around him like a flag around a standard. He, too, knew what he wanted, and his arms were waiting to haul her flush against him, his lips were waiting to claim hers. They stood in the middle of the sidewalk and let the dark yard hide them while they gave their open mouths to each other. Since midafternoon they'd known this would happen; suppressing their attraction at every encounter through the long, long evening had only fueled the tinder. They stood foursquare against each other, one of his shiny black shoes planted between her glittering blue ones. She was shorter and when he bent to her, her hand went to his head, holding him while they kissed and kissed, with neither of them denying the other anything, least of all the admission that lust had come a-calling sometime since he'd pulled her around to face him.

What they had imagined, they brought to life. Her head nestled against his shoulder and his arms crossed her back while the kiss continued as if the wedding dance and all those left behind did not exist. Their lips got wet and their breath got short and the back of her dress got twisted beneath his hands.

She doubled her arms around his neck and he lifted her free of the earth, held her fast against him with the kiss still unbroken. Like a key in a lock he swung his head the other way and carried her across the grass to the blackest shadow next to the back steps. There, beside the crickets and the hydrangea bushes, they kissed some more, first with her shoulder blades against the wall, then with his.

It was better, though, with her against the wall. He was stronger, could exert more pressure, so they rolled to reverse positions, his hips pinning her in place. Once he put his hands against the house, bent low and ran his mouth over her collarbones, then up to her ear before the kiss resumed, mouth to mouth. And once she put her hands inside his suit coat and felt his warm back, and let her nails mark it through the white cotton. He shivered and undulated against her, full length, one time only, and made a sound against her lips.

Then he dragged her backward with him onto the grass, and fell, carrying her along onto the cool soft turf and made a cradle of his legs where she lay upon him in the star- light. Her hair tumbled and covered his face, and he held it back as he rolled her over and lay half on top of her with his hand just below her left breast. He might have covered it, and she might have let him, but by some unspoken compact they had come to understand that kissing was all they'd al- low tonight. But kissing—maximized by moonlight and movement—would be thrill enough. They would use it and wring from it every pleasure they had imagined, and revel in temptation for temptation's sake. With open mouths and straining bodies they trod that delicate balance where indulgence and suppression vie for the upper hand. And when indulgence threatened to win and carry them beyond a state of grace, he fell to his back on the grass beside her. There they lay with cricket song pulsating in their ears.

It took a long time before either of them spoke. Finally he breathed, "Whoa."

"I'll say," she managed. Her left arm was outflung, caught beneath his sleeve. She moved her thumb, just to keep the connection with him, scraping it across the fabric of his suit. She smiled to herself, then rolled her head to look at him.

"What do we think we're doing?"

He continued looking at the stars. "I think they call it necking. It used to be popular back in the fifties."

"I like it."

"Me, too."

She sat up, languid and liquid-limbed, and pushed her hair back and put her face to the sky.

He sat up, too, and they remained side by side, thinking about what they'd done, still enjoying the aftereffects that had changed the inner rhythms of their bodies.

"There'll probably be grass stains on your dress."

"I'll have it dry cleaned."

"But what about going back to the reception?"

"Funny thing . . . I really don't think I'm in the mood anymore."

"Me, either." He drew up his knees and draped his arms over them, bobbed his head forward and smoothed the back of his hair. She ran her hand down his near sleeve and over the back of his hand, and pushed her fingers between his, working them in his palm like a cat's paw in carpet.

"Hey, if we're going to do stuff like this I've got a right to know—do you and Faith sleep together?"

"Yes."

Her fingers stopped working and she sat very still. Then she stretched out on her back again, linked her hands at her waist and crossed her ankles. Gazing at the stars, she said, "Well, she's very lucky, I must say. I haven't been kissed that thoroughly since . . ."

"Since when?"

"I don't know. I don't make a practice of this."

He stretched out on his side propping his head with one fist, and laid his spread hand in the center of her ribs with his thumb on the underside of her breast. "Neither do I."

She covered his hand with one of her own, enjoying the warmth of it through her clothing. "Then why do you suppose we did it?"

"Look," he said, "I'm not married to Faith. I've had this thing for you since high school, and I wasn't going to pass up the chance. We both knew this was coming."

"But she won't find out about it, will she?"

"No."

"And neither will Casey."

"No."

"No reason for either of them to know because it's just a crazy fling. Lots of people probably have crazy flings at weddings."

"Probably." He moved his thumb, merely scratching the cloth of her dress.

She emptied her mind and reached up to riffle her fingertips through the hair at his temple. It was fine and short and slightly curled. She realized how much she missed having a man whose hair she could touch whenever she wanted to, who would kiss her and make her feel womanly and wanted for more than her talent as a singer. She pulled his head down and whispered, "Then kiss me some more."

He dipped his head and did as she asked, crooking a knee across her legs and staining one elbow of his suit jacket on the grass. Six minutes later, when they had tested their resistance again, he dragged his mouth away, deposited a parting kiss on her lower lip, then on her neck, then on her right breast, just one brief touch through her dress before drawing back to survey her face again.

"I think we have to get back to the dance now."

"Mm . . ."

"If we don't it'll be all over and everyone will be asking why we never came back."

She sighed and sat up with an effort, hands behind her like a girl on a beach towel. "You're right."

His pose curled him around her, his left arm caught over his updrawn knee, his other hand on the grass behind her stained skirt. It took only a turn of her head to put her lips next to his, to rub without kissing, suggesting further intimacy.

"But I don't want to," she murmured, tasting his breath.

"Neither do I."

They lingered, mouths scarcely brushing, his fingertips stroking her throat so faintly they might have been touching her, might not. "But we have to. Come on." He took her hand, pulled her to her feet and they paused on the grass they had flattened, shaking their clothes back into place. She brushed off her skirt, he unbuckled his belt and tucked in his shirt. He did not turn away while he did it, but let her watch as he ran his hands inside his trousers, then buckled up again.

When they were both back in order they imparted one last lazy kiss, standing close without caressing. *It's been fun,* the kiss said, *and we won't ever forget it.*

"I'll drive," she said, and in very slow motion turned toward the car.

"You sure?"

"Yes. I'm perfectly sober now."

The speed of their footfalls slowed with each step that took them closer to parting. The car doors sounded like explosions in the quiet night, and the engine, when Tess started it, like thunder.

Kenny glanced beyond her to Mary's dark house. "Your mother is probably wondering why we're just getting going."

"My mother is probably asleep."

They wondered about it though as they drove back out to Current River Cove, wondered about the future when Tess would be back in Nashville and Kenny would resume his life with Faith—would they look back upon this night and smile inwardly? When they were halfway to their destination Tess said without preamble, "When I get back to Nashville I have a date with my boyfriend, Burt. I figured that would do the trick."

Kenny had slumped down in his seat and managed to get one long leg hitched over the other, his knee on the window ledge. He rolled his head to look at her. "Do what trick?"

"Get you off my mind."

He replied, "I'm pleased to know I've been there."

They reached Current River Cove and the car bounced as it entered the pitted gravel parking lot. She pulled up before the door and the entry lights from the building shone into the car.

"Aren't you coming in?" he asked.

"I don't think so. I think it's best if I go straight back. If anybody asks, just tell them I thought I should stay home with Momma."

Their gazes lingered, but both were determined to keep this light.

"Come to church tomorrow and sing," he encouraged.

"It's better if I don't."

He studied her a moment before deciding she was right. All they'd want to do was spend the day together afterward. "All right, then. When are you going back to Nashville?"

"Tuesday."

"Will I see you again?"

"I'm sure we'll run into each other in the alley."

"Yes, we always seem to, don't we? Well . . ." Some wedding guests came out of the hall, laughing, heading right past them en route to the parking lot.

"I'd better be going," Tess said.

A light kiss seemed in order, but the wedding guests were close enough to see into the car, so they desisted. Their pact continued: neither of them was going to get maudlin or clinging. They were going to take away some provocative memories and no regrets. They were going to part smiling.

"Well, it's been fun," he said, opening his car door. "See ya, Tess."

"Yeah . . . see ya, Kenny."

He got out, slammed the door and she watched him walk toward the building. When he'd opened the hall door, he stopped for a moment and looked back at her. His smile was gone. She could hear the music from the band and see the amber light behind him, then the door closed and he was gone. Back to Faith.

FOURTEEN

ON SUNDAY Tess avoided Kenny by attending the earlier church service once again. In the afternoon she and Mary went to Renee's house, where the bride and groom opened their wedding gifts. They ended up staying for supper and got home late.

On Monday morning shortly after ten o'clock, Tess's business manager, Dane Tully, called.

"Tess, where have you been? I've been trying to call you all weekend."

"My niece got married and I was at the wedding. What's wrong?"

"Papa John died. His funeral is tomorrow."

"Oh, no . . ." Tess sank against the kitchen cabinet, fingers to her lips. Papa John Walpole was a sour-faced, sweet-hearted, leather-skinned old promoter who'd run a little dive called the Mudflats for over thirty years. It was said that in the last twenty, every successful recording artist coming out of Nashville played the Mudflats Thursday night picking parties at one time or another on his way to signing with a major label. If it weren't for Papa John, Tess would not have met Jack Greaves, or Dane himself, or the folks who'd signed her on at MCA. She'd walked into the Mudflats one hot July day in 1976, a brash know-it-all from the show-me state who looked Papa John straight in the eye and said, "I've got nothin' to pick but give me five minutes and the key of G and you don't have to show me anything. I'll show *you!*" Eighteen years and thirteen platinum albums later, she had *shown him* too many times to count, going back and playing the Mudflats whenever she had a night to spare, always gratis, always unadvertised.

She was stabbing at tears as she asked, "What happened?"

"A guy with a nylon over his face came in the back door when Papa John was counting the day's take, pointed a gun at his head and demanded the money. Papa John told him to go piss up a rope."

Through her sniffles, Tess let out a cough of laughter. "Sounds just like him. I'd expect him to go out talking back. Did they catch the guy?"

"Damn right. A waitress was still out front and heard everything. She was dialing nine-one-one before the gun went off, and a prowl car happened to be two blocks away."

"Oh, my God, Dane, I can't believe he's dead."

"Neither can anybody in Nashville. He's being cremated, but there's a memorial service tomorrow at ten A.M. and everybody he ever helped is singing at it. It'll be the biggest choir ever assembled in this town. Can you be here?"

"I've got to be."

"Your mother will be okay?"

"Sure. I've got sisters here. It'll take me a couple hours to make some phone calls and get packed, but I'll be rolling by noon today. The truth is, Dane, I'm more than ready to get out of here. I'll see you tomorrow."

She called Renee, who said, "Oh, Tess,

I'm so sorry. Yes, go ahead and take off. If I'm not there by the time you leave, I'll be there shortly after. And don't worry about Momma. There are plenty of us to watch out for her and drive her wherever she needs to go."

Mary was dismayed. She'd planned on having Tess for one more day, and grew twittery at her sudden announcement of departure. Though she couldn't follow her up the stairs, she followed her to the foot of them and called up while Tess was packing, "Should I fix you a sandwich to take along? Will you be all right driving alone? You're awfully upset, Tess."

When Tess came downstairs for the last time with her duffel and her oversized gray leather bag, Mary was waiting at the bottom, looking gloomy, wearing a pilled polyester knit slacks outfit that was about the same age as Papa John had been. The staples had been removed from her incision a week ago and she had graduated from the crutches to canes, which gave her much more mobility. But she seemed rooted with sadness as Tess hugged her good-bye.

"Now, you call the girls whenever you

need anything. If they can't come, one of the kids will. Promise?"

"I'm no baby. It's not me I'm worried about, it's you, driving all that way crying your eyes out."

"I'm not crying my eyes out. I'll be fine."

"You sure? I don't see why you don't wait till morning. You could get an early start and be there by ten."

"Momma, it's time I go."

"Well . . . yes . . . I suppose it is. I just thought . . . one more day I could have my little girl here."

There had been some changes since she'd been home, but this remained constant: Mary would always call Tess her little girl.

"Gotta go, Momma," she whispered, and pulled back. Mary stumped along behind Tess to the kitchen, and took a sandwich bag off the counter. "Here. It's just pressed ham and cheese, but it might taste good on the road."

Pressed ham and cheese. Couple hundred calories, Tess thought wistfully, recognizing that what she was taking along was a love sandwich, not a ham and cheese.

"Thanks, Momma, I'm sure it will. Well

. . . gotta hit the road." There were tears in both women's eyes. "Listen, you don't need to come outside."

"Of course I do."

"But, Momma . . ."

Mary had her way, following Tess down the crowded step to the back entry, then outside onto the concrete stoop. There she stood, balancing on two aluminum canes and resting her backside against the thick handrail while Tess loaded her car, put on her sunglasses, got in and started the engine. She looked over her left shoulder. The noon sun turned Mary's hair to the color of cooked squash. Her ancient slacks had shrunk and showed her ankles, still bound in support stockings. The house was in need of painting and the lawn needed mowing. But the cabbages in the garden had doubled in size.

Tess called through her open window, "Don't you go bein' sad now, Momma, you hear?"

Mary had hung one of her canes on the handrail to wipe her eyes with a tissue. "Oh, go on with you," she said, flapping a hand, then wiping her other eye.

"Love you, Momma!"

"Don't be gone so long this time!"

"I won't."

Tess hit the gas pedal twice—a real smart aleck trying to lighten the mood. The muffler rapped like strafing and Mary pressed the tissue to her quivering chin. Tess pushed a tape into the deck, cranked up the volume until it nearly broke her own eardrums, backed into the alley, then roared away with her own recorded voice belting out a diminishing farewell for the little squash-haired lady on the high back step.

IT WAS ROUGHLY ONE MILE from her mother's house to downtown. Tess cried all the way, partly for the loving and lonely mother she'd left behind, partly for Papa John, and partly for herself because she was leaving Kenny Kronek. She should not stop at his office; what purpose would it serve? But the thought of driving away without bidding him good-bye caused an actual ache in her breast. It felt as if some force greater than she controlled her will as she pulled up in front of Kenny's office, raised her sunglasses, checked her eyes in the mirror and found she'd cried off all her mascara. Hiding behind her shades once more, she got out and stood for a moment studying his building. It had a gray wooden facade with the door in the center and, on either side, a white window box filled with red geraniums. The geraniums looked like Faith's work.

She nudged the legs of her jeans down off her calves and headed for the plate-glass door that said Kenneth Kronek, CPA. Her sensible self half hoped he'd be gone to lunch, but her sentimental self yearned for a personal good-bye.

She stepped inside and there he was, working at a desk beyond an open doorway of a private office that stretched across the back half of the narrow building. Out front a small reception counter had been abandoned by his secretary, leaving him alone in the place.

He looked up and his fingers stalled above the buttons of a calculator. She took her glasses off slowly and stared back at him while time froze and neither of them flickered a muscle. Finally he rolled his chair back and rose, impaling her with his eyes as he walked through the doorway and stopped behind his secretary's empty chair. He was dressed in gray trousers, a white shirt with a pen in his pocket and a mul-ticolored tie with an equestrian motif. His sleeves were rolled up several inches, but the tie was knotted tightly and fell straight down his flat front. She was dressed as she'd been the day she rolled into town—in cowboy boots, jeans and the Southern Smoke T-shirt with the sleeves rolled up.

"Hi," she said.

"Hi," he answered, and she could tell from the thick-throated syllable that her appearance had generated the same tumult within him that was going on within her. "What's wrong?"

"I have to go back to Nashville today. Something came up very suddenly."

"You've been crying."

She pushed the glasses back on. The lenses grayed his face and clothing.

"A little, yes . . . but it's . . . I'm okay." She rubbed the underside of her nose with the back of her hand.

"Come into my office."

"No." She started rummaging in her purse, seeking a distraction from the awful stranglehold he seemed to have on her heart. "I just wanted you to know I was leaving so you can tell Casey. And I wanted to give you my card so that—''

He came around the desk and gripped her arm. ''Come into my office, Tess.''

''Kenny, I didn't come here to—''

''My secretary's gone to lunch, but she could come back any minute.''

He hauled her into his private domain, shut the door and they stood behind it, facing each other, mixed up and frenzied inside. He dropped her arm the minute the door closed, and asked, ''What happened?''

''A man who got me started in this business was killed by a robber.''

''Who?''

''His name was John Walpole. We called him Papa John.''

''Yes, I know about him. I can imagine what he meant to you. I'm sorry, Tess.''

''You know about him?''

''I've read about what he did for you, lots of times, in magazine articles.''

''You have?'' Her grief over Papa John, and her sadness over saying good-bye to her mother—and him—became momentarily eclipsed by wonder at this man. She had peeled back so many layers of him that she thought herself foolish to be amazed by what this new layer revealed.

Wordlessly he went to a file cabinet, opened the drawer marked M and pulled out a manila folder. He tossed it on his desk and its contents fanned out in a crooked train, half exposed. Tess glanced down at an array of press clippings she recognized—portions of photos peeked out, one behind another, tear sheets from newspapers, and articles from glossy magazines. She opened the folder and saw a headline and picture of herself from *USA Today,* and a much smaller piece from the *Wintergreen Free Press* telling about her singing with the First Methodist Church choir directed by Ken Kronek. She closed the folder again and met his eyes.

They were leveled on her without the slightest embarrassment.

"All right," he said, "now you know."

She was stunned. "How long have you been collecting these?" she asked.

"Right from the beginning of your career till last week. There are two more folders in the drawer."

"But what was the point?"

"Maybe none, I don't know. Maybe just

that you were a hometown girl who made it, somebody I took inspiration from, somebody I tried to kiss one time on a school bus. Hell, I don't know. Old crushes die hard." He scooped up the file and turned away to put it back in the metal cabinet. When the drawer closed he remained facing it, hands bracketing his belt, breathing deeply. She studied the smooth surface of his white shirt back, the rim of his shoulder blades pushing against it like a kite frame in a gusty wind, the neatly trimmed hair above his white collar—so much more conservative than the Nashville shags worn by most of the musicians she hung around with. He could not help himself from giving away the fact that saying good-bye to her was turning out to be far more difficult than they'd expected.

If it was difficult for him, it was no less difficult for her.

"Look, Kenny, I have to go," she said quietly, trying to keep her voice from breaking. "I just wanted you to tell Casey that I'm sorry I couldn't talk to her before I left, but here's my card. It's got my unlisted phone number on it, so she can call me anytime. And I just want you to know that when she comes down to Nashville I'll take very good care of her. She's going to be living with me for a while at least, and as soon as she gets a job I'll help her find someplace to live. I'm going to try to talk her into getting into Vanderbilt in the fall, just in case the music career doesn't fly, and even if it does, she'll never regret college. I'll introduce her to good people and I'll always be there for her, so you don't have to worry, Kenny, honest."

He turned around at last and she saw the pent-up emotion in his face, equal to that within her.

They both spoke at once.

"Tess—"

"Kenny—"

They barely got the names out before she was in his arms, not kissing him, but drawn up high and hard against his chest in a painful good-bye. She clung to his shoulders, her business card bent in half, the pen in his shirt pocket biting into her right breast. He smelled so familiar, and felt so stable and reliable, the rock upon which her mother had leaned long before Tess had learned what a wonderful man he was.

"I'm going to miss you," she whispered.

"I'm going to miss you, too."

She pulled off her sunglasses and they hung against his back while their eyes began to sting. After a long time he put a hand on the back of her head and pressed her forehead against his neck, very tightly, so she couldn't look up. When he spoke, his voice sounded tortured. "On Saturday . . ." he managed, and swallowed as if unsure he could go on. "When I said to your mother that I just might fall in love anyway, I was talking about—"

"No, don't." She lurched back and covered his lips with her hand. "Don't say it. It's not true anyway. This was just a . . . a crazy fling at a wedding reception—we both agreed, right?"

He reached up for her wrist and dragged her hand down, freeing his mouth. He held her hand over his hurting heart as they drank each other in, saying good-bye with their eyes and realizing no other ending was possible. "Yes," he whispered sadly. "We both agreed."

When they kissed she was crying and his chest hurt so badly he felt as if he had broken a rib.

The kiss was bittersweet, and when it

ended the embrace continued for several more heartbeats.

"Watch after Momma," she whispered.

"I will," he whispered back.

Then she withdrew, letting her palms slide down his arms until only their fingertips touched. They each tried smiling, doing terrible jobs of it.

" 'Bye," she whispered.

" 'Bye," he mouthed, his voice failing at last.

She took a step back and the contact broke, leaving his arms outstretched before they fell uselessly to his sides.

She opened his office door and looked back at him one more time before walking out of his life, back to her own.

FIFTEEN

SHE REACHED NASHVILLE at a quarter to five, exited I-40 and wound her way toward Music Row, southeast of downtown. Home could wait. Right now she needed an infusion of what she had missed, the vitality and energy flowing from those twelve square blocks south of Division Street where the business of record producing created the heartbeat of Music City. As if its lifeblood seeped into her own and powered her, she felt invigorated as she approached her office. At the foot of Demonbreun a larger-than-life-sized likeness of Randy Travis welcomed her from a red-brick wall. Tourists moved in and out of souvenir shops and climbed the ramp into the Country Music Hall of Fame. In front of Sony's offices a sign promoted Mary Chapin Carpenter's latest album. MCA lauded Vince Gill's. Along Music Square East and West, headquarters of industry-related businesses lined both sides of the street—law firms, recording studios, video production companies, music publishing companies, ASCAP and BMI, who tracked radio usage and collected royalties, booking agencies, offices of various record labels, offices of America's best-known country recording artists, and restaurants where number-one parties were thrown for the most successful.

Her own office was located in a century-old Victorian house on Music Square West, a three-story monstrosity painted several shades of yellow with a parking lot shaded by four huge basswood trees that were nearly as old as the house itself. Out front on a wooden signpost, an oval brass plaque announced, simply, Wintergreen Enterprises. She had chosen the name to remind herself of how far she'd come from that little burg in Missouri to the top of the country charts and her place as a respected businesswoman in an industry that for decades had been dominated by men. Under the umbrella of Wintergreen Enterprises fell several individually successful companies that had each been born out of necessity or common sense. Her music-publishing company came about when she realized how many talented writers were approaching her to sing their songs, many of which had neither been copyrighted nor published yet. She figured, Why pay another publishing company royalties on her records when she could be collecting them herself? Her specialty clothing operation created custom-designed concert costumes not only for herself but for other recording artists as well. Five years ago when she'd run into a scheduling snag and been kept on tenterhooks not knowing if her posters and buttons would be made in time for one of her concerts, she had purchased a small printing company that created posters, buttons, fan club newsletters and concert programs for her, and did some highly profitable contract work for other performers as well. There was also the small fleet of jets she used and leased to others.

All of this remained secondary, however, to the phenomenally successful operation that kept Tess McPhail on top of the country charts. That operation scheduled roughly a hundred and twenty concert dates a year and provided the essential organizational force allowing her to coproduce her own albums and videos, act as talent in those videos, do publicity, keep contact with fan clubs in every major city of America, and pay the salaries of over fifty permanent employees required to keep such a behemoth operational.

And Tess McPhail oversaw every aspect of it herself.

When she walked into Wintergreen Enterprises, she walked into the hub of her success.

Physical coolness struck her full force when she opened the back door and stepped from the private rear entry through the kitchen that was now used as a copy room and canteen. She passed the former servants' stairway, the one she commonly used to reach her second-floor office, and heard the hum of various conversations as she entered the central hall. The walls throughout the house were cream, the floors were hardwood, and the windows shuttered in white to hold back Nashville's intense summer heat. Country music played softly on a built-in sound system as she entered the main hall where oversized reproductions of her album covers trimmed the walls.

Her receptionist sat at a desk with her back to the ornate stairwell, her blond hair twisted up high in back but left to trail to her shoulders from the temple.

"Hey, Jan, I'm back."

Jan Nash swiveled her chair slowly and broke into a smile. She was in her mid-thirties, pretty as a Barbie doll and shaped like one. Jan looked smashing in a black scuba dress, her makeup fresh and flattering, silver loops at her ears. She rolled back her chair without hurry and rose in black high-heeled boots.

"Hey, Mac, welcome back. We sure missed you." She had a pronounced Southern drawl that made "you" sound like "yeeuuu."

"Thanks, Jan. It feels great to walk in here. I can't wait to get back to work."

"Sorry to hear about Papa John."

"Isn't it awful?"

Others heard Tess's voice and came out of the various downstairs offices to offer much the same greeting. Soon Tess moved on to her own office upstairs. It occupied the entire width of the rear, which faced east and enjoyed the dappled green shade from the basswoods outside. In a smaller adjoining office Kelly Mendoza was talking on the phone, and turned to smile when she saw her boss approaching through the connecting doorway. Kelly was Cuban, twenty-nine, five feet eight and regal, with a mass of long black hair as shiny as spilled ink, worn today in an explosion of ringlets. Her jet eyes tilted up at the corners and her skin was smooth and dark as a pecan shell. She was dressed in a silk suit the color of green tea with a multicolored silk scarf caught under the collar.

"Mac . . . welcome back."

"It's good to be here."

After seven years of working together, the two women hugged, but not for long. They both were geared to accomplish more in a single workday than most people accomplish in two.

Kelly said, "I'm sorry about Papa John."

"We all are. Do you have details about the memorial service?"

"Tomorrow morning, eleven A.M. at the Ryman, singers gathering one hour beforehand for a brief rehearsal."

"Good. What else?"

"I've sent flowers in your name, as well as some from Wintergreen Enterprises, but you'll want to sign the sympathy card on your desk. Burt Sheer called three times since lunch and Jack wants you to call him the minute you get in. He's got studio time scheduled for Wednesday and wants to talk to you about who you want for backup singers. Peter Steinberg got a call from Disney World asking if you'd be interested in them doing a Tess McPhail day sometime next year—short performance, be in the parade on Main Street U.S.A., do an autographing—that sort of thing. He wants you to call him. Cathy Mack has five dress designs she wants you to look at and Ralph wants to start concert rehearsals as soon as you feel like your head is above water."

Kelly went with Tess into her office, indicating the stacks of correspondence on the console beside her desk. "There are notes on everything I've told you. This stack needs immediate attention, this stack could wait a couple of days, and this one I've already seen to. Oh, one other thing—and this one isn't good—Carla's got an appointment with a throat specialist. That problem with her voice is still hanging on."

Concern crimped Tess's brow. Carla not only sang backup on some of her recordings, she was also supposed to go on this tour.

"Still?"

Kelly nodded solemnly.

"Is it worse?"

"Not worse, just the same. But she's worried, I can tell."

"No wonder. It's been bothering her for at least six months."

"Closer to a year, she said."

The phone chirped softly, and Kelly picked it up at Tess's desk.

"It's Burt." Kelly handed the receiver to Tess and returned to her own office, giving Tess privacy.

"Hi, Burt," Tess said, dropping into her familiar leather chair.

"You're back. Figured you would be when I heard about Papa John. Hey, I'm really sorry, Tess."

They talked for a while, then Burt said, "I really missed you, babe."

His voice raised within her none of the longing that it had when he'd called her in

Wintergreen, before she'd kissed the man across the alley. Though they were supposed to have a date that week, she canceled it, using her sadness over Papa John as an excuse. Whatever feelings she'd had for Burt Sheer had been dulled by the memories she now carried of Kenny Kronek.

But it became clear to Tess within an hour of her return that she was right about Kenny's place in her life. There was none. Though at times over the past four weeks she'd questioned where she belonged, she had merely to face catching up with business to understand that her place here was fixed. She belonged here in Nashville—absolutely—where her career continued to click along even during her absence, where her staff knew her needs even before she could voice them, and where her future was already mapped out.

The latest *Gavin Report* sat on her desk, faceup, and beneath it *Billboard,* and *Radio & Record.* Her next single would be released in mid-June and another one in August (hopefully the one she and Casey hadn't even recorded yet!) before the September release of the new CD. It was expected to go platinum, maybe double platinum—four million fans waiting to buy her songs. The producer of the Super Bowl halftime show wanted to know if she'd headline a year and a half from now. Her major sponsor, Wrangler, called to set up a photo session in some place called the San Blas Islands, where they proposed to photograph her in a pair of their jeans in the surf. They wanted the ad campaign to hit the newsstands at the same time her new CD hit the stores. And Nissan had somehow found out she owned one of their products and wanted to discuss the possibility of a contract for television commercials.

There was no place in her life for a man.

Nevertheless, if one in particular phoned, she didn't want to miss his call.

"Kelly?"

"Yes?" Kelly appeared in the open doorway.

"Phone calls from either Casey Kronek or Kenny Kronek are to be put through to me immediately, no matter what's going on, and if I'm not here, make sure I get the message as soon as possible, okay?"

"Will do."

"Casey is a graduating senior from my hometown who'll be staying with me for a while in June. She's going to do the harmonies on one of my songs."

"Lucky girl," Kelly remarked.

"Talented girl," Tess replied. "She helped me write it."

"Wow." Quiet surprise lit Kelly's face and made it even more attractive. Without asking questions, she returned to her desk and made a note of the names, amazing Tess again not only with her proficiency, but with her ability to keep her nose out of Tess's personal business. In Tess's line of work, this kind of tactfulness was invaluable.

Tess worked till eight o'clock, discovering, to her surprise, that after a month at her mother's, her body clock demanded supper at six. She ignored the hunger pangs until she could no more, and by the time she was heading home her stomach ached. But she bypassed fast food in favor of familiar surroundings and pointed the car southwest.

She lived in the city of Brentwood, in a subdivision called Woodway. It was announced by a lavish brick entrance surrounded by sculptured shrubbery and flowers of red, white and blue on either side of the gilded sign.

As Tess neared home she lowered the windows on the Z and breathed in the warm, humid southern air, something she would not have thought of doing a month ago when she drove out of here. A month ago she would have sped up the road with her tinted windows up and noticed little of her surroundings.

Tonight she noticed . . . and appreciated.

It was one of those evenings when twilight refuses to hurry, and as her car climbed up Heathrow Boulevard, the oaks and elms spread like black chapel veils against a butter-yellow sky that thickened to peach at the tree-caps. In front of the house two doors from hers, Mr. Ruddy had just finished waxing his classic '68 Corvette. He waved as she passed, but she encountered him so seldom that she didn't even know his first name. She thought he worked at NationsBank but wasn't sure. Two boys came coasting down the hill on bicycles, and she waited for them to pass her driveway before pulling in. It struck her that she knew neither of the boys; knew, in fact, no children in the neighborhood, or any of the homeowners.

She couldn't help recalling Mrs. Perry reminiscing at the wedding reception about how Tess, as a little girl, had come to her door asking for English toffee. She thought of the view out her mother's kitchen window and how she herself had watched the comings and goings at the house across the alley.

So different here. So isolated by success.

Her towering living room windows faced the street, and through them Tess saw that Maria had left a lamp on. The garage door rolled up at the touch of a button, and Tess noted, to her surprise, that Maria's little blue station wagon was still inside. She hauled her duffel bag and a green suitcase through the back entry, calling, "Maria, are you still here?"

"Miss Mac, welcome home!" Maria was in the kitchen, topping off the water in a bouquet of red zinnias that sat in the middle of the the table.

Tess dropped her gear. "Lord o' mercy, what are you still doing here?"

"Waiting for you. Nobody likes to come home to an empty house."

"But I always come home to an empty house."

"Not after you've been gone this long. I'll take your bags upstairs, Miss Mac."

"Thanks, Maria, but I can do it myself."

"Nonsense. Give me that."

Maria was Mexican, in her fifties, spindle-legged and bantam-sized. Her hair was streaky gray and held back in an unceremonious French roll. Though she looked about as strong as a ten-year-old boy, she had no trouble wresting the suitcase out of Tess's hand.

"All right, then, we'll each take one," Tess conceded, hauling the duffel bag herself. "But your family will be expecting you."

"I told them I might be late. I didn't know what time you'd get in. How is your momma?"

"She's doing very well, walking with a cane, getting happy on wine at weddings."

"And your sisters?"

"They're fine. I saw them a lot while I was gone. Maria, thank you for staying."

Maria flapped a hand as if no thanks were needed, and the pair climbed an open, flying stairway that curved up to the second story, where a C-shaped landing overlooked the living room. The guest suites lay straight ahead and to the right. Tess turned left through double doors into her own bedroom suite. Unlike at Mary's, everything here was new, bright, coordinated, all the decorating done in neutrals with only touches of pastel color here and there.

Maria had made sure lamps were lit everywhere, and Tess paused to let her eyes wander over the black metal crown bed with its canopy frame looped with yards of white gauze that trailed on the floor at the four corners. Other than that gauze and some throw pillows on the bed, the decorating was spare, the windows were naked, the walls ivory, the carpet and sofa white. Double doors—closed tonight—led to a balcony overlooking the pool.

Tess dropped her bag onto an upholstered bench at the foot of the bed, and there beside it stood her brand new M. L. Leddy boots. They were made of green ostrich skin and brought a smile—everything perfect here, so different than at Mary's. Everything seen to for her.

She sat on the bench to try on the boots.

Maria said, "I saved the box in case they have to be sent back." She went around the room lowering white pleated shades.

"Thanks, Maria."

"You want me to help you unpack?"

"No thanks, tomorrow will be time enough. You can go home now."

"I'll go home when I think I should," the woman said with her back turned as she headed downstairs again. Tess smiled and took a walk across her bedroom to the white marble bath/dressing room, sampling the fit of the new boots, smiling at the bud vase with a single peach-colored rose that Maria had put on the vanity, the fresh salmon-colored towels on the racks, her favorite robe lying on a bench in the corner. Though she was used to living alone, she was remarkably happy to have the garrulous housekeeper here tonight to make some noise around the place and create a welcome. She went back through her bedroom to the central balcony and stood looking down into the living room. It had sixteen-foot ceilings and was decorated in tones of white ranging from snow to oyster with only a touch of peach in the furniture. A cream-colored grand piano—one of two in the house—stood at the foot of the immense front windows. A white-brick fireplace on the left was flanked by floor-to-ceiling bookshelves. A giant slab of glass resting on two short white plaster columns created the coffee table between two sofas that faced each other at a right angle to the fireplace.

It was as different from the houses in Wintergreen as Picasso is from Renoir. The contrast struck her fully, and for only a second, left a faint emptiness.

Leaning over the railing, she called, "Hey, Maria, anybody call?"

"No," Maria shouted back from the depths of the kitchen, "just Miss Kelly this afternoon to let me know you got in."

"Nobody named Casey?"

"No."

"Casey Kronek?"

"No."

"Anyone named Kenny?"

"No."

"Oh," Tess said softly to herself, disappointed. She raised her voice and bent over the rail again. "If either one of them calls—whenever—you're to put them through to me immediately. Casey or Kenny Kronek—got that?"

"Got that, Miss Mac."

Like Kelly, Maria knew how to keep

Tess's personal life personal. She did her job, refrained from gossip and didn't ask what was none of her business. If she garnered inside information during the general day-to-day activities around the house she treated it all as confidential. At Christmastime she got a bonus that many executives would envy.

Upstairs, Tess washed her face, stripped off her jeans and put on a one-piece cotton lounger, then returned to the kitchen, a tile-floored room with copper pans hanging over an island stove, and French doors set into a bay that jutted into a screened porch. Without a word of instruction, Maria had set out a Caesar salad topped with grilled Cajun chicken, a cobalt-blue goblet of water, a smaller goblet of skim milk and an inviting plate of fresh fruit. It waited on a blue placemat on the distressed pine table where Tess ate her informal meals. In the center of the table was the pitcher full of zinnias, more than likely picked from Maria's own garden.

"Maria, bless your soul," Tess said, sitting down immediately and stabbing a forkful of crisp romaine.

"Looks like you put on a couple extra

pounds," the housekeeper noted. "I'll get you back in shape in no time. I pressed your midnight blue suit for the memorial service tomorrow. Too bad about Papa John."

"Thank you, Maria. Now will you please go home?"

"Yes, Miss Mac, I believe I will. You can put your dirty dishes in the dishwasher when you finish."

"I'll be sure to do that."

Maria found her sweater and purse. "Well, good night, then. It's nice to have you back. There's fresh-squeezed orange juice in the fridge and bagels in the drawer for morning."

"Thanks again, Maria."

When the back door closed and the garage door quit rumbling, Tess was left in silence. She stopped chewing and listened to the hum of the refrigerator. She glanced at the copper pans above the stove, at the uncluttered cabinet tops—perfect order everywhere—and sat motionless in her chair, experiencing nine-thirty on a week night in a 1.4-million-dollar house big enough for eight but built for only one. She had resisted building it, but her accountant had advised her she needed to diversify her investments, and since real estate would appreciate, why not have the comforts of a nice house at the same time that her money was growing? She had bought the first jet by then so she could be home more nights, even during concert season, and she'd thought, why not?

But as she rinsed her plate and put it in the dishwasher she wished for her small apartment up on Belmont Boulevard where she could hear the owners' television through the floor and the occasional sound of voices drifting up from an open window.

She turned out the lights downstairs and went up to take a whirlpool bath in the marble tub that could easily hold two but never had. While she was sitting in it with the jets on, the phones rang—seven of them, all over the house—and she answered the one on the wall at the foot of the tub.

"Hello?" she said, killing the jets.

"Hi, Mac, it's me, Casey."

"Oh, Casey, it's good to hear your voice!" Joy sluiced through her, coupled with the realization of how lonely she'd been. "Hold on just a minute, will you?"

She got out of the tub, wrapped herself head and body in thick white terry, and transferred to the bedside phone, tossing five assorted pillows onto the floor and sitting back against two big square European jobs with custom cases. "Casey? I'm back. Listen, hon, I'm sorry I had to leave Wintergreen so suddenly without telling you."

"It's okay. Dad told me about your friend. I'm sure sorry, Mac."

"I won't be brave and pretend he wasn't important to me, because he was."

"I know. Dad told me you were crying."

"Yes, well . . ." She'd been crying not only for the loss of Papa John, but because she was leaving Kenny. "It's good to be back and keeping busy. It takes my mind off things."

"You still working?"

"No, I'm done for the day. I just had supper and took a bath."

"I hope it's okay that I called there . . . at your house, I mean."

"Of course."

"I know it's your unlisted number and everything, but Dad said—"

"It's fine, Casey, anytime. I told both Maria and Kelly that they're to put you through anytime."

"Great. Well, listen, I just wanted to let

you know I was thinking about you. I can't wait for June. Now Dad wants to say something . . . talk to you soon. 'Bye, Mac.''

Before she could prepare for the impact of his voice it came across the wire, subdued, hushed, somewhat thick-throated like his good-bye this morning.

"Hi," he said, nothing more, only the single, lonesome word. It filled her heart with an amazing rush of emotion as she sat in her big empty house missing him, wishing she could see his face, touch it, talk, laugh, maybe ride out to Dexter Hickey's and scratch some horses' noses.

"Hi," she managed at last, feeling her senses reaching out to him even from two hundred fifty miles away. Seconds passed while neither of them spoke, only pictured themselves as they'd been in his office, kissing good-bye.

Finally he said, "You got home okay?"

"Yes, just fine."

"I worried about you."

There were men who worried about her daily—her producer, her business manager, her agent—but they were paid to. Nobody paid Kenny Kronek to worry about her. The very notion brought pressure to her throat and lowered an anvil to her chest.

"You mustn't worry about me, Kenny."

"You were crying."

"No, I wasn't."

"Yes, you were. Why won't you admit it?"

"All right, I was, but not for long. I put a tape on and just drove it out of my system."

"Drove what out of your system?"

"You," she admitted. At the other end of the line she heard only his breathing, and thought how pointless this was. "Is that what you wanted to hear, Kenny?"

No reply came, only the electronic hum of the phone, and finally, the sound of Kenny clearing his throat. "I'm shuffling around here looking out the back window at your mother's house and it seems like I should be able to walk over there and knock on the door and you'll answer."

"Kenny, that's never going to happen, not . . . not like it did this past month."

"I know," he said, so quiet and forlorn she could almost picture his chin on his chest.

"It was a fling at a wedding, nothing more. We agreed, remember?"

"Yeah . . ." He cleared his throat again. "Yeah, right. We agreed."

Yet another silence crawled by, filled with useless wishes.

"Well, listen . . . I'm bushed, and tomorrow's going to be rough, so I'd better say good night."

"Sure . . ." he said. "Well, take care. I miss you."

"I miss you, too. Tell Casey good night."

"I will."

"Are Momma's lights still on?"

"No. It's dark over there."

She smiled. And closed her eyes. And realized there were tears on her lashes. "I forgot to call her and tell her I got here okay."

"I'll tell her in the morning before I go to work."

"Thanks, Kenny." Dear Kenny, always concerned about Mary.

"Sure. Well . . . sleep tight, Tess."

"You, too."

When she'd hung up she remained on the bed, heart-heavy, the phone on her stomach, her ankles crossed, still wrapped in her white terry robe, aware of her nakedness inside it, and of how much she missed sex, wishing she'd allowed herself to have it with Kenny last Saturday night.

Two tears rolled down and stung the skin beside her nose. She swiped at them with the tail end of her terry-cloth belt, and sniffed once, then sat on, staring through a blur at the end of the belt while working it over with a thumbnail. She wondered if Faith had been at Kenny's house tonight. Had they eaten supper together like a regular little Cleaver family? Had he kissed her hello when she arrived? The thought made Tess angry and depressed by turns. She wondered if he'd call here often—she hadn't expected him to do so at all—and if he would continue his plaintive pursuit which could not, must not, lead anywhere. She wondered if, when Casey came to Nashville, he would bring her or if she'd drive down alone. (In that rickety pickup truck? No way.) So if he came, and if the opportunity presented itself, would they take this ill-fated affair to bed the way they wanted to?

She sighed, tipped her head back against the wrought-iron headboard and closed her eyes.

There were no answers, of course, only the enormity of her obligations, the silent luxury of her home, and the confusion in her heart.

SIXTEEN

THEY LAID PAPA JOHN TO REST but kept his memory alive—Tess McPhail and a list of mourners that read like the *Who's Who* of country music: Garth, Reba, Vince, Alan, John Michael and more.

Congregating with her peers, sharing music with them again, even if for so sad a reason, pointed out to Tess that she had been out of the mainstream too long. She was back. She had music to make, work to do, work she loved. She'd better get to it without mooning about Kenny Kronek.

She did exactly that in the days that followed.

On her first full day back in the office she had an intense six-hour meeting with her business manager, Dane Tully, to go over everything that had happened since she'd been away. She met with Ross Hardenberg, Ralph Thornleaf and Amanda Brimhall, respectively her road manager, producer of her upcoming tour and clothing designer to discuss the show in detail before rehearsals began. She went into the studio and recorded the overdub for "Tarnished Gold," so Jack Greaves could complete the vocal comp of the song, then went back afterward to give her final approval of the finished product. Working with Jack, she chose the background singers and studio musicians for "Old Souls," the new song by Ivy Britt, and spent a day in the studio recording it. Seven record label executives—from the president down to the vice president of marketing—came by to hear the album in progress. Tess and Jack met with them to discuss jacket photo, jacket design and the release dates of individual singles from the album. Tess explained that they had one more song to record and she wanted it to be the title song—could they wait till they heard it?—because she thought it would make the best video off the entire album. They listened to the rough cut of "Small Town Girl," the one made in Mary's living room, and agreed to wait until it was recorded and mixed before deciding on the album title. She and Jack discussed sequencing (the order in which the songs would appear on the album), which everyone considered vital to an album's success.

Tess met with Sheila Sardyk, the woman who coordinated all of her fan clubs, so Sheila could compose the next newsletter for fans and get it out to club leaders in all the cities around America. She spent two days on the photo shoot, for which a photographer, his assistant, and a stylist were flown in from New York. At the end of the shoot she took them out to dinner.

She had her quarterly meeting with her CPA to project both her income and her quarterly taxes, and to discuss the changing laws regarding payment of contributions into the retirement funds of her employees. She talked with her advisor from Merrill Lynch about long-term investments and the constant shifting and diversification of Wintergreen Enterprise's financial portfolio.

She received a treatment for a video, which she read and disliked, and called the MCA marketing department with ideas of her own. She did an interview with *Good Housekeeping* magazine for an article that would run in September, to coincide with the release of her new album. She posed for their photographer for two hours, then played hostess over luncheon with the *Good Housekeeping* crew at her own home before they flew back to New York.

She signed over three hundred autographs (in six batches) on post cards and publicity photos for fans who had requested them by mail and had sent in their requests through the clubs.

Concert rehearsals began.

On the personal side, she went to the doctor complaining of fatigue. He took a blood count and ordered her to eat more red meat. She received a beautiful letter and card from Mindy Alverson, complimenting her on her singing at the wedding, promising they would not lose touch again, and asking for a luncheon date the next time Tess came to Wintergreen. She answered Mindy's letter with a handwritten note, accepting the invitation for next November (after the tour ended) and offering free concert tickets anytime Mindy and her husband wanted them, in any city they chose. She lost the five pounds she'd gained in Wintergreen. She made sure she called her mother every other night, and Renee on the weekends. She received a graduation announcement from Casey—she would graduate the Friday night before Memorial Day—and put off answering it, wanting to fly up there and see Momma and Kenny, too, but afraid she couldn't afford to take the time off.

Burt got back in town and called again, and she finally agreed to go out with him. They met at the Stockyard and sat in one of the small, intimate dining rooms fashioned from yesteryear's cattle exchange offices. Burt ordered the Cowboy, a hearty beef steak with grilled onions, and Tess ordered the live Maine lobster from the tank up front. They toasted each other with wine, and caught up on each other's lives, and after dinner went downstairs to the Bull Pen Lounge and danced a couple fast ones to the house band until some tourists who'd been eyeing her finally got up the courage to come over and ask for autographs, then she and Burt left.

At Tess's house Burt sat down at the piano in the living room and said, "I wrote a song for you. Come here and I'll sing it." She sat beside him on the sleek cream-colored bench and watched his blunt fingers move over the keys while he sang a song that would have swelled the hearts of most women. It was called "I Wanna Be There When You Come Home," and when it ended Burt Sheer took Tess into his arms and lowered his bearded face and kissed her with enough feeling to raise the fine hairs all over her body. But while he did so, she pretended he was Kenny Kronek.

She forced Kenny from her mind, giving the kiss an honest chance, kissing Burt back the way he wanted to be kissed. But the beard, though soft, somehow no longer appealed. And the taste, though pleasant, was not the one she knew. And his beautiful musical accolade, though touching, was eclipsed by the kind deeds of another for her mother, and even for herself.

Burt ran his hand to Tess's breast and she thought how ideal that the hand played music, like her; that he sang, like her; that he was part of the close Nashville family of musicians, like her. How simple it would be for them to slip into each other's lives, two who understood the performers' lifestyle and all its demands and vagaries.

But nothing happened inside Tess. In that

visceral, carnal core where sexual abstinence should have created a quick starburst . . . nothing happened.

She caught his wrist as it descended toward her stomach, and said, "No, Burt."

He drew back and looked into her eyes. "I thought you wanted it, too."

"I thought I might, but . . . I'm sorry."

He returned his hand to her ribs and said, "The last time we were together I thought this was where we were headed."

"The last time, maybe. But things happen."

"Things?"

She took his hand from her ribs and held it, dropping her eyes while the two of them remained side by side on the piano bench.

"You met someone," he said.

"Sort of."

He studied her downcast face, then hooked both hands over the edge of the bench and hunched his shoulders.

"So is it serious?"

"No."

"Well, if it's not serious, then what's going on here?"

"It's someone I knew when I was young.

Someone from back home. He's sort of a friend of the family."

Burt studied her in silence awhile, thoughtful. Then he raised his hands and let them slap his knees. "Well . . . how can I compete with that? You and I haven't got a history."

"I enjoyed supper though, and dancing."

Paltry crumbs, her words, and they both knew it.

"Well . . ." He sighed and pushed himself up. "I know when it's time to make an exit."

She walked him to the door. Their goodbyes were stilted until he took her hand and looked down at it while speaking. "You probably think that every struggling musician who comes along is playing you for how you can boost his career. I just want you to know I'm not one of 'em."

And with that he walked out, leaving her to realize that what he'd said was true, and had been for years. Every struggling musician who paid her attention became suspect for exactly the reason he'd cited. Though she'd had a gut feeling Burt's motives were honorable, how in the world could she tell, when she was worth upward of twenty million dollars? When she could spark a career with little more than a word to the right label executive?

But Kenny had no musical career. He didn't want her money or her fame or a home in Nashville. He wanted exactly what he had in Wintergreen. He'd told her so, and that's why she hadn't called him or answered Casey's invitation, afraid that he might be the one to answer the phone and she'd get all soft and mushy about him again.

SHE PUT OFF MAKING THAT CALL until it absolutely could not be avoided. Casey would graduate on Friday night. At nine on the preceding Tuesday night, Tess was exhausted. She had just finished another hundred signatures and writer's cramp had set in. She had a bad case of PMS that had given her the disposition of Joan Crawford, and she wasn't too crazy about the haircut the New York stylist had given her. Kelly had had to leave the office early to go to the dentist, and Tess, forced to do her own dialing and waiting, had been put on hold by a new secretary who forgot her on the line.

Shortly after that Carla Niles had called with the news that her regular doctor said there was nothing wrong with her throat, but she still had a raspiness in her voice, so she had set up an appointment with a throat specialist. Until she saw him the rehearsals for the concert were in limbo. Then, to top it all off, Tess had run out to grab a sandwich for supper and on her way she caught the handle of her favorite big gray bag in the car door and it had trailed on the blacktop all the way to the restaurant and gotten rubbed in half. Returning to the office, Tess made the mistake of reading a batch of fan mail in which one letter chewed her out for insulting half the women in the world by using the phrase "just a housewife" in one of her songs. Did she think being a housewife was easy? If so, she should give it a try and find out what real work was!

All in all, it had been a horseshit day when she picked up the phone to dial Casey's house at nine o'clock that night.

As she'd feared, Kenny answered.

"Hello?"

Perhaps she was working too hard, perhaps it was the PMS, but for whatever reason, hearing Kenny's friendly voice unglued

her. Without the slightest warning, she began to cry. Trying to disguise the fact, she
failed to reply immediately.

"Hello?" Kenny repeated, sharper. Then,
growing irritated, he barked, "Hello, *who is
this*?"

"Kenny, it's T-Tess," she managed.

"Tess, what's wrong?" he said, the
change from irritation to concern immediate
in his voice.

"N-nothing," she blubbered, then,
". . . everything. Hell, I don't know. It's just
been an awful day, that's all."

"Tess," he said, the way he might to a
child, soothing. "Hey, come on, darlin',
nothing's so bad it won't feel better if you
talk about it. I'm here, you can talk to me."

She felt better already, so decided to
baby herself a little, something she rarely
did. "Hey, Kenny, would you call me darlin'
one more time? It sounds good tonight."

"Darlin'," he repeated matter-of-factly,
"now you go ahead and talk. What was so
awful today?"

So she talked. She admitted to Kenny
that her empire was getting to be more than
she could handle without relinquishing personal control. But there were so many sto-

ries about superstars whose dominions had crumbled under mismanagement, whose agents or accountants or business managers had cheated the stars they worked for, undermining them to the point of ruin.

"I'm not going to let that happen to me!" she vowed. "And the surest way to let it happen is to give over control to someone else. That's why I watch everything so carefully." Under questioning, she admitted she was keeping tabs on more than any one human being should be expected to, and she'd been doing it for eighteen years while her business concerns grew and grew.

"You've got to learn to delegate," Kenny said. "That's what you pay these people for."

"I know. But look what happened to Willy Nelson. He's probably still putting on concerts to pay off his debts."

"Is there someone you employ whom you don't trust?"

"Well . . ." She thought for a second. "No."

"There," he said reasonably, "it's you, not them. You know, Tess, it's possible that you think of yourself as omnipotent, and when you come right down to it, that's a pretty egotistical attitude, isn't it? Did you ever think that by not trusting them more, you undermine them? By placing your full, unadulterated trust in them you might get more production out of them, more cooperation, certainly a pride in their work that will boost their egos. And you know what happens to output when egos get boosted."

She knew he was right, knew, too, that most people wouldn't have had the temerity to say something like that to Tess McPhail because of who she was. She respected him for his honesty as well as for his sound advice. "How did you get so wise, Mr. Kronek?" she asked, feeling much better, her frustration and weariness dissipating.

He chuckled quietly. "By running a two-person office with such a grinding routine that the last time either one of us surprised the other was when Miriam came out of the bathroom with the hem of her skirt accidentally hooked up on the waistband of her panty hose." Tess burst out laughing while Kenny went on. "She turned her back to me to sit down in her desk chair and I looked through my office door and raised a finger as if to say, 'Hey, Miriam, guess what?' but, hell's afire, you ever tried to tell your secretary that you just got a wide-angle shot of her hind end? Wouldn't have been so bad if it was a shapely one, but you've seen Miriam, haven't you?''

"No, I haven't." Tess was still laughing.

"You haven't! Well, Miriam's the kind of woman that if you ran into her at a bar you'd say, 'Hey, Miriam, pull up a couple o' stools and let me buy you a drink!'"

Tess's laughter billowed once more, igniting his own, and they spent some enjoyable time letting it pour forth across a couple hundred miles of telephone wire. When their mirth wound down, Tess wound right down with it. She released a huge breath, stretched out in her chair and ran a hand up the back of her hair. "Gosh, I feel so much better."

"Well, of course you do," he said smugly. "I'm good for you."

"You really are, Kenny. Too good."

They enjoyed the thought for a few beats before he inquired, "So tell me—where are you right now?"

"Still in my office on Music Row."

"Time for you to call it a day, isn't it?"

"Yes. Actually, I'm really tired tonight, and kind of cranky. At least I was until I talked to

you." They were both affected by the signif-
icance of what she'd said and sat awhile
absorbing it.

"So," she asked, more quietly, "is Faith
there tonight?"

It took him a moment to answer. His
voice had grown subdued. "No, just Casey
and me."

"I really called to talk to Casey. I got her
graduation announcement and the invitation to the party on Saturday. Wish I could
be there, but . . . I'm afraid I can't." Her
disappointment was unmistakable.

"I wish you could be here, too."

Tess knew she should end the conversation and ask him to put Casey on the line,
but she simply could not let him go yet.
Outside, in the distance, a siren cre-
scendoed and faded, and down the hall a
fax beeped and started printing while she
imagined the sound of crickets in the backyards in Wintergreen, and him on the
kitchen phone, and Casey in her room playing her guitar, and the soft summer evening
settling blue upon the gardens. She pictured the houses with their backs to each
other, and the aged, narrow sidewalks that
had carried them toward one another dur-

ing their many encounters in the alley. She wanted with incredible intensity to be there, to step out onto her mother's stoop and see him walking toward her through the warm May night. She wanted to glide into his embrace and feel and smell and taste him once again. Instead, she could only imagine him and wonder if he'd detected the slight tremor in her voice, if he understood how valiantly she was trying not to be jealous, to be realistic about what could and could not happen between them.

"I suppose Faith is doing the party for Casey."

"Yes. She's been making grocery lists, and ordering party trays, and the two of them have been digging through old photo albums and putting together a bulletin board of old pictures."

Tess had never longed to be a mother, but at that moment she would cheerfully have traded places with Faith Oxbury. On Tess's desk were pictures of her nieces and nephews, the only "children" she would probably ever have. Her eyes lingered on them, then she drove another thorn into her own flesh with a question that had been hovering in her mind for some time.

"Kenny, may I ask you something?"

"Sure." Funny how a single syllable with sandpaper edges could give away how a man feels.

"When Casey moves away, will Faith be moving in with you?"

He took some time answering, time while Tess discovered she was holding her breath and cataloguing each beat of her heart.

"I don't think so, Tess. This is a small town. Living arrangements like that are frowned upon."

She released the breath slowly and closed her eyes while they clung to their phones and listened to the clanging silence of things unsaid. It was torment and bliss reading between the lines, learning that each of them had missed and been missed, wondering how far to go in this conversation, which was getting dangerously intimate. Finally, when the ache in Tess's throat became too great to disregard, she clamped a hand across her forehead and uttered, "Jesus, I miss you, Kenny."

Like the rests in music, the silences in the conversation had become as vital as the spoken words. This one held them both by the throats. When he spoke at last, his voice held a note of frustration.

"I've already told you, I miss you, too, but what do you want from me, Tess? I can't stop my life for you!"

"I know. I know! I don't expect you to. But what if . . . what if . . ."

Silence.

A great, groaning, silence reaching across the distance.

"What if what?" he finally said.

"I don't know," she admitted haltingly. "I want . . . I want . . . to . . . to be with you . . . sometime . . . that's all. Just to be with you, do you understand?"

"To do what? Have an affair?"

"No!" Then more honestly, "I don't know, but a piece of my heart stayed in Wintergreen when I left, and I feel as if I left it there with you for safekeeping. Nothing's the same since I came back to Nashville, but I'd die without this, Kenny. I'd just die. This is my life! Yet I'm dying without you, too. I'm just so mixed up."

They thought for a while, groping for a solution, finding none.

Finally he spoke. "Maybe you love me, Tess. You ever think of that?"

"Yes, I have."

"But you wouldn't allow yourself to say it to me before you left, and you wouldn't let me say it to you."

"It's too scary. It would bring too many complications."

"For who? You or me?"

"Both of us."

"And you won't say it now."

"Because I'm not sure!"

"But you want me to end it with Faith—why?"

"I didn't say that!"

"No, but you hinted at it. You don't seem to understand that while Nashville and your career are your life, I've got one, too, and Faith is a big part of it."

"All right, all right! I don't want to argue, and anyway, it's silly, because we're arguing about something that's not even logical. I mean, I'm here, you're there, you have your business, I have my career and I'm gone a hundred and twenty days a year! Anybody with half a brain can see that what we've got here is a logistical stalemate, so I don't even know why we're on the subject!"

"Because we miss each other, that's why. And because maybe—just maybe—

we really are falling in love, so the question is, do we run away from it or face it?''

"Kenny, I called to RSVP an invitation to a graduation party. How did this conversation get so complicated?''

"What I'm trying to get you to understand is that it's complicated not only for you, but for me as well. And you know what? We *are* starting to argue, so what do you say we wish each other good night and I'll put Casey on? We can talk about this another time.''

"Fine,'' Tess retorted with a note of stubbornness.

"Fine,'' he repeated.

Then nothing happened.

"So put Casey on!'' Tess ordered.

"Okay,'' he barked, equally frustrated. "But let's get one thing straight. It was more than a roll in the grass and we both know it!'' The phone clunked and she heard him holler, "Hey, Casey, it's Tess!''

Casey came on quickly, exuberant, a big smile in her voice. "Hey, woman! Less than a week and I'll be there!''

"I know. Can't wait.''

"I'll be there Sunday afternoon—no, wait! Monday. Memorial Day.''

"Your room is waiting. I won't be able to get up there for your party on Saturday though. I'm sorry, hon."

"Aw, shoot, I knew that," Casey said cheerfully, "but I wanted to send you an invitation anyway."

"I should have called earlier, but I was trying to think of a way to work it out."

"It's okay."

"I thought of something I can send you for a graduation gift though, but you'll have to keep it to yourself."

"What's that?"

"How would you like to hear the songs from my new album before anybody else outside of Nashville gets to hear them?"

"Oh, my gosh, Mac, are you serious!! You're sending me *that*?"

"I can't wait to have you hear them, but you have to promise me you won't let anybody else hear the tape. Jack would have a shit fit if he found out I'm letting it go out. Promise?"

"Not even Dad?" Casey sounded disappointed.

"Well . . . maybe your dad, but nobody else. Not Faith, not Brenda or Amy, or anybody else. Just you and your dad, okay?"

"You got my promise, Mac."

"All right, then. I'll see you next Monday, and you and I will celebrate your graduation when you get down here."

"Darn right. When do we get to go into the studio?"

"On Tuesday. Jack's got it all scheduled."

"Jeez, I can't believe I'm even having this conversation! It's just too awesome to believe."

"Well, believe it. Now let me go. It's late and I'm still at the office and I want to go home."

"Okay . . . six days, woman!

"Six days. See you then."

THOSE SIX DAYS PASSED as swiftly as fallen leaves on a river. A blink of the eye and another day was gone. Another blink, another day. Tess express mailed a tape of her album-in-progress to Casey. She had Maria stock one of the guest suites with bathroom sundries, and the refrigerator with foods that a teenager would like. She tried not to think of Kenny, and for the most part, succeeded. There were major concerns that kept her mind occupied, the most important of which was the continuing throat problem of Carla Niles.

Nobody had thought much of it months ago when her voice began cracking and turning hoarse. A cold, they'd thought, or some upper-respiratory thing. But when it kept on, she'd begun voice lessons, hoping that proper technique might help. Several weeks into the lessons, when the problems continued, she'd consulted a doctor, who'd told her, "There's nothing wrong with your voice." So she'd gone on using it, which— in the end—turned out to be the worst thing she could have done.

Carla finally saw a throat specialist. His report came in on the Friday afternoon before Memorial Day. He told Carla she had a hypothyroid condition, that her body had quit producing thyroid hormones, affecting her vocal chords. The doctor ordered her to quit using her voice—not even to whisper!—for one month. After that, he said, even with medication it could take up to two years for Carla's voice to return to normal.

The news threw the McPhail camp into a tizzy. With rehearsals already begun for the concert tour, Jack Greaves, Dane Tully, Ross Hardenberg and Tess brainstormed about who they could get as a replacement. The town was full of girl singers playing the small clubs who aspired to get a record contract. A stint as backup singer for Tess McPhail could jump-start any one of their careers. Ross came up with a list, and at the top was a twenty-two-year-old named Liza Lyman whom Tess had heard and liked.

"But I'm not sure her range is right," Tess said.

"We can get her in and give her a try," Ross suggested. "Think about it over the weekend, and we'll talk about it again Tuesday at the session."

SEVENTEEN

IT WAS A HOT, BRIGHT AFTERNOON when Casey was expected. Maria had the holiday weekend off, so Tess had the house to herself. Given the size of the place, it seemed a shame it had held so few overnight guests, and none who had been as eagerly awaited. Tess found herself happy and anxious as she checked the house one last time. She had chosen the light blue suite for Casey. It had furniture of natural pine. On the bed a puffy coverlet of oversized blue-and-white checks brought the Tennessee sky into the room through lots of windows whose white shutters were folded aside. Tess gave the room a quick perusal: the flowers on the dresser, the blue towels in the bathroom, the shampoo and soap in the shower, the bubble bath on the tub. She turned on the sound system and two lights in the bedroom as well, just to give it that welcoming feel.

The guest wing held three suites, and maybe Tess had been foolish, but she'd also prepared one for Kenny.

He hadn't said a word about driving Casey down; neither had Tess asked. She regretted it now. Why hadn't she? Afraid he'd say no, maybe, and take away her anticipation.

She'd always referred to his suite as the dark blue one, though it was not dark at all. It was done with eggshell walls and shutters and navy blue paisley bedding, a more masculine room with mission-style furniture and terra-cotta accents. She had gone downtown Friday, to a little shop in the District, and bought talcum and soap wrapped in oatmeal brown paper that smelled woodsy—something a man would like. And she'd taken one yellow lily out of the bouquet in Casey's room and put it in a bud vase beside the navy blue hand towels in Kenny's bathroom.

She stood in his bedroom doorway with her hands knotted together, wondering what he would think if she invited him to

stay overnight before heading back to Wintergreen.

She realized, with some surprise, that she
wanted him to see her house, wanted him
to observe firsthand what she'd achieved,
what kind of lifestyle her success had af-
forded her—this cool, neutral place of spa-
cious comfort that she'd never actually
wanted much until now. Now she wanted it
so that she could show him she was capable of choosing, staffing and decorating a
place like this. A home.

She entered his room one last time and
turned on the sound system beside the
bed, leaving the volume low. At the west
windows she adjusted the banks of shutters to let in the afternoon light but keep out
the sun.

Bring her, Kenny, she thought. *Please
bring her yourself.*

But at two-thirty, when a red Ford Bronco
pulled into her driveway, Tess saw only one
person inside. She had been sitting at the
piano, playing, where she could see out the
front window, and when Casey alone got
out of the Bronco, Tess's heart grew leaden.
Her chest felt as if it were caving in upon
itself.

He had not come. Only Casey, slamming the door and walking toward the house in sunglasses, shorts and a straw cowboy hat, smiling.

Ah, well, Tess was a performer, was she not? She could hide her disappointment for Casey's sake, and make her welcome as exuberant as the girl expected.

She threw open the front door before Casey could ring the bell.

"Hey, honey-child, you made it!"

Casey catapulted into her arms, and when they'd hugged and laughed with pleasure at seeing each other again, Tess asked, "Where'd you get the Bronco?"

"Dad surprised me and bought it for me for graduation! Can you believe it?"

"Very nice."

"He said my old pickup would never make it, and if I was going to be out on my own I needed reliable transportation. Pretty great dad, huh?"

"Yeah, pretty great. Well, come on in and I'll show you the place, then we'll get your stuff unloaded and stashed in your room."

At her first sight of the living room Casey stopped and crooned in an amazed Missouri drawl, "Oh, my Looord in heaven, I've never seen anything so beautiful in my entire life! Mercy, woman, this is where you live?"

"This is where I live."

"And that piano . . ." Casey moved toward it as if mesmerized, touching its shiny ivory surface as if to ascertain it was real. "And these windows." She looked up. "Would you look at 'em! Why, I betcha you can see into God's living room from the top of that."

She followed Tess between two neoclassical columns into the dining room, whose ceiling created the second-story balcony that overhung the living room, and into the rear kitchen, through the French doors onto the screen porch, from where they looked down at the pool area below. Next they checked out Tess's home office, tucked behind the triple garage, then retraced their steps to the front of the house and went up the curving stairway to the second level. All the while, Casey never stopped babbling, admiring the house, exclaiming over everything. Lordy, could that girl talk. Incessantly! But Tess enjoyed it, and the feeling she got from watching her experience true luxury for the first time in her life.

In the open doorway of her own bedroom suite Casey halted and said, "You mean I get to stay *here*?"

"This is your room. And that's your bath."

"My *own bathroom*?"

"That's right . . . take a look."

Casey entered as if it were a sanctuary, halting in the bathroom doorway, peering around it at the glass-walled shower, the marble tub, the long vanity and giant mirror. "This is bigger than my bedroom back home. My gosh, Mac, you mean I could own a house like this someday if I make it big?"

"Someday, maybe. Why not? A major part of achieving success is believing you can."

Casey gazed around, and said, "I wish Dad could see this. He wouldn't believe it." She roamed back into the bedroom and investigated the panel on the wall beside the bed. "What's this?"

"A sound system."

WSM country radio was tuned in, and the voice of Wynonna came softly through the speaker. "You mean you've got it piped all through the house?"

"Well, I'm a musician." Tess flapped her hands. "Got to have music in the place. The components are in the living room, in the built-in cabinets beside the fireplace."

"What's playing now? Radio?"

"Yes."

"Can you play CDs or tapes or anything?"

"Anything."

"So, how come your new tape's not playing?"

"It can be, in a second."

"Well, put it on!" They clattered back downstairs, and as Casey hustled after Tess, she said, "Hey, I really love your new album. Thank you so much for sending it to me. It's going to be a great seller. Platinum! Double platinum! Dad says so, too, and I never played it for anybody else, just him, like you said." Tess started the tape running and Casey ordered, "Turn it up!" The volume got rowdy and Casey started singing along. Tess sang, too. They sang all the while they left the front door open and went outside to empty the Bronco; while they hauled Casey's stuff upstairs, and hung her clothes in the closet and stashed some cardboard boxes in a corner, and set her suitcases at the foot of the bed. The tape finished and Casey yelled through the house, "Hey, run it again! I love it!"

Tess was downstairs in the kitchen, taking out some chicken enchiladas that Maria had left in the refrigerator, topping them with salsa and cheese and popping them into the microwave. Casey bopped in and said, "What can I do?"

"Fix us some ice water."

The sound system was piped into the kitchen, too, and they sang along while Casey dispensed ice cubes and ice water from the door of the refrigerator, pausing to exclaim, "Hey, way cool!" and while Tess chopped up lettuce. They sang while Tess diced some green onions and pointed to the cabinets where napkins and silverware and plates were, and while Casey set the table. They sang while they carried their steaming Mexican food to the table, and pulled out their chairs, and sat down and picked up their forks and . . .

And finally they had to stop singing to eat.

Being together was every bit as much fun as it had been in Mary's kitchen the night they'd discovered they really liked each other. Sometimes the music would over-come Casey and she'd break into song with her mouth full. Then Tess tried it, and some food fell out of her mouth and they both laughed, and Casey said, muffled by a mouthful of her own, "Pretty rotten manners, huh?"

Tess, with her cheek still bulging, replied, "Uh-huh. My momma would chew my butt good!"

"So would my dad, but what they don't know won't hurt 'em."

When they finished their enchiladas they each ate a banana. It was easier to sing in between bites of banana, and sometimes Casey would direct with hers, as if it were a baton.

The lightning bolt struck Tess when she had half her banana still left in its skin: Casey knew every word to every song on the tape! She forgot all about finishing her fruit and fixed Casey with a stare. Casey was directing and singing at the same time, hitting only the licks the backup singers hit.

"Hey, Casey, how many times did you listen to this tape in the last six days?"

"Heck, I don't know. Fifty? Sixty? I wasn't counting."

"You know every word, don't you?"

"Yeah, I guess I do."

"Put your banana down and sing this with me, just the way you were." It was a fast cut called "Last Chance to Boogie," with scads of words. They sat at right angles to each other at the kitchen table, inched forward in their seats, eyes locked, singing to the end of the number.

Then Tess got up and went to the kitchen speaker and lowered the volume. In the rest of the house the next cut began at full volume as Tess returned to the table.

"Why weren't you singing lead?" she asked, resuming her chair.

"Well . . . I don't know." Casey looked confused, afraid she'd done something wrong. "*You* were singing lead."

"But everybody sings lead when they sing along with a song on the radio, don't they?"

Casey shrugged. "Not me, I guess . . . I sing alto in choir."

A bizarre, fortuitous, exciting idea hit Tess, but it was too soon to pose it to this seventeen-year-old girl. *Whoa,* she told herself, *hold on! You haven't even heard her in the studio yet!* But with Carla out of commission for at least one month, possibly for years, Tess needed a replacement for the tour that would begin in late June.

Frowning, Casey said, "What's wrong?"

Tess relaxed and answered, "Nothing. You're amazing though, memorizing all those words so fast."

"Heck, I know the words to all your songs."

"You do?"

"Uh-huh. I've been playing some of your albums since before there were CDs."

"*All* the words?"

"What? You doubt me, woman? You don't believe that you were my idol since I was old enough to operate a record player?"

Tess decided it was time to let the subject rest for the time being. "Come on," she said, rising. "Let's put our dishes in the dishwasher, then you'd probably like a little time to unpack or kick back, or maybe take a swim."

"A swim! Wow! You mean it? That'd be great!" Carrying her dishes across the kitchen, Casey recanted, "I really should call Dad first though. I promised him I would, the minute I got in."

"Go right ahead. There's a phone in your room, if you want privacy."

"Why would I need privacy?"

Casey dialed on the portable kitchen phone, and Tess listened while putting away the salsa and wiping off the tabletop. The conversation was the usual got-here-just-fine sort. Then Casey added, "Hey, Dad, you should see this place. It's like a palace! Everything's painted either ivory or white. She's got a cream-colored grand piano in the living room, and a sound system piped into every room in the house, and there's this huge dramatic open balcony that looks down into the living room from the upstairs hall, and I have my own bathroom, and she put flowers in my bedroom, and all this fancy stuff in the bathroom—you know, like little bottles of stuff. And she's got a swimming pool! And you know what? I'm talking on a portable phone! Gol, Dad, it's way too cool."

The conversation continued for a couple more minutes, then Casey said, "Yeah, she's right here. Hey, Mac, Dad wants to talk to you."

Whereas Casey had not felt the need for privacy, Tess could have used some. But it would have looked strange, her holing up to talk to Kenny, so she took the phone from Casey's hand and spoke while the girl listened at close range.

"Hi, Kenny," she said brightly, trying to act unaffected in front of Casey. This was the first time they'd talked since they'd had the tiff on the phone the other night.

"Hi, darlin'," he said, and her heart went *ka-boom* with relief. "You still mad at me?"

"No."

"Well, that's better. My daughter likes your house."

"Yes, but she's easy to impress."

"It sounds like *Lifestyles of the Rich and Famous* over there."

"I suppose it is. I thought you might drive Casey down and see it for yourself."

"I might have if I'd been invited."

She didn't know what to say, so she changed the subject. "Pretty nice Bronco you bought this girl."

"She loaded it to the hilt. I told her that was too much stuff for her to take to your house—she should wait till she found an apartment of her own. But you know teenage girls. She said it was all stuff she couldn't live without."

"There's plenty of room here, don't worry about it." Casey wandered off into the living room, so Tess asked, "How you doing, Kenny? I mean, with her gone?"

He waited a beat before answering, dropping his cheerful banter. "Worst day of my life."

She felt a surge of empathy and drew a mental picture of how he used to walk Casey to the house with his arm slung over her shoulder. "I can imagine."

"I can't seem to stop myself from walking into her room and looking around at the empty spots. Where her guitar used to be, all the stuff off the top of her dresser. Hell, she even took her bed pillows."

"Is Faith there?"

"No, not tonight."

"Why don't you call her up and be with her for a while?"

"Because I don't feel like being with Faith. Funny thing is, I've felt like it less and less since you went away. I was thinking I might go across the alley and visit with Mary for a while. Maybe see if she wants to play a hand of cribbage or something."

"She'd love that, I'm sure. Well, listen, I

should . . . I should go. Casey and I might take a swim or something."

"Yeah," he said, forlorn.

"I'm sure she'll call you again tomorrow after the recording session and tell you all about it."

"I told her she can call anytime, collect. I'm getting her an AT&T credit card of her own, but it isn't here yet."

"That isn't necessary, Kenny, she can dial direct from here whenever she wants to."

"No, no, you've done enough, taking her in, giving her this break with her music. She doesn't need to run up your phone bill, too."

"Well, let's not argue about it." Casey had returned and was listening again.

"If she needs anything, you'll let me know, won't you?" Kenny asked.

"Of course. Now, you take it easy, and don't stay around the house moping. I'll put her back on so you can say good-bye."

"Hey, Tess, wait!" Casey was standing right beside her waiting to reclaim the phone when Kenny said, without warning, "I love you."

Tess was so stunned, she froze, staring at

Casey while his words drove her heart into a backbeat and threw heat into her face. Just like that—when she was least expecting it—"I love you." With as little compunction as he'd say "See you around." She stood rooted, gripping the phone, unable to respond with the same words. They were not words one took lightly, or spoke without absolute certainty, and she certainly wasn't going to say them the first time with his daughter standing four feet away. She struggled to come up with some fitting response without giving away how flustered she was.

"I think it's just the loneliness, Kenny. It'll get better with time."

"Is Casey listening?"

"Yes, she's standing right here."

"All right, then, I'll hope that the next time I say it, you'll say it back."

What could she say? She took the easy way out. "Here she is. . . ."

Casey frowned at her, and whispered, "What's wrong?"

"Nothing," Tess mumbled, handing over the phone and turning away.

———

IT WAS HARROWING trying to hide her over-
wrought emotions from Casey when her
deepest instinct was to talk about the whole
situation with her, which Tess could not do
yet. They swam, and looked forward to tomorrow, and Tess answered questions
about what it was like in a recording studio.
They went back inside and played a bunch
of other artists' CDs that Tess had gotten
free at a trade show, and she told Casey
about that type of promotion and how it
helped a career to meet the big distributors
who handled your products. They talked
about when and where Casey should look
for an apartment, and about Fan Fair, coming up soon, and about the concert schedule and when it would begin and where it
would take Tess, but she never mentioned
the possibility of Casey singing backup on
the tour.

They retired near eleven, and only then,
after the house was quiet and dark, while
Tess was lying wide awake in her own bed,
did she examine what Kenny had said. She
drew his words, like polished stones, out of
the secret satin drawstring bag of her memory, and with them the image of his face as
it had been the last day she'd seen him, in

his office, rising and coming toward her wearing the tortured look of good-bye. *"Hey, Tess, wait! . . . I love you."* She heard again his words coming over the phone in that offhand fashion that had caught her off guard. In her imagination she kissed him again as she'd kissed him then, and wondered if this was love, this underlying emptiness that marked each day spent without him, this feeling of jubilation upon hearing his voice at the other end of a telephone line, this urge to go back into her stored memories of him and draw them out into the light to be examined, then filed carefully until next time.

Hey, Kenny . . . maybe I love you, too.

Or was she idealizing him simply because he'd spoken the words? She didn't think so, for she was not an idealizer, but a realist, always had been. So, *realistically* speaking, what hope was there for any sort of relationship with Kenny when he staunchly refused to get rid of Faith? When Tess was committed to her career and he to his? When they lived in two different places with two wholly different lifestyles? And what about the difference in their incomes? Was there even the remotest possibility he was pursuing her because she was rich and famous? No—she felt absolutely certain about that. But perhaps the opposite was true. Perhaps he was the kind of guy whose pride would not allow him to live off a woman's income. And did she have the right to ask him to?

She hadn't even admitted she loved him and already she was suffering some of the pangs that poets wrote about. Her disappointment today when he'd failed to show up with Casey had been sophomoric and uncharacteristic, not at all the kind of thing she was accustomed to doing: building something up in her imagination, then suffering a letdown when it turned out differently than she'd hoped. If that wasn't idealizing, what was?

Simply being with Casey presented its own peculiar pang, a little more difficult to psychoanalyze, but a pang, nonetheless. It sometimes felt as if being with her was a substitute for being with her father. Sometimes Tess saw a reflection of Kenny in Casey's facial expressions or body language. Sometimes the things the two women talked about harked back to Wintergreen, where Tess had spent time with

Kenny, and kept those memories green. Also, being Casey's benefactor practically assured Tess that she'd see Kenny in the future, away from Wintergreen. Did all this make her a schemer? Unworthy of the trust both Casey and Kenny had placed in her? Was she using the girl to woo him?

Disturbed by her thoughts, she turned onto her stomach in bed.

The moon was up, painting the window frames the faded purple of the irises that her mother had grown when Tess was a girl. And in

Wintergreen, Missouri, that iris purple moon was shining on Kenny's house . . . and on Momma's house. Had the two of them played cribbage tonight? And was he back home now, maybe lying awake, too, feeling the emptiness of the house without Casey in it? Was he missing Tess McPhail, and wondering what she thought of his bold admission of love? Was he waiting for her response?

At eleven-fifteen she could resist no longer. She picked up the phone and called him. He answered on the first ring, in a clear, unsleepy voice. The mere sound of his hello raised a clamor within her, which she schooled her voice to hide.

"Hi. Did I wake you?"

"No. I was lying here awake."

"Me, too."

"Casey in bed now?"

"Yes. We swam, and talked, and listened to CDs, and she had a thousand questions about what it's going to be like in the studio tomorrow. Did you go to Momma's and play cribbage?"

"Yes. She whupped me three games out of four, then fed me rhubarb pie and ice cream and sent me home."

"Did you feel better after getting out of the house for a while?"

"Temporarily. It's awfully quiet here."

A lull fell while she pictured him in his old-fashioned upstairs bedroom with the window overlooking the backyard and alley.

"Kenny, about what you said ear-lier . . ."

She hadn't planned exactly what she was going to say, and stumbled into silence.

"It just sort of slipped out," he said.

"Is it true?"

"Yes."

"Are you sure it's not just that you're lonesome tonight?"

"Some, maybe, but the groundwork was laid down long before Casey left."

"Then maybe it's because I'm different from Faith, and because I'm helping your daughter, and because I'm rich and famous and supposedly unattainable, and—"

"Of course it is!" he interrupted, his anger flaring. "It's all those things! If you expect me to deny it, I'm sorry to disappoint you, but I can't divorce myself from the knowledge of your fame and success any more than you can undo all that for your sister Judy. But if you're suggesting that's all I'm in love with—Mac, the public persona—you're wrong! And by the way, if you think it's easy being an ordinary guy falling in love with a multimillionaire recording star, guess again. It's pretty damned terrifying because of everything you just accused me of. But I've been doing a little sorting out of my own, and examining my motives, and what I come back to time and again is this great big lump of emptiness that's lodged in my gut since I said good-bye to you in my office. Tess, it's like . . . it's like . . . hell, I don't know." His anger was gone, and in its place borderline misery. "I have to push myself to go to work in the morning, and there doesn't seem to be any point to my day. Every day's the same—no highs, no lows, no laughing, no anticipation. I miss you. And every day I think about driving down to Nashville and ringing your doorbell, and then I think, that's dumb, because what would happen then?"

"Then we'd probably go to bed together, and that wouldn't solve anything, would it?"

"No, but it would sure feel good."

The line hummed while both of them realized they were laying their wishes bare for the other to see.

"I never told you," Tess confessed, "that I went out with that guy I'd been dating, Burt Sheer, and I tried kissing him, hoping it would chase you from my mind, but it didn't work. Kissing him was just awful compared to you, and I don't know what to do about it any more than you do."

She heard him draw a deep, unsteady breath, then he asked, "Do you love me, Tess?" He paused, and added, "I'd like to hear you say it if you do."

She lay in the dark, staring at the black

ceiling, afraid to say it, knowing it was unfair not to, feeling as if her heartbeat were punching the stuffing out of the mattress beneath her. Saying it was inviting all that turmoil into her life.

"I do . . . I must, because I'm feeling the same as you, like my life is this chord with one note missing that wasn't missing before. I always thought . . . I thought my career was enough, that it would satisfy me in so many ways, and bring so many fascinating and talented people into my life that I wouldn't need one specific one. But since I came back to Nashville . . . it's . . ." Her throat got thick and she had to stop talking.

"Since you came back to Nashville . . ." he prompted.

"I miss you, Kenny."

"But you still didn't say it."

No, she hadn't. She was deathly afraid to let the words out of her heart, because once she had she might begin those insufferable daydreams again, and what if they didn't turn out the way she imagined? How could they turn out the way she imagined?

"All right," he said, sighing, sounding tired. "I'll let you off the hook. It doesn't mean anything anyway if it's forced. Well, listen . . . it's late. We'd better say good night."

She rested the back of her hand across her eyes and felt tears gathering in her throat, disliking herself for withholding the words. The minute he hung up it would get worse, and she'd probably roll over and bawl when she had her life just the way she wanted it. Just the way she'd dreamed it when she was clear back in high school! Mac! Superstar! Millionaire! In absolute control of her career and her future! Mac, who didn't want to be derailed by a husband, or marriage, or a family, or any of the baggage that went along with them!

"Kenny, I don't mean to hurt you."

"It's okay, I said."

"But I feel like such a shit."

"Hey, are you crying again? You are, aren't you?" She heard a sad smile come into his words. "Well, that's something anyway."

"Kenny . . ." There was appeal in her voice, but she didn't know what she was pleading for, so how could he answer? "You were right before. It's time we said good night."

"Good night, Tess," he said, "I love you."

Then the line clicked and she rolled over and did exactly what she'd feared she'd do. Mac . . . superstar . . . millionaire . . . with her prized life mapped out before her, bawled into her pillow.

bawled into her pillow.

EIGHTEEN

IT WAS QUARTER TO TWO the next afternoon when they arrived at Sixteenth Avenue Sound, a converted bungalow not far from Music Row. Tess led Casey inside through a small, unimpressive reception area to a room with sofas, tables and chairs, but no windows. A Pepsi machine threw red light over the L that served as a canteen, and the coffee warmer sent out the smell of burned coffee. Country music played softly from some unseen speakers. A huge man with a receding hairline, flowing gray beard and streaked gray ponytail sat on one of the sofas extracting an electric bass from its case, whistling to the music.

"Hey, Leland! How ya doin'?" Tess greeted. "You've got to meet this pretty young *thang* who's gonna be doing harmony vocals for me today." Her intentional drawl made Leland smile. "This's Casey Kronek. Leland Smith."

While they were shaking hands a red-headed guy about thirty, with hair as trim as Johnny Carson's, dressed in neat blue jeans and a polo shirt, came out of the lavatory. He was the keyboardist, Dan Fontaineau, and he shook hands with Casey, too.

"Come on," Tess said, "I'll introduce you to Jack."

Jack Greaves was already in the control room at the console, a fifteen-by-four-foot wedge of electronic wizardry with so many buttons, knobs and zinging orange lights it looked like the flight deck of a space shuttle. Beside him the sound engineer was deciding which of the fifty-six tracks he'd use, while the engineer's assistant sat nearby loading a tape machine. Through an immense window the recording studio was visible, a gray cube of subdued lighting where some studio musicians were warming up playing riffs, which came through the wall-mounted speakers along with their voices as a pleasant cacophony. A couple of the guys noticed Tess and gestured in greeting through the window. "Hey, Mac."

She leaned over, held a switch on the talk-back, and said, "Hey, guys."

Jack, a trim man of medium height with meticulously trimmed brown hair, beard and mustache, turned in his swivel chair. Though he smiled and kissed Tess's cheek, and shook hands when introduced to Casey, it was clear he had business on his mind, and little time to waste. As a record producer he controlled the session, which was costing Tess plenty. He himself earned some thirty thousand dollars per project plus a percentage of the royalties; the studio rental ran close to two thousand dollars a day; the sound engineer got eighty dollars an hour, his assistant twenty-five; the studio musicians—all of them double-scale caliber—commanded over five hundred dollars apiece for each three-hour session. Given that today they'd work for six hours, the cost of this day's session, even before mixing and mastering, would run over ten thousand dollars.

Jack Greaves had been in the business long enough to realize that each minute lost meant big bucks. He wasted little of Tess's money before asking Casey, "Did you sign your AFTRA card yet?"

Casey looked nonplussed, and replied, "Excuse me?"

"Union stuff," Tess explained. "American Federation of Television and Radio Artists insists that all singers' performances be documented." To Jack she said, "She doesn't need to today since it's her first time. She gets one free session, then she's got thirty-one days to join. Don't worry about it," she told Casey, "I'll have my secretary help you get in touch with the union later."

Jack went right on with business. "You want one box or two, Tess?"

"One, I think. Might be easier for Casey the first time."

"You get that, Carlos?" he inquired, turning to the sound engineer while Leland went into the studio and began tuning his bass.

Tess leaned over and whispered to Casey, "Never mind Jack. When he gets in here he's got a one-track mind. Come on, let's sit down and go over our parts."

A row of high-backed leather stools stood behind a desk facing the control board and window. They climbed onto two of them, and Casey whispered, "What's a box?"

"The recording booth—see?" Tess pointed through the window at a pair of doors leading to two tiny black-walled rooms off the left side of the studio. "Isolation booths to help keep the tracks from bleeding into one another. We can use one or two, but until we get used to each other I figure it's better if we just use one. You sometimes get better synergy with close eye contact."

Jack kept the talk-back on so the conversations were audible as they passed back and forth between the two rooms. The musicians kept tuning, occasionally breaking into spontaneous warmup music that would suddenly acquire harmony and rhythm and might run for sixteen or twenty bars, then be broken up by laughter. Conversation, when it happened, was spoken in a lexicon peculiar to musicians—short, brief colorful phrases that would make no sense away from the studio. Somebody said, "You hear that pork chop sizzling in Lee's bass?"

"Got us a buzz fly here."

"Try another track."

"Okay, I'm putting you on sixteen, Lee."

And after Leland ran a riff, "Hell, it's still here."

"Try another patch cord."

The assistant engineer left the room and appeared on the other side of the window o change the cord.

Leland played once more. "Better now," he engineer said.

The drummer put in an earplug, ran his sticks across his snares and tenors, hit the cymbals, and sampled a few thuds on the bass drum. Two guitarists were soundlessly tuning their instruments with electronic tuners. The piano player, behind a black grand facing the window, executed a quick smattering of Gershwin that segued into a few bars of boogie-woogie, followed by an arpeggio that took his fingers sailing off the end of the keys. Another guy on electronic keyboards had them sounding like bells. Leland, still monkeying with his bass guitar said, "The humidity's got my axe going sharp today. I can't keep it down." A saxophonist had set up his music stand in the hall between the two rooms and through the open doorway the sound of his bluesy wail added to the noise.

Jack said, "Somebody do the charts?"

"I did," the pianist said. "Got 'em right here."

"What do you say, should we look at 'em and give this demo a listen?"

Casey took it all in, mesmerized by her first experience in a recording session, still awestruck that she was actually a part of it. Staring at the lead guitarist, she whispered to Tess, "My gosh, that's Al Murphy. I've seen him on TNN. And Terry Solum on keyboards! He used to play with John Denver!"

"These guys have all been around awhile. You're gonna love what they do. The road musicians are essentially copyists—they can recreate the licks that are put on the albums. But these guys—the studio musicians—are the ones who have the originality to put them there in the first place. And we hire the best. Every one of these guys is a double-scale musician. Wait'll you hear them work."

"Double-scale?"

"They earn twice what the regular ones earn and twice what the union demands."

The musicians all came from the studio and crowded into the control room. Casey beamed with elation as she was introduced to all of them. The pianist passed out cop-

es of the charts—a Nashville number system that transcribed chords onto paper,
creating a crib sheet for sessions players
who sometimes were unable to read music.
The number system had been created in
the fifties by a member of the Jordanaires
and allowed for improvisation and immediate key change without rewriting the charts.
Casey looked at the ranks of 1s, 4s, Cs and
Vs, and Tess pointed, giving a quick explanation. The assistant engineer ran the demo
tape and it took less than half the song for
the chart to make sense to Casey.

Keys were named. Numbers indicated
how many lines would be done in that key.
V indicated "verse," C indicated "chorus,"
and B meant "bridge." It was like looking at
the frame of a house before the siding was
put on: the structure of the song was all
there waiting for the musicians to do it their
way, with all the improvisation they pleased.

The demo ended and a bunch of musicians voiced approval. "Hey, nice song.
You two wrote this together? You ought to
collaborate some more. This thing is gonna
cook. Lemme hear it again."

"What key are we doing it in, Tess?"

"F," she answered.

Everybody wrote F on the top of their charts and the guys took them back into the studio where they sat listening to the demo tape a bunch of times while noodling around on their instruments. At first they paid no attention to one another, turning within to find their own personal musical take on the song, but soon they became aware of the others, discussing licks, intros, runs. Talk and music. Music and talk. It sounded like a jumble.

Meanwhile, Tess and Casey huddled over a lyric sheet, writing in the margins who would sing which lines. Sometimes, from inside the studio, snatches of the song would resurrect in new form, pulling together as the guys got a handle on their individual parts.

"Come on," Tess said, "let's go in." She led the way through the studio into one of the recording booths. It had black walls of acoustic paneling, two music stands with lights on them, and two mikes in stands. A pair of headsets hung over each music stand. The engineer said, "Let's do a sound check," and the women clamped them on.

It took a while for the engineer to set the volume levels, then the women did some scratch vocals, working out their parts, annotating their pages here and there. After several minutes of sound and flurry Greaves took control and said into the talk-back, "Okay, everybody, why don't we do a run-through for nothing?"

Tess could see Casey getting nervous, and said, "Just relax and sing the way you did back at Momma's house. We'll do plenty of run-throughs before we record."

The drummer gave the standard downbeat and the intro began. Tess watched Casey's face light up as the mix of instruments came through her headset, filling her head with full-bodied sound. Wow, she mouthed, wide-eyed, and Tess smiled as she began singing.

Suddenly Jack's voice interrupted in her ear. "Oh-oh, what's the deal? We've got vocals in the sax. How can that be?"

The music fell away and the first engineer suggested, "Let's try taking the direct out of nineteen."

There was some scrambling around at the console and the problem got solved.

"Okay, let's go one more time," Jack said, and they began again with a new downbeat. Tess hit her cue, and when

Casey came in it sounded sensational through the earphones. Their two very distinct vocal qualities blended like smooth chocolate and rough peanuts, coming out sweet to the ear, and Tess knew beyond a flicker of a doubt that she and Casey would do many, many songs together after this one.

Watching Casey's face as she sang for the first time with these extraordinarily talented pros made Tess smile. Hearing the song they'd composed coming to life was incredible. She remembered her own first time, and saw in Casey's radiant expression her own excitement, years ago, when she'd stepped into a recording studio as a beginner. The girl was good. She had a natural feel for which words to sing and which to drop; which harmony note would sound best; when to crescendo and when to hold back. Nashville had a clever, oft-repeated answer whenever an out-of-towner inquired if a musician could read music: *Not enough to ruin the song.* Casey was that way; Tess had recognized it back in Wintergreen and it was reinforced again today.

They finished their first run-through, and Casey exclaimed, "Far out! This is way too incredible, Mac! When did I die? 'Cause if this isn't heaven, I don't know what is!"

"It'll get better."

"Better! You're kidding! It don't get no better than this!"

Chuckling, Tess replied, "No, I mean the music. We've got some kinks to work out yet. I was thinking, here where we break into the bridge . . ." They dissected their parts while the musicians did the same.

Over the talk-back Jack said, "Sounding good, ladies. What would you think about running the last note of the second verse over onto Mick's solo for a couple beats, then fading?"

And so it went. Jack interacted with everyone, and everyone with him, and with each other, trying various spots in the song, experimenting with rhythm and technique. The quality of the talent in the studio made the work inventive and mercurial as the song started coming together. The blank audiotape alone for any project could cost some three thousand dollars, and Jack didn't want to waste it recording takes that were too unpolished, but after ten minutes of experimentation, and a second run-through, which sounded far smoother than the first, he said, "Okay, everybody, should we record one?"

Dan Fontaineau said, "Hell, yes, we're professional musicians. We can knock this thing."

"Okay, Tess, Casey? . . ."

"We're set."

Dan gave the downbeat and the second engineer started the tape running. The first engineer operated the board, and Jack concentrated on listening, one finger crossing his lips and a scowl on his eyebrows— his usual expression when he was concentrating. The music was sounding very smooth, but, unfortunately, halfway through the take Dan's earphone fell out of his ear and he stopped playing. The sound swooned and the song fell apart. Naturally, the guys—they had a great collective sense of humor—gave him some shit.

"Hey, way to go, Dan."

"Yeah, we're professional musicians," someone mimicked. "We can knock this thing."

"Knock that earphone into his head, you mean, so it'll stay there."

"Anybody got some Super Glue?"

Everybody laughed and relaxed as Jack,

ever the overseer and prompter, got them
back to business. "Let's save what we got
and start again. Whenever you're ready,
Dan."

This time they completed the song, got it
on tape, and afterward everyone piled into
the control room to give it a listen. The
women sat on the leather stools, leaning
forward with their elbows on the slanted
desk. The men gathered around the control
panel and while they listened some played
air guitar, some studied the floor, some
mouthed words. Everybody in the room had
a knee, a foot, a head or a hand keeping
time to the music.

The playback ended and chatter broke
out.

"It's solid."

"What we've got here is a fresh ballad
with a heart."

"Nice way to start a career, Casey."

Though they liked the start they'd made,
they had a long way to go. Everybody exchanged ideas. "You think that solo was
too Las Vegas? . . . In the fourth bar of the
intro the sax is resolving too fast . . . I
wonder if we should pull back the tempo a
bit."

They worked this way for two and a half hours, back and forth between the studio and the control room. Record it again. Listen again. Record. Listen. Record. Listen. Finally one run-through seemed to ignite a specific spark in everyone. They'd got it: they all felt it simultaneously, and the charged atmosphere was palpable as the playback ended.

"This one's got the edge."

"We finally filled that deep pocket."

This was the best cut so far, and everyone felt the diminished tension and a sense of self-satisfaction.

"Time to break bread," Greaves said. "We'll pick up again at seven o'clock."

While they'd been recording, a caterer had come in and set up food buffet style on a large table in the lounge. As most of the group headed toward it, Mick Mulhall asked Jack, "Can I put a fix on that line where Tess sings, 'Say good-bye, mustn't cry'?"

He went back into the studio to rerecord the section while the other musicians wandered out into the lounge, put quarters into the Pepsi machine, loaded plates and sat around on the sofas talking mostly about the song in progress.

Casey was so fired up she found it hard to sit.

"Jeez, this is *wild!* I never had so much fun in my life!"

The others remembered what it was like to be breaking in, hearing yourself for the first time, and they humored her.

"Hey, Mac, you're gonna have to tie an anchor to this one's tail or she's gonna float right on outta here, she's so high."

Tess smiled, and said, "Better eat something, Casey. We've got three more hours of work before we call it a night."

Mick finished his fix and came back into the lounge area with Jack, who was so intense he didn't take time to eat. Instead, he told Tess, "We're still getting a little creep in the vocals. You want to come in tomorrow and lay down a new track, just in case?"

"Sure, if you think we need it. What about Casey?"

"Casey, too. I think we'll get a cleaner sound if we use two boxes. Okay with you, Casey?"

The girl's eyes were so wide and excited, she couldn't believe she was being asked to come back again. "Yeah, sure . . . heck, yes!"

Tess told Jack, "We'll be here."

They sat around eating grilled shrimp, rice pilaf, salad, green grapes and watermelon, all of it served in very utilitarian fashion: this was a work session, not a party: remaining in the studio was essential to keeping the musical urgency alive and pulsing. Leaving to eat elsewhere, they all knew, sometimes managed to subdue that drive. When that happened, the lifelessness came across on tape.

Jack barely ate. He remained in the control room, working with the first and second engineer on the tracks they'd already recorded, listening for anything that might possibly need fixes.

Tess left Casey visiting with the guys and went into the control room to speak privately with her producer.

"Can I talk to you a minute, Jack?"

"Sure," he said, turning from the control board on a rolling chair, hooking another with his foot and inviting her to sit.

The engineer and his assistant went out to catch some supper, leaving the two alone.

"I want your opinion, Jack," Tess said

when the two had the control room to themselves.

He could tell from her demeanor that whatever she was going to ask was important.

"That's what I'm paid for."

"It's not about the album, it's about the tour. Carla's throat problem's not going to be straightened out anytime soon. I want to ask Casey to go on tour with me and sing backup vocals."

He considered for a moment, then said, "She's young."

"She's talented. And she knows my music. Jack, we were playing my old albums around the house yesterday and she's got the backup cues cold on every one. Every lick—exactly like the record! I know she's inexperienced, but we don't have much time left for rehearsals, and sometimes the hungry ones are willing to work even harder than the experienced ones. Besides that, I like her and we get along like two cats in a litter. What do you think?"

"Shouldn't you be talking to Ralph about this?"

As her road show producer, Ralph Thornleaf would have the final say. "I will, but I wanted your opinion, too. I just got the idea last night and I haven't had a chance to call him. So what do you think?"

"You know what I think. I trust your instincts, Tess. If I didn't I wouldn't be letting you coproduce your own albums. I like the girl's voice."

"How do you think it would blend with Diane's?" Diane Abbington was one of Tess's other two backup singers.

"Her voice is actually a lot like Diane's. I think they might sound all right together."

"And Estelle?" Estelle Paglio was Tess's other harmony singer.

"Estelle can blend with anybody. Why don't I see if I can get those two in here tomorrow when you and Casey are coming in, and we can dream up some excuse to get the three of them singing together, then you'll know. If you want to, we could use them for a little additional backup vocal on "Old Souls." I've been thinking about it anyway, like maybe if we drop some three-part harmony into selected spots we could get a little deeper sound. What do you think?"

"I think it's a good idea. While we're at it, I'll see if Ralph can casually drop around, then we'll all know what the four of us sound like together. Be a good chance for him to meet Casey."

Tess returned to the lounge to join the others. The sax player went home and a fiddle player arrived to work on the next song. Everyone returned to the studio for the evening session. "Don't Leave Me High" was the last song, the spare one they'd record for the new album. The session followed the same pattern as the earlier one—charts, demo, working on parts, laying down tracks until finally, around nine o'clock, the last fixes were put on and Jack called the session over.

WHEN THEY WERE DRIVING HOME, Casey said, "That's the most fun I've ever had in my life."

Her adrenaline was still pumping, Tess could tell. Casey threw her head back and stretched herself out like a surfboard against the car seat. "I want to do this till I'm ninety."

Tess laughed. "You'll need some bionic parts if you do it till then. Like a larynx and lungs, for instance."

"I feel bionic right now! Like I could go all night! Tess, I love you!"

"Well, that's good. I love you, too."

"What can I ever do to pay you back?"

"The truth is you won't pay *me* back. Someday when you're forty years old and a superstar you'll give some other beginner a break and pass along the tradition. That's how all of us handle our paybacks."

"I'll remember that. I promise I will."

When they got home Casey called her dad immediately. She used the phone in the kitchen while Tess leafed through the mail that Maria had left on the counter.

"Jeez, Dad, it was so great! I mean, when I heard the sound coming through my earphones it was like, wow—I mean this really major rush, you know? And we recorded it again and again and again, and everybody was really nice to me. Dad, the studio musicians were guys who played with Ricky Nelson and Graham Nash and everybody you could think of! The best talent in town, and they treated me like . . ." Casey went on and on, filling her dad's ear while Tess moved in and out of the kitchen, to and from her office. After about ten minutes she heard Casey call, "Hey, Tess, Dad wants to talk to you!"

Tess was sitting in her office so she answered there.

"Hi." She grinned. "How's your ear?"

He laughed, and said, "That's one excited girl."

"Hey, I wish you could've been there. She did great. Our voices are really good together."

"I know. She told me. And told me and told me."

It was Tess's turn to laugh. In the living room Casey started a CD playing and the sound of Tess's voice spilled through the house at high volume. "Just a minute . . ." She swiveled around in her chair and turned it down on the wall speaker. "There, that's better. Your daughter likes her music loud, plus she's making herself right at home."

"Hey, if she's too—"

"No, don't worry," Tess interrupted. "Casey and I get along just fine."

"Well, thanks again for today, for everything you're doing for her."

"Kenny," she said, and tipped her chair forward, elbows to the desktop. "I'm going to try something tomorrow. We have to go back into the studio to lay down another vocal track and I'm going to have Casey sing along with two of my backup singers— I mean the two who go out on concert tour with me. There's a third one, Carla, but she's got a thyroid condition that's taking her out of commission for maybe as long as two years. The long and the short of it is, if Casey's voice blends as well as I think it will, I may be asking her to go on concert tour with me, starting at the end of June."

The line went silent.

Finally Tess asked, "Do you have any objections, Kenny?"

"You're moving kind of fast with her, aren't you?"

"Yes," she admitted honestly, and waited for his response.

"This scares me, Tess."

"I imagine it does."

"Too much too soon."

"She knows every word of every song I've ever recorded, and not only that, she knows the backup vocals to a T. The plain truth is, she'd be doing me a favor. I wouldn't have to go through all those tedious rehearsals to train a new girl. We could do it quite easily in a week or two."

Silence passed again, and she wisely let it.

After a long time, he released a pent-up breath . . . then nothing.

"We open the concert tour at Arrowhead Pond in Anaheim on June twenty-eighth. The first concert is already sold out, so we've agreed to do a second one on the twenty-ninth. Can you imagine your daughter singing in a place with eighteen thousand ticketholders filling the seats? I have this fantasy, Kenny," she went on, "it's of you, sitting in the front row of Arrowhead for Casey's first public performance, then coming backstage to hug her and congratulate her and drink champagne with us. What do you think?"

Again he let out a breath, then an uncertain laugh. "You've caught me so off guard here."

"Think about it. I'll send you tickets for the gold circle. Maybe you can bring Momma, too. She just might be persuaded to come, if she could travel with you and Faith."

"Faith, too? You want Faith to come?"

"Well . . . no, not especially, but how could I send tickets to you and not to her?"

"Tess, listen, it's . . . I don't know what to say. Besides, you haven't even heard Casey sing with the others."

"No, but I have an ear. I think I can tell what she'll sound like. Tell me yes, Kenny, so I can ask her with your blessing. It's important to me."

"All right, then, yes. Hell, what am I saying?"

Tess smiled. She knew when she'd see him again!

"All right, then!" she said with excitement in her voice. "Save June twenty-eighth and I'll see you in Anaheim!"

"Tess, wait!"

"What?"

"Call me tomorrow night. Tell me how it went in the studio."

"Of course. Do you want to talk to Casey again?"

"No, just tell her good night. And one more thing . . ."

"What's that?"

"I think I love you. Last night I was sure. Tonight I'm not so sure . . . depending on what happens to my daughter's life because of you."

She laughed, and said, "I'm not going to let anything happen to her. I love that girl."

"Oh, you love her but not me?"

"I didn't say that."

"So you love me, too?"

"I didn't say that either. Good night, Kenny."

"Good night, Tess."

She was smiling as she hung up. And, actually, she was pretty sure she loved him.

NINETEEN

THE SECOND DAY'S SESSION went the way Tess expected. Casey's voice blended with the others so well that there was never a question she was the right choice. When they all sang together it clicked. Tess could tell by catching the eyes of Diane and Estelle that they, too, liked what they heard. When the song ended Diane said with engaging sassiness, "Whoa, you cook, girl!"

With the approval of Jack and Ralph, Tess asked Casey right there in the studio if she wanted to go on tour, starting at the end of June. It was fun watching her face suffuse with shock.

"You're kidding," she said. "Me?"

"Yes, you."

"But . . . but why?"

"Because you know my music. Because

your voice blends. And because you're easy to get along with."

Casey dropped onto a chair, and whispered, "Holy shit."

And so began one of the busiest months of Tess's life. June was traditionally a wild month in Nashville anyway, kicking off with the Summer Lights festival—a three-day street fair down by the capitol—and a celebrity softball tournament at Greer Stadium. Then came the TNN *Music City News* Awards, followed by the most intense week of contact with fans to happen anywhere in the world, namely Fan Fair, when twenty-four thousand of them paid admission into the Tennessee State Fairgrounds to pay homage to their idols at close range, at booths set up in the cattle barns; to shake their hands, have snapshots taken with them, bring them homemade pies, tell them their babies were named after them, buy T-shirts, caps, coffee mugs, and albums, and have all these moneymakers signed, signed, signed!

There were times during Fan Fair when Tess did nine or ten radio interviews a day, plus a three-hour stint at her own booth and sometimes another at the label's booth.

There were also newspaper and TV interviews, autographings at record stores and, of course, some performing. She lost track of how many times a DJ with a tape recorder stuck a microphone in her face, and asked her to say "Hi everyone! This is Tess McPhail coming to you from KMPS, Seattle!" Or perhaps he was from Tulsa, or Albuquerque or Sweetwater, Oklahoma. Wherever the DJs were from, during Fan Fair, when they asked you to give them a recorded message to take back home to your fans, you did it. There were meetings with fan club leaders from all over America, even special awards for some of them, dinners with disk jockeys, and special get-togethers with managers of record shops.

It was a grueling week, but Casey stayed beside Tess through its entirety, and Tess was grateful to have her there. She ran errands, brought cold Cokes, sold T-shirts, made phone calls, took snapshots with the cameras the fans handed her so they could have their picture taken with Tess. But most importantly, she smiled through it all and brought along her boundless energy to lift Tess's spirits when, at the end of an eighteen-hour day, the overworked star wanted nothing so badly as to cry with weariness.

For Casey it was novel, exciting. Every new experience was reason for rejoicing: she was getting a firsthand look at the hard work of being a country music star, and deciding it was definitely what she wanted for herself.

When Fan Fair ended, concert rehearsals began.

Mac's stage show was an extravaganza of lights, costumes and equipment requiring a dozen semitrailers to haul it all, and fifty employees to make it work, as well as another twenty local hands in each concert venue. Everybody worked hard preparing for the tour, and Casey was no exception. Since time was tight and workdays long, she continued to live at Tess's house.

She called her father every night, or he called her, and at the end of each conversation he asked to speak to Tess. Often the two of them were on the line longer than he'd been with his own daughter, and it seemed they never lacked for things to talk about.

He told her about his business.

She told him about hers.

He talked about the church choir.

She talked about the concert rehearsals.

He kept his eye on Mary.

She kept her eye on Casey.

He said he'd ordered a new car.

She said she'd ordered her road manager to set aside three tickets in the gold circle for him and Faith and her momma, for the concert in Anaheim, even though Mary hadn't committed yet. Then she asked, "You're coming, aren't you?"

He paused a telltale beat before answering, "Yes . . . I'm coming."

Her breath seemed in short supply and the one thing she wanted to say was much too significant. She said it anyway.

"What about Faith?"

"I haven't asked Faith."

"You haven't?"

"No."

"Why?"

During the long pause before he spoke again, they felt the leap of awareness that signals change. At his end of the wire Kenny leaned back against the kitchen counter, staring down his legs. At her end she was lying on top of her bedspread, staring at her index finger lying motionless in a curl of the phone cord. Both of them were reliving the night of the wedding reception. His voice, when he finally answered, was slightly gruffer, slightly quieter.

"I think you know, Tess," he said.

A long silence passed, filled with the intimacy of the unspoken. It was the first moment they seemed to run out of things to say.

Finally he said, "Tess?" as if she might have gone somewhere.

"I'm glad," she admitted.

Then she heard him release a breath as if he'd been suffocating, too.

Plans began racing through her head. "I'll get you rooms at the Beverly Wilshire, where Casey and I will be staying. It's an hour's ride in to L.A. from Anaheim, but I want to show you Rodeo Drive and take Momma to lunch at Ivy—if I can get her to say she'll come—and buy you something exquisite at Battaglia. I'll have my road manager take care of everything—limos, tickets, backstage passes, everything. Kenny, I'm so happy."

"So am I," he said. "And I'll work on Mary."

"Yes, do. Well, listen . . . it's late."

"Yeah."

"I guess we should say good night, shouldn't we?"

"Yes, we should."

"Well . . . good night then."

"Good night."

"Kenny, wait!"

He waited. "I'm here."

"About Faith . . ." She felt obliged to add, "Just make sure."

"I'm sure."

"All right, then. See you soon."

"Good night again."

" 'Night, Kenny."

At last they hung up, reluctantly, as always.

THE DAYS FLEW between then and the Anaheim concert. Tess spoke to her mother almost daily, trying to convince her to come with Kenny. Mary kept saying, "Well, I'll see how my hip feels. That's a long plane ride, you know."

"Momma, please?"

"Well, Tess, now, I told you, I'll just have to see."

She was still saying the same thing the

day Tess headed for L.A. on her private Hawker-Sidley jet, taking Casey with her, because she was still having fun thrilling the kid and showing her what her future could hold if she worked hard enough and got the big breaks.

ON THE NIGHT BEFORE KENNY FLEW to L.A., he and Faith were scheduled to play cards, their regular Thursday-night game. The bridge group had met at Faith's house, and Kenny had played poorly. Though Faith had not chided him, sometimes she'd looked up over her cards with wry disapproval at his absentmindedness, bitten the inside of her lip and stared at him corrosively. At ten o'clock she served warm peach pie à la mode and by ten forty-five everybody had left except Kenny. He was helping her clean up the kitchen and put away the card table and folding chairs. He stuck the four metal chairs behind the coats in her small entry closet and returned to the kitchen to find her storing away her good forks and spoons in a silverware chest. He picked up a stack of dessert plates and put them in the cupboard.

"Kenny," she said, examining each fork before putting it in the velvet-lined box. "Maybe we should talk about this mistake you're making."

"Mistake?"

"I wasn't born yesterday, Kenny. I know why you didn't ask me to come along to L.A. with you." She shut the silver chest and looked at him, her hands curled over the edges of the box.

"She's sending me the tickets, Faith, and there are only two."

"Kenny . . . please," she said, as if he'd insulted her intelligence. Carried the chest away into another room and he waited, chastised, for her return. She came back removing an apron, opened a drawer, tucked it away, then stood looking down at the drawer instead of at him.

"I guess I realized it within two weeks after she got home. I know you well enough that I could tell the minute you started to fall for her. But, Kenny, think . . ." She turned to him, slightly imploring, resting one hand on the cabinet top. "What is she going to do with you when it's over?"

He thought for a moment, and answered honestly, "I don't know."

His admission of guilt, coming so soon, quite stunned Faith. Her expression flattened and her chin drew back an inch. She had expected him to deny any involvement with Tess. When he did the opposite, it left an emotional gap in the room.

Faith said, "You're willing to give up everything we have to pursue this hopeless affair?"

"Everything we have? What do we have, Faith?"

"We have eight years of loyalty!" she replied, sounding a little panicked. "At least, I've been loyal to you."

"And how many times have we talked about getting married, and how many times have we both decided not to?"

"I thought you liked our situation the way it's been."

"We've become a convenience for each other, admit it, Faith."

"Well, what's wrong with that?" she snapped, irritated.

He hung his head and wobbled it from side to side without answering.

She moved a step closer, her hand still extended on the countertop. "I don't want to lose you, Kenny. And that's what will happen if you go to L.A. and go to bed with that woman again."

He showed a first hint of anger. "Let's get one thing straight, Faith. I've never been to bed with her."

"No, but you're planning on it, aren't you?" When he refused to answer she demanded, louder, "Aren't you!"

"Faith, did you ever stop to think that we've been heading toward this day for eight years, and neither one of us could find the courage to end it? I don't want to be a seventy-year-old man who's been dating you for half of his life. Don't you realize how ridiculous that would be?"

She retracted her hand and straightened her spine. "Well, I can see you're not going to change your mind." She crossed the room and switched off the overhead fluorescent light, leaving a smaller one on over the sink.

"No," he said quietly, remaining where he was. "I'm not."

"You're going out there, and you're . . . you're going to start an affair with her."

"I think I love her, Faith."

"Oh, don't be ridiculous!" she retorted in

the most disparaging voice she'd ever used on him.

"You think I'm ridiculous?"

"Believing she'd fall in love with you? Doesn't that sound a little ridiculous, Kenny? A woman like that—rich and famous—how can you help but suspect her motives?"

Faith was not by nature a cruel person, but her remarks cut deeply. Did she see him as a man who would have no permanent value to another woman, especially one like Tess McPhail?

Faith continued badgering him. "And have you stopped to ask yourself why she's taken such a sudden interest in Casey, if she might be using Casey to get her hooks into you? It sure looks like it, doesn't it?" She paused a beat for effect. "So when she's done with you, will she be done with Casey, too? Oh, Kenny, don't you realize how that girl could get hurt? She's fallen under Tess McPhail's spell even harder than you have."

Anger boiled up in him suddenly. He kept it under tight control as he told her, "You know, Faith, you and I have been together all these years and hardly ever had a fight

. . . but you're really pissing me off right now. So before I say something I'll regret, I'm getting out of here." He headed for the door, informing her over his shoulder, "I'm going to L.A. tomorrow and I'll be there for three days. Maybe while I'm gone you should take your extra clothes out of my house and leave the spare key on the kitchen table."

She watched him in stupefaction as he broadsided her screen door with both hands and let it slam behind him.

"Kenny!" she called, bolting after him. "Kenny, wait!"

Outside she changed her mind about chasing him down the sidewalk and stopped on the steps, bent urgently toward his disappearing form as it was swallowed by the night shadows. "Kenny, please, can't we talk about this? Don't go."

"I have to, Faith," he called without turning back.

"Kenny, this is silly! We can't end it like this without even talking about it!"

"The neighbors are going to hear you, Faith. Go on back inside."

Some time later, when he'd driven away and left her standing on the steps pleading, she wandered inside feeling dazed and somewhat dizzy with the sudden shift her life had taken in such a few short minutes. She should have let him go without saying a word. Should have let him fly off to L.A. and get it out of his system without ever finding out she suspected.

Touching her lips, she looked around the kitchen as if searching for something. But everything was in its place, everything put away neatly, everything in order.

"Oh, Kenny," she whispered, wilting back till her hip bumped the cabinets. "You're going to get so hurt." But what she really meant was *I'm going to get so hurt.*

TWENTY

THE ANAHEIM CONCERT was scheduled to begin at eight the following night. At seven, backstage at Arrowhead looked like backstage at NASA—confusion to the untrained eye, complexity within order to the trained. The sound check had been done that afternoon, but technicians darted everywhere, stretching cables and communicating on walkie-talkies. The floors looked like jungles, twisted with electric cables that resembled tree roots, some as thick as a man's arm. The curtains were closed. Dim canister lights dropped blotches of illumination from the gridwork of metal that hung from the blackened ceiling. On the stage wings immense black speakers were piled like tall buildings, and everywhere in the dimness small red lights peppered the scene. Members of the band gave their instruments one last tuning. A faint electronic buzz could be heard over all, punctuated by the hollow thud of footsteps hurrying over the elevated wood floor. Some people wore headphones with mouthpieces fixed before their lips, like telephone operators. Some people wore tool belts. Some wore suits and ties. Some ran around with flashlights, shining them into dark corners.

On stage right, beyond the circuitry and circus, a corridor between the curtains led to a large windowless room completely curtained in white. Ceiling to floor, the drapery covered every wall. Against one, a long table held a bouquet of enormous white lilies. The lilies—dozens, arranged with pure white snapdragons and clouds of airy sprengeri—filled the room with an overpowering fragrance. Beside the table black-clad members of the caterer's staff stood awaiting requests for anything not already provided. There were cold drinks on ice, bottled water, a variety of sodas, fruit juices and milk, but nothing alcoholic. There were a dozen kinds of finger foods, including specific favorites of Tess and the band, from salmon sandwiches on dilled bread rounds to miniature quiches. There were berries and cubed fruit and a tray of gooey brownies and hot coffee.

But no one was eating a thing.

A half dozen reporters milled in a corner where torchères spread rosy light onto the draped wall above their heads. Two long white sofas were unoccupied, but near them stood the executives of the MCA record label and their spouses. Yet another group of top DJs waited around while a pair of uniformed, armed guards stood with their hands linked at their stomachs just inside the door. A woman with a clipboard came in and glanced around and went back out, remaining just beyond the door. A different woman—younger, dressed in a black leather off-the-shoulder dress, high black spiked heels and a rhinestone belt slung low on her hips—approached the woman with the clipboard, and said, "Hi."

The woman smiled. "Hi, Casey."

"She in there?"

"Yes. Go right in."

"Thanks."

Casey passed between the guards, who smiled and nodded and relaxed their knees a little. "Hi, how's it goin'?" she said to them nervously, then, scanning the table as she passed, "Hey, this is really somethin', isn't it?" She veered over to the food and pointed. "Is that pizza?"

One of the caterers, happy to see any interest shown in their handiwork, answered, "Yes, mushroom and sausage miniatures . . . please, help yourself."

"Oh, I couldn't eat a thing." She pressed a hand to her stomach and made a face. "Too scared. But thanks anyway. Maybe afterwards."

The curtained walls were interrupted by a single door. Affixed to it was a small brass plaque that said Mac, in the same signature typeface as that used on her album covers. Casey knocked and stuck her head inside.

"Okay if I come in?"

Tess was sitting at a dressing table having finishing touches put on her hair. Her face had been illumined by stage makeup— a thirty-five-minute application that Cathy Mack had done with brushes and a palette, like an artist doing an oil painting. The freckles were gone, covered by an alabaster base. The lipline was perfect, enlarged slightly, and flattering. The lips themselves had been darkened to plum. Her eyes, shaded and mascaraed to appear larger, became vibrant with welcome as she caught sight of Casey in the mirror. "Of course. Hey, you look sensational!"

"So do you."

They truly did. Casey's hair was done in shiny loose locks, drawn back behind one ear. Tess's was a longer version of the hairdo on her upcoming CD photo, a sexily disheveled shag that was made to look un-styled but had—in fact—taken Cathy an-other thirty minutes to arrange.

Cathy said, "Hold still . . . just one more minute."

Complying, Tess followed Casey with her eyes. "They taking care of you okay?"

"Everybody's been just great."

"The dress looks fabulous."

"Now I know what Rowdy feels like when I've got him saddled." She put a hand on her trembling stomach where the leather dress clung.

"Scared?" Tess asked, smiling a little.

"Shitless."

Tess laughed, relieving a little of the ten-sion. "That's all right. When you get on that stage you forget all about it."

"I know. Hey, have you seen anything of Dad and Mary yet?"

"Not yet." *Where are you, Kenny, where are you?*

"Gol, you don't suppose they missed their plane, do you?"

The tension was back, full force, greater than ever before in Tess's life. She hid it for Casey's sake. "If they did they'd have called." But inside, her stomach trembled, and every time anyone came to the door her heart jumped into her throat.

"Do you think Mary will be with him?"

"I can't even guess. She absolutely refused to commit."

Hurry up, Cathy, I want to be perfect when he walks in, and not anchored here in this chair. Tess sang a few lines from her opening number, to relax and be certain she was in good voice.

Finally Cathy said, "That's it for hair and makeup. Now for the suit." Tess got up and Cathy went to pull a white satin trouser suit off a hanger. Tess dropped her dressing gown and stepped into the pants. They were trimmed with a strip of clear sequins down the outsides of both legs. The jacket had an oversized collar, a nipped waist and was covered all over with clear sequins that glittered as she moved.

"Earrings," Cathy said, and handed Tess a pair made of white egret feathers dusted with the same iridescent sequins.

"Shoes," Cathy said, and produced a pair that had been custom-made to match the suit. They, too, glittered when she walked.

When Tess was dressed she faced the mirror, which was surrounded by lights. *All right, Kenny, come now . . . please!*

Casey appeared in the mirror beside her. They checked each other out.

"Wow, fresh, huh?" Casey said.

"A couple of real eye-catchers, ain't we?" Tess joked.

"I say we look like a pair of Saturday-night hookers."

They were both laughing when the door opened and made Tess's heart go *ka-wham.* But it wasn't Kenny and it wasn't Momma. It was the woman with the clipboard. "Time check, twenty minutes," she said.

Twenty minutes . . . where could he be?

Then it seemed like everybody came in at once. Estelle and Diane, also dressed in black leather, styled differently from Casey's. "Just wanted to say break a leg, Mac. You, too, Casey." And behind Estelle came Charlotte Carson, Tess's publicist, who told her, "Got the press and a few people from MCA out here waiting whenever you're ready."

"Okay, be right there. Cathy, something's scratching my neck back there. Will you see what it is?"

Cathy was checking the neckline of her dress, and the room was filled with chattering people when Charlotte answered a knock and Ross Hardenberg stuck his head in, announcing, "Somebody special to see you, Mac."

And into the dressing room walked Kenny with her momma.

It wasn't at all the way she'd imagined, seeing them again, not with her chin down while Cathy snipped with a scissors and held her prisoner. Not with a half a dozen chattering people filling the room, and a bunch more waiting outside for her attention. Not with all this commotion!

She had wanted to be relaxed, and poised, and smiling, and to walk straight to him with her hands reaching out for his. Instead, she could only stand with her head down, able to see nothing but the black silk stripe meeting the hem of his trousers, next to Momma's green silk pantlegs.

A tuxedo? He'd worn a tuxedo?

Cathy finally said, "Okay," and Tess was free.

She looked up and felt the impact in her throat, chest and lungs. All over. A full-body charge. A tumult of joy and relief and promise: *Tonight we're going to become lovers.* They both knew it in that instant when their eyes met across the crowded room, and she wondered how in the world she'd manage to sing with everything inside her seized up this way.

Then she was moving toward him, toward them—*Momma* first, she reminded herself.

"Momma, you came!"

"Kenny wouldn't have it any other way."

"And you look so pretty!"

"Well, so do you, honey. That's some outfit you're wearing."

She was dimly aware of people stepping back while she embraced her mother, and of Kenny and Casey hugging, too, and of the fact that Mary was decked out in the green suit and emeralds she'd worn for the wedding, and that Mary's hair had been fixed in a beauty shop and looked absolutely lovely. But all of this was secondary to the man she was dying to touch.

She gave him her hands at last, and smiled up at him, and said, "Kenny," in some strange, emotion-pinched voice, and read the look in his eyes that said, I missed you, I can't believe I'm touching you, this is torture not kissing. And oh, he looked elegant, though his face was flushed above the white collar and black bow tie of his tux.

"Hi, Tess," he said simply. But he nearly broke her knuckles, he was squeezing them so tightly.

She stretched up to him and he lowered his head and they gingerly touched cheeks, protecting her stage makeup, hair and sequins.

"Thank you for bringing her," she whispered, leaving a tiny trace of lipstick on his cheek, taking away the suggestion of sandalwood from his skin.

"Thank you for arranging it. You look beautiful."

"So do you. The tuxedo is smashing."

It was as much as they dared say under observation. She stepped back dutifully, longing only to grab his arm and haul him out of this place, away from obligation, and the crowd, and the press and the craziness—anyplace the two of them could be alone. Instead she told him, "Someone will bring you back here afterwards. Just wait in your seats."

"Time check, ten minutes," a voice warned, and she squeezed his hands and released them.

Kenny and Mary were ushered away, and Tess was separated from everyone else and taken into the anteroom where the press, the DJs and the hierarchy from her record label were waiting for a five-minute audience. She shook every hand, beamed her famous smile, remembered the first names of a couple of the DJs, answered a couple of questions, charmed the gold out of everyone's teeth, and wondered again how in the world she'd be able to sing with this swollen feeling in her throat.

At her side, someone spoke quietly. "Three minutes."

Her show producer, Ralph, always went with her right to the edge of the stage, and Cathy Mack did as well, checking her hair at the last minute, maybe whisking a brush over her nose. Tonight, as they reached the wings, Cathy sensed that Tess was more tense than usual, and stood behind her, reaching her thumbs deep down into Tess's back neckline to give her an impromptu massage. Tess let her mind go blank and her shoulders relax for thirty seconds, willing the tension away.

"Two minutes." Again, quietly, in a tone meant to calm.

There was one last thing she had to do.

"Thanks, Cathy," she said, and went out among the black-and-silver cubes holding her band members at various heights, and reached up to the one where her three backup singers stood high above her in black leather. She squeezed Casey's hand, and said, "Just like in Momma's living room, okay?" Then she gave Casey a wink and went back to stage right.

The same calm, quiet voice advised, "Okay . . . anytime."

Tess took a huge breath, shut her eyes, emptied her lungs in a long, slow stream, and opened her eyes again. The drummer was waiting. He caught her nod, gave a *tak-tak-tak* on the rim of his snare, and out beyond the curtains the music rattled to life.

The crowd burst into applause that nearly covered up the drummer's backbeat, and the curtain lifted as a gorgeous male voice boomed, "Ladies and gentlemen . . . America's leading lady of country music . . . *Tess McPhail!*"

Deafening applause surrounded her and carried her to center stage. The beat kicked ass. The spotlights blinded. Her cordless mike was waiting. She grabbed it and started giving these people what they'd paid to hear.

All dressed up and howlin' on a
Saturday night,
Creeping down the alley toward your back
porch light,
Woo-ooo (the girls sang)
Mee-yew (they jutted their hips)
Gonna dress in satin,
Gonna go out cattin'
With you.

The playbacks carried her own voice back to her as she sang for an audience that remained invisible. She could see nothing beyond the blinding footlights. But during rehearsal she'd marked the spot below the stage apron where Mary and Kenny would be sitting, and now, as she sang the chorus, she pointed a long copper fingernail at where he must be, just as she'd done at the wedding dance: *with you.*

She wished she could see his face. But he could see hers, and it was heady knowing he was there, eyes lifted, while she telegraphed her intentions before eighteen thousand fans.

She never opened a concert without a modicum of angst. It was customary. And, granted, tonight it was worse, but, as always, the music grabbed her, controlled her, and midway into the first number she had forgotten everything else.

The song ended. Her arms were extended in the air over her head. The crowd went wild with applause as she stood center stage wishing more than ever that she could see Kenny and Momma. Even though she couldn't, the knowledge of their presence fired her performance as never before and brought her a satisfaction that superseded any she'd ever felt about her work.

The concert flowed seamlessly. Tess's professional side took over, entertaining her fans, yes, but analyzing everything at the same time. Casey did a remarkable job, considering how little rehearsal she'd had. Tess could watch the show on an closed-circuit TV screen that hung from the catwalk above the audience's heads, of which they were unaware. She was pleased with what she saw. The lighting was innovative, rhythmic, and effective on her shimmering costumes. The three backup singers had their licks and movements down cold, and against the dull black leather of their dresses, their rhinestone belts accented each maneuver when the powerful spots hit them.

There were cold audiences and warm ones. Tonight's audience was warm: polite and quiet during the numbers, explosive afterward.

When the band took over during the first costume change, Ralph Thornleaf was waiting in the wings to give her the thumbs-up. "You got 'em, kid! Dynamite!" Cathy Mack skinned her out of her white suit and zipped her into a green beaded gown held by an assistant. She put a quart bottle of cold Evian water into her hands, and Tess drank half of it, then climbed into a Stutz Bearcat that drove her onto the stage for the next sequence. There were six other costume changes, and six other bottles of cold Evian water. There were dancers and graphic effects, and a slide show of Tess at all ages, reproduced from Mary's old home photographs. There were blowups of all Tess's album covers on nine huge squares arranged like a tic-tac-toe board, automated to turn individually like those on a game show.

Midway through the show she introduced the members of the band, saving Casey for last. She told the audience, "This little girl is special. She's from my hometown of Wintergreen, Missouri, and this is her first time ever onstage with me. We've been writing music together and our first collaborative effort will be the title song on my new album in September. You're going to see a lot of this young woman in the years ahead, and I have a feeling she won't always be backing me up. Won't you give her career a big send-off . . . here's Casey Kronek!"

The audience responded with an enthusiastic ovation, and Tess felt the vicarious thrill that she saw in Casey's face as the applause swelled for her alone. When the auditorium quieted Tess moved close up to the footlights and spoke into her mike with an air of sincerity that silenced every rustle in the house.

"Tonight is very special for me because there are some people here I love. People from back home." A spotlight hit row one on cue and Tess saw Mary and Kenny for the first time since walking on stage. She let her eyes pause briefly on him before settling on her mother. "One stands out above all the rest for what she's done for me my whole life long. This lady sat on the front steps and let me serenade her when I was six. She bought me a piano and paid for piano lessons when I was seven. She overlooked my terrible grades in every other class except music, and allowed me to join a little band when I was much too young to legally do so. She suffered through all those awful rehearsals in our living room long before there ever was a record contract. And she watched me pack my suitcase and drive away to Nashville the very week I graduated from high school, without once letting me see the tears in her eyes, or hear the voices of misgiving that surely must've been busy in her head. She always said to me, 'Honey, I know you can make it. There's not a doubt in my mind.' "

Letting her gaze rest tenderly on Mary, Tess said, "Momma, won't you please stand up so these people can honor you?"

Mary made one false attempt to rise, but her hips were a little stiff, then Kenny graciously took her arm and helped her to her feet. She never even straightened entirely, but raised one hand and flapped it while sitting down again quickly—as if to say, All this fuss over an old woman. The audience caught her wry unconcern over being spotlighted, and a ripple of laughter brought a down-home feeling to the fading applause. Then Tess confided in the audience, "Momma's got two new hips so the plane ride here wasn't too easy for her. Thanks for coming, Momma."

She let a beat pass.

"And beside her is someone else from my hometown who is also special to me. He's the proud father of Casey Kronek, and an old classmate of mine. Kenny . . . so glad you're here." To the audience she said, "Both Kenny and Momma know the genesis of this next song. They heard it performed for the first time in Momma's living room last spring, the very week that Casey and I wrote it. It's got a new verse written especially for tonight that they've never heard before . . . comes straight from the heart. It's the title cut I just told you about, and this is our first time performing it in public. It's called 'Small Town Girl.' "

There had been special moments in Tess's career, songs that meant more than others. But singing this one in public for the first time truly was the emotional high of her life. The words seemed to run a thread through her and Casey and Momma and Kenny that bound them, inexorably, forever. Not another soul in the place mattered during the course of that song.

One-way traffic crawlin' 'round the small-town square,
Eighteen years've passed since she's been there,
Been around the world, now she's coming back,
Wider-eyed and noting what this small town lacks,
Can't return,
Too much learned.

Mama's in the home place, never changed
a lick,
House as worn and tattered as a derelict,
Same old clock a-tickin' on the faded
kitchen wall.
Mama won't replace anything at all.
Mama's fine,
Can't change her mind.

How we change
As we grow,
Rearrange
What we know.

Heard a lot of talk about the boy next door,
He's a part of yesteryear I see no more.
Circumstances took us eighteen years apart,
Took him just one night to soften up
my heart.
Say good-bye,
Mustn't cry.

Home-town girl departing on a
one-way flight,
Something deep inside her somehow
set a-right,
Runs her tearful eyes across the faded
kitchen wall,
Whispers, Mama, please don't change at all.

Must return,
There's more to learn.

One-way traffic crawling' 'round a
small-town square . . .

When the song ended, there were tears in Tess's eyes and a great fist seemed to have seized her heart.

The audience response was thunderous. With a flourish of her hand Tess guided the sweeping spot to Casey at rear stage, so she could accept her share of the applause. Casey smiled and bowed, experiencing the most heady moment of her life, and Tess wondered when—if ever—she herself had experienced a moment this perfect.

The remainder of the concert seemed almost anticlimactic. Though the program included louder songs, faster songs, songs that had built her career and that were more familiar to the audience, none had the impact of the new ballad that showed where her heart was.

They did two encores, and when the curtain lowered and the house lights came up, Tess felt victorious. The adrenaline rush was still buzzing through her as the armed guards escorted her among a swarm of others to the same white-draped room where a hundred twenty-five people had been invited for a postconcert champagne reception. Tess was taken straight through to her dressing room, where Cathy was waiting with yet another bottle of chilled water, and to remove her gown and replace it with a tailored trouser suit and silk blouse of Tess's favorite midnight blue—not a sequin or rhinestone in sight. Cathy also had lower-heeled pumps, and her ever-handy makeup bag with her powder brush at the ready. She blotted Tess's hot face, dulled her shining skin with translucent powder, ran a lipstick brush over her lips, hooked a silk scarf beneath her jacket collar, and said, "All ready to meet your public."

There were only two members of her public in whom Tess was interested tonight, and when she emerged from her private dressing room her eyes sought them out immediately. Mary was seated on one of the white sofas, surrounded by reporters who were asking her questions. Kenny was handing her a glass of champagne while Casey was standing by with two plates of food. She gave one to Mary, then sat down beside her while Kenny remained standing, drinking champagne.

Tess went straight to them.

"Hey, Momma," she greeted, and leaned over to kiss her mother first.

"Oh, honey, here you are. Say, that was some concert. I'm sure glad Kenny made me come."

"So'm I." She slipped her arm around Kenny's waist and smiled up at him.

He looked into her eyes and said quietly, "I'm awestruck," in a way that excluded everyone else in the room. His low-key compliment was all she needed to gild the moment. That and the arm he dropped casually around her shoulder.

But obligations still waited, so she told him privately, "I've got things I have to do, but we're all riding back to the city in the same limo, so don't go away."

"I won't."

Later, his eyes promised.

Hurry the hour, hers replied.

Louder, for the benefit of the press as well as the girl, Tess said, "Casey, honey, you were sensational," and leaned over and kissed her, too. "Promise you won't sign any record contracts till I get back, okay?"

Then, holding Casey's face, she asked softly, "You happy, sugar?"

"Oh, Mac, you just can't know."

"Me, too." And after a pause, "Gotta talk to some of these people, then I have to do the usual fan thing out front. If you want to come out there with me you can. I'll keep it short tonight though." She caught Kenny's hand again, and told him, "Watch over Momma just one more time, then I'll be back. Thirty minutes max."

"Hurry," he said as their hands reluctantly slid apart.

There were people she simply had to pay attention to—the executives from the record label were at the top of the list; the mayor of Anaheim; the top brass from Wrangler, her sponsor; syndicated columnists and concert reviewers; Tanya Tucker was there, and Clint Black with his wife, Lisa Hartman Black; Emmylou Harris; Kevin Costner; the members of her own stage band who'd made tonight such a big success. In the midst of all these well-wishers, she would look up and find Kenny watching her, and their gazes would lock and they'd exchange that same unspoken message: *Later. Tonight.* And it would be difficult to

look away and pay attention to what someone was saying.

But after the backstage obligations were
fulfilled, there were still the fans.

It was her custom to allow all active
members of her fan clubs to remain in the
auditorium after each concert for a private
greeting from her. These women and men
were the heart of her support structure, and
they deserved every minute she gave them.
She took Casey along to show her how this
aspect of business was handled. But part of
Tess's reason for having Casey along was
selfish: leaving Kenny, even for only half an
hour, was a sacrifice. With Casey beside
her it seemed less of an imposition.

It was just past midnight before Tess's
obligations had been fulfilled and they finally walked out the stage door and got into
the waiting stretch limousine. It was upholstered in leather, and the seat felt wholly
welcome as Tess sank down beside her
mother, facing front, while the other two sat
opposite, facing backwards.

The driver had left the courtesy lights on.
They formed a dotted line around the pe-
rimeter of the interior while champagne,
bottled water and canned soft drinks waited

in the coolers on the doors. Tumblers and stem glasses stood securely in their rosewood holders as the car pulled smoothly away, heading north.

Casey was still wound up. She jabbered, making everyone laugh, and Kenny put an arm around her while they rode. Mary, having sampled the champagne, was soon nodding. Tess, welcoming the quiet, mostly let Casey do the talking, indulging herself in her absorption with Kenny and the fact that they could, at long last, look at each other. He stretched out one long leg and his black tuxedo cuff deliberately touched her ankle. She rubbed against it like a cat preening, then rested her head back against the leather seat and closed her eyes, still connected to him by that tenuous link.

When they pulled up between the buildings at the Regent Beverly Wilshire it was after one o'clock in the morning, the place quiet, deserted, the doormen gloved and gracious. Mary, aroused from sleep, toddled up the steps on Kenny's arm, with Tess at her other elbow. She groaned a little, and said, "Oh, thank you, kids. Land, but I'm tired."

They walked through the lobby, past the

silent restaurant, between the brightly lit windows where gems and clothing were artfully displayed by the upscale shops on nearby Rodeo Drive, and took the elevator up to the fourth floor where they unlocked Mary's room.

"Are you on this floor?" Mary asked Tess.

"No, Casey and I are up on the sixth."

"And I'm right here across the hall from Mary," Kenny said. "But I'll walk you ladies up."

They bade Mary good night and when her door closed the three of them rode the elevator to the sixth floor, where they reached Tess's door first. Kenny kissed her cheek in brotherly fashion and thanked her, and she thanked him for bringing Mary. Next came a heartfelt hug from Casey, who said, "As long as I live I'll never forget this night. I never thought I'd do anything like this in my life. Thank you again, Mac."

Tess told her, "You're going to be a star in your own right someday, Casey, I just know it. And don't forget, bringing you into the music business has been fun for me, too. See you in the morning, hon." She put her key card in the slot, and added, "Good night, Kenny."

"Good night."

When Tess's door closed, Kenny slung an arm over Casey's shoulders and walked her farther down the hall to her room, saw her inside, then took the elevator back down to the fourth.

TWENTY-
ONE

IN TESS'S SUITE, a single lamp glowed softly in the sitting room at the far end of the sofa. She left it on and walked through to the bedroom where the maids had provided turn-down service while she was gone. The bedspread had been removed, the sheets folded down from the center like a paper airplane. On each pillow waited a good-night wish: two chocolate coins wrapped in gold foil.

The sight of the bed, waiting, prepared, raised a fine and welcome tension within her, a sexual impatience that pressed up insistently, bringing his visage to mind— Kenny, in a sleek black tux, come to gaze at her across a crowded room with eyes that matched the suppressed desire in her own. Like water above the rim of a cup, she felt as if the mixture of emotions she held were more than the human vessel could contain. It trembled there, close to overflowing, as she removed the makeup from her flushed cheeks; as she showered and washed her hair; bound it in one towel and dried with another; put on a freesia-scented splash and stared at her dilated, dazzled eyes in the wrap-around mirrors.

She touched the freckled hollow between her breasts, her trembling stomach . . . and assessed herself through his eyes, wanting to please him.

Tonight, she thought.

She put on the thick white robe provided by the hotel, dragged the towel from her hair and finger-combed her damp curls, impatient for his return.

IN HIS ROOM Kenny hung up his tuxedo jacket, removed his bow tie and cummerbund, washed his face, then sat down with a magazine and checked his watch. He'd give her ten minutes before going back up.

He lasted six before realizing he hadn't read a word or turned a page. Tossing the magazine aside he bolted from the chair and pocketed his key card on his way out the door.

The suites at the Regent had doorbells. When he rang hers it was 1:27 A.M.—a bizarre hour to go courting, he thought, but then her lifestyle was bizarre. He wondered how he'd get along blending into it once they were married.

"Kenny?" her voice said softly from inside.

"Yes."

The door opened and there she stood, in bare feet and an oversized white robe, her damp hair rollicking around a scrubbed and shiny face, the smell of flowers coming to the door along with her. Without a touch of the artifice she'd worn onstage she was even more beautiful to him.

She said very simply, "I thought you'd never get here," and he stepped inside, against her, blindly swatting the door closed behind him. Their embrace was a collision with her up on tiptoe and his arms lashed hard around her, lifting her free of the floor. Their first kiss was a desperate thing without finesse—two starving people with mouths open and bodies straining to make up for all the time apart. Then he lowered her till her toes gained purchase again, and like bends of a knot they turned into one another, trying to make two halves into a whole. The kiss changed directions as they tried a new slant on an old pleasure. She made a tortured sound, burrowing upward as if close were not close enough.

There were words pressing to be spoken, but their lips scarcely parted. "I thought I'd die before we could do this," she said within the satin folds of the kiss. "All those people . . ."

"And all I wanted to do was this." He wandered her face, his teeth taking nips of her upper lip, the edge of a nostril, her eyebrow—illogical places that only a man in love would prize. "I wanted to kick them all out!" he ranted. "Every last one of them! I kept thinking they didn't have any right to you! You were mine, not theirs!"

She smiled, loving how he'd felt exactly as she had.

Enough talking. Talking wasted lips that had better things to do, randy, wild things they'd been imagining doing together. He found her mouth again and covered it, tasting, holding nothing back. His hands slid down her back and captured her low, like an inverted heart, hauling her high and hard against him.

The intensity, of course, could not be sustained. Like any glut, it filled them, and soon they needed something less. His embrace slackened and her heels touched the floor. They drew apart and their gazes caught at close range. One of them laughed—it was he, murmuring, "We're awful, aren't we?"

She laughed, too. "Yes, and isn't it wonderful?" His arms were doubled lightly beneath her shoulder blades while they took the time to gaze at each other as they had not when he first came in, to appreciate the face of the other, turned perfect by love. The kiss resumed, gentler than before, now that the first desperation was gone. Their hands began roving. His back was smooth cotton, hers was rough terry. They explored with palms spread flat, reacquainting, thrilling each other with the simplest of touches. Time flowed into the wee minutes of the night while they remained near the door where only dim light found them from the lamp across the room. He reached to untie her belt, but she caught his hand between them and looked into his eyes.

"I have to know first . . . about you and Faith."

He said, with neither smile nor regret, "I've asked her to take her things out of my house. It's all over between us."

"Really? All over?"

"I'd never lie to you, Tess, not about that." Then he added, "Not about anything."

She knew he wouldn't. He had never been anything less than truthful about himself and Faith, right from the beginning.

She released his hand and a moment later the belt dropped to the floor. He reached inside and found her warm skin. Fragrance lifted from it as his hands caught her waist and his wrists parted the terry robe. He gave a gentle tug and she bumped up against him, resting there lightly while their bodies formed a wishbone and their eyes engaged in playful approval, just this side of full intimacy. She was supple and compliant, catching him behind the neck and leaning back while they swayed a little, all hurry gone.

"You smell good," he murmured, still gripping her waist as if to lift her into a carriage where none waited. Only her bed waited in the other room. And they, in this one, pretended nonchalance.

"I put something on for you. Freesia."

"Freesia. Where?"

"Everywhere."

They took some time to flirt with the suggestion, to let it play upon their libidos while their bodies swayed in a lazy figure eight. She thought he would bend down and kiss her, perhaps between her breasts, but instead he gathered her close once more, and putting his face to her neck, threaded his arms inside the robe, caressing her sleek warm back not only with his hands, but with his starched sleeves as well. He ran them along her sides, a crisp contrast to the smoothness of his palms as they slid down the slope of her spine to her naked buttocks. And from there one hand shifted at last to her breast and held its precious weight like a fruit warmed by the sun. It seemed forever they'd been imagining this first naked touch. Now it was here, better than imagined, spreading warmth and want deep within them. For a long while they paid homage to the moment, holding still everywhere else, absorbed in the pleasure of nothing more than his hand cupping her breast. Then her head fell back, her eyes closed and she put her hands in his hair, holding his head while down the gap in her robe he fit her bare body to his clothed one.

"I missed you so much," she told him.

"I missed you, too," he said, bringing his other hand into play. "So much . . ."

"After I left Wintergreen it was . . ." His thumbs moved and she shuddered once, and lurched, then let herself fall forward against both of his hands. "It was . . ." The word escaped her. All words escaped her. "It was . . ."

"It was hell," he whispered for her.

"Yes . . . it was hell."

Her forehead rested against his chin and his breath beat against her uncombed hair. Her hand dropped between them, playing over the worsted wool of his trousers, learning his shape within his clothing.

"Tess . . ." he breathed, before silence became their ally. Only silence, mingling with his disbelief that he was here with this woman, doing this incredible thing, feeling her hands on him after all the years she had been far, far beyond reach.

"Take me to bed, Kenny," she whispered.

He was struck by a broadside of awe, realizing who she used to be—the Tess from his past. Who she'd become—Mac, the superstar, adored by millions. And who he'd become—the man she wanted as fully as he wanted her.

She sensed a change in him and looked up. "Kenny?" she whispered, "What's wrong?"

"Nothing. It just . . ." He appeared momentarily beleaguered. "It just hit me where I am, and who I'm with, and what you just said . . . and I'm human enough to be a little stunned by it, that's all."

"Don't be too stunned," she murmured softly. "It's just me, Tess."

"Just you, Tess. The girl on the school bus. Then you became Mac, the woman so far beyond my reach that all I could do was cut out pictures of you. And now you're Tess again, and you want to go to bed with me. I don't think you can quite realize how incredible this seems sometimes."

"No more incredible than you are to me. Kenny Kronek, the boy next door. Who'd have believed it?" She smiled and repeated, "Take me to bed, Kenny . . . please."

He picked her up like a groom carrying a bride from a church and headed for the brighter light of her bedroom, her arms coiled around his neck and her mouth pressed to the warm hollow behind his jaw. His skin smelled like sandalwood. She tasted it, made a small wet patch on his smoothly shaved neck, and the scent became flavor on her tongue.

"You taste good," she said.

Above her head, he grinned. "You're getting ahead of me."

"Hm-mmm," she singsonged, meaning, *No I'm not.* "And I know whereof I speak, Mr. Kronek."

He was still grinning as he reached their destination and released her legs. She landed on the foot of the bed, kneeling, the robe puddled around her, and lifted her hands to the black onyx studs down his shirtfront. While he began freeing his cuffs he let his knuckles bump her breast—a pebble over a washboard—bringing them both smiles.

She smiled at his shirtfront.

He smiled at the top of her hair, then kissing it, bent at the waist and got rid of his shoes.

"We both knew this would happen to-night, didn't we, Kenny?"

"Yes, we knew." He found a condom in his trouser pocket and tossed it onto the bed behind her. She undid his waist button, he the zipper, and together they got rid of everything but his shorts. They were silk. Green silk with orange cats on them.

"You wear silk shorts?" she said, surprised, delighted, sitting back on her heels to ogle them. "With *cats*?"

"They're new. I figured that's what a guy should wear to take Tess McPhail to bed."

"Don't say that as if all kinds of guys have figured the same thing, because there haven't been that many."

"We can talk about that later, Tess, okay?" he said, drawing her back up to kiss her.

"There are lots of things we've got to talk about later."

"Mm-hmm."

He was naked and she was just about as he went down on one knee and plunged his face into the gap of her robe to take his turn at tasting. A very slow sweet turn before pushing the robe off her shoulders and tumbling her sideways onto the smooth ecru sheets. They fell in one swift motion at the same moment that they touched each other intimately for the first time—a sweep, a fall, a lunge—it was all of these, and silent except for their harsh breathing.

They explored with a shared sense of wonder, first with their eyes open, then with eyes closed, kissing tenderly, then not so tenderly as some primal force took control.

Once he whispered, "Oh, Tess . . ." because there were no other words in this foolish man-made language to do justice to what he felt.

And she answered in kind, repeating his name, "Kenny . . . Kenny . . ." because she, too, found no other words adequate.

Much later, he whispered, "Like this?"

And she breathed, "Yes . . ." arching her throat.

And later yet she found the foil packet in the sheets and said, "Put this on now . . . please," and watched, unashamed, as he did.

As he knelt to her she reached up and touched the hair at his temple, feeling a compulsion to say to this man something she'd said to no other. "Let me say it now, Kenny . . . I love you."

She loved the look that overtook his face: joy and disbelief after her long refusal to admit it.

"Say it again, Tess."

"I love you," she repeated, with wonder seizing her soul, quite stunned by the force of the words, spoken at last. "Oh God, I do, I love you!" she rejoiced.

He turned his face into her palm and kissed it.

There were tears in her eyes as he entered her and elevated them both to a state of splendor. Then he pressed deep, past the flesh, into the soul, into the heart of her.

There had been, in Tess's life, no moment as magnificent as this, saying the words, meaning them, manifesting her love in this most perfect way.

"I love you, too," came his jagged whisper as he began moving, finishing what they'd started one dark spring night in a backyard on the grass beside some crickets.

IT WAS TWO-FIFTEEN. They lay in the lamplight, tired but unwilling to admit it, wanting to waste not a minute of this night. Their faces were close on a single pillow, and their bodies scarcely linked. Gravity pulled at the skin beneath his eyes and showed her where a wrinkle would lie in the years ahead. She followed it with one fingertip and repeated what she'd said earlier. "Kenny Kronek, the boy next door—whoever would have thought it?"

"Not me," he said with his eyes closed. "Not in a thousand years. Not with Tess McPhail."

"I'm just flesh and blood like anybody else."

"No. Not like anybody else." His eyes opened. "Not to me. I've loved you so long that I can't remember when I didn't."

She thought of the file of newspaper clippings he kept in his office, and believed him. "Oh, Kenny."

"It's true. You were the one I never forgot."

"I'm sorry I can't say the same thing back to you. But I only found out how wonderful you are this spring, and even then I resisted falling in love with you." Her fingertip trailed down to his lower lip and rubbed it softly. "Wanna know something?"

"Hm?"

"After I left Wintergreen I kept remembering that night of the wedding dance in Momma's backyard, and wishing we'd done more."

"You, too?" he replied lazily. "I'd think to myself, man, how stupid can you be? Why didn't you do it while you had the chance? Tess, I wanted you so much that night."

"I wanted you, too."

"Then all of a sudden you were gone and I'd lost my chance. After you left I'd look across the alley at your mother's windows and get so damned lonely knowing you weren't there anymore."

"And whenever my phone would ring my heart would leap, thinking it was you. And when it wasn't, I'd feel so unbelievably let down. It was this new and . . . and almost *consuming* feeling, missing somebody that much."

"Why didn't you say so?"

"I don't know." She shrugged. "Scared, I guess. Because of the intensity of my feelings. Doubting they could be real."

"It was different for me. I knew it so soon after you came back home."

"Even though you were living with Faith?"

"Faith and I had become a huge convenience. She ironed my shirts. I mowed her lawn. But you can't build a lifelong relationship on convenience. At least, I can't. I knew I had to make a break with her, and when you came back to town I began to realize that with Faith, this part of it . . . the sex was . . . well . . . it was . . ."

"Go ahead. You can say it. You can say anything to me."

"All right. Unsatisfying. It had become . . . well, mechanical, sort of."

"Mechanical," she mused aloud.

He considered what might be construed as a breach of confidence and decided he could say this much: "She didn't like to get messed up."

His frankness caught Tess by surprise. She felt a grin threatening but pulled it back into line. Though she tried not to laugh, a little snort fizzed up, and she covered her mouth too late to hold it in. Above her hand her eyes danced with mischief, and finally she said, "The woman didn't know what she was missing."

At first she thought she might have offended him but then he, too, caught the bug and laughed—a big, hearty one that threatened something else entirely. "Oh, Lord, don't laugh!" she warned, clutching him tight around the middle.

But it was too late. The link was lost and they were forced to make repairs.

It took a few minutes then before they were back in bed, snuggled up against three stacked pillows, covered by the smooth sheets with Tess tucked comfortably under Kenny's arm and one knee pulled up over his thighs. Behind her shoulder he unwrapped the last piece of chocolate, gave her the first bite, then popped the rest into his mouth.

"All right," he said, tossing the foil ball onto the nightstand, "What about you?"

"What about me?"

"I'm asking about your former sex life. How many before me?"

"Do I have to tell?"

"No."

She peered up at him, surprised by his answer.

"Four."

"Four!"

"All before I was twenty-eight. That's the year I hit it really big and realized I had to be more cautious. Fame works against you in that way. You never know what men are after. It gets . . . very lonely."

"Were any of them serious?"

"No."

"What about this musician you were seeing lately?"

"No. The truth is, he tried, but that was after I'd been back home and seen how good you were to Momma and sung in your choir and rolled around with you in the backyard and you made other men seem icky."

"Icky?" He grinned at her choice of words. "I did that?" He pulled his chin back to look down, but could see only the top of her head.

"Absolutely."

"So are you saying you've never been in love before?"

"I didn't have time to fall in love. I had places to go, things to accomplish. And then I accomplished them and . . ." She absently rubbed his chest before continuing thoughtfully. "It's a funny thing . . . I used to think my life was so full without this, without you, and I never knew how I was fooling myself. I thought I had it all . . . till now."

The chocolate was gone from their tongues. They lay for a while in the smug afterglow of first love, feeling lucky, and sated, and very reluctant to part, come Sunday. They had tomorrow to spend together, then her concert tomorrow night, but after that he'd have to go back to Wintergreen, and she'd have to go back to Nashville. And what then? A long-distance affair?

Kenny brought it up first, what they'd both been thinking of.

"How do you think it would work if we got married?"

She reacted without the least surprise, remaining where she was, nestled against him as if this were not the most important conversation each of them had ever had.

"I don't know, but I've been thinking about it, too."

"That's *all* I've been thinking about, but there's a lot to work out."

"Where would we live?" she asked.

"In Nashville."

"And in Wintergreen?"

"What do you mean? We can't live in both places."

"Why not? We can afford it."

"I never thought of keeping both places."

"We could if Casey wanted us to. For a while anyway, until she got used to the idea of her childhood home being sold out from under her. We have to be careful about that."

"Yes, I suppose we do."

"We could use your house whenever we went back home to visit Momma. But what about your business?" she inquired.

"I'd sell it and take care of yours for you."

"You would?" This surprised her. She drew back and stared at him.

"It struck me one day when we were talking on the phone and you said how many things you have to keep tabs on, and how risky it is for you to delegate the money matters. I thought—hey, I could do that for her! I'm a natural, Tess. I'm a certified public accountant. Who better to see after your financial affairs?"

She sat up and looked at him in rank amazement. "You mean you'd do that? You'd actually give up your business to marry me?"

"Why, of course I would."

"And you'd move to Nashville? Without batting an eye?"

"Of course I would."

"Wouldn't you worry about being called a kept man?"

He burst out laughing and hauled her down where she'd been. "No offense, Tess, but that is one of the stupidest questions I've ever heard. I know how much work there'd be, and believe me I'd be anything but kept. I'd probably end up putting in more hours than I do now, judging from what I know about your success."

"You *have* spent some time mulling this over, haven't you?"

"Think about it—everything I do all day long is something you pay somebody else to do. Why shouldn't I be doing it for you and making your life easier?"

She *did* think about it. It sounded too good to be true.

"Boy, wouldn't it be wonderful if I could just hand over all the business management to you and I could just concentrate on the creative end?"

"I could take care of your taxes, your payroll, your accounts payable, your incoming royalties. I could handle your employees' retirement funds and their insurance, and all the financial arrangements involved in running a production the size of your show. Who does all that for you now?"

"A bookkeeper named Sue."

"Sue, huh?" They both thought about firing Sue; then he said, "She could show me your computer system, get me started. Would there be enough work to keep two of us busy?"

"I don't know. Maybe."

It was a minor hitch and they knew it. He rubbed her arm and assured her quietly, "You could trust me, Tess."

"Oh, heavens, I've known that since you counted out Momma's change the night you brought her softener salt in. You gave her every last penny." The mention of her mother brought another thought. "Boy, Momma would sure miss you if you moved away from Wintergreen."

"We'd go back to see her often though. More often than you have without me. I'd make you."

She chuckled, and said, "I know you would. And it'd be good for me, too. I need to see Momma more often."

They imagined it for a while and it began to seem entirely feasible.

"What about Casey?" she asked.

"Would you want her to keep living with us?"

"I don't know. What would you want?"

She gave it some thought, and remarked, "I sure love that girl."

He kissed the top of her head, and his tired eyes closed. "I know. That's what started this whole thing, isn't it? And that's one of the reasons I love you so much."

"But I'll confess to you that I don't want to have any kids of my own. My career is too important to me."

"Then Casey can be your kid. It's perfect." He yawned.

She imagined Casey as her kid and loved the idea. "I think I would want her to live with us for a while. I'm not tired of her yet."

He chuckled and rubbed his cheek against her hair. It was dry now and curled up like Little Orphan Annie's. He yawned again and her voice began fading away as she went on talking.

"I want you to see my house, Kenny. It's really beautiful. It's two stories with this fantastic overhanging balcony and a grand piano in this immense front window."

"Mmm . . ." he mumbled.

"I have an office there, and Casey has

her own bedroom, and our bedroom overlooks the pool."

Our bedroom, he repeated to himself, while from the wispy world of semiconsciousness, he smiled.

"When can you come and see it, Kenny?" Tess said, and getting no answer, "Hey, Kenny?" Drawing back, she discovered he'd drifted off to sleep. She smiled and studied his face in repose, loving what she saw, imagining that face on the other pillow for the rest of her life, knowing it was exactly what she wanted.

"Kenny," she said again, simply to speak his name one more time before spending the night beside him. "I love you."

She reached across him and turned out the light, then dragged the extra pillows from behind him and threw one on the floor. He roused slightly as she wriggled down into a comfortable curl at his side and turned her backside against him. Mumbling something unintelligible, he hooked an arm around her waist and pulled her back into his warm curve.

She smiled, closed her eyes and thought, Now I have everything.

AT DAYBREAK she awakened right where she'd fallen asleep, snuggled in the Z of his body. It was an exquisite place to be, and she closed her eyes and waited for a sign that he was waking up.

When he wiggled, she rolled over to face him and snuggled her kneecaps smack up against his stomach with her feet hooked over his knees.

"Hi," she whispered, and he opened one eye.

"Hi," he said in a voice like a galvanized bucket dragging on concrete.

"Still respect me?"

He closed the eye. "Uh-huh."

"Still wanna marry me?"

"Uh-huh."

"Still wanna keep my books?"

"Not right at this moment."

She giggled and kissed his chin. His eyes remained closed. She poked a finger into his mouth, and said, "Let's call room service and order breakfast for four, then tell Momma and Casey to get up here and tell them what we're going to do."

Biting her nail, still with his eyes closed,

he said, "Mm-kay. But do I have to put up with this intrusive behavior every morning?" The words came out muffled before he spit out her finger.

"Nope," she said. "Some mornings I'll be gone, singing in some faraway city—who knows? Could be as far away as China maybe—then you'll be so lonesome you'll wish I was there to pester you."

He smiled and pushed her knees down and rolled over on top of her. "Darlin'," he said, stretching out full-length, fitting his fingers between hers and burying her hands in the pillow, "You can pester me anywhere, anyway, anytime."

She took him at his word, then and there.

Afterward, they did exactly what she'd suggested, calling the two people they loved most and inviting them up to breakfast in Tess's suite, then they showered and dressed and tried to contain their excitement about telling Casey and Mary.

At precisely ten, the doorbell rang and Kenny answered.

"Room service, sir." A white-coated waiter rolled the table up to the sofa, lifted its drop leaves, and pulled four side chairs up to it.

"Would you like me to open the champagne, sir?"

"Yes, please."

The young Asian man wrapped a white napkin around the bottle of A. Charbaut et Fils and popped the cork. "Shall I pour, sir?"

"No, thank you. We'll wait till our guests arrive." The waiter put the bottle back into the footed silver wine cooler and Kenny saw him out. When he opened the door he found Mary and Casey just ready to ring the bell.

"Heyyyy . . . good morning!" he greeted them jovially, kissing their cheeks as they came inside. "How did everybody sleep?"

Casey gave him a curious glance. "Gee, you're in a good mood this morning."

"You bet," he said, clapping his hands once and shutting the door.

More greetings and kisses were exchanged with Tess while they got Mary seated on the sofa.

Casey eyed the ice bucket. "Champagne? At ten o'clock in the morning? What's the occasion?"

"Sit down, honey," Kenny said. "Tess?"

He pulled out a chair for her, then seated himself.

Casey eyed them both suspiciously while Mary lifted silver lids and sniffed the food.

"What's this? It looks good."

"A ham-and-cheese omelette," Tess answered, hoping she'd guessed right, for Kenny had placed the order.

"Who's for champagne?" he said, pulling the green bottle out of the ice.

"Not me," Casey said. "I can't stand the stuff."

"None for me, either. Gets me goofy," Mary said. "I'll have some coffee, though."

Kenny began filling everyone's cups and Casey watched him curiously as he came to hers. "Dad, what's the matter with you? You know I don't drink coffee."

"Oh!" He stopped pouring and set the silver pot down. "Well . . . then drink your orange juice, because Tess and I want to make a toast." He sat down and caught Tess's eye, giving her the go-ahead.

She lifted her flute. "Momma . . . Casey . . ." Another flute, a stem glass and a coffee cup joined it. "The toast is to all of us, and to our future happiness. We called you down here to tell you that Kenny and I are going to get married."

Mary looked stunned, as if she'd drop her cup.

Casey exclaimed, "I knew it!"

"How did you know it?" Kenny said.

"Well, you've still got your tuxedo pants on, Dad," she said, leaping to her feet to hug him.

"Oh . . . so I do."

"It's obvious you didn't spend much time in your room last night. Oh . . . sorry, Mary."

"Married?" Mary interjected belatedly. "But . . . but when did all this happen? I thought you two . . . oh, my . . . oh, gracious . . ." She started crying.

"Momma, what's wrong?"

"N-nothing. I'm just so happy." She covered her nose with a linen napkin. "You're really going to marry Kenny?"

"Yes, I am." Tess touched her mother's hand tenderly while the old woman stuck a stiff napkin under her glasses and dabbed at her eyes. Then the two shared an awkward hug across the corner of the table.

"Oh, my gracious me, this is too much."

Next, Casey threw a hug on Tess, and

both of them felt tears gathering in their throats. "You guys . . ." she said, growing emotional, "you sure know how to make a girl happy." When the emotional level got critical, she cracked a joke. "Does this mean I have to call you Mother, Mac?"

"Mother Mac? Oh, please, no." They all laughed, because there were tears in a lot of eyes.

Then Mary said, "Kenny, come here," and put her arms up. He left his chair and went to hers, leaned down into her embrace and felt her loving arms fold around him as he dropped to one knee. "Oh, Kenny," she whispered, but could say no more. She could only feel her tears roll over her downy cheeks as he held her.

"I love her very much," he whispered, "nearly as much as I love you." He pulled back and looked up at her, squeezing her hands hard.

"It's just so unbelievable."

"It is . . . I know."

Mary freed one of her hands to take one of Tess's. "You and Kenny," she said.

"But the hard part is, Momma, I have to take him away from you."

"Oh, don't be silly." Finding her spunk,

Mary released their hands and flapped her napkin impatiently. "I can get along just fine without him. I've got two sons-in-law and those big, strapping grandsons. They can help me when I need it."

"But you'll miss him."

"Well, of course I will. But—oh, my—how happy you've made me."

Suddenly Casey had a thought. "Oh, my gosh!" she exclaimed. "You'll be my grandma, Mary!"

"Well, now, that's a job I'll like!"

It took a while before they got around to eating breakfast. Who could eat breakfast with happiness like this chasing everything mundane from the mind? But finally somebody realized the food was getting cold, and they removed the lids and were two minutes into the meal when Casey stopped, and said it for all of them.

"Hey, you know what? This is going to be absolutely perfect—I mean, all four of us as a family. It's like it was meant to be."

It certainly was, their smiles all said.

Meant to be.

TWENTY-TWO

THEY WERE MARRIED less than two months later in the church where she had sung in his choir. The wedding was scheduled for one o'clock on a Wednesday afternoon, because the church was booked for all the weekend days that month, and so was the bride. She had sung in Vancouver the previous weekend, and would be singing in Shreveport the next.

But on this day—a hot, late-summer, high-sky day with the temperatures in the nineties and the cicadas singing in the backyards—she would belong not to her fans, but only to her man.

One hour before the ceremony was scheduled to begin, Mary was in her kitchen, all dressed, when she heard Tess and Renee coming down the stairs. She'd been listening to the two of them talking and laughing and traipsing through the house most of the morning. Now here they came, ready at last.

"Well, Momma, here I am," Tess announced from the doorway.

The old woman turned and put a hand to her mouth.

"Oh, land . . . oh, me . . . I think this is the happiest day of my life. I believe I'm happier today than I was the day of my own wedding."

"Don't you go cryin' now, Momma, not after Renee and I got your makeup all pretty."

Mary got control of herself and made a stirring motion. "Turn around. Let me see."

Tess turned a full circle, showing off her bridal dress. It was very simple, made of white linen, with cap sleeves, a square neck, and a stovepipe skirt whose hem was created by points of open cutwork that overhung her ankles by three inches. On her feet she wore white linen pumps, on her head, instead of a veil, a circlet of baby's breath with her hair pulled up high inside it. Her only jewelry was a tiny pair of sapphire ear studs matching the ring Kenny had given her: an emerald-cut sapphire surrounded by diamonds.

"Isn't she gorgeous?" Renee said, leaning against the doorway.

"Lord o' mercy," Mary said.

The bride was definitely the prettiest thing in that kitchen, which hadn't changed a whit. The same ugly wall clock pointed to the hour. The same curled-up plastic doily sat on the same old-fashioned table. The same wounded Formica bled white up through a thousand scratch marks.

But the house was a cool seventy-two degrees, because Tess had said, "Momma, if you want me to get married at First Methodist you're going to have to let me put air-conditioning in that house, 'cause if you think I'm getting dressed in that attic in the middle of summer, you're wrong. I'll melt like an ice cream cone and you'll have to pour me into that church!"

So Mary had called Clarence Spillforth down at the plumbing and heating store, and said, "Clarence, I want you to come up here and put me some air-conditioning into my house because my girl Tess is gonna get married here. She's marrying Kenny Kronek, you know, and he's moving to

Nashville to take care of her business for her, and his daughter, Casey? Well, she's been singing on Tess's records, don't you know. So, Clarence, when can you be here?"

Everybody in town knew what was happening over at First Methodist an hour from now. There would be lots of reporters at the church, and Tess had no desire to encounter her groom for the first time with shutters clicking from fifteen directions. So she and Kenny had made their secret plans.

She took Mary's hands, and said, "You understand, don't you, Momma? Kenny and I just want a few minutes alone together before we go to church."

"Well, of course. You got a right to do your wedding day the way you want. I'll get my purse, then I'm all ready to go."

While she went off to the bedroom, walking with scarcely a visible hitch these days, Tess and Renee exchanged a sentimental smile.

"Thanks so much for being with me this morning," Tess said, going to hug Renee, who rubbed her back.

"I wouldn't have missed it."

"You sure it's okay that I didn't ask you to be my bridesmaid?"

"Absolutely. You picked the perfect ones."

"Thanks for understanding."

"All ready," Mary announced, returning. "Let's go, Renee, and leave these two to do whatever it is they want to do."

At the back door, Renee paused, the last one out, and looked back at the bride. "It *is* the happiest day of her life, and it's no secret who's going to be her favorite son-in-law from now on. We're all happy about it, Tess."

"Thanks, sis."

They went out and the house grew quiet. In the alley the car doors slammed, an engine started, then disappeared. The only sound in the kitchen came from the humming of the clock. Tess went to the window above the sink and looked out. The back lawns were neatly mowed. Heavy red tomatoes hung on the vines in the garden. Up the side of Kenny's garage a huge purple clematis vine cascaded with brilliant blooms. The sun shone on his back porch where she and he had played together when they were children. His garage door was up, and inside she could see the tail end of a brand-new Mercedes she'd bought him for a wedding gift. It was a smart buy, he'd told her, for it could be legally written off on her taxes as a business expense, since he was now a vice president of Wintergreen Enterprises.

She smiled, realizing how perfectly his life was meshing with hers, and how much help he'd be to her in the future.

Then she checked the time again, and got her gardenia out of the refrigerator.

"Well, here goes," she whispered to herself, and headed from the room. But reaching the doorway, she turned to scan her mother's kitchen one last time as a single woman. She had no inkling what prompted her to pause and look back, but doing so, she experienced an unexpected bolt of nostalgia, and thought, *Let it never change, let me always come home and find it just this way, plastic doily and all.*

Outside on the stoop the sun was hot on her head as she paused and looked across the alley. It took less than five seconds before Kenny appeared on his back step, too, dressed in a gray tux with a cutaway jacket and a pleated white shirt. Even from this distance, his appearance made her heart race, this man she'd taken for conservative, who was constantly surprising her with his clothes.

They stood for a moment, studying each other across the depth of two backyards, recalling a dawn with the sun coming up through the trees behind him, and the sprinkler fanning the garden while Tess jumped the rows of wet vegetables, barefooted, and Kenny stood watching her with a cup of coffee in his hand and his bare toes curled over the back step.

No bare toes today. Instead, two enchanted people in their wedding finery, initiating a ceremony of their own design.

They walked slowly down their respective steps, across the backyards, between patches of summer grass. Instead of an organ, the cicadas piped a song from somewhere among the rhubarb leaves. Instead of bridesmaids, a pair of white cabbage moths fluttered along in front of Tess. Instead of an aisle, a coarse concrete sidewalk; and instead of an altar, an alley.

They met in it, dead center, halfway between his house and hers, where they had met so many times during the weeks when they were falling in love.

The sun lit his dark, neatly combed hair and put little flames into her red curls. It picked out the intensity in his eyes and threw it into hers.

He took her hands lightly, the single oversized gardenia falling back over her knuckles.

"Hello," he said softly.

"Hello."

"Happy wedding day."

"Happy wedding day to you, too."

"You look . . ." He searched for a word. "Radiant."

"I feel radiant. And you look exquisite."

"I feel like the luckiest man on earth."

They smiled some, then he asked, "Are you ready?"

"Yes."

"So am I. Go ahead."

She dropped her gaze momentarily, composing her words, then looked up into his eyes.

"I, Tess McPhail . . ."

"I, Kenneth Kronek . . ."

"Take you, Kenneth Kronek . . ."

"Take you, Tess McPhail . . ."

"To be my beloved husband for the rest of my life."

"To be my beloved wife for the rest of my life."

"To love you as I love you today . . ."

"To love you as I love you today . . ."

"Renouncing all others . . ."

"Most definitely renouncing all others . . ."

"And we will share all that we have, and all that we will have . . . the joys and the sorrows, the work and the play, the worries and the wonders . . . and your daughter . . . and my mother . . . and all the love and commitment it will take to see them through the years ahead . . ."

"And we'll be kind to each other . . ."

"Yes. And respectful . . ."

"And I swear to love you, sustain you, be your strength when you need it and your ease when you need it."

"And I'll do the same for you."

They tried to think of anything they'd missed. He thought of something. "And I renounce all jealousy . . . of your fans and their demands on you."

She smiled, and said, "Why, Kenny, how sweet of you."

"That might be my hardest part," he admitted.

She rubbed his knuckles, and replied, "For me, too . . . being away from you."

They paused once again, adoring each other without smiles, because the moment seemed too sacred to diminish with smiles.

"I love you, Kenny."

"I love you, Tess."

"Forever."

"Forever."

He leaned down and kissed her lightly while bluebottle flies buzzed nearby and the white summer sun lifted the scent of her gardenia and mixed it with the dusty smell of the graveled alley.

When he straightened, they smiled fully, as they had not earlier.

"I feel as married as I'll ever feel," she said.

"So do I. Now let's go do it for everybody else."

IT WAS, TO THE SURPRISE of many, one of the most modest weddings ever held at First Methodist. Some expected luminaries from the recording industry to sing at the ceremony. Instead, only the First Methodist choir sang, directed by Mrs. Atherton, who was back as their leader. Some expected an entire chorus line of attendants, but there were only two. Some expected the attendants to be both male and female. But tradition was shot to the four winds when Casey Kronek and Mary McPhail, smiling fit to kill, each walked up the aisle solo. And when the bride appeared, everyone craned around, supposing she'd be decked out in several thousand dollars' worth of wedding finery shaped like a mushroom cloud. Instead she wore the simple white dress and the simpler ring of girlish flowers in her hair.

She smiled at Kenny all the way up the aisle. He was waiting at the chancel with Reverend Giddings, and when Giddings asked, "Who gives this woman to be married to this man," Mary answered first.

"I do."

Followed by Casey, "And I do."

Though smiles were exchanged behind them, and a soft ripple of amusement lifted from the congregation, everyone thought, how perfect that these two should give their public blessings to this match, because everyone in that church knew how Kenny doted on Mary, and took care of her, and how she'd practically been a grandma to the girl since Casey's own grandma had died. And who but the famous Tess McPhail would have had the temerity to have two women as attendants at her wedding and get by with it? She spurned tradition once again at the traditional giving of the roses. Normally the parents of the nuptials couple received them. But while Kenny gave one to Mary, Tess gave one to Casey, and as their cheeks touched, most eyes in the house got misty.

The wedding guests had one more surprise in store when, after the exchange of vows, the bride took a microphone and sang to her husband. They shouldn't have been surprised by the time Casey took another microphone and sang backup harmony. After all, what about this wedding ceremony matched preconceived notions? Furthermore, the word had spread that the song was co-written by the new "mother-daughter" duo, and that it would be released in the fall as the title song from Tess's new album.

There was, at the Kronek–McPhail wedding, one element of glamour. Among the guests were a bunch of Tess's friends who had flown in from Nashville. Their names were household words, and their faces were recognized in airports and restaurants wherever they went. They were the crème de la crème of the Nashville country music scene, the stars whom Tess numbered among her friends.

When the bride and groom swept jubilantly out of the church to form the receiving line, those stars took their turns just like all the other guests, being dismissed by the ushers and congratulating the newlyweds while the townsfolk from Wintergreen grew rattled, being elbow to elbow with them.

While their presence at the wedding was notable, the presence of another was even more notable. Faith had come. There had been a question about whether or not to invite her, but in the end Kenny and Tess had decided that, given how important she'd been in Kenny's life, she certainly should be asked.

She was every inch a lady, doing the proper thing as she came through the receiving line, taking Tess's hand and smiling. "Congratulations, Tess, you look lovely. Thank you for inviting me." She took

Kenny's hand, too, and kept her smile intact, giving away nothing but pleasure in being here, no matter what heartbreak might be lingering. "Kenny, I hope you and Tess will be very, very happy together."

The bride and groom rode in a white limo out to Current River Cove where their reception was little different than hundreds of others that had been held there. The fried chicken dinner was geared for down-home tastes. The dance, however, turned out to be the talk of the year. Tess's own band played, and a slough of Nashville stars got up, one after another, and sang their hits for the dancers. In the middle of this spontaneous show, Judy got huffy and stalked off to the ladies' room to fluff her hair and fume.

"Showing off all her *famous friends*!" she hissed to two women who were in there freshening their lipstick. "It's sickening."

Judy would never accept the facts of Tess's life: many of her friends *were* famous, just as she was. Many of them *were* idolized on albums and magazine covers just as she was. Many were millionaires. But for Tess not to invite them today would have been a snub. And for them to adjust their schedules to be here was a measure of their affection for her.

Vince Gill and Reba McEntire were singing together on his old classic "Oklahoma Swing" when Judy came out of the washroom. From the dance floor, Tess saw her and said to her new husband, "There's Judy . . . in one of her jealous snits."

He smoothly turned her so her back was to Judy and said, "You know what, darlin'? You're never going to change Judy."

"I know that by now."

"And you're not going to let her ruin your wedding day, are you?"

She flashed him an honest smile without undertones. "Absolutely not." She had come to accept Judy's insecurities as the root of her jealousy, and to pity her instead of getting angry. For there, on the other side of the dance floor, was her sister Renee dancing with Jim, and Renee counterbalanced all of Judy's jealousy with a sure and constant love that looked beyond superficiality. And there, too, was Momma. . . .

Flirting with Alan Jackson!

She was sitting at a table surrounded by her friends, who were all making a big fuss over him and gathering enough fodder for a year's worth of card-party table talk.

"Look at Momma," Tess said.

Kenny looked. And chuckled. "I think she's half-shnockered up on champagne again."

"Six months ago I'd probably have gone over and apologized to Alan, but now I don't see any need to apologize for anything on Momma's behalf. She is what she is, and I love her."

She told Mary as much soon after that when they went to wish her good-bye and sneak away without farewells to the crowd in general. Mary said, "Now, you kids come home soon as you can."

"We will."

"And I'll keep an eye on Casey while she's here." Casey was staying in Wintergreen for a week before driving Kenny's new Mercedes back home to Nashville.

"Thanks, Momma," Tess said as they exchanged a kiss.

"Thanks, Momma," Kenny said, and made Mary all emotional, calling her that for the first time.

She grabbed his face in two hands and planted a kiss on his cheek. "You dear thing," she said. "I'll bet your own Momma is smiling down from heaven at this very moment. Now go on, take your wife and go."

They found Casey and told her they were slipping away. Kenny handed her the car keys, and said, "Be careful with my new Mercedes."

She gave him a smooch on the cheek, and said, "Be careful with my new mother." Then she added, " 'Bye, Mother Mac, have a nice honeymoon."

On their way to the airport—lo and behold—the limo got caught behind Conn Hendrickson's lumbering fuel oil truck.

Tess threw her head back against the leather seat and laughed.

"What's so funny?"

"Just like the day I came back home last April. I followed Conn's truck all the way around the town square. That was the day I met you."

"Mmm . . . not exactly," he added.

"Again," she amended.

"There ya got it."

Her private plane was waiting at Three Rivers Airport and flew them to Nashville, where her Z was waiting at another airport.

She gave her hubby a smirk, and asked, "How'd you like to drive?"

"Wow," he said drolly, accepting the keys, "this is really true love after all, then, isn't it?"

Some would have thought that a millionaire like Tess McPhail Kronek would choose to spend her wedding night in the fanciest bridal suite of the most exotic city in the world, but she'd spent enough time in hotels that home was her idea of luxury.

Besides, though Kenny's things had been moved in, *he* had never moved in. They'd decided for several reasons that he would not sleep there until their wedding night. One reason was Casey, whose respect he still valued, who lived down the hall and *should not* witness a bad example, no matter *what* he'd been wearing that morning in L.A. Another reason was the "rags" and their trade gossip, ever watchful of people of Tess's fame, just waiting to print a dirty headline. But most importantly there were Tess and Kenny themselves, who chose to have a wedding night complete with anticipation.

When they reached her house, Kenny said, "May I do the honors, Mrs. Kronek?"

And she answered, "I wouldn't have it any other way, Mr. Kronek."

When he carried her inside, the built-in sound system was playing softly—not country or rock, but Debussy's "Reverie." They paused to kiss just inside the entry before he set her down and they went exploring. Maria had left walnut chicken breasts in brandy sauce ready to warm in the oven along with a crisp French *boule,* and an artichoke-heart salad in the refrigerator. A table for two was set with candles and a single white rose floating in a glass compote. In the living room they found some wedding gifts piled up on the piano bench, and upstairs, the double doors to the master bedroom suite stood open, while inside, on a dresser, a bouquet of red roses filled the room with scent.

Kenny stopped in the doorway, holding Tess's hand.

He was filled with a sense of excess that seemed, momentarily, beyond accepting.

"I can't believe I'm going to live here with you."

"Sometimes I can't believe it either."

"That we're this lucky . . . that we have all this."

"And love, too. It does seem a bit much, doesn't it?"

But it was theirs to accept, and they stepped inside to begin their life together.

Later, when they'd consummated their unity in bed, and eaten Maria's delicious walnut chicken, and taken a swim in the pool, and opened the pile of wedding gifts, they were sitting on the floor among the wrappings with one small gift unopened.

"Momma said to open it last," Tess said.

"Well, go ahead," he said.

She began pulling at the Scotch tape. "What do you suppose it is?"

"I don't know." It was no bigger than a billfold. When the wrapping was off, she opened the end flap of a small cardboard box and tipped it till something slid out into her hand: a picture frame, and in it a photograph of Tess and Kenny at about ages two and three, eating watermelon on the back steps of Mary's house, their knees together, feet bare, toes hooked over the edge of the step, faces sunburned and dirty, as if they'd been hard at play just before the picture was taken.

Tess's reaction to it was as emotional as

Mary's had been to the announcement of their wedding plans.

"Oh," she said, a hand going to her lips and tears stinging her eyes as she turned the picture his way. "Oh, look . . ."

He looked. And got a lump in his throat, too.

"Have you ever seen it before?" she asked.

"I don't think so."

She dusted the glass lovingly. "I wonder where it's been all these years."

"In your mother's bureau, I suppose, tucked away with the precious things that mothers keep."

"Do you suppose they planned this day back then, when they used to watch us play together?"

"Maybe they knew something we didn't."

They kissed, feeling special, and loved by more than each other, and magically fated to end up together.

"What time is it?" she said.

"Nearly eleven."

"Oh, I don't care. Let's go call Momma."

He beamed, and leapt to his feet and pulled her up after him. "Yeah, let's!"

They took the picture along, and went together to wake Mary and thank her, and to tell her how happy they were. And then they simply had to call Casey, too, just to say good night and that they loved her.

When they finally went upstairs, they took the picture along and set it on their bedside stand where it would be when they woke up in the morning.

And the morning after that, and the morning after that.

And often, when they would look at it, in the years ahead, one of them would say what Casey said that morning in the hotel, "It's like it was meant to be, isn't it?"

And the other one would smile.

For no other answer was necessary.